Kate Rose has a first class degree in Human Biology and an MA in Creative and Life Writing. She has written for various publications and her short stories have been published on various platforms and within anthologies. *The Angel and the Apothecary* has been long-listed for both the Aurora Metro International Novel Writing Competition and the Mslexia Women's Novel Writing Competition. Kate lives in London. When not immersed in the past, Kate ghostwrites biographies. This is her first novel.

'The Angel and the Apothecary is a rich, dark and wholly
compelling story of pain, passion, healing and hope.
It powerfully and wittily evokes a world in flux, as the
Enlightenment comes to terms with the wisdom of the ages.
I loved it.'

Emma Darwin,
author of *The Mathematics of Love*

D1437996

KATE ROSE

The Angel and the Apothecary

EWING ROSE
PUBLISHING

LONDON

EWING ROSE
PUBLISHING

ER Publishing
41 Panmure Road
London SE26 6NB

First published in Great Britain by ER Publishing, 2020
Published in Penguin Books 2014

Printed in India by Chennai Publishing Services Pvt. Ltd.

A CIP catalogue record for this book is available from the British Library

ISBN: 978-1-5272-5740-5

www.ewingrosepublishing.com

For my
parents and Saskia

If half the world knew how the other strives,
T'would spoil the comfort of their easy lives.

Picture an angel looking down upon this city, what would it see? Street lamps burning in yellow constellation? The serpentine swirl of the river with its floating wilderness of masts? And what if this celestial being were to walk the city's streets: would it marvel at the labyrinth of alleyways, the hotchpotch of buildings? Or sigh in disbelief at the rammed slums, places where even the rats fared better? For in this city sickness seeps into the bodies of rich and poor alike: cankers, fistulas, dropsy, consumption, the pox, agues and bloody fluxes, all seize their opportunity. But for an angel observing such suffering, it might be almost too much to bear...

December, 1741

Feet meeting with London clay, we find ourselves in the parish of St Giles-in-the-Fields. Built on marshland there are no fields to speak of, and despite its new church it remains a poor parish, thronged with vagrants, plentiful gin lovers. But walk this way, eyes to the cobbles to avoid any shit getting on your shoes, and just up from Seven Dials, where seven streets converge on a pillar topped with six sundials, you will see an alleyway. From here, slip within the cramped triangle of Neal's Yard. And here, between the premises of an astrologer and an alchemist, sits the apothecary shop of one.

Jeremiah I. S. Goode

The shop front comprises wood in a state of disrepair, its bowed plate-glass windows smeared with soot. Just visible behind are the common Cure-alls; the flint glass bottles of the travelling salesmen: *Daffy's Elixir, Evan's Worming Powder* and *Turlington's Balsam*... Behind, stand the blue and white gallipots of the apothecary's trade: jars decorated with baroque scrolls, exuberant plant life, exotic birds and heavy-winged angels, oddly reminiscent, one might say, of the details embellish upon tombs.

Now duck beneath the emblem of the Worshipful Society of Apothecaries—Apollo, they say, overcoming pestilence straddling a wyvern—and enter a black door delicately trimmed with gold—mind your head! A melodious bell, wouldn't you agree, for so sombre a façade? See the dust motes hanging inert, as if distant stars! After the stench of the streets, the aromas of cloves, cinnamon, lavender and liquorice combine in olfactory harmony. And when eyes adjust to the light, it is evident that its humble frontage belies the scope of its owner's ambitions. Above a counter of mahogany, hangs a puffer fish whose marble eyes are doomed to eternal vigilance. In the shadows beneath, lurks the desiccated remains of—could it be?—yes, indeed an *alligator*.

Dozens more Delft apothecary jars from the Lambeth potters stake their claim to walls space. Behind the counter, further shelves are loaded with syrup bottles, curved spouts, unguent pots with bright metal lids, bottles of cordial waters, perfumes, ointments, plasters, razors, vials of oil, bags of sugar; a small central space reserved for the expensive drugs—*Paracelsian, Helmantians*—favoured by the physicians. Whilst presiding over all, layered with the thickest dust and surveying the room with a distinct sneer to his skull, stands Nicholas Culpeper!

The shop is otherwise empty. But wait a moment. Grinding and tapping: the ubiquitous sounds of the apothecary's trade. Let us slip behind the counter, through a doorway hung with rich red velvet, and what do we find? The light is still dim but if you peer closer you will see two men, both so absorbed in their tasks neither has noticed us enter.

Jeremiah regards the quivering feathers of his quill.

'A customer in the shop perhaps?' he asks his apprentice.

Boswell—the boy has long forgotten his age—puts down the pestle and mortar he cradles. 'The wind, I expect, sir.' He brushes cinnamon from his nose with a swipe of a grubby shirtsleeve. 'Shall I take a look?'

Jeremiah listens to the shop bell trill. Does not look up. The boy drags his boots across the *elaboratory,* sliding back the velvet drape as if drawing a sword; Jeremiah returns his attention to his accounting ledger. He frowns at the balance at the bottom of the page. Amount owing to the druggist and other creditors: *£240 4s 6d.* Amount due from customers: *£250 3s 4d.* He runs a hand across his face. He need only turn back a few pages to see how this has come about. Barely a handful of customers have paid him in a year with the three previous years being no better. *Two hundred and forty pounds.* A small fortune and yet, if he does not find it, he will soon be sleeping like a hog upon a dunghill in a close ward of nine feet by six, with a gaol sentence ahead of him as extravagant as the unforgiving nature of his creditors.

He slams the accounts book shut, releasing a dark cloud of dust. He sits back in his chair to survey his *elaboratory*. By the guttering light of two cheap tallow candles, its once ordered contents appear neglected. The massive mortar squats in pride of place on the workbench, its pestle hanging overhead; a condemned corpse from its gallows. Of late, they have had no reason to grind ingredients in large quantities. Rather, Boswell's grinding seems to stem from habit as opposed to necessity. For Jeremiah, it is a continual battle to push back guilt.

Amongst the ledgers, on a table in the centre of the room, are stacked a variety of books—*A Methodical Introduction to the Theory and Practice of Physic*, Nicholas Culpeper's *Complete Herbal,* and the giddily titled Parkinson's *Paradisi in Sole Paradisus Terrestris*—essentially a gardening book. They sit beside the elixirs Jeremiah fears may bring harm to his customers: *Elixir Proprietatis, Vatican pills, Fioravanti's Balsam*; the most fanciful of the *Cure-alls* imposed on him by the more insistent salesmen. He has found them effective in staving off rats.

Before the fire a great copper crucible for making tinctures. Like so much else it sits empty. Distillation is the best way to concentrate a plant's essence. Scales and weights, funnel, flasks, alembics and curcubits—all gathering soot.

As if in prayer, the young apothecary now clasps his hands before him. Not much given to moments of piety, however, he daydreams, musing with unabashed sentimentality about his childhood home, his siblings. Then his smiles fades as he remembers—in unrelenting detail—the December day in Dulwich when his father threatened to disown him for his love of botany over physic. He had set off to forget his hefty sorrow, roaming the woods in search of fresh specimens. He had stopped to catch his breath, gazed up through the blocks of low winter through the encroaching branches towards a patch of cerulean.

'What am I to do?' he spoke aloud.

As if in response, the wind picked up. Fallen leaves began to eddy around him. A vortex formed with the young man at its centre. He stood, arms outstretched and neck extended, gazing past the skeletal branches to the heavens above. Three words gradually swum at the forefront of his mind. He craned back his neck and cried as loud as his lungs would permit:

'Yes! I will serve. *I will* serve!' he cried.

Abruptly, the wind died. Leaves ceased their whirl, drifting to the ground. Jeremiah looked down. Before him a single *galanthus nivalis*, had broken through the soil, a month or so early. The snowdrop: a flower of hope; the first plant Eve saw after leaving the Garden of Eden. Snow transformed by an angel had flowered. Something stirred in his breast, a momentary easing of the burden of perpetual guilt. It was then that he first began to feel aligned with a far greater force than that embodied in his father, *the eminent* Dr. Robert Goode. It was not too farfetched to see this moment as the beginning of an intense communion with Nature; mind and body willingly rendering into a vessel through which She could effect her Cures.

Yet, a shortness of investment that had brought Jeremiah to St Giles, rather than the Strand—where any physician worth his weight might be found. Though he quickly became known as a miracle-maker, his purse, under the weight of such a title son became irrelevant. Only time revealed that miracles and money were bad bed partners. Four years of Curing hundreds, if not thousands, who had nothing left to give, and little choice but to become sick again, had left him deep in debt and as devoid of hope as those that he laboured to Cure.

Go to St Giles and disappear! He opens his eyes and pushes a finger into his ear, attempting to dislodge the echo of his father's curse. The shop bell ceases to ring and a rare silence scatters his thoughts. He opens his herbal compendium, admires a sketch of Archangel: a plant with crumpled, hairy leaves, adorned with hooded flowers of red, white or yellow. He is at least content with the drawing, but as for the plant's uses… well, they remain a little disordered, so far undocumented. After Archangel comes Arrach, good for yellow jaundice and for cleansing of the womb. He pictures its small round leaves: a little pointed and without serration or lobe, a dusky mealy colour, displayed on slender stalks. He can see the clusters of small flowers, even smell its rotten fish-like odour, the result of roots deeply embedded in dunghills for Jeremiah has a memory for plants like men of this city have for women of pleasure. The rest is derived from scraps of paper, scattered about his elaboratory; hasty notes recorded at times of revelation or inspiration, many more inscribed upon his bedchamber walls.

Asparagus, he hopes, shall prove less taxing. He picks up his pen, dipping it into what remains of his ink, and recommences—with the fervour of a dying man digging his own grave—a record of his findings. He reminds himself of both his grit and gift for Curing, a thing he does not properly understand, despite its unfailing accuracy. He rejoices in its imperviousness to his humble surroundings and, slowly but surely, finds the courage to press quill to paper.

Some time later a shrill cry of '*Potecary? Potecary?*' carries through from the shop. Another customer unable to read the Bailiff's note no doubt.

'She insists upon seeing you, sir,' says Boswell, appearing at the curtain, 'I think this one's a Covent Garden nun, sir.'

Jeremiah lifts his brow enquiringly.

'A bat, a punk, a bit of laced mutton,' his apprentice elaborates with a wink.

'Ah,' says Jeremiah, sitting back in his chair and lacing hands behind his head, 'another goat's intestine sheath before the evening's venereal adventures' He smiles, mischievousness warping his face. 'Adventures, Boswell, that kept the men of the city wedded to their wives. I shall let you tend to her.'

'But that's just it, sir, she's insisting on seeing you and you alone.'

Jeremiah shakes his head as Boswell grins.

'Do you think that you and this quean might be already—how shall I put it?—acquainted, sir?' the boy asks.

Forgetting gratitude and allows his respectful manner to slip, Boswell in turn becomes the ragamuffin he might have remained had his grandfather never fallen sick, had opportunity never plucked him from the streets.

'Explain to her that I am busy.' Jeremiah, straightens his notes on Asparagus. 'Tell her that I trust my well-trained apprentice to deal with her condition.'

'I have tried, sir. But this one, well, she does insist, sir.'

Jeremiah runs a hand across his face. '*Trying,* by its very nature, has no limits, Boswell. And remember—'

'To demand payment and on no account to give herbs on credit, sir?'

'Very good.' The Bailiff had said credit was to be extended only to those credit-worthy, a phrase Jeremiah has still to properly understand. 'Now go!'

The boy exits the elaboratory as another shrill cry of '*Potecary, Potecary!*' threatens to separate the ceiling from its gilded cornice. Jeremiah writes, *Asparagus produces fragrant urine*, and regrets that he has made his quill too sharp for it scratches across the page, doing little to alleviate his present irritation.

In theory, all he need do to finish the compendium is find enough paper and ink and a little sobriety—of which he presently has plenty—and fill 500 or so blank pages with his account of medicinal herbs. Following that he must publish it. Thus described, it seems almost achievable.

So far he has reached Asparagus. To complete studies of 500 or so herbs, at such a rate, will take him the best part of a year, and a year, he is quite certain, he does not have.

Boiled with white wine or vinegar, Asparagus could relieve pain in those troubled by hip-gout or sciatica, though in certain individuals, that are susceptible, it may worsen such pains.

He crosses out this last part, searching his memory for something more uplifting. The exigencies of serving the superior physic have steered him from the individual towards the general, so that every person—whether their disease is ague, dropsy, pestilence or ulcers—is expected to be healed by similar means. Physicians who come to his shop (admittedly few of them nowadays) dispensed a word or two of medical verbiage and expected it to be interpreted instantly into a cure. If Jeremiah enquired as to whether the patient was young or old, fat or thin, happy or sad, whether he ate mostly meat or bread, whether he walked 10 miles a day or barely got out of bed, he would be scorned for wasting time. Physicians believed that for every disease there was a specific, unchanging (and usually ineffective) medicinal cure. They treat every ill and pain of each body part individually, when what they needed was to see each bodily part as making up the whole, growing out from a fundamental cause. With this in mind, Jeremiah writes hoping his compendium will one day serve the need for self-physicking by those who cannot afford to consult neither physician nor apothecary (preferring to forget that most of his parish cannot read, nor afford a book!). His theory stands, however, that a cure operates primarily through the dispensing healer's understanding of the individual, as well as the nature of plants. Admittedly, on occasion, he has himself relied on emetics, purgatives and a little luck too—for this is often the way when healing—but in final analysis it is always the individual who matters most. And in the interstices where neither cure nor hope can, there is laudanum.

He reaches for the bottle now, savouring the tonic's bitterness upon his tongue, watching as the fog forms intricate droplets on the plate glass in the haze. Distant hooves clash against cobbles, awakening something in his breast. Unread notes on Asparagus amassed at his elbow, Jeremiah begins picturing her red mouth… the way the tip of her tongue touches her upper lip… the way she tips her head to one side as she studies a plant… Temptation along the path of Salvation! Far better to turn his thoughts to the compendium and this last chance he perhaps has of evading debtors' prison.

He opens his eyes, scratches his hair—a head shave being long overdue—and picks up his pen.

Asparagus: a plant good for cancer of the breast, the larynx and lung…

What else? He riffles through further scraps of paper strewn across his desk, comes across: *Stirs up lust in man and woman,* and is struck, quite suddenly, by a vision of her ears: pale, intricate whorls like the outer edge of a South Sea shell once seen in a museum of curios. He drops his quill, pressing a thumb and forefinger to the corners of his eyes. Three times he has seen her at the Chelsea Physic Garden, three times dressed invariably in a long black cloak, plucking herbs, rubbing fragrant leaves between her fingertips and bringing them to her lips… three times and each sight more entrancing than the last. He checks his pocket watch. Perhaps, he might reach the Garden before dusk. He could find an Asparagus plant to draw…

'*The Potecary! I must see the Potecary!*' The woman's cry carries through his Elaboratory like a giant winged irritation.

He abandons Asparagus, skips over Autumnal-water Starwort, and moves straight on to Avens, an excellent plant for dissolving bruises.

'Sir?' Boswell asks as he runs a hand through his hair. 'She will not let me serve her, sir. I have but tried.'

Jeremiah sighs. No avoiding it. As promptly as he allows it to enter, discomfort swells in his abdomen. He sets down his quill. He burps. Regurgitates a little food. A moment later his feet start to swell in his shoes and a nettle-like sting sears at his anus.

'What in God's name must a man do for peace in this city!' he says, pushing back his chair. 'Cut off his ears?'

Of course, it was not that he did not wish to heal these women; it was that they did little to prevent themselves from falling sick again, or with child again, or drunk again, or succumbing to whatever other vice they used to brighten their miserable days. And in a state of despair they flocked to the threshold of his shop, passing on their symptoms with poorly conveyed astonishment. So it is with some reluctance that Jeremiah clears his throat and with his head a great cathedral of resentment, steps upon his stage.

'Madam! How may I be of any assistance?'

The woman, standing on boards worn pale by the sick, pushes matted hair from her face. She looks from Boswell to Jeremiah and back again, shuffles her feet and appears to point to a sleeve heavily stained with blood. 'Can I shew it to you or need we be alone?'

Jeremiah nods whereupon, rather than the sleeve, the woman lifts the hem of her skirt. She tucks the fabric tucked beneath her arms, exhibits, with the modesty of a cow offering full udders (for she wears not a thread of undergarments) the tips of pendulous breasts and a belly a month or so from parturition. Jeremiah experiences a sharp, yet definite, internal kick in his own gut and leans across the counter to conceal Boswell's eyes with his palms.

"E not seen mama's belly afore?'

'Is this your mother, Boswell?'

'No, sir.'

'You happen not to be that particular woman, madam. Examinations are conducted here at my discretion and always in private.' Jeremiah waits for her to lower her skirts before removing his hands from his apprentice's face.

'You want to go somewhere and take a better look?' she offers, with an intonation of promise.

'No, madam. I already have a clear idea of your condition.'

A slight huff. 'Then what shall you give me?'

'You must find a country nurse.' He removes a jar from a shelf. 'That is, if you will not keep the child.'

The whore laughs. 'In this town?'

'Many here do manage.' He thinks: Pepperwort, its potent juices... and Butcher's Broom for haemorrhoids...

The woman clucks. 'But I have no husband to depend upon. Being up all the night until I can barely depend upon my own wits. How must I manage?'

'Alas, I am an apothecary not a politician as such I try to change health, not habits.' At least this had been his ethos upon arrival. He holds up a jar. 'Some juice of Pepperwort, taken in ale to quicken the delivery. Butcher's Broom to be taken as a tea, seep for fifteen minutes before drinking.'

The whore shakes her head. 'Eleven foundlings God has cursed me with and every one a wretched birth.'

'Then let us hope number twelve shall be your lucky number.'

'You misunderstand, Master Potecary. I don't want it born—I wish to be rid of it.'

They all want to be rid of these unborn children but it is not a thing he enacts. 'Then you must visit a wise woman.'

'For her to put a live toad on my back and make the child kick? This one is already quickening... quickening like a beast. The fellow who usually cuts them says it's too late, and besides I can ill afford a month off work. I must be rid of it. Rid of it quick!'

Doubtless, the wise woman and abortionist would prefer to be paid for their services. 'I cannot help you,' he affirms. 'Two, perhaps three, more weeks and Nature will do the job for you.' He returns the herb jar to the shelf. 'An apothecary is in the business of saving lives, not ending them.'

The sound his customer makes next is the snort a donkey might make. Jeremiah shifts the thought that not a gentleman in the whole of London could deny some accountability for the birth of such children. Uncertain whether the woman laughs or cries, he nods conspiratorially to Boswell, who ventures around the counter and places an awkward hand upon her shoulder.

'The Apothecary knows his business,' says the boy with practised intent. 'You would do well to take his advice.' He pulls a flat lipped smile that serves as a closed door for the more discerning.

'But the hospital will not take it, and if it goes to a parish workhouse it shall perish, or be sold into work before its bones have hardened. I will leave it upon no man's door—not even yours, Master Potecary.'

Jeremiah is having difficulty following the woman's argument. It seems she will be content only if she were the one to kill her child. 'But with the child placed in the workhouse, you shall never know if it lives or dies.'

'I shall know. I'm its *mother*.'

He is fighting for the life of a child already doomed. If it does not suffer now, it will assuredly suffer later. He fetches down two jars and, unable to meet the woman's accusing eyes, weighs out a penny's worth of herbs.

'A pound of raspberry leaf tea. Boil and drink hot, thrice daily,' he tells her.

'God bless you, sir! And what of this other herb, what do I do with it?'

9

'Seep for a quarter of an hour and apply directly as a compress to your haemorrhoids.'

'To my what?'

'The condition affecting your…' he seeks the correct medicinal term '… *bum*. Porridge oats to break fast and your bowels will empty as they ought. Asparagus, or sparrow-grass, will aid. And plenty of boiled water. But no gin.'

The woman gives a toothless grin and extends both arms. '*Potecary*! How can I possibly show thanks?'

'Money is the usual means,' he says, dodging the embrace.

'Well, I shall give you plenty—'

'Settling your account in coin shall alone suffice.'

'I mean to say, I shall give you plenty of money just as soon as my customers return. Sailors who want to blow off loose corns have no liking for a whale. Sailors see enough whales out at sea! You must understand that as well as the next man, Mr Potecary.'

She laughs her peculiar laugh, or perhaps cries. Jeremiah only wants to get rid of the woman now so he can work on his compendium undisturbed and forget for a time the shambles that lies beyond his threshold, the confusion he had once considered himself capable of righting.

'You have a kind face and good teeth, Master Potecary. A lucky convenience I am certain you must have.'

'She speaks of *your wife*, sir,' Boswell winks.

'There is no Mrs Goode, madam.'

'Not with those comely blue eyes and black curls!' Concealing her bulging belly under a stained mantle, the whore snatches the bag of herbs from the counter. 'I should say you'll have no trouble finding yourself one, being a clever gentleman with a proper gentleman's voice. You don't see many of your kind in St Giles. None, I should say. Good day, Potecary!'

Jeremiah opens the shop door and the whore leans towards him.

'Every man needs a good woman.' She fingers the ends of his hair, kisses his cheek and steps out of the shop. Boswell continues to stare.

'Do I have ink on my face?' Jeremiah asks him.

The boy shakes his head. 'No, sir. But I have not seen you do such a thing before as you did with that woman, sir.'

'Pray, what?'

10

'You have always taught me to do whatever it takes to make a man, woman or child live a day longer in this wretched world.'

A chuckle catches in Jeremiah's throat. Brief theatre and a good lesson were provided this afternoon. He sometimes forgets that despite the boy's attentiveness and enthusiasm to siphon every bead of information from his employer's mind, Boswell cannot in fact read it.

'No cause for concern,' Jeremiah assures him. 'Raspberry tea strengths the uterus. The woman should have a soon and swift birth. The easier the birth, the easier it should be for her to love the unwanted child. Perhaps number twelve she shall keep.'

When a boy with a bleeding nose has had it packed with yarrow leaf and Jeremiah has seen to a case of *la grippe* in the baker's wife and the King's Evil in a beggar, the shop slumps into quiet. A surprising amount of custom has reaped the grand total of two ha'pennies. A familiar problem: too much sickness and too little money.

He returns to his elaboratory and sits at his desk, staring at the Bailiff's order to cease customers' credit—*in the midst of winter*—screws it up and tosses it into the dwindling fire. He makes a note: *Asparagus heals haemorrhoids, serves the heart and rids the body of hope salt*. He remembers the favour promised the night soil man and, at this prospect, drains the last of his laudanum.

'I must depart.' He checks his pocket watch.

Boswell looks up from bagging herbs. 'Going abroad, sir?'

'To Southwark, Boswell. Familiar with Southwark?' Jeremiah wrestles with his coat.

'I've never had much reason to cross River, sir.'

Jeremiah suspects his apprentice has never gone farther than the parish of St Clement Danes. 'Southwark is best known for its houses of correction—its prisons,' he says.

'Be that your reason for you journeying there, sir?' says Boswell.

For a moment Jeremiah's tongue twitches with the truth. 'No. I have an errand to run.' Is all he is able to confess. 'My hat?'

'Behind you, sir.'

'I shall not be back for supper. If you could convey my absence…' He cuts short his request. Given the difficulties of informing his maid about anything, it would perhaps be easier for the boy to consume two suppers. Jeremiah searches for the key to his drug cabinet.

'Mary's hearing is much improved, sir.' Boswell picks up the pestle and mortar as well as the train of Jeremiah's thoughts. 'Lately, she has been faithfully…'

But now distracted by the found key, Jeremiah opens a drawer in his drug cabinet where he stores his most valuable ingredients—silver, gold leaf, exotic seeds and roots from the Orient in row upon row of miniature drawers—that is, he *used* to. The chest now lies almost empty aside from a purse of coins from pawning his grandfather's ring. He misses the ring upon his finger with it generous brilliant set amid gold. Naturally, the money could well be spent more wisely. A muscle twitches in his shoulder and involuntarily lifts as though body and mind had temporarily parted company. Ignoring the irregularity, he tells himself he should be able to make a swift profit on the transaction at the port. By selling some of his supply onto druggists, it should help to keep the bailiff from the door. He wipes off a rim of grime from his finger where the ring once sat, places the purse in the inner pocket of his breeches and spends an age fastening the many buttons of his fashionable waistcoat.

'I have finished Archangel,' he muses aloud as he rights his wig.

'I am glad to hear it, sir.'

'Well, you needn't be. I have an entire alphabet ahead of me.' As well as a Bailiff in his shadow and a list of debtors as long as his waistcoat. What man could complete a great body of work without money? What man could complete a great body of work *for* money! 'But Archangel,' he tells Boswell, 'is good for the spleen. Remember that.'

'Aye, sir.' Boswell pulls back the curtain for him. 'There are more requests for laudanum at the Rookery, sir. A fellow lost his leg after he was hit by a carriage. His wife says he cannot drink enough to drown such suffering.'

Gin was cheap. A large bottle could be bought for a penny. In St Giles people piled up outside the grog shops, barely alive. Drunk for a penny, dead drunk for two.

The boy returns to the elaboratory. Jeremiah's shoulder flinches once more. He takes a handful of bagged herbs from the shop counter and stuffs them in his coat pocket. By the time the debt collector is in possession of his drug jars they shall, if nothing else, be empty.

Nicholas Culpeper grins at him from the corner.

'Shall they not be satisfied until I am a bag of bones like you? You lived until seven and thirty. If I am sent to gaol at four and thirty, I tell you, I shall not be far behind. Confess, did you feel their pain as if it were your own? Did walking these streets fill you, at times, with unbearable agony? Too late to recommend a bottle of laudanum and tell you it is a better Cure than gin.' He laughs at a joke that seems to be at his own expense. 'Methinks, God took pity on you with an early death.'

Resting his hand on the once gleaming brass door handle, Jeremiah stands for a moment on the threshold of his shop, observing the drizzle trickling from the waterspouts. Not another sound can be heard from the yard. A place so quiet it hardly seems to exist. Yet, if he were to cup a hand to his ear and listen carefully, he is certain he would hear the city spitting his failings back at him, its message as clear as the water splatting on the cobbles: *Time is running out.*

To the right of his shop lies the astronomer: an eccentric fool, who makes up stories about what he finds in the skies or on his absurdly imaginative charts. The shop to the left belongs to the alchemist: another fool who claims he can prolong life with a band of angels and a philosopher's stone. People assume Jeremiah's beliefs strike a chord with his neighbours. They could not be further from the truth. For his cures he relies on plants and instinct. He has no concern for the stars or whatever else lies hidden by perpetual fog above his head. His interests lie solely people and their peculiar habits.

'Evening, Apothecary Goode,' says Ludwell the astronomer, appearing on the threshold of his shop, pipe smoke curling into the air around him. 'Saturn is in the fray and thus one never truly knows.'

'Evening, Mr Ludwell.' Jeremiah wonders, as he often does, what exactly it is that the fellow smokes. 'But one always knows. Inevitability is our greatest enemy, rarely uncertainty, Mr Ludwell.'

'Mr Goode, you of all people should know that plants fall under the dominion of the planets. An apothecary cannot Cure if he does not recognise that Taurus has dominion over the neck, ears and throat, for Dygges in his 1555 manuscript…'

Jeremiah lifts his hand. 'Good evening, Mr Ludwell!'

Naturally, he knows that the body must adapt to an ever-changing environment, knows it to be in a state of flux just like the heavens. He knows too that keeping it in balance is important. From this context it is indeed an astrological arrangement—but what Jeremiah does not believe is the popular dogma that planets govern bodily parts or, for that matter, the doctrine of signatures that states that herbs resembling body parts can be used to treat ailments of said body part. Personally, he had never found God to be so blatantly helpful. To his mind, it was merely wishful thinking and if they put him in the stocks for his beliefs then so be it; his cures work which is more than can be said for most so-called healers in this town.

At the corner of Neal's Yard he passes the lamplighter, who stands with one foot resting on the bottom rung of his ladder, eating an apple.

'How's Mary?' the boy asks.

'My maid keeps well.' Jeremiah watches a moth pointlessly flap around the edges of the lamp's flame.

'I try to see her at the window of your house…' The lamplighter's face twitches as he blinks convulsively. 'But it is too dark.'

'You are spying on us?'

The boy resumes control of his features with dignity. 'No, sir, but on the occasions I look up to see her face at the window, it is dark… I mean, for a house belonging to a gentleman such as yourself.'

Jeremiah turns back to look at it. Indeed the place appears empty. It seems even constant twilight one may adapt to. 'Spearmint and ground fennel seeds. Boil up and drink as a tea.'

'Sir?'

'For the twitching. My maid will not look at you with a face that dances about like a mad March hare.'

He heads towards Queen's Street before the boy, or anybody else, can bother him further. The watchman—the third St Giles has seen in the space of a year—stands on the corner, swinging his horn lantern, pent-house hat worn to guard against the unrelenting weather.

'*Hang out your light so that honest men may walk along, may see to pass safe without wrong...*'

At Seven Dials, Jeremiah realises he has forgotten his hat. Too late. He must press on. At least the extortionate price he once paid for his wig means it is warm, impervious to the rain.

'Going begging, Master Goode?'

'Not yet, Manners. Not yet.'

The Bailiff's vein-cracked eyes appear wilder than usual and his mop of red hair is raised as if in tentacles. 'I was just coming to visit you at your shop.' He speaks as if conferring a favour.

'For any particular reason?' This pot-bellied wisp of foulness has been tailing him around the parish for a month or more and they both know why.

Manners scowls at the bag of 'herbs' in Jeremiah's hand—remaining scraps from the bottom of his drug jars. 'I come looking for anything you have left to give, Master Goode. Anything at all.'

'Then I must disappoint you for you have already taken it all.'

The bailiff's eyebrows wiggle. 'Everything, Mr Goode?'

Manners was not a real Bailiff but a *bum-bailiff*, a term Jeremiah now fully understands for the man has grown closer to him than his own shadow. He knows, however, of the 1706 Act of Anne, and that he still stands a chance of discharging himself from debt and avoiding gaol if luck—*God*—is on his side. Once deemed insolvent, however, he will be sent to prison to serve a term dependent upon the forgiving nature of his creditors. In the meantime he must pass on any earnings—however pitiful—to Manners, or else be found guilty by the courts and swiftly hanged.

'Everything of value, aye.'

Manners shakes his head. 'What is not of value to a gentleman may be of great value to a pauper such as myself.'

'Is that so?'

'Aren't you a Good Samaritan!' Manners swipes a bag of herbs from Jeremiah's grasp and tucks it into his belt. 'But what you really need is to Cure yourself, Master Goode. Cure yourself of the disease of penury. There is none sicker, you understand, than the fool who gives away his money. The Bailiff has permitted you one more month of living like a free man. One more month afore you stroll the Fleet's moat to its tower. Might I suggest you waste no more of it on acts of charity.'

Discreetly, Jeremiah tucks the rest of the herbs into the lining of his coat. 'And the ten pounds paid but three weeks ago? Does it not bide anymore time?' He had paid Manners ten pounds from pawning a looking glass; a twenty first birthday present from his mother.

'Aye, plenty more… once you fetch me the remaining two hundred and forty pounds due. Speaking of time, how shall you be spending your last hours?' Manners' tongue hangs limply from his mouth. 'Kissing your lover's wet lips?' He cackles. 'You have a lover I assume?'

Bile rises in Jeremiah's throat. 'I have work to do.'

Manners' hand falls heavy on Jeremiah's shoulder, fingers appearing to grip his very bones. 'I don't require money, sir, not like the women of the parish.' He smiles, revealing six blackened teeth, as he continues to grotesquely bat his eyelashes. 'Maybe you and me could come to an arrangement. Why don't you have a think about it. Have a *good* think.' The fella spits laughter. 'For I am certain we could come to some mutually beneficial arrangement.' More laughter thick with artifice. 'Eh? A gentleman—a clever one too— choosing the life of a pauper?—I shall never understand it. One more month, Apot'cry. One more month to Cure your thyself!'

As abruptly as he appeared, the bum bailiff enters the Angel Inn, laughing like the Devil's own.

Suffering angels

For eight months of the year, thick fog hangs over London like flies hovering around shit. With no sedan chair or horse of his own, and with Hackney coaches costing little less than sixpence per half mile, Jeremiah must walk. He does so, head bent before the December cold. There is in an art to walking these streets. A man must negotiate broken cobbles, open sewers and all manner of filth without losing his balance, arms pressed to his sides to deter pickpockets and, whenever possible, avoid meeting another's eye, attempting—in Jeremiah's case—to prevent further ills blighting a body too willing to receive.

He reaches the Rookery, a place pinched between St Giles Church and Great Russell Street. Despite the new laws following the Great Fire, the Rookery is constructed from wood; a muddle of blind alleys and half-finished buildings propped up against one another like drunken men at a tavern. Its windows are boarded up, lamps perpetually unlit. There is only one way in and no way out. The Rookery: the lowest point a person can sink with breath still left in his lungs.

Before his shop opened, the only remedy to pass beyond the Rookery's walls was gin, freely dispensed for every complaint suffered by man, woman and child. But looking down the narrow alley, between the part-derelict hovels—places that would go up in flames at the blink of an inebriated eye—strewn with filth, and with the cries of suffering babes piercing the unaccustomed ear, it is hard to blame the inhabitants for finding a little comfort in Madam Geneva.

Behind a blanket, in a place where an outside wall ought to be, Jeremiah discovers the source of the crying and the reason, most likely, for this visit: a baby of a month old, no more, in its mother's arms and, as was the custom for ones so small, bound to a board.

Taking out two bags of herbs, Jeremiah introduces himself. 'I am an apothecary, madam. I understand your family could benefit from a Cure.' A favour begets a favour. For three long months he had been searching for illicit opium since his druggist cut off his credit. The night soil man has tipped him off to a likely source and in return Jeremiah has undertaken to treat the inhabitants of this single room.

The woman of the wretched household stares back at him, startled. 'I have no care for what you are. We have not sent for you.'

Her eyes wander from his hat to his shoes, coming to rest on the bags of herbs he holds in his hands. She wears a nightshirt, or so it seems. He imagines she was handsome once. Now her hair hangs loose to her waist, so matted that its colour is no longer discernible, and on her cheek is a tender pink scar three inches long, woven tight into a grimace.

'I am not looking for business. I bring remedies. That is all,' he assures.

The woman's lips tighten, emphasising her scar. 'We have no need for your remedies here.'

'Even if they are dispensed without charge?'

17

She turns to hang the baby from a hook in the centre of the ceiling then faces him, tight lips replaced by a frown. 'What kind of remedies?

Jeremiah glances around at her children sprawled over the dirty floor, forming a living, breathing drugget. The elder ones play pick-up-sticks. There is a whoop as somebody wins but the stale air and gloom quickly dim their joy. Windows are bricked up to avoid the tax. Water drips along the walls and in one corner appears to lie an open cesspit. It is not a home, thinks Jeremiah, but a cave.

'Tell me first, madam, what is ailing you?'

The woman laughs, hand on hip. 'Ailing me? Where do I begin? My children.

My hunger. My pesky husband. Have you any drugs for that, Master Apot'cry?'

'I have herbs to strengthen,' he says and searches through pockets, playing for a little time. Then it comes, as it always does: a pain striking his ear with such sharpness he rubs at it, seeking relief. 'Boil it up and drink in the morning.' He hands the woman a bag of meadow-sweet, casting an eye about the room for the source of his pain. 'Do you have a child with a sore ear perchance?' he asks tentatively, not wishing to cause alarm.

But the woman's eyes narrow. 'If you have been watching us so that we'll part with money on your next visit, then you are wasting your time. I've come across your sort before.'

'I do not wish for payment.'

She studies him, biting her lip, wags a finger at a child.

'Come here, John, see the Apot'cry.'

A young boy of four or five, with deep black circles rimming both eyes, drags his feet in boots that are too big for him across the room. The pain in Jeremiah's ear grows to a steady, throbbing ache. He leads the boy by the arm towards the entrance, to where light pricks holes in the tattered blanket.

Jeremiah's so-called *gift* had started during his apprenticeship under Mr James in his Fleet Street shop. Whenever he had so much as tapped the shoulder of a patient a tingling sensation would commence in his fingertips and spread to specific regions of his body. He would then know—in an instant—what ailed the sufferer and what herbs were required to heal it and,

18

in time, became able to diagnose without any contact, purely by listening to his own body as it transmuted into suffering. On certain days, when having cured the apparently incurable, he imagines such a gift to be a sign of God's mercy, possibly even His forgiveness. Did God not take pity on His sinners? But with some sources of pain borne only briefly, becoming unbearable, what was easier to imagine was that this gift was a curse, an affliction, dispensed by a vengeful God; one he had long ago disappointed.

'How old are you?' he asks the boy.

'That one don't speak. Lost his tongue when his father left these two years past.

He's five or maybe six years old, I forget.'

Jeremiah looks back at the child. 'Which ear?'

The boy points to his left ear. Jeremiah peers inside, at a boil the size of a large acorn. He takes out a quill knife—a man ought never to walk the streets of London without a knife. He presses the boy's face against his leg as he cuts into the protuberance. Pus bursts free, splattering his lips. The rest oozes down his hand and the side of the boy's face. Using the tail of his shirt, he wipes it from the boy's skin then cleans his own mouth.

'It needs to be bathed, day and night.'

The boy presses a finger to his ear and Jeremiah whips it away.

'But not with hands covered in dirt.' He turns to the mother. 'You must bathe their bodies once a month. Dirt left to fester will form boils and much worse.'

'Bathe them with what?' She looks towards the crying baby, hanging from its hook. 'You are like my man: never knowing the work a mother must do, and with no water at the pump and most of the time no light to see by. I tell the eldest ones and Mark there that they must seek work, but there is too much of their father in them. Rather be playing with sticks or stones than out earning their keep.'

He asks, 'Where is your husband?'

'Lost.'

'You mean dead?'

'I wish that he were. He left to find work and never returned. Eight children he left me with.' She whips the wailing baby from the hook. 'Besides this one. This one's not his.' She tugs down her dress and presses the child

19

against a shrivelled bosom. 'You've a lot of herbs in those pockets of yours,' she says. 'You like plants, don't you?'

'I do.' He shrugs. 'For every sickness there is a herb to Cure it.' This thought never fails to bring solace. 'You see, madam, Nature's overarching instinct, so I have discovered along this path, is to heal. It does not care for what we think or feel about this, it heals all the same.'

'Come across anything on that path of yours to help with feeding this child? Some days my milk just won't come. I give him plenty of gin but that he vomits it back up. All night he cries, wanting more, and I am too tired to do anything about it.'

'I have fennel seeds. But you will need the boys to fetch you clean water. The pump at Broad and Cambridge Street is working. Boil the seeds up and drink as tea. You have coal?'

'I can find some.'

He has grown used to the hopelessness of such lives, though not without reminding himself that there is only so much comfort he is capable of supplying.

'Mister Apot'cry, there is another woman in the room next to this, Mrs McKenzie. Her third child has turned yellow. If it does not get better quickly she intends to kill it with kindness. Can you help her? Please.'

Murder was often considered their offspring's best fate by mothers in the Rookery.

'Tell your neighbour to take the child into daylight as often as she can. The sun will see to its colour.'

'Visit her before you go, Apot'cry. She could do with some laudanum, that I do know.'

'No laudanum today,' he says, as his stomach tightens. Unless his dockside meeting goes well, his supply will soon run out and then there will be no ease neither for his neighbours, nor for himself.

He dispenses herbs for the boy's ear and then inspects the rest of the children. All appear filthy, ridden with worms and fleas, but no serious ills. He witnesses this often: children adapting to squalor and surviving; some as young as two, climbing a cellar ladder with the dexterity of a young man. Few, however, grow safely to adulthood, and the workhouse—where unmarried women with children end up—was a place where every 100 children that enter, fewer than five leave alive.

The woman sits dazed by the suckling of her child, wearing a look of helplessness. 'I don't mean to be ungrateful, Mister Apot'cry.' She looks across the room, her nursing expression softening into a half-smile for each individual child sewn up in its winter clothes—a brief picture, thinks Jeremiah, of maternal contentment, something even the deprivations of poverty could not completely destroy. 'But d'you really think that a bag of herbs is enough?'

After seeing to a man with a gangrenous leg and a woman with not an inch of bodily hair, Jeremiah makes his way out of the half-lit warrens of the Rookery, the pains in his ear and legs beginning to subside. Having tended to several hundreds in this parish in the past four years, he can concede that bags of herbs are by no means enough. The government recruited men for the country's battles whilst people in the Rookery—in all the Rookeries in England—waged war daily against poverty and death. But slums were too far from the politician's eye. Even for the policy makers leaving the clubs of St James's, the poor were ugly blemishes, useful only for carrying their chairs homeward or rowing them across river. The Gin Act was not drawn up from consideration for the health of the poor but passed to keep them useful. The alternative: the workhouse and who in their right mind would go willingly to a life in gaol?

Jeremiah pulls an elderly man out of the path of a Hertford stage. As he picks up the man's cane he flinches as pain momentarily emanates from every joint in his body. He closes his eyes against the grinding of it.

'White willow bark tonic,' he says, opening them again. 'Go to my shop in Neal's Yard. Tell my apprentice I sent you. You must drink it thrice daily in order to heal.'

'I do not understand,' says the elderly man.

Jeremiah hands him back the cane. 'You have no need to live with your pains, sir.'

Not as he must do.

'God bless you—our parish angel!'

Despite Jeremiah's reassurances to his apprentice, it seems likely that gaol shall be his home in the New Year four weeks hence. Hardly a fit setting for an angel! And after gaol, and beginning again with nought, prison for him will no longer be a threat but a continuing state of mind. Jeremiah salutes the old man and briefly envies him his faith.

It grows dark in London's narrow streets. He checks his fob watch beneath a lamp: almost five of the clock. The Physic Gardens must wait until another day. He continues south, towards the Thames, picking up his pace, finding, to his surprise that thoughts of Southwark, and what he shall obtain there, brings little comfort.

One month of liberty remaining and then who will tend to the suffering?

More than a messenger

Robert Goode once told his son that people walk in direct proportion to their intelligence, a slow gait corresponding to a state of stupidity. Jeremiah walks briskly and frees his limbs, in the hope that his mind shall soon follow. He crosses from Lincoln's Inn into the City's square mile where streets widen into vast stretches of opportunity. Chairmen and hackney coachmen vie for their fares. All kinds of vendors with quick hands and grubby faces pester the living daylights out of him. The pains in Jeremiah's body grow in intensity.

'Twelvepence a peck of oysters! Four for sixpence...'
'Mackerel!'
'Muffins!'
'Sausage fryers!

Jeremiah's every sense is offended indiscriminately. Fried eel. The grunt of swine. The din of ballads doing battle, enlivening beggars and children alike. He walks in time to one particular rhythm, before a child—quite healthy from a rudimentary assessment (though with freckles barely visible beneath the grime)—blocks his path in an attempt to sell him a lifeless nosegay.

'Mister, mister, a pleasant smell for a gentleman's delicate nose?' the girl croons.

How is it possible that he still appears a gentleman? He shakes his head. But the child blocks his path. He knows better than to push her aside. One wrong move in these parts and he is likely to be flattened by the mob. Thus, with head stooped lower, he dodges her and walks faster, for as with thieves, purpose and vitality are the best deterrents against beggars.

He reaches London Bridge at dusk. By the clock hanging above a watchmaker's shop, he sees he has made good time. He strolls through the bridge's piazzas, peering through shop windows. With his bag of coins he could purchase gloves, jasmine-scented, in the softest calfskin, for 30 shillings a pair. In the face of such luxury, obligations and responsibilities seem suddenly absurd. The solution to all his problems now seems to be a handsome Staffordshire pig in glazed ebony and a watch with an alarum at 12 shillings apiece.

But these cravings are surely for the small-minded. His desires belong to a grander, more enduring plan. Admittedly, he struggles to recollect the pristine blueprint he had once held for his life. Thoughts of debt, of sponging houses and of gaol, have a habit of stripping a man's existence to its bare essentials, and recently the idea of a *prospect* makes him think only of a thick rope tightening about his neck. But, alas, avoiding debtors' prison requires more than his habit of letting the days unfold, blossoming or perhaps withering as they do. Cleverness is required. Cunning transformation. He must become much more than apothecary; he must become a man of *business*.

For the merchants are the clever ones, understanding the sensitivities of their fellow man, his weaknesses, his petty longings. Some are already wealthier than earls. Indeed, if only he possessed their cunning, their insatiable greed, he might then invent a remedy comprised of pig's fat and arsenic, place a large notice in the *Public Advertiser* and have Boswell walking the streets selling the stuff. Eventually, they would all become rich. Thus, he would sleep easy at night as the successful purveyor of a useless Cure-all and would soon be able to buy himself a shop on The Strand, as originally intended, rather than curing hundreds, if not thousands, in a parish of people with nothing left to give.

He swerves, stepping off the kennel edge and into the road to pass a gentleman holding out a penny to a beggar. The fellow sits naked to the waist, his bare flesh tinged duck egg blue.

'What shall you do to earn it?' the gentleman bellows to the mendicant. 'Money does not fall from London's elms.'

A sudden burst of heat emanates from beneath Jeremiah's chest and he knows that the lad suffers from livergrown—the horribly swollen organ rotting to its death.

23

'What shall you do for this?' booms the gentleman. He extends the penny, waving it ever so slightly.

Jeremiah steps back behind the pavement posts just in time to preserve his life, or at least his stockings. A Hackney coach flies past, scattering chicken feathers in its wake and spraying the back of the gentleman's coat with mud. Although the Lord Mayor has decreed carts are to pass into the city on the west side and into Southwark on the east, it seems a man still cannot cross London Bridge without fearing for his life.

The beggar cups his hands, a serene expression briefly crossing his face. The gentleman returns the coin to his pocket, departs, brushing down his coat in disgust.

'Come to my apothecary shop in St Giles tomorrow afternoon,' Jeremiah tells the lad.

'Sir?'

'I shall have some herbs for you and something else for the pain.'

If the exchange at the port goes to plan.

He reaches into his pocket and tosses a hemp bag of milk thistle into the beggar's lap—an action all but useless to a man inhabiting the alleyways of the bridge. 'Get yourself to a water pump and drink as much as you are able,' he says. Even London water was of benefit to the dying. 'Then come to St Giles tomorrow and if you find hot water, in the meantime, steep the herbs.'

'St Giles? I live in St Giles.'

'Then ask for Jeremiah I. S. Goode when you visit my shop.'

'Thank you, thank you, sir.'

From a gap between buildings he takes in the lifeblood of London, the eastern stretch of its river: a place through which it seems the entire world flows daily. A muddle of red and green-painted wherries, yachts and water taxis steer reckless paths through heavy currents of commerce. At least a thousand boats must be moored in the Upper Pool, some waiting many weeks to berth at a quay. Coals from Newcastle. Timber from the Baltic. Cheshire cheese destined for the Royal Navy. It is a sight to set any Englishman's heart aglow until Jeremiah reminds himself of the essence of this monstrous city: *every man is out for himself.* Catching the pervasive stench of the roaring current cascading through the water wheels, he steps off the far side of the bridge and into Southwark.

He heads east, past a dogfight, past sailors alighting from ships, unsteady on their feet. He had once considered sailing the high seas. Even now at four and thirty, if sought out by the press-gangs for compulsory service, he would not object to discovering the world's wonders. It appeals more than the thought of sinking in its quagmire. But to choose escape is to neglect one's purpose on this blessed Earth. Thus he takes opportunity in whatever unlikely place it is to be found.

He waits on a wharf. The gilded hull of the East India Company's *Sussex*, gleams in the setting sun, its sails briefly cast a dazzling white. Snuffle hunters, the port's helpers, unload cargo: tea, cotton, spices. How much easier his life would be as a gentleman of the road, or better still a pirate: shooting at sailors with a pistol and floating downstream buoyant on a barrel, all his troubles ended.

His shoulder twitches as yet another yelp from the dogfight carries to him on the wind. He rubs his gloveless hands together; looks up at hull of the *Sussex*, feeling small, insignificant. He puffs out his chest, attempting to stand taller. He wears a lavishly embroidered waistcoat. He often tells his sister, Rose, whose diligent hands embroidered the waistcoat, that a great mahogany counter exists between him and the rest of the world, that waistcoats pale to insignificance in St Giles. The only people that appreciate such grandeur in St Giles, he tells Rose, are the thieves.

'Goode?'

A man bearing an uncanny resemblance to the skeleton in the corner of Jeremiah's shop appears beside him. He carries a paper-wrapped parcel pressed to his chest.

'Joe Smith sent you?'

'Aye,' replies the fellow whose face is partially covered by his hood.

'You have come from the *Sussex?*' Jeremiah takes in the stench and regrets not purchasing the nosegay earlier.

'The money?' White wisps leave the mouth of this human cadaver.

Jeremiah stalls, 'Remind me of the sum?' He is certain the stench emanates from the fellow's cloak, but at least the amount is less than he thought. He is perhaps cutting somebody out of his share but this is no place to consider another's carelessness.

With yellowed bones poking through his flesh, the fellow holds up the package.

'From India,' he says, as if Jeremiah had just demanded to know its origin when he was instead picturing the tight little balls of resin, remembering how Linnaeus—the father of botany—first classified the poppy, *Papaver somniferum*, as sleep-inducing, in his book *Genera Plantarum*.

A tricky manoeuvre follows, one in which each is afraid to take their eye off the other. Jeremiah hands over the money remaining from the sale of his grandfather's ring. He peels back the wrapping, estimating the parcel's weight whilst the cloaked man counts and recounts, jangling guineas.

'Shall you be needing more?' the fellow eventually asks.

Jeremiah wants to laugh. Aside from spending the last of the money from his grandfather's brilliant on the stuff, he now holds enough opium in his hands to put to sleep half of St Giles. 'Not for a time.'

The man, clearly adrift from the mechanics required for smiling, continues to nod. Feeling something more is expected, Jeremiah turns to the *HMS Prince George*, looming overhead with its three square-rigged masts, so close to the *Sussex* that the snuffle hunters jump between decks.

'A vessel that has no doubt travelled many a stormy sea,' he says, jovially—too jovially perhaps. 'Trade, it would seem, is much recovered since the bursting of the South Sea Bubble.'

He has heard that the port is too overcrowded for the customs officers to cope. The *George*, perhaps, was the vessel this fellow had alighted from. The opium might have been destined for the Royal Navy. If Jeremiah is caught by an inspector from the Worshipful Society of Apothecaries he shall have his license revoked, be fined enough to sink a whole fleet of these ships.

He turns back to the cloaked figure to express his thanks but the fellow is already, his silhouette quickly engulfed in the fog. If not for the package held in his hands, Jeremiah might believe him to be an apparition of impending death.

There was certainly unexpected good to be had from friends in low places and there was perhaps none lower than Joe the night soil man and father of the child he was requested to visit at the Rookery. Yet the Pool is no place to linger in gratitude. Jeremiah shoves the package down his breeches and soon turns his attention to food.

Having a deaf and dumb maid has its drawbacks. Everything works smoothly only so long as he keeps to a routine that is by now so enmeshed into his existence he feels unsettled when straying from it. He checks his watch, decides Boswell will have already eaten his meagre supper, and heads south.

He walks inland. The miasma from the Southwark tanneries grows steadily stronger. Southwark is a place of timber yards, of factories making vinegar, dyes and tallow. A place of prisons and asylums. Yet, there is always a good inn to be found too.

In the yard at The George, coach boys in smock-frocks nest in the thick straw, clutching their few belongings around them. In the Parliament Bar passengers await coaches to Kent, sleeping on benches or in small spaces between trestle tables. Stepping over several such bodies, Jeremiah continues down a number of corridors and darkly panelled bars until he reaches the coffee room at the back of the inn: a large parlour pungent with ale and thick with tobacco smoke. Yet beneath, lies an aroma capable of enlivening the most downcast of Englishman: *roasting beef!*

Jeremiah chooses a quiet and dimly lit table, away from a group of ruddy-faced men playing piquet, and sits opposite a more soberly dressed man, a lawyer—or so Jeremiah guesses by his dark attire and his elaborately full wig. Too hungry to wait to be served, he quickly makes his own way down to the scullery where he comes across a bald-headed cook, crouched low to the sea-coals, blowing into the flames.

'I would like some of that beef,' Jeremiah states, as an Englishman might declare his need for fresh air.

Perhaps mute, or on the other hand French, the cook wipes his brow on his sleeve and points towards the steaks lined up on the gridiron from which Jeremiah selects the largest and waits whilst it is sprinkled with breadcrumbs and a little pepper. He requests honey sauce for it is winter and the beef will be heavily salted. As the cook ladles, Jeremiah experiences a painful burning sensation along both arms. He notices the skin shrivelled on the man's arms by scars old and new.

'Some witch hazel, St John's Wort. Your cuts will heal quickly with these herbs.

Nod if you understand me.'

27

The fellow nods. He hands Jeremiah some chalk and he follows the cook's gaze to a wooden board where ingredients are written in French. He adds his own list of recommended herbs asking, '*Comprenez?*'

The man bows his head. Feeling a favour has been enacted, Jeremiah requests vegetables: a meal for him being incomplete without them. He is gestured towards a pan of sooty mush. Impatient with hunger he declines these, asking for more recognisable specimens to be brought to the table. When finally seated with his food and a bottle of thick Rhenish wine, he drinks an entire cup in one grateful gulp.

'Animal fodder,' says the plump-faced man seated opposite.

'I beg your pardon?'

'Vegetables are mere animal fodder. A man must eat meat.' The fellow's periwig slips low over his brow. 'Flesh feedeth flesh.'

Jeremiah tries a mouthful of steak, thankful, as he often is on such occasions, for his teeth. After swallowing some surprisingly good meat, he says, 'Vegetables save a man money in purging. That is why I do eat them.'

The man appears interested to hear this.

'You are a physician?'

'An apothecary.' There was no surer way to ruin a good meal than with pointless prattle—not to mention the discomfort felt in the company of a man of Law whilst carrying three pounds of illegally acquired opium in one's breeches.

'A tradesman. Well, you neither look nor speak like a tradesman.' The fellow leans across his plate. 'Tell me, the money in your trade… is it good?'

Jeremiah slices off another mouthful of beef. He regrets not choosing the table with the gentlemen absorbed in their game of piquet rather than an argumentative fellow on the brink of gout. 'An apothecary might make two hundred pounds a year.' He shrugs. 'If you consider that good.'

'Two hundred is excellent but you do not strike me as such a gentleman.'

Jeremiah's shoulder performs another involuntary flinch. 'I might make such a sum, if people felt inclined to pay me,' he grunts. Whom was he fooling? All the money in St Giles would not amount to two hundred pounds a year.

'You have a shop?'

'For my sins.'

'Where?'

'St Giles-in-the-fields.'

'And you wonder why people do not pay you?' The fellow laughs.

Jeremiah shakes his head, wondering if he is losing track of the distinction between rich and poor, or at least which category he occupies, no doubt some great deep abyss between the two.

The lawyer sits taller. 'For a gentleman such as yourself, I see the profession of physician as being more suitable.'

Jeremiah takes another gulp of wine. 'I have a preference for plants over people.'

'But physicians are rich.'

Jeremiah thinks of his father, the 12 bedrooms of his childhood home with its extraordinary collection of books and plate, as well as the comfortable, though stifling social arrangements of the village of Dulwich. 'They can be, that is true,' he says. 'But you, sir, what is it you do?'

The man puffs out his chest in anticipation of his reaction. 'I am a footman—a footman most loyal.'

'A footman?'

'Aye.'

'A footman,' Jeremiah repeats with a smile.

'And I do know that apothecaries do rob a man of a small fortune and leave him no better than when he stumbled sick into their shop. If they make two hundred a year it is by no other method than robbery.'

'Indeed.'

The footman adjusts his wig to an angle that better suits his vehemently nodding head. 'If I am sick, I should personally prefer to go to the Dispensary at the College of Physicians to find myself a Cure.'

'I see.'

'For there I should be Cured quickly, and without further assault to my body, for no more than forty shillings a sickness.'

'Forty shillings?' Jeremiah picks something unwanted from his teeth and discards it.

'All said and done, a man would do better seeking help from a travelling mountebank and his bothersome monkey than to go visiting an apothecary shop. That I dare swear my life upon!'

29

Jeremiah shrugs, affirming how healing not persuasion is his art. 'Agreed. Some apothecaries do err toward quackery. Thankfully I do not count myself amongst them.' He picks another piece of meat from between his teeth.'

'No? Well, you must be on the wrong side of something… for a rich man when dying will always call for his physician, never an apothecary.'

'Having money makes a man rich but not always right.'

'What of physician's drugs?'

'What of them? Plenty of physicians turn their patients green from excessive doses of arsenic or mercury. If they concentrated their efforts less on the capabilities of a drug and more on the patient's particular constitution and the intricacies of his maladies, sicknesses would succumb to a Cure. The physicians might then spend less time holding the hand of the dying, lucrative though such work is to them. My herbs, in properly calculated doses, at least heal without harm. Arsenic, I keep for the rats.'

'All tittle-tattle. That's what my employer would say.' The footman flushes. He sits back against the wooden panelling and for a moment Jeremiah thinks him on the retreat. The man rallies, then makes a disparaging sound.

Jeremiah senses he is all puff and no clout. 'Then 'tis good fortune your employer is not here,' he says and eats the last mouthful of beef, wishing he could eat it all over again.

The footman points to his plate. 'Tell me, if all those vegetables do a man good, then why are the poor still sick?'

'The poor eat too little and drink too much gin. And get sick from watching footman catching the farts of the rich.'

The man's fat lips pucker in wordless indignation and Jeremiah turns his attention to the wine. It is thick and strong and with any luck suitably numbing. He takes a gulp and sets down his glass. He had not expected the fellow's sudden solemnity. No matter. Jeremiah prefers to eat in silence— talking whilst eating plays havoc with his gut. He finishes his skirrets and steak with contentment, savouring a food he has not had opportunity or money to eat for many months. Yet, once his plate is empty, the footman resumes conversing as if they are now on friendly terms, no doubt adept at living in the gaps between another's life.

'I wish Her Ladyship went abroad more often,' he sighs, 'but she has been bedridden for two years now. Two years and three months. And I am a fish swimming around a small pond, holed up in that great house day after day. I only wish she would go abroad—*anywhere*—so long as she went somewhere. I never thought I'd see the day where that big mansion would feel like a goal, but that's exactly how it does feel.'

Jeremiah drains his glass and pours himself another. 'Naturally, I have often pondered the wishes of footmen,' he says, and fortified by a full belly offers his dining partner a glass. Any such extravagance can be justified by the prospect of the compendium it seems he must very soon complete: the herbal that shall one day surpass Culpeper's. Not to mention the several pounds of opium tucked away in Jeremiah's breeches, which he will use to relieve the sickest in his parish, and with luck make a handsome profit on from a druggist or two. A cheer of 'Caput!' rises from the piquet table. Life following the intake of beef and liquor brightens immeasurably, perhaps even enough to make the company of a quarrelsome fart-catcher tolerable.

'I have done my duty,' the fellow drones, bulbous lips moving apparently faster than his words, 'performed more than was expected of me. But life cannot forever be so dull. I deserve more than an ailing employer, of that I am certain.'

'So find a position with another employer.'

The fellow's face sinks as low as the table-top. 'I signed a pledge to stay at the side of my mistress until death. I saw remaining loyal as an opportunity and a well-deserved one. Now, of course, I see better.'

'Your mistress…' says Jeremiah, uninterested in what the fellow imagined he deserved; living in St Giles revises any thoughts on deserving. '… does she live in Southwark?'

'Little Chelsea, not far past the Queen's Elm. Away from the hurling and burling.'

'I know the Physic Garden at Chelsea very well.' He would certainly not object to having further opportunities to visit the place *en route* to the footman's sick employer.

'Lady Soloman is presently seeking a physician at Saint Thomas's Hospital. A Dr Edward Michaels.'

'She must be in a state of desperation then.'

'Indeed, but there are few medical men remaining in London she has not consulted.'

'Is she dying?'

'I think not. She is too strong in her mind for death.'

'Distemper, consumption… what ails her?'

'Lady Soloman only converses with physicians regarding her ailments and what with you being a—'

'Member of the Worshipful Society of Apothecaries.'

'It is not fitting for me to discuss Her Ladyship's condition with the likes of you and your trade.'

The footman purses his lips. Jeremiah wipes his hands on his waistcoat: in this city black clothing is worn for good reason. He finishes off his glass.

'Then I hope that your employer soon finds her Cure,' he says, standing. 'I, however, must depart for the hurling and burling.' He pulls on his coat. He now wishes only to be home, to lock the opium safely away and to sleep without dreams. He takes a last look at the footman; though it is a curious analogy, with those bulging eyes and those great gawping lips of his, he does seem to possess a piscine sort of quality.

Outside, in the courtyard, in the rain, the bawdy cries of sailors carry from the galleries above. Jeremiah relieves himself in an alley and in the fug of alcohol it slips his mind to settle his shilling bill.

He stumbles north, past the leather works and the bookbinders and glove makers, alcohol now providing relief, in the form of euphoria, from the usual pervasive maladies. His own emerging melancholy, however, is less easily remedied. Having perfected the art of living in the here and now, it comes as some annoyance that the threat of gaol has scattered his thoughts both forwards and backwards. It is as if he has awoken from a long dream, a delusion in which he had healed the sick without care for his own prosperity, only to discover it to be a nightmare for all concerned; a task rendered impossible without money. The poor needed free medicine, a halfpenny for a bag of herbs being beyond the reach of most. The parish angel! He is but a hopeful dolt, and dolts—*it is becoming clear*—do not benefit from the divine protection extended to angels.

With thoughts of frugality washed away by wine he decides upon a sculler to take him across the river, to part with sixpence and put up with complaints about weather and *trafique* for the sake of a hastier journey home.

He turns into the High Street and just as he does a hand crashes down upon his shoulder.

O, spirit of Divine Retribution, of all the nights to be robbed!

'Did I mention that Her Ladyship is offering a reward?'

Jeremiah's heart continues to thunder in his ears and he grips his chest.

'Any person able to restore Lady Soloman to good health shall be handsomely rewarded,' continues the Fish—from the gilt cord visible on his shoulders beneath a harvest moon it is, of course, obvious he is a footman.

'If you consider wealth a measure of success, what makes you think I am capable of Curing your employer?'

'Your phiz.'

'What about my face?'

'You look,' the man's eyes are directed to the ground as, in the rain, the powder from his wig runs in white rivulets down his cheeks and onto his coat, 'filled with good health, sir. And your voice, though a little worn, tells me you are a gentleman.'

The man has drenched his pride in wine or else is a molly. Then a thought occurs to Jeremiah. 'What do I owe you for dinner?'

'You are willing to surrender an opportunity that fate has thrown your way?'

The glint in the footman's eye puts Jeremiah on his guard. 'No, but *a reward* might mean anything.'

'Her Ladyship's husband has been dead two years. She has only one surviving relative and dependent, a niece who has proved to be more than a disappointment.'

Jeremiah had not asked who would inherit the woman's fortune. But he has tired of conversing in the rain. If the Fish talks sense now he will still talk sense in the morning. 'Come to my shop on the morrow,' he says, lifting his collars. 'We will talk then.'

'Where shall I find this shop?'

'You have to ask? You laughed loud enough when I told you! *Jeremiah I. S. Goode* of St Giles.'

'I like that!' The man laughs again, swaying on his heels, righting himself and crying still louder, 'I like that. I like that a lot. And are you?'

'Am I what?'

'Any *good*?'

Jeremiah doffs his absent hat and turns on his own well-worn heels. 'Let us leave that to your employer to decide.'

'I might add, she is a difficult woman.'

'Then we shall get along well.' Head bent to the rain, Jeremiah sets off towards the bridge.

'*My name is Farley*,' the footman bellows.

'Do not fear, I shall tell my apprentice to expect a Fish!'

Dwindling flames

The lamplighter lingers in Neal's Yard. Theirs must be the brightest, most reliably lit yard in all of London. Jeremiah searches on his threshold for his key.

'Evening, sir.'

'Waiting for daylight to extinguish them again?'

The boy grins. 'Nay, sir, I have lit half of St Giles since you been gone.'

'Go on then. What else do you wish me to tell her?'

'Tell her…' the boy scratches his matted head. 'Jack says she's pretty.'

One day the boy will realise that the only flames he kindles in this yard flare at the top of lampposts. 'Hardly a sonnet!' Jeremiah scrapes his boots on the metal scraper. 'That is all?' It is not the first time he has passed such a banality on to his maid. Last month the watchman had provided a list of his meagre plate, anticipating her hand in marriage. Fortunately, some favours in this parish were not in Jeremiah's power to enact. 'Proper regard for another is more than a chance to lie together. It is a matching of minds. It is respect. Admiration.' He tries recalling what else he had told the last watchman. 'It is moreover the opportunity to see yourself reflected by the light of high regard in another's eye.' Such lies Jeremiah wishes he still believed. The only matching that had taken place between himself and his almost-fiancée Lucy Aldridge had come down to income and income alone. It did not matter that he knew so much about her, even to the arrangement of the freckles scattered about her décolletage. The wheels of society, after all, ran along the ingenious matching of a wife's dowry to a husband's income and prospects, and little else besides.

'Tell her,' says the boy, 'that Jack loves her. He *really* loves her.'

'One day you shall realise that love does not exist, not when a man is full-grown. What we are speaking about here has nothing whatsoever to do with love.'

'A gentleman has other things to consider that are more pressing than love?'

Other things more pressing? Jeremiah wipes the last of the shit from his shoes. 'Indeed, many things more pressing,' he says, 'like discovering ways of paying one's lamplighter!'

The shop bell trills. The boy groans, 'Why does she never come to the door?'

Jeremiah never tells them that Mary does not hear the bell, could not hear a gun fire if it were let off next to her ear.

'Ask her to smile at the window for me, sir.'

Jeremiah closes the door, wondering briefly if Lucy ever loved him. He suspects he loved her in that familiar, comfortable, way born of knowing someone since childhood. Lucy, on the other hand, seemed only to love his prospects—which he had destroyed—that and the softness of his hands.

A burning candle awaits him on the shop counter. The silver holder was a present from his sister Blanche—or was it Violet?—engraved with the proper arrangement of his initials: *I. J. S Goode.* Indigo, as part of the rainbow of colours bestowed upon his mother's children, and Samuel from his father's father, also a surgeon; a man who had claimed to come from a long line of others such as he, capable of performing immeasurable acts of goodness, all the way back to the Domesday Book. The *goodness* of surgeons was to Jeremiah's mind questionable. The definition of the family name, however, was not. It would be preferable if names could skip a generation, as success often did. Then, he might not feel so put upon.

The back room, his elaboratory and office, is fragrant with liquorice and fennel. His pocket watch sits on his desk, tardily ticking. He places the candle on a pile of books and, careful to avoid smudging any pages with London filth, opens his compendium. At such moments he finds himself wishing for a hat with candles attached to it, like those that artists wear, but then wax marks are worse than inky fingerprints and even now the Great Fire is never far from any sane man's thoughts. Every so often, he will take the herbal outside to examine it. On sunny days finds himself surprised by what he finds there splattered, amongst his hesitant script.

He takes the opium out and sets it upon his desk. He takes out the bottle of laudanum from the drawer. He administers three drops from its pipette upon his tongue, to aid a body still recovering from the day's dis-ease. He dips his quill—turkey feather, chosen for reliability over finesse—and pauses, pen aloft. Each time committing his thoughts to paper requires him first to surmount self-doubt, like a man climbing aboard a giant steed. Most people, he believes, think him gifted at curing the poor and the poor alone. Perhaps, they are right. What if the bodies of the poor do differ from those of the rich? Worse still, what if there are no cures, only luck or what God has decreed for every man and woman at birth? It would make Jeremiah a quack on the right side of chance, nothing more but also nothing less. Then a particular patient will enter his thoughts and he will remember how he had cured a chairman's sciatica with kidneywort, how the man's chilblains had likewise benefitted, how he had luxuriated in a month of free chair rides, going abroad simply for the sake of it, and how he had been baked enough pound cakes by nursing mothers to fill a barge. Small victories, but enough to allow nib to engage with paper.

But one solitary month remaining to accomplish his work. A blessed month!

Once the text for a particular plant is finished he will move on to the drawing. If the plant is not in his yard he will hunt it out at the Physic Garden at Chelsea and, if he cannot find it there, he will roam countryside. In his earlier, more enthusiastic days, he spent his Sundays combing the forests and fields of Hertfordshire and Kent, and as far afield as Sussex, picking samples, recording, later distilling, infusing, grinding, and finally testing the herbs on himself. He had pricked his finger with poison from a spider's tooth and watched his body repair; drunk infusions of antimony in order to understand the way the stomach rapidly vomited it up. He had made modifications to what he had learned during his apprenticeship under Mr James. He liked to think he was making a still somewhat fanciful trade more exact, that he was replacing the unknowns Culpeper had filled with the likes of Libra and Uranus, with earth-based facts. Slowly, his personal method became more efficient, less conventional, becoming—as he was presently discovering—*impossible* to record.

'Sir?'

36

His apprentice stands silhouetted in the doorway.

'What is it Boswell?'

'We have no more candles.'

'I beg your pardon?' Jeremiah replaces the quill in its stand, lifts up his periwig and scratches his head.

'I have been teaching Mary to read, sir.'

It is beyond Jeremiah how anyone might teach a deaf girl to read. The prospect of one day communicating with his maid nonetheless allows him to overlook this.

'One must sleep if there is no light,' says Jeremiah, thinking that at times it is as if he is an actor playing the part of employer.

'Sir?'

'Look, what is it, Boswell?'

'Do you think, sir, you shall finish your herbal before the bailiff takes everything?'

'So delicately put.' Jeremiah stares at the blank page. 'Miracles, isn't that what this shop is known for?'

'Aye, sir.' The boy grins. 'Me and Mary do not know what we would do without you, sir.'

'No?' He wipes a hand across his face, dispelling any unnecessary sentiment at the same time, guilt always being harder to bear at night. He scowls at Boswell's pestle and mortar. 'I smell liquorice.'

'A lady came in requesting it for her wheezing, sir.'

'And something else?' His nose was altogether too fine for this city.

'She also wanted rosewater and gum tragacanth and did pay me a penny for both.'

A *penny for tragacanth*, thinks Jeremiah too tired to complain. 'Lady?'

'No, not a lady. A girl. A country girl.'

'Well, she is not wrong. Country girls learn a thing or two about healing from their grandmothers.' Jeremiah scents the air again. 'But I smell fennel.'

Boswell's eyes drop to the boards. 'Mary is feeling a little nauseous, sir.'

'You wait upon her these days?'

'Not often, sir.'

'Freely dispensing my herbs to my maid?'

'No, sir. Yes, sir… I suppose I am.'

'Mary may have her fennel tea, Boswell. Where would we be, after all, without her?' Jeremiah picks up his quill. 'Now leave me in peace so that I may save us from gaol.'

The boy's head continues to hang. 'That is the difficulty, sir.'

'Difficulty?'

What must a man do for peace in this city?

'Yes, sir. We cannot make tea in the dark, sir.'

Jeremiah curses. 'For Heaven's sake, Boswell, take the damned candle!'

'Thank you, sir.'

Jeremiah stumbles to be. He was wrong to think there was nothing to stop him from transcribing his compendium when he is subjected to the whims of his servants and the cost of candlelight.

He takes off his shoes. He is perhaps too soft on Boswell, perhaps driven by the presiding force in his life: that of guilt. Two years ago the boy had come to his shop looking for drugs.

One day he had visited three times, and Jeremiah had told him, 'Your employer will send you to an early grave.'

The boy had said he was waiting on his grandfather. ''E's a tailor,' he'd explained, 'not my employer.' Adding with a sniff, 'He's a Jew who wants to live forever, sir.'

Jeremiah did not discriminate between the ideologies of his patients. Perhaps, another defining mistake. He had given the boy nettle tea and sent him on his way. The following day he had come twice more, looking for remedies for his grandfather's gout. Jeremiah had told the lad in jest, 'Ask him to apprentice you here. Then you may Cure him yourself,' a light comment thrown like pollen into a breeze. He had not expected the boy to return enquiring how much an apprenticeship might cost. At that time Jeremiah had prepared his own tinctures, served his own customers. The meeting seemed too fortuitous. A devil's trap. Nonetheless he suggested two hundred pounds (a sum he now regrets as trifling) for seven years in *loco parentis*, later learning that the boys' grandfather owned three further tailor shops in the city. By then Boswell was installed in the attic. As for the grandfather: his gout was cured free of charge in a month—though six months later he died from falling down his stairs. If there had been any will, Boswell did not benefit.

In the faint glow cast by the street lamps, Jeremiah gets undressed. The laudanum has rendered him soporific. Lured by the prospect of sleep he closes the shutters and gets into bed. Lying on cool linen behind closed bed curtains, he slides a hand beneath his pillow and encounters the crumpled outline of Lucy's last letter.

… and as I am sure you are aware, a physician—like your father—Papa might accept, but not a man engaged in trade. I know you must understand his sentiments, Indigo, for an apothecary is little more than a shopkeeper after all. Thus I implore you to reconsider your decision so that we need waste no more time…

He closes his eyes but rather than Lucy he sees the cloaked woman from the Physic Garden, sees her thickly lashed and inquisitive eyes, brow gently creased as she studies a plant. He sees her moving between flowerbeds, the black fabric of her cloak billowing behind like the mythical sail, until she is, as always, just beyond reach.

Old friends, new eyes

Silently his brother lies slumped over the pail, his head in the water, meadow flowers scattered about his oddly shaped feet. His head lifts. Ducks. Lifts. Ducks again. His gasps for air seem deeper than his lungs. His eyes bulge. A dandelion petal, that had clung to his eyelid, falls into the water. 'Help,' he says. 'Help!' But Jeremiah's hands remain clasped behind his back in a position of stultified fear.

Swimming. Limbs freely negotiating the waters. No need to breathe. Amphibian-like, weightless, perhaps even limbless. He does not care, for this is where it all began. A weightless womb. The waters his three sisters swam through, his brother too. He stretches out a hand—he has hands! He wades onwards, upwards. There is light now. A little speck. He moves quickly, gathering agility. Gathering hope. Nearly at the top. A surface. Beyond lies something wondrous: a golden hue… But wait! A pair of black hands, flashes of pink palm, stretching down; gripping tightly about his neck. A black face, black pupils: two bottomless wells. His gasp for air is feeble but he fights, thrashing with all his might. Too late. He is no more than a fish dying aboard a ship's deck. A last twitch, then nothing.

Jeremiah is awake, scrambling about for the absent candle. He wipes sweat from his brow, catches his breath. The dream flickers between his thoughts like the world observed through the spokes of a carriage wheel. It's as dream him as long as his teeth; a never-ending reminder of his young brother part-drowned, rendered an idiot. Just he regains his breath his heart is awoken again.

Thump.

Thump… thump.

When the next thump rattles the glass Jeremiah throws back the shutters expecting to find the window shattered.

'Who goes there?' he asks, his breath fogging the air as he opens the window wider to find it mercifully protected by its thick layers of grime. *That lovelorn lamplighter will have no rungs left on his ladder by morning.* But leaning out of the window, he sees not the whey-faced suitor but a white-wigged head wreathed in fog.

'It is I, your faithful friend!'

Jeremiah cannot help but smile. 'You! What do you want?'

'A fine welcome for your friend returned from his travels. Come! Time we went to White's. Tis a full moon and I feel Lady Luck must be on my side.'

'What of my sleep?'

'Forget about your sleep! Sleep when you are old or sick and you are neither yet, my friend. Though, I must say, it won't be long, living in this place!'

'And earning my living?' Jeremiah asks, watching his breath hanging uselessly in the bitter cold. 'Perhaps you recommend I do that too when I am old?'

'No, I recommend you don't do that at all! Now hurry or we shall both be old and dead from this cold. My driver waits in Mammoth Street.'

Jeremiah glances back at his warm bed. 'Is there no one else you can bother?'

'Plenty but none such convivial company as yourself…' His old friend scowls at the shop front. '*Mr Jeremiah IS Goode.*'

Or none so conveniently and reliably at home in bed, he thinks.

Jeremiah closes the window and begins dressing. His friend, Lord Frederick Wordsley, belongs to a breed of man so unfamiliar with his own company as to fear it. But of all the places Jeremiah should be avoiding, White's presently rates highest. With the sale of some opium to a druggist or two he might manage to pay off some of his debts, keep Manners from his door until the weather becomes milder and employment improves for the poor. Little building can take place when the mortar freezes beneath the bricklayer's trowel, and until the poor find employment he has less hope than ever of avoiding gaol. Yet despite his drowsiness, there is reassurance to be found in Wordsley choosing his company over that of half the lords in England: society then has not disowned Jeremiah Goode completely. Whether he should on such nights be going to the Chocolate Club is another matter entirely, but with one foot still mired in his troubling dreams he would sooner grasp at present opportunity.

Jeremiah takes the stairs, feeling his way through his elaboratory and into the shop. Here, he unlocks the door.

'The lamps burn well in this yard,' says Wordsley, standing on the threshold, wafting a nosegay beneath his long pointed nose: an immaculate flash of cream silk, shaped like a May pole bare of ribbons. 'You must have a reliable lamplighter.'

'Who is in love with my maid,' Jeremiah replies, stepping into the yard where he finds the temperature differs very little from that of his bedchamber.

Wordsley slaps his back. 'How fares that young Abigail?'

'*Mary* is well. But I have come to believe beauty is a form of revenge upon man.'

'Revenge for what, my friend?'

'For too many things than I care to list.'

'Come, your spirits are low.'

Wordsley gestures him towards the coach. 'I had a fascinating tour, I must say. It has certainly enlightened me as to the wonders of our Empire.'

'I'm sure,' says Jeremiah as he places one shoe on the foot-iron of Frederick's coach and four, fog eddying about his head as he realises he ought to have remained in bed, risen virtuously early so that he could write his compendium in a good light.

He mutters, 'I ought not to be here.'

'What? When we have Lady Luck to court?'

'Look around you, Wordsley. What do I know of luck?'

'Luck does not discriminate my friend. That is her beauty.'

It is also a lie. In St Giles, even colours discriminate. From the windows of Wordsley's carriage, their surroundings appear as an insipid sketch, one the artist has neither inclination nor materials to paint.

As they travel down poorly lit streets, Wordsley passes Jeremiah a fur-lined rug.

'I saw Lucy Aldridge at Vauxhall last night,' he says, 'she asked after you.'

'Lucy is well?'

'Well and handsome. Naturally, I told her that you were working all hours God sent. But must you keep her waiting, my friend? She is such a lively, pretty young thing, not to mention superbly rich. She will be quickly taken if you do not act soon. Shall you marry her?'

'I think not.'

'You think? Ah, but "think" is a word able to prise open a small door of opportunity. Let us head to White's and discuss further what you *think*.'

The carriage's iron wheels scream on the uneven cobbles. Jeremiah stares out at the elaborate façades of the Leicester Square houses where the Prince of Wales' mansion burns brightest.

'You know that Lucy is not without attention from other admirers,' Wordsley continues.

Jeremiah wipes a hand across his face. 'Circumstances have been against me of late.' When had they not been against him—that was the sting of it?

Wordsley smiles. 'And circumstances can change, my friend.'

At one time Jeremiah had written Lucy many letters in which he tentatively spoke of their future together, despite his inability to imagine Lucy Aldridge ever living the life of an apothecary's wife. After a seven-year apprenticeship, his greater inclination had been to explore the world: to discover rare plants and their cures from far afield places such as India and Egypt, yet the match with Lucy had been secured many years previously on account of her father's respect for and gratitude towards physicians, namely, Jeremiah's father. And so—going against Robert Goode's wishes once more—Jeremiah had not travelled to the four corners of the Earth but had rented an apothecary's shop in St Giles. A decision, it seems now, only marginally less rash than renting a shop in India.

'Circumstances may change but in my case for the worse,' he shouts over the din of carriages along Piccadilly. 'And Lucy is not the kind of girl to sit by a fire darning a man's stockings.' Then, curiosity gets the better of him. 'Did she... did she speak of me?'

'You speak of ladies, my friend. They reveal so little these days.'

Jeremiah sighs. 'I suppose I am but a stranger to her now.' He was certainly no longer the person who spent his nights indulging in flirtatious conversation whilst dancing corantos and gavottes at Vauxhall Pleasure Gardens or the person who told the same tireless anecdotes to crowded tea tables, dinner or gaming tables as if life were not held together by charity and love but by fickle conversation and wine. Living in St Giles, his life had become measured by what was necessary and what was not.

'You are right, Wordsley, I cannot expect her to wait for me.'

His friend toys with his frilled cuff. 'Well, she still has not become engaged to anybody else *and* there are worse things that might befall a man than an income of two thousand per annum. Her heart still yeans for you, Goode!'

Jeremiah pauses to search for the appropriate sentiment, knowing all he says will eventually reach Lucy's ear. 'She must not give up her future for me,' he says, aiming to be forthright. 'What I mean to say is that I am quite certain it would be an act of... desperation, for us both, if we were to marry. I wish it could be different but... but apothecaries are not... well, they are not welcomed by Society as the physicians are.'

Wordsley shakes his head. 'You're relinquishing a grand opportunity you know. In the south of England, there is no larger dowry than that of Lucy Aldridge.'

The carriage's axles let out a low groan. Jeremiah regards the blind at the window, half-drawn, the gold tassel at the bottom flicking incessantly. 'So you have called to persuade me into a quick marriage, is that it?' snaps Jeremiah.

'Lud, no!' Wordsley's thick white Rosa Solis face powder begins to crack under the force of his exclamation. 'That would make for a dull evening. I have taken you out to game. Lucy is by the by. I only wanted you to know that you do possess a means of leaving St Giles. Life cannot be enjoyed if one's regrets are too burdensome. I *know*.'

'I have no regrets.' He has made mistakes, of that he is certain, but nonetheless does not wish to compound them by starting again. He was not of the opinion that he had another life, running parallel to this one, and into which he could jump at any given moment. The truth is, he is a different person now. His past he views as a line of discolouration surrounded by solid rock. To examine it, one must first smash it, and since he is not given to violence, he would rather regard it for what it is: set in stone. 'I have seen more sickness than Lucy would see in a hundred lifetimes. I converse with the night soil man and my lamplighter as equals. More to the point, I am practically penniless. What kind of matrimonial prospect is that for an heiress?'

'Irrelevant to a girl who has spent her entire life admiring you.'

'For God's sake, Frederick, Lucy has spent a lifetime *being* admired.'

'And yet she waits for you, my friend. I am certain of it. Going against your father is one thing but turning your back on a grand fortune, well, that is quite another. How fortunate that you have *me* to remind you of your folly.'

Jeremiah takes a deep breath. 'I would prefer to *enjoy* the pleasure of driving about town in your carriage, Frederick.' Opulence, in small doses, can be an agreeable distraction from his daily routine of suffering and curing.

'Well, you are wrong in another respect.'

He slumps a little in his seat. 'About what?' He has been wrong about so many things lately.

Wordsley adjusts his periwig. 'About beauty, my friend.'

'How so?'

'It exists to remind men of love's importance. Otherwise we might spend all our lives at the gaming tables. Is that not the truth?'

Jeremiah laughs as one does at the verity contained in wit.

His friend leans closer. 'And love is entirely necessary in order for women to be able to tolerate us!'

'Love is mere delusion,' says Jeremiah, 'indulged in to ensure the populace increases and keeps breeding like animals.'

'My friend, you have gone too long without the company of a good woman.'

'By *good* I take it you mean rich?'

'There are plenty of women who are both.'

Jeremiah smiles, thinking of the cloaked woman he has observed at the Garden. 'And do you know the difference between loving a good woman and lying with her?'

Wordsley shrugs. 'I suppose not. Let's say then that love is reserved for the poets and the fairer sex. I shall immediately confirm this with one of those who should know beyond dispute.' He lowers the window. *'Madam, pray would you tell us if a man is as capable of love as a woman?'*

The sleepy whore first raises her fist at him and then flashes her bosom.

'Fine girl.' Wordsley dusts off his gloves and closes the window. 'Our city streets are lined with such toothsome delicacies. No doubt it is a fault of my character that I cannot resist gorging.'

Jeremiah suspects it is rather the result of having too much time and money that Wordsley spends his days pursuing leisure, studying books such as Seymour's *The Complete Gamester* or else philosophising about pleasure and pain, his overriding vista being that of the sublime. Devoted as he is to theories of solipsism, evenings out with him are unpredictable at best. He had married Agnes eight years earlier, shortly before her brother had lost the family's fortune in the South Sea Bubble. There were plenty in society willing to ignore his *mistake*, the accoutrements of his own large fortune—the house in Grosvenor Square and frequent balls—far outweighing any ideal of matched incomes. But doubtless his father had worn a hole through his coffin at his son's behaviour, and viewing Wordsley as one black sheep does another, Jeremiah suspects even death does not free a son from the burden of paternal expectation. But these women of the streets tempt rich and poor alike, as sweetmeats tempt children, as a bejewelled woman named Lucy Aldridge had once tempted him at Vauxhall Pleasure Gardens (though, Jeremiah concedes, that hardly seems believable now).

'I am perhaps too driven,' Wordsley is saying, marvelling at another cluster of whores. 'My umbilical cord was cut too long and you know what they say about that!'

'No. Enlighten me.'

'Long cord, long…' He takes hold of his breeches. Jeremiah rolls his eyes, turning back to the window. 'But you, Goode,' says Wordsley his tone becoming serious, 'you deserve a proper marriage.'

Jeremiah loosens his neck scarf. 'Why are those tethered by wedlock so intent on inflicting the same curse upon others? Must a man be deserving of marriage when in the long term he is to be shackled by it? I *am* happy,' he says, the words settling like dust upon the carriage interior. 'I have been absent from Society so long, I doubt I possess the patience or even the desire for courting anymore.' Besides, whores, he had recently discovered as the hypocrisy of this city permeated his bones, required little more preamble than a conversation about the weather and weren't inclined to make one feel so useless, not to mention guilt-ridden.

Wordsley shakes his head. 'Happiness disguised as martyrdom is a cheap way of purchasing one's place in Heaven, my friend.'

'In truth? Well, perhaps I have fewer means at my disposal than most!'

They reach White's Chocolate House. Wordsley straightens his hat and, before alighting, tosses a heavy object into Jeremiah's lap. Gold coins glint at the neck of the purse. Jeremiah sighs. All men have their weaknesses. A deck of cards and a pair of dice had once been his.

'I cannot take it,' he says, joining Wordsley outside the club. 'I gave up gaming when you left for the Continent.'

'See it as a loan, my friend.'

Jeremiah shakes his head. 'My pride I can still afford.'

'Forget your foolish pride and marry Lucy!'

Jeremiah looks at the heavy purse in his hand. 'Wordsley, if I accept your loan, will you drop the subject of marriage?'

'Do I have my gaming partner for the evening?'

'No. I must use your money to settle my debts, and in time shall pay you back with interest.'

'Goode, have you forgotten how to live in my absence? I cannot give money to a coward. What next? Abstinence from whores?'

'Your purse,' says Jeremiah, offering it back to Wordsley who affects not to notice.

'You are too hard on yourself, Goode. Do you see yourself as less deserving of happiness than others?'

'Perhaps.' But Jeremiah is no longer thinking of matrimony but of simpler pleasures: of hot chocolate—there is no chocolate like a White's: imported from Spain, mixed with just the right amount of milk, a little

46

citrus peel and vanilla—and the warmth of a fire, not to mention the sheer joy of *illumination*. He will request a quill, some paper, and continue with his herbal compendium, undisturbed by customers.

'Happiness need not end when a man reaches thirty, my friend,' Wordsley says. 'Life's greatest purpose is joy, after all.'

'Well, I shall reacquaint myself with happiness once I have completed and sold my herbal for a profit. That is if I am not firstly locked up in the Fleet.'

'You require a bookseller to publish it?'

'Indeed I do.'

'I know of such a gentleman!'

Jeremiah had hoped as much.

'And in the meantime,' says his friend, sensing a shift in his direction, 'you will accompany me tonight in a little—'

But the club's door is thrown unexpectedly open. The two men step inside and the warmth hits like the blast from a stove.

'Good evening, gentleman,' says the footman. 'May I?' he adds gesturing towards their coats.

And for a moment, Jeremiah is caught up in the persuasion of comfort; a sensation that only grows as they are ushered into a room so convivial, so warm and red and pulsating with life, they may well have entered the pulsating heart of the city.

Bled Dry

Now that he is living outside society, Jeremiah can see White's as if through the lens of a reflecting telescope. This is a club where few fortunes were won and many were lost. Pharaoh, basset, baccarat: all as unavoidably addictive to the rich as gin to the poor With odds invariably favouring the banker, the weak were defrauded of their fortunes. Trouble was, most considered luck their right. In fact, some time ago, in his carefree years, just before settling upon the profession of apothecary, Jeremiah had watched a friend stake his entire fortune on a five.

'You know what you are taking on?' Jeremiah had warned him as the bet was placed.

But his friend had merely shrugged. 'I do but I am powerless to control myself,'

And in the throw of the dice he lost an 1800 acre estate that had been in his family for 400 years. He had perished not long afterwards on Grubb Street, his decomposing body discovered amongst dozens of gin bottles. Sometimes Jeremiah thinks Wordsley shall meet the same fate. As for himself, a Grubb Street rent already lay beyond his means, his gamble already staked, not on a card but on a profession.

Yet the atmosphere at White's is convivial, a chamber orchestra playing above the din of bets. Somewhere amongst the gathered groups, sits the infamous bet book and amongst its many forbidding entries the name of the first baronet who might one day be hanged—Sir William Burdett—and the accompanying odds. Approaching the throng Jeremiah and Wordsley learn that the cause of this present commotion: whether a certain earl will arrive in a carriage drawn by bay or grey horses.

'Wordsley, how good to see you,' says a man in a full-bottomed wig. 'Do join us. Odds are in favour of the grey.'

'Sir Robert,' says Wordsley, 'you remember Mr Goode?'

The older gentleman raises a brow. 'Son of the eminent Dr Goode?'

'Yes, sir.'

Sir Robert Walpole takes Jeremiah's hand in his. 'Your father is a damned first-class blood-letter. Knows precisely the point at which I am about to become unconscious, thus precisely when to stop bleeding. He does so without fail. A rarity amongst barber-surgeons and physicians alike. A true rarity!'

Wordsley swipes a glass of wine from a passing tray. 'My esteemed friend advises me not to go in for bloodletting,' he says. 'He believes it may damage my health, though I must say on account of his advice, or merely good fortune, I have not been burdened by sickness for an age and, well, the ladies certainly do not complain!'

The *de facto* Prime Minister, Sir Robert shakes his head, sending ripples along his periwig. 'As long as bloodletting is required,' he says, 'it can be borne; and as long as it can be borne, it is required.'

'A pernicious myth,' says Jeremiah, arms folded tightly against his chest. 'And one all too frequently presented as the truth.'

'A myth?' Sir Robert Walpole frowns. 'Look here! There is nothing I enter into without seeking the assurance from past advocates and there is none more reliable in antiquity than Hippocrates, of that I can assure you.'

'To whom no specific text on bloodletting is attributed.' Jeremiah might as well be conversing with his father through the medium of his patient so familiar is the upbraiding. 'Hippocrates believed in Nature and its ability to Cure. Above all else, he did not believe in inflicting harm on people.'

Walpole's face puckers. 'You know that your views go against the doctrines of an entire medical profession.'

'Oh indeed he does! But my friend is prone to going against many a grain,' cuts in Wordsley.

Jeremiah's liver burns and for once it is his own liver. 'The point is, a return to bedside observation is necessary, together with a reduction in hazardous intervention,' he says, quietly yet firmly. 'Physicians are, in short, killing their patients.'

Walpole's eyes widen in the manner of man whose authority is rarely questioned. 'That, young man, is precisely why a physician such as your father has plentiful experience in using the right-sized lancet for the specific part of the body needing to be bled. He knows with the utmost precision— *the utmost precision!*—where lies the swiftest currents of the blood. It is a considerable art to perform well with the lancet, to be able to support the arm of the patient with delicacy and grace through his moments of uncertainty and Dr Goode, your father, has proved himself more than adequate to the job, time and time again. I have nothing but his praises to sing.'

His father's *job* relied on patients becoming inured to the potential danger and unpleasantness of repeated bloodlettings and forgetting how weak they were rendered the last time they had been bled. However, realising his words incapable of moving a fortified wall, Jeremiah acknowledges another truth. 'I am not at all surprised to hear my father's proficiency at bleeding people dry,' he says. 'But of more relevance to me than blood-letting is the idea that many crippled by their poverty do die yearly of a Curable disease, for want of timely advice and suitable medicine.' To whom better than the future Prime Minister should he vent his concerns about conditions in St Giles and many other poor areas? 'As for myself, I no longer have the means or ability to keep the poor of my parish alive, sir—not without assistance.'

'So you a physician yourself, young man? I do recall your father speaking of a son he had high hopes for.'

Jeremiah lifts his chin. 'No, an apothecary, sir.'

Sir Robert laughs loudly. 'A true wit!'

'Goode the Younger speaks the truth, Sir Walpole,' says Wordsley, intervening, quickly realising his mistake in opening up this topic of conversation. 'He is indeed an apothecary. Not only that, he has the shop to prove it.'

The elder man takes a gulp of his wine upon which he promptly chokes. Once recovered, with some enthusiastic back patting from Wordsley, he tells Jeremiah, 'Young man, do not let envy come between you and your father. You will not be the first, nor the last to envy a father's success, but such feeling can only produce a lifetime controlled by the most destructive of forces. You would do better to admit to your inferiority and to stake your ambitions in another profession entirely.'

'*Envy?*'

'Indeed! It happens more often than you can imagine, particularly in cases of sons living in the shadows of respected fathers whose professions they aspire to. Find you own merits, is my only advice. Do not attempt to outdo him, for as I can attest to tonight, the slighting of an eminent physician's skilful methods will only put a strain upon your own reputation. It certainly will not cause any harm to his. Now you must excuse me, gentlemen, for I have plenty of losses to recoup.'

And plenty of lost blood too.

Wordsley leans closer. 'Joining the First Lord of the Treasury, the man who has the country's purse strings at his disposal, will surely bring us some luck, do you not agree, Goode?'

'I think,' says Jeremiah, watching Sir Robert half-stumble to the gaming table, 'I should rather work on my herbal.' He looks to the sofa beside the fire equipped with an adjustable writing table on its arm, at the mantle, candelabras burn brightly: six blessed candles apiece. *Oh precious, precious light.* All he needs now is to find a servant from whom he can request paper and pen.

'Goode?' says Wordsley, prodding him. 'This is not the place for work. Work tomorrow when you are too tired to do anything else. Now, bay or grey pulling this damned carriage? Prove to Wimple you are, at least, better at gaming than your father? What do you say bay or grey?'

He watches Walpole place his bet.

'Chestnut,' Jeremiah replies with complete lack of interest.

'Chestnut? Eh?' repeats a fellow who staggers past, so drunk his eyes appear to have crossed.

'The Duke has thirty horses there must be some chest…chest…some of those beasts,' hiccups another.

Wordsley pats Jeremiah's back. 'That's the spirit!' And he pulls his friend closer to the gaming table and with practised intention extends his purse of sovereigns. Jeremiah, one eye still on the country's future Prime Minister, places a bet on Earl Sandwich arriving with chestnut horses and lets the gold coins slip silently through his fingers on to the cloth.

Miss Heart's visit

On his back, the draft tickling his nose, Jeremiah appears as serene as a church effigy: carefully sculpted, unblemished, deemed handsome by some, beautiful by others. Yet, there's no time for the looking glass, whose spots and smears only irritate. Besides, what use can handsomeness be to a drowning man?

Before settling upon the profession of an apothecary, when his father still provided him with an income, Jeremiah's measure of a night's success was determined by the days it had stolen, three days being the longest, and on the third day—drunk to the point of sobriety—he had won 500 pounds at Newmarket Heath on the Duke of Queensbury's stallion. Such nights, however, did not always end so fortuitously and, despite his efforts, the end of last night remains as blank as an artist's unmade canvas; it is, he fears, the worst of all signs. Thus, he seeks the ultimate escape: that of sleep and with any luck the dreamless kind.

Some time later, at the whine of a milkmaid's cry he opens his eyes and lifts a finger from beneath the cover to stab at the air, his scowl ruining illusions of serenity. Unimpressed, he retreats back into the warmth of the four-poster, sinking into horsehair, into the rare optimism of his dreams with the sense that things might be righted again, that a few keys must be inserted into appropriate locks and that somehow, by some means, he will find the determination to complete his herbal.

When it begins to get dark, Mary comes to check on her employer. She sets down his broth, firmness causing it to form a pool upon the chair from where it drips steadily upon the boards. Mary's actions speak where she cannot. A slight, dainty girl by nature, she is not given to clumsiness unless her employer is deserving of it. Thus, he suspects he has awoken her in the early hours.

Once Mary has exited his bedchamber (with a slam of the door), Jeremiah looks about for his waistcoat before realising he is wearing it. He finds the key in his pocket, where it should not be had it been used, and realises he woke the household by requesting to be let in. Then a more sobering thought washes from the crown of his head to the holes in his stockings, a sensation not dissimilar from bedbugs: *the bag of money won in a game of Hazard?* The wind had come with a flurry of back-patting. As caster in a game of Hazard, the odds had been staked at 10 pounds. With a main of seven and a chance of five he had won 15 pounds in addition to the stake of 10. A total of 25 pounds.

Twenty-five pounds!

Unsteady on his feet, and with a pounding head, he retrieves his coat from the floor and searches its lining to see how much he has left. It is apparent the garment is too light. He checks the waistcoat again, knowing there is barely room in its pockets for a penny. He must have dropped it. His actions become ineffectual means of delaying the inevitable. He searches beneath chairs, beneath the bed, amongst the bed curtains, even lifting up the mattress. Then, he stands in the centre of the room gripping his head, silently blaspheming.

Oh, the effort to stop after only one win!

Once downstairs, he continues his search in his elaboratory, crawling on his hands and knees to discover a candle, a chipped pestle, a lid to a drug jar and a rock of chalk as well as spider upon spider and the remains of their webs, but no purse. In his angst he cannot even appreciate the discovery of a penny. Evidently, Mary had not cleaned the floor for many months. *Might the girl at least use one of her God-given senses?*

'Sir?'

'What is it Boswell?'

'There is a lady here to see you, sir.'

Jeremiah sits back on his heels.

'Lady or woman? As I have remarked on numerous—'

'*There is immeasurable difference*, I know, sir. You taught me well, sir. The point being that this one I believe to be a lady.'

Brushing dust from his hands, Jeremiah stands, scratching his head, flagrantly wigless.

'Lost something, sir?'

'Aside from my mind?' Perhaps, he dropped the purse in the shop. What if it had caught beneath the whore's skirts? Most customers were whores looking for a cure-all for distemper. What if one of them swept it out onto the streets to be lost in the muck?

He stands, and in too much haste to brush dirt from his breeches, pulls back the curtains to which on most days is his stage but unfortunately for this customer they have entered not the performance but the rehearsal, and with eyes scanning the boards, he crouches at her skirts. The woman's cry fleetingly cracks open his wine-weary head. Yet, violet silk does little to deter him. His chest now pressed to the boards he grapples with handfuls of hem and pushes aside a pair of silk shoes asking, 'Could you please step to one side, madam?'

Boswell clears his throat, 'The erm…lady is here about her aunt, sir.'

'One moment, Boswell.' *How damned wide were these skirts? What possesses a woman to wear such volume of fabric in a city of filth?*

But at last, and not without a short gasp, the woman obligingly shuffles her feet.

'Sir? You spoke to the lady's footman…'

Jeremiah stares at his knuckles whitened to the bone. 'Footman?'

'Yes and he did mention the lady's aunt.'

Having straightened any creases as best he can Jeremiah fixes his face with a smile—at least he hopes it resembles a smile. Slowly, painfully, he rises from the floor.

'How do you do?' he says, bowing as low as he can given the state of his head. 'Jeremiah Goode.'

'The lady's aunt, sir, is offering a reward for the person who might restore her to health,' interjects Boswell.

'Ah!' says Jeremiah, flattening his wayward curls, last night's excesses still gripping his head like a vice as well as producing a peculiar soreness over one of his eyes. 'Forgive me. I was expecting to see somebody else.'

The lady—for there is no mistaking that now—already has a hand to the door.

'Madam,' says Jeremiah, sweetening his tone, 'you have come about your aunt?'

'That had been my intention.'

'Then how might I assist?'

The shop bell trills as she opens the door and Jeremiah is brought back from his lost winnings to the present: to a lady standing in his shop visibly trembling. But taking in her plain face and tightly pursed lips as she stands with one hand on the door handle, he notices one of her eyes: mossy green, no lashes to speak of, but startlingly red and greatly swollen. He blinks back the pain in his eye, a raw throbbing sensation which prompts the first of the day's gambles.

'Your eye, how long has it been that way?'

'My eye?'

'You must allow me the liberty of recommending a herb,' he says, shame lifting the end of each sentence to the pitch of a choirboy. 'Raspberry leaf tea? Bathe the eye thrice daily. You will find it righted before the week is through.'

'I think…' she half pants, reaching again for the door handle, 'it is you who are deserving of the most pity, sir!' She raises a hand to her bonnet as she negotiates cobbles, crossing the length of Neal's Yard. Jeremiah watches this figure in violet, a knuckle pressed hard to his lip.

'I did tell you she were a *lady*, sir.'

'That's not the sting of it!'

'You have lost something of importance, sir?'

He watches opportunity disappear around the corner, before considering the boy. 'My mind. I have lost my mind.' He pats the skeleton *Nicholas Culpeper*. 'Suffice to say it has been a time of vast disappointments, Boswell.'

Boswell brushes herbs from the counter. 'That's what Mary said this morning, sir. How disappointed she was.'

'Mary?' He swings round to face the boy. 'How was Mary disappointed?'

'When she came down to open the shop for you at sunrise.'

'Well, you tell her that she is the least put upon maid in the whole of Christendom!'

'You certainly put upon her last night, sir.'

Jeremiah pictures Mary's face, pale and innocent. 'How?' he asks, a scattering of heartbeats catching in his throat. 'Did I put upon Mary?'

'You and Lord Wordsley put upon her very much indeed, sir.'

Of all the disturbing things today had brought this is surely the most shameful!

'You both did insist Mary dance, sir, and she hates to dance. She said you pulled her onto the counter and made her dance an Irish jig for an hour. Me, I had to scrub the counter for a further hour this morning to remove the blessed dirt.'

Jeremiah sighs. 'Then apologise to her sincerely on my behalf. I need tea. Meadowsweet, black horehound and a little honey to sweeten. Bring it up to my chamber.'

'What is it you taught me, sir? That alcohol is but a poison to the body?'

Jeremiah recoils from the stabbing pain at his temples, from these moments of piety when he feels inclined to preach. 'Or was it that insolent apprentices are wholly replaceable!'

To truly remain alive, one needs hope just as one needs breath, hope in all its myriad forms. Jeremiah—or so he likes to think—instils hope in his customers, for hope alone holds power to heal. Yet how can he be expected to give hope when he no longer possessed it? How does a man so perpetually struck down continue to proceed through life on his knees? He is not angry at God. If anything, God has offered him this very morning an angel; an angel in the form of a rich lady's niece and what had he done?—abused her skirts and causes her to flee. No, it was not in the direction of God that his anger ought to be vented.

He checks the drawer of his cabinet for the opium. It is still there, pungent, raw, a collection of comforting amber coloured tears. Later, he shall prepare a tincture with alcohol turning it to laudanum, a rusty-brown liquid capable of improving the lives of even the most wretched. Laudanum, from *laudare*, the Latin for *to praise* though Jeremiah calls his tincture *Goode's*, for

55

he adds cayenne pepper, a little citrus like Paracelsus, the Swiss alchemist, leaving out his recommendation however for pearls and amber—plants being Jeremiah's belief, not stones. Yet believing a little in Galen, he can see why the Roman physician saw the poppy as dangerous yet but, in truth, he is too weak to leave a man writhing in agony; certainly too weak to bear witness to his own suffering. If he could not provide hope, relief would do. Yet for his patients it is last resort; opium if the dose is large enough can kill a man in less than an hour.

His mind returns to the lost money and his own descent into hopelessness. He had planned to return the purse to Frederick, and the profit—the sum he had made from the chestnut horse and the game of hazard—he would keep for himself or rather hand over to Mary for food and the rest to Manners, the debt collector, keeping a small sum back for ink and for candles and coal to last throughout winter. He also had Wordsley's promise to find him a bookseller with whom to publish his herbal compendium. In short, the win at White's, had provided an opportunity to save himself from gaol and what had he done? *Dropped it.* He must add the sum to the rest of his debts, piling up around him like corpses in a common grave. The sting of it all: he finds himself in a worse predicament today than he was yesterday!

For supper he eats a meal, comprising entirely the foods he dislikes. Though Mary may be mute she possesses certain power. She lifts her chin and refuses to meet his eye. She is a woman now, he thinks taking in her posture, her generous bosom. Gone is her former childlike desire to please, a thing brought with her from the Female Orphan Asylum. But her beauty still remains. A beauty he had once wanted to protect. He was sure it had made the workhouse weary of him; there were, after all, too many gentlemen in London willing to take advantage of such a beauty, in spite of or even because of Mary's limitations.

But Mary has become a good maidservant, one who takes pride in his home, and this is of more value to Jeremiah. At times he wishes he had the means to make it a proper home for her, occasionally entertain guests. His family were not permitted to visit, a rule enforced by Jeremiah's father, and aside from Wordsley there were no remaining friends. In truth, Mary and Boswell were his family now.

After settling at his desk, he finds his earlier state of misery alleviated by smoking *just a little* of the opium—in a pipe—followed by concentrated work on his herbal.

Artichoke, *Cynara scolymus*. A tonic for the liver. An aid to digestion. A plant capable of making any man fart from here to kingdom come!

Having accepted his apology—she can lip-read when she wishes—Mary brings him tea.

'I am weak when it comes to the gaming tables,' he says. 'Wordsley is not the best influence on my life.' He clears his throat. 'When my father provided my income Wordsley and I did gad about town for a time, but...' Mary regards him; head tipped to one side wearing an expression of genuine concern. Does she understand him? He often feels she understands him more than he understands himself. 'I had no inclination to become a physician like my father. Naturally, he was unwilling to support my gaddingindefinitely and so I had to do something with my days and here... well, here I am, Mary.'

Mary smiles. In the light of that smile he thinks forgiveness from one so sweet might almost be enough. As soon as he had set eyes on her at the Female Orphan Asylum, he had sensed her purity, something he worked hard to distil in his elaboratory. In time, they managed by various forms of communication until they had built the scaffolding of routine. But Mary has not been paid for the last month. And though Jeremiah is certain that if he were to look closely he would find a discreet halo beneath Mary's lace cap, he knows too that it will not be long before she seeks a new position.

Wearing her serene smile, Mary exits the room. Jeremiah sips his tea, staring into the dwindling fire. To detract and perhaps prevent the collapse of his household, he thinks about visiting Miss Heart for he must apologise to the woman. Can the village of Chelsea be so large? He remembers her aunt's name: Soloman. *Lady Soloman*. Yes, on the morrow he will depart for Chelsea and seek out his salvation. It will provide an opportunity to call at the Physic Gardens on the way, where he might give Boswell some further, much needed, instruction and if, by chance, he happens to see the cloaked woman, he shall insist upon knowing her name. So happy is Jeremiah at this decision, it quite slips his mind to take any more opium. He subsequently retires to dreams that are not so much brimming with dread, but offer instead a thing so foreign to a man standing on the edge of an abyss: that he sleeps far too late, enveloped in comfort.

The Physic Gardens at Chelsea

But by mid-morning Jeremiah's yoke is firmly in place. After the loss of his winnings, further disappoint arrives in this morning's post from his druggists who refuses to purchase opium from an unknown source. Jeremiah holds the crumpled letter in his fist, staring out into dismal light of Neal's Yard.

'Damn the Law,' he tells Nicholas Culpepper, to which the skeleton appears to grin in earnest.

Jeremiah briefly wonders if he should visit his father and ask him for the money, he has enough of it. Trouble is, the prospect of returning home remains only slightly more attractive than gaol.

He has commenced 'B' today in his herbal compendium, though frequently himself questioning what qualifies him to write such a great body of work, which does nothing to hurry its completion. Yet in bilberries he holds certain faith, faith in its ability to potently creep along the earth, and to capably cease a woman's menses in a matter or weeks. He shall make a sketch today at the Physic Gardens. Fresh air and nature, that is what is needed. Besides, he cannot neglect his duties as Boswell's tutor, the gardens serving as both garden and schoolroom. He has neglected too much of late. Besides, a visit to the Gardens might relieve him of his recent passion for a cloaked woman, a thing that inhibits him at times more than the lack of candle light.

Half a mile from Neal's Yard and Boswell is shedding his cloak of courteousness like a wet dog drying itself, delighted to be out of the confines of the shop. His sleeves are rolled, brown eyes a sparkling. Piccadilly and the Hay Market become places rife with street sellers and ragamuffins.

'Rosemary, sage or thyme, come buy my knotted marjoram?' says a simpler pointing to his basket.

'Not for us,' says Boswell, firmly.

'*Dandelion, houseleek, pennyroyal and marygolds,*' the simpler continues, ranting now prancing beside them, holding up limp bunches of his leaves, '*Water-cresses and scurvy grass, dragon's-tongue and wood-sorrel. No need for a physician or an apothecary, not with my herbs. No need to look to distant shore with my herbs to explore.*'

Boswell groans 'He tests my patience, sir!'

'A penny is a small amount,' the simpler drones. 'Some parsley, some winter-savory? What say thee to some thyme?'

Despite the stains on his clothing, Boswell is too well dressed. He wears an old waistcoat of Jasper's and coat with gold brocade and buttons, appearing more of a gentleman than a lowly apprentice and sellers liked to assume well-dressed customers had their purses wide open to every hawker that accosted them. 'You must remember, Boswell,' Jeremiah tells him, patience is a virtue to cultivate, as assiduously as we cultivate our tenderest plants.'

Boswell spits. 'Patience is a thing I have ran out of, sir. As yours too must be wearing thin.'

'God demands faith. He does not state for how long it must be applied.'

How much easier to preach than enact!

'*Sell them to your master. Make a handsome profit,*' sings the simpler.

'My master gets his from Covent Garden where they not be *dying*!'

Jeremiah lowers the brim of his hat. Truth be told, these outings abroad were often better amusement than a trip to the Theatre Royal.

'*Lovely pair of diddleys!*' Boswell shouts.

'*As sweet as you will ever taste,*' shouts back a gingerbread girl.

Jeremiah hits his head. 'Can you not keep your mouth shut for a moment?'

'I confess it is difficult, sir.'

In the shop the boy remained charming to customers, listening attentively to some of the biggest bores. He possessed the ability—one Jeremiah lacked—in getting them to part with their pennies with youthful enthusiasm, but out here on the streets he was inclined to express himself too freely. Jeremiah suspects such brawls serve as a necessary release for his truer, brusquer nature, leaving his countenance on their return somehow cleansed and unsullied.

But acting as the boy's guardian—as Mr James had once acted as his—it was Jeremiah's responsibility (at least occasionally) to instil moral as well as herbal guidance.

'You,' Jeremiah tells the boy. 'Are a damned nuisance!'

Boswell grins. 'But life, would it not be dull without me, sir?'

Jeremiah feels like ringing his apprentice's neck. 'Hurry!' he orders, he hopes with some authority. 'It shall be dark before we leave this wretched city.'

They walk on, silence occasionally interrupted by Boswell's bursts of admiration. They pass the new St George's Hospital at Hyde Park Corner and the tollgate. Eventually they reach the King's Road—the King's own road to Kew—walking through twisting lanes at a steady pace just beyond tiredness. Now and again the boy stops and checks his teeth. Jeremiah tastes the salt on the air, blowing in from the marshes. What's left of the season's greenery creates space inside his head for new thoughts. He listens to the call of a blackbird, admires later flowering heliotrope and wonders, as he often does, why he insists on suffering this city.

To begin with London had offered the promise of infinite business, then he discovered its snares. What business came his way was quickly spent on the business of living. London was little more than a leech, sucking the lifeblood from its inhabitants. It was foolhardy to think he might one day win; far easier to imagine a lifetime of having one's blood sucked dry.

'You shall accompany me after the Physic Garden to visit Lady Soloman, the rich widow aunt of Miss Heart,' he tells the boy.

'Is she dying?

'Not immediately. She has been bedridden some time. I suspect she suffers from melancholy.'

Boswell stops abruptly and grips his chin. 'Of low spirits. In women it is often confused with hysteria. There are two types of melancholy, sir, natural and unnatural. Natural is brought on by black bile, often dried up in time and caused by the eating of certain foods and strong wines.'

'And also indulgent and compulsive behaviours,' adds Jeremiah, pleased to have his apprentice back again. 'Treatment for melancholy?'

'A balance of good sleep, play, exercise, company—' Boswell pauses, wiggling his brows—'and carnal dealings.'

'Correct,' says Jeremiah. 'Stimulation of mind and body, and a pressing need to keep the patient from being sad. If any one of these elements is absent the black bile will surely rise.'

'But there is a second kind of melancholy, sir, for you have not mentioned corruption from demons and spirits.'

'I do not think we need to consider that here.'

'The devil, sir, he comes in many disguises.'

He likes that the boy strives for independence, for in striving the seeds of self-reliance are sewn but bring the Devil into the fray and one may as well be craning a neck to the skies like Culpepper.

'I am prone to thinking Lady Soloman's melancholy is the kind in which the mind becomes fixed on one particular object,' he tells the boy. 'She doubtless mourns for her dead husband and this melancholy has created internal bitterness. I have seen it many times in widows who take to their beds. It makes little difference whether the husband was worthy of such mourning. In fact, I suspect it is possible to grieve even for the absence of one's hatred.'

'Why does she not rise from her bed, sir?'

Jeremiah takes in winter aconite, golden yellow, offering certain hopefulness beneath a copse of oak trees.

'Without daylight,' he says, 'people, like plants, wither and die, though more inconspicuously than most people. I suspect this is the reason. I shall dispense some angelica for her lungs. If I can persuade her to sit in sunshine I am certain she will heal quicker.'

'And if she is bitter as widows are wont to be?'

He briefly laughs. 'Plants, I am afraid, can only do so much.'

The boy counters his smile with seriousness. 'But on this occasion they must do everything, sir. For if they do not then you shall not be saved from gaol.'

At times he preferred the boy as an urchin. 'Thank you, Boswell.'

'Is this your alternative plan, sir, if your compendium is not finished in time?'

'With a thousand pounds I am inclined to think of it as a premier plan.'

The boy lets out a long whistle. 'A thousand pounds! Well I be kicked in the teeth, sir.'

'Not yet but anymore bad behaviour on the city streets and I may very well be doing that myself. Now, we have work to do.'

The garden behind the shop in St Giles was pitifully small, barely able to provide enough room for 30 or so herbs. The light it received was inadequate, the plants stunted, blackened by smoke and eaten by vermin, the rosemary and mint the only species to thrive. In short, life in Jeremiah's yard proceeds as it did in the rest of the parish: with a struggle. Yet at Chelsea, flourishing simples fill the well-tended gardens and once a month or more Jeremiah instructs the boy here on medicinal plants, preparing him to collect from fields in the summer and perhaps one day he will tend to his own garden. Lately he has been teaching the boy about plants from the continent, from the Americas and the Orient, ensuring he will be as familiar with tea seedlings as with *Yucca filamentosa* or *Madagascar periwinkle*. But over the 12 years Jeremiah has been coming here, the garden has altered, becoming unrecognisably exotic in parts so that he often finds himself learning alongside his apprentice. He learns from gardeners, recalls what he can of his studies under Mr James, and in this pleasant state of remembering and absorbing invariably forgets the existence of time; problems becoming as relevant as the green fly crawling from leaf to leaf. Such moments provide him with reason why he has chosen the pitiful life of an apothecary.

He had first come here with his father, jogging after Dr. Goode as he marched about the garden's pathways in his red coat, clutching his gold-headed cane, looking not for a particular plant but for an apothecary he might trust. When he found the face he was looking for he would say, 'I have a patient. Interested?'

If the apothecary indicated an interest—sparing his father with any luck from details such as his name or where he kept shop—symptoms would be shot at him: *cachexia, dropsy, palsy, ulcers, gout, consumption,* like acorns dropping from oaks. A patient's pain would be turned into words as English was turned into foreign tongues, and Jeremiah would listen in wonder, imagining what such words meant or meant to his father the physician, the surgeon. It seemed to Jeremiah that his father considered the apothecary's job to remove such words, as the man came at night to remove effluent from the cesspit and, from the tone of his father's voice it seemed there were parts to sickness his father did not comprehend, as if he preferred passing these symptoms onto others so that he could sit and reap vast sums per annum instead. However, it was not the sickness that appealed to Jeremiah. He had little interest in such words. It was the plants: their beauty, their simplicity. It was the state of magnificent awe held for a thing so unassuming, so apparently powerless yet capable of ridding a man of his every disease; for every disease there was a cure—a delusion, perhaps, but one he was willing to stake his life upon because his belief in Mother Nature never wavered. But if these plants had not held powers to heal, the language spoken by his father all those years ago would have remained strange for, unable to tolerate further ridicule and punishment, Jeremiah had been too cowardly to announce his desire to study botany. Thus, his father continued dragging his son to the gardens and to the coffee shop where he practised his trade, to Westminster and Guy's and the newly opened St George's Hospitals to remove the usual gallstone, assuming he was preparing the boy to become a physician or at the very least a surgeon. What Robert Goode had not counted upon was a son having a mind of his own.

Inside the red brick perimeter wall of the Physic Gardens, a man with a bulbous nose rakes the soil in furious motions. Protected by tall walls and the heavy trafique on the Thames, medicinal plants remain unaltered by the harshness of winter. Jeremiah looks with satisfaction across the four well-tended acres. His shoulders drop a little and a rare smile crosses his lips.

'What shall I draw today, sir?' asks Boswell, yawning at his side.

'Wormwood,' Jeremiah tells him, exhaling deeply, 'Common wormwood and Roman wormwood.' Wormwood is a herb that he drinks with rosemary, blackthorn and saffron; a herb to keep a man's body in good health, though it was also a herb to give him impossible dreams. 'Tell me of its uses.'

Boswell's hand shades his eyes from the sun. 'Mothers do give it for their children for the worms, sir.'

'Correct, and remember too that it strengthens the weak. Roman Wormwood, it often grows on tops of… ?'

'Trees, sir.'

'No, mountains.'

The boy cranes his neck.

Jeremiah follows his gaze. 'Pray, what do you keep staring at?'

'That woman again, sir.'

Jeremiah looks again. The third time he had seen her she appeared in the kitchen garden, wondering a pathway in a long black cape, hood pulled up over her head. He was struck by the way she held herself, the way she moved—without inhibition—hair hanging loosely over her shoulders. A woman in the gardens was as rare as a bearded tit, a beautiful woman akin to an apparition. Briefly he had followed her, seeking, when necessary, refuge behind an elderberry bush. He had seen her twice since and the last time, and perhaps the reason why his mind kept returning to her, she had been conversing with the Head Gardener, Mr Miller, on the subject of *Ammi majus* and its effectiveness against the scaly skin condition *psora*—a herb Jeremiah had also found helpful for the condition, though it was not incorporated under his apprenticeship with Mr James. She had spoke in a lively, self-assured fashion despite Mr Miller's dismissiveness but before Jeremiah could contribute, she had bid Miller farewell, pulling her cloak over her loose, raven hair. Though he had searched the gardens many times over, he had not seen her again, nor since.

Jeremiah follows Boswell's finger to a small Yellowroot bush. 'You are correct, there are no women apothecaries in the whole of London,' he says, 'I expect she comes for another reason, to draw flowers or pick them but today you are mistaken.'

'I did see her,' says Boswell, continuing to point. 'Now disappeared behind that tree.'

Jeremiah screws his eyes against a brief burst of sunlight but finds only plants and the garden's greenhouses. Besides he has previously seen her on Thursday. 'There is a time for imaging women and a time to draw.'

'Sir, I saw that woman again, the one in the black cape. I know I did.'

'And there are ghosts in the St Giles' cemetery! Roman Wormwood, it is good for…?'

'Sleep.'

'Jaundice! Do I teach you nothing?'

'No sir, I mean yes… sir.'

'A good Cure for the sting of a wasp or a scorpion!' He slaps the boy hard on the back. 'And Skullcap tea works wonders for a mind that roams!'

Jeremiah takes out a sheaf of paper—cannot presently spare more—and hands Boswell the quill and ink from his coat pocket. He smiles at the thought of seeing the woman again within these four walls (and he casually looks for her). The Physic Gardens after all was a place for seriousness, not for appreciating the prettiness of flowers or discussing the frivolities of fashion. No matter their enthusiasm for botany, no woman's mind cannot help ponder such things.

But was it any wonder the boy was distracted? He had spent a week sitting behind the counter of an empty shop, waiting 12 hours a day for a handful of customers who fled (few could read the sign) once they realised that rumours were true. In refusing customers more credit in the midst of winter, Jeremiah might as well have put a sign above the door reading: 'Open only to the rich.' But, of course, he has no further say in the matter. The bailiff has given his orders and until he could pay off his debts he was little more than the dun's reluctant puppet.

'Go and at least draw correctly,' he instructs.

'If my hand is not frozen first!' replies the boy.

Jeremiah gives him a shove and takes out his own quill and paper. Although he too has come here to sketch—specimens for his compendium—he had also hoped to see her face. But his herbal is a means of ordering his mind. Arranging it is an onerous task, a matter of gathering discoveries made upon scraps of parchments, empty boxes, the walls of his elaboratory. It has brought to light his unorthodox methods. He cannot say for certain that the cure for one person will work for another or that one person will react to a herb in the same manner as his brother. He has, as he preaches often to Boswell, always treated the individual, not the sickness. For this he relies heavily on instinct, though it seemed more complex than that. To the onlooker it might appear he was making it up as he went along. Perhaps, he was. He could only describe it as a *knowing,* in the way one knew there was a God but was at pains to prove so and most days he feels plants and their powers is the only thing he knows at all.

He draws steadily the leaves of woody nightshade, a plant Mr James had used for relieving obstructions. It was useful as a tincture: four to six ounces of twigs added to a quart of wine. He has a mind full of such measures. Rarely does he forget a recipe. His head is a place for doses, for weights and for other memories he should rather forget.

In a half-daze he sketches the windy, woody stalk, thoughts turning to his brother Jasper. He shall take him more herbs. It has been too long since he last visited, since he last stealthily crept into his childhood home when his father was out tending patients. This time he shall take some passionflower, a little hawthorn, calming to the nerves. 'Each time something new and each time a little eased.' But after Violet has said these words Jeremiah will look to his younger brother unsure if his sister merely humours him. He has been treating Jasper since he was apprenticed under Mr James. Perhaps there was slight improvement, perhaps Jeremiah's visits to Stony Hall were too infrequent to be of much use but if the sun burnt itself out of the sky he would bring him tinctures, tonics, rubs, together with his merciless guilt. Besides, he has healed sicker than Jasper. And though his brother may be sick in both body and mind, the mind cannot be so very different from the body. The two were inextricably linked by one insufficient neck after all. Could not the healing of one contribute to the healing of the other? Jeremiah attempts holding this belief but at times it is a little like grasping a dream once the shutters are drawn back. It returns to him every now and again, muddled. *If I can heal the mind I can heal the body, or the body can be healed and the mind will follow.*

I can heal, he tells himself. *I can heal. I can undo all that I have done…*

Woody nightshade at high doses could lead to vomiting and convulsions; its bitter berries poisonous.

He looks up, shading his eyes from the sun and for a moment thinks, in a greenhouse originally built for conserving evergreens, he sees her dark silhouette moving through it like a shadow.

'Precision is the point to this exercise, Boswell. *Calendula officinalis* has very different petals to *Borago officinalis*. God is in the detail. This is not an approximation,' says Jeremiah, examining Boswell's drawing.

'I will look again at God's details, sir.' Boswell grins. 'This time I did see her, sir, over there.' He points to greenhouse, Jeremiah had been observing not 30 minutes earlier. 'There she is. See?'

Jeremiah's squints past the statue of Sir Hans Sloane, the garden's founder.

'I expect she is an acquaintance of Mr Miller's?' he replies, quite fascinated.

'Nay,' a nearby gardener replies, leaning against his rake as the woman exits the greenhouse and stoops to pick a sprig of rosemary. 'She is acquainted with the *Praefectus Horti,* Mr Rand…She travels up from Dorset. Calls herself an… *herbal healer.*' The fellow speaks slowly, cautiously. Jeremiah holds his breath, waiting for him to continue. 'What she does not know about plants…God does not know about 'em neither. Mr Rand, he gave her a corner of the garden to manage for herself … Mr Miller, our head gardener, was not happy with such an arrangement though… But it flourishes, and better than the rest. We have learnt much from her methods.'

How had he missed this flourishing corner?

They watch as she rubs the herb between her fingertips, bringing it to her nose, eyes partly closed. Her lips part as she takes in its scent. She was, Jeremiah decides, a woman straddling the living and the divine: an earthly goddess, one permitted within unreservedly masculine walls.

'Are you regarding me?' she says looking up and frowning at the slack-jawed men.

'Forgive me…us,' Jeremiah steps forwards. 'We, erm… like yourself, are here to study plants. May I introduce myself, Jeremiah Goode.'

The woman does not move. She stands tall, spine proudly arched. 'You cannot claim to know why I am here,' she says—her voice deep, commanding, not a lady's voice but not a peasant's either. 'And besides, you were staring at me, not the plants.'

Jeremiah remains speechless, struck by the darkness of her eyes, the thickness of her lashes, even the delicateness of her earlobes. He wobbles like a man attempting to balance his toe on a penny, racking his mind for something of intelligence. Too late, she has lifted the hood of her cape, and exited the kitchen garden.

'Always the way,' says the gardener. 'Here, then she is gone again.'

Jeremiah replaces his hat. 'Her name?' he asks, watching her enter a glasshouse, cape ballooning behind like a ship's sail in some mystical, magical wind.

'We call her…the Angel… the Dark Angel,' the gardener replies.

'But what of her name?'

'That, sir, I do not know.'

'Does she come here alone?'

'Aye, though some say she has a dog, a black dog, that accompanies her, though I have never seen such a creature.'

Jeremiah strides up the garden path, feet crunching over gravel.

'Are you following her, sir?' says Boswell, trotting at his side.

'What?' says Jeremiah, wishing that the boy would disappear.

'We have almost reached the glasshouse, sir, where that lady—'

'Boswell pay attention. I am searching for a Cure for the old hag.'

'Sir?'

'Lady Soloman.' Jeremiah stops dead, pointing at random. 'Kidney wort. Effectual for inflammations and unnatural heats. Also helps cool a fainting stomach, a hot liver...' He squints as he regards the dark aura of her cloak, observes her graceful, gliding movements as she moves about the glasshouse as if on ice. He can picture her dark, thickly lashed eyes, can hear the distinct strength to her voice. But it is not enough to recall these things from memory. He wants those eyes to be looking at him, for the voice to address him...

'Liver, sir?'

Jeremiah turns briefly back to the clumsy, round leaves of the plant. 'Yes, liver. It cools a hot liver...and heat in the bowels. Useful in treating swollen...'

She has exited the glasshouse, is coming his way. He straightens his hat, stretching his face with a smile.

'Swollen, sir?'

She passes them by, eyes not straying from the path. Jeremiah inhales something of her wake, shudders involuntarily, repressing the urge—more an instinct than an urge—to call out her name, her epithet: *the Dark Angel. The beautiful Dark...*

'Swollen?' repeats Boswell.

'Scrotum, Boswell. It eases swellings of the damned scrotum.'

Boswell looks at him strangely. 'Very good, sir.'

Jeremiah removes his hat and wipes his brow. How was any of this *good*?

I assume you know of the reward my aunt offers

'Sir, we have called at eleven houses so far and it is getting dark.'

'A thousand pounds is at stake,' Jeremiah reminds his apprentice, gritting his teeth and lifting yet another knocker. 'So we will call at every house in Chelsea until we seek Miss Heart.' He blows into his hands. Five or six floors of Palladio-style mansion loom above. For some reason instinct tells him this might be it and if so, the Fish indeed has a wealthy employer.

'You again!' says the fish-like footman, correcting himself with a hiccup and an unctuous, 'Good day,' preceded by a clandestine wink. He ports black satin breeches stretched over ample thighs with blue stockings squeezed between a pair of elaborately buckled shoes, the fat of his anatomy bunched here and there at regular intervals. He is, Jeremiah notes, as flushed as when they first met.

Jeremiah takes in the receiving hall, agleam with pale pink marble. Gold-topped Corinthian columns support a staircase as tall as the tallest building in Neal's Yard. He tries to ignore the taunt of his thoughts that warns of rich old widows rarely parting with their husbands accrued wealth. And it smells like an abandoned church, air so cold it mists before his face. 'I was looking for Miss Heart,' he says.

'Ah, good afternoon to you, Mr Goode,' says Miss Heart, who appears as if by some miracle from a door beneath the staircase.

'Good day, Miss Heart,' replies Jeremiah, bowing low.

'I was going to call on you, Mr Goode.'

'You were?'

'Indeed, for you have healed my eye. In fact, I was quite impressed with the speed of recovery.' Eyes, practically bare of any lashes, search his expression then turn rapidly towards the floor. 'I wanted to say, thank you.'

Jeremiah finds himself wary of shyness, his sisters having furnished him with the belief eloquence to be evenly distributed between the sexes. Though quite unremarkable in appearance—pasty skin, hair the colour of a brown rat—there lies something in the woman's features, which Jeremiah struggles to grasp. 'I wished to apologise in return, Miss Heart. My profession does not always involve rearranging of skirts you understand,' he says, sounding a stranger even to himself. 'We were calling to… to in fact check upon your eye,' he says, lying fluently enough.

'That is a coincidence because my aunt has once more requested to see you. She was, well, curious, after I explained about my eye. I assume you know of reward my aunt offers?'

Jeremiah clears his throat. 'Your aunt's footman mentioned something.'

Miss Heart comes closer. 'Well, my aunt is offering one thousand pounds to the person that can cure her.'

His first instinct is to ask for the sum to be repeated. 'A thousand pounds you say?'

'Indeed. It may appear large but it is, you understand an amount relative to the time my aunt has spent already looking for a Cure. It is a figure to encourage only the best, only the true healers, Mr Goode.'

Jeremiah bows again, hoping to properly surrender his mind as well as his body to this unbelievable opportunity. 'What is it that ails your aunt?' he asks.

'A great deal but I would like to mention a demand that accompanies the reward, if you do not mind.'

Jeremiah nods in agreement.

'My aunt has her own beliefs about what it is to be Cured. She must be out of bed and able to descend to the bottom of her staircase… unaided.'

It seems the most reasonable demand in the world! He has served men wishing to build a house in a week, or wishing to lift sedan chairs and carry a lump of a lord across the city when half-crippled. A staircase by comparison is trifling. 'That seems quite reasonable,' he admits.

Miss Heart looks up, eyes wide. He sees kindness in her features, wavering there as if misplaced, like a haze of heat over a hot paving stone, as if dependent on something external, something beyond her reach. Her hand rests again against her bosom and Jeremiah comprehends the action: she protects her heart, but from whom? Her aunt?

'But, alas, my aunt has been bedridden these past two years, Mr Goode, and during that time, well, in that time she has not attempted to leave her bed chamber once. What keeps her alive are private reasons she has for becoming well again and without such reasons, well, I suspect she would have perished long ago. The difficulty is I am no longer certain whether her body is anymore capable of health than the wretched alligator that hangs above your shop counter can swim.'

A creature Jeremiah had once named Robert, after his father. He considers grief, exhaustion, consumption sickness of the head and asks, 'Would your aunt permit me perhaps to administer a tonic?'

'A tonic? She is quite unwell, Mr Goode. She may need more than a tonic.'

'Does one question whether arsenic kills rats, Miss Heart? I do Cure, Miss Heart, and herbs are my tools. Into each and every one I pour my faith entrusting them to perform the small miracle Mother Nature has assigned them. They rarely, if ever, let me down.' *People not plants were the thing to do that.* 'If I furnish you with a tonic, your aunt will be in better health tomorrow than she is today. You must trust me on this, Miss Heart.'

'Mr Goode, will you please accompany me upstairs?'

'Have you been an apothecary for very long?' asks Miss Heart, as they climb the seemingly endless stairs, Jeremiah's apothecary case rattling objectionably as he takes in the lifeless landscapes lining the walls.

'Four years, but I trained for seven,' he says.

'Seven years, that is, well, indeed a long time.'

'It is the usual period.'

'I mean to say,' Miss Heart clears her throat, 'I mean to say it is a long time if one is not to be recognised in the way one ought to be… recognised.'

He wonders if she attempts to flatter or encourage him to play the fool, or perhaps it is a carefully concealed insult. Either way he has been away from society too long to care.

'An apothecary may not be a physician, Miss Heart,' he says, his voice raising an octave as he attempts to add freshness to an argument he's repeated more times than the Lord's Prayer. 'And I have not been to Oxford or Cambridge for my degrees but it is my belief a hundred thousand do die yearly of a Curable dis-ease for want of timely advice and suitable medicines as a result of their poverty. I reside in St Giles, where I do what I am able.' He turns to her. 'You see, physicians, Miss Heart,'—she recoils at the use of her name, at the way his voice pushes against the walls and up to the domed ceiling—'they do not treat the poor, rather they will do their utmost to avoid treating those who lack the money to pay them.'

'I see,' she says.

'I believe, Miss Heart, in the power of plants, not in the persuasiveness of the travelling seller.'

'Is this then what distinguishes you?'

'No.' He smiles at the prospect of indulging his own wretchedness. 'What distinguishes me is my refusal to give up.'

He glanced at her as they reach the first floor. From the curve of her cheek, the small creases beside her eye, he assumes her to be smiling. Somewhat pleased, he continues with what is obviously an examination.

'Aside from not letting a dis-ease get the better of me,' he goes on with only a hint of his father's pomposity, 'I believe, Miss Heart, that God intends us all to be happy.'

She turns to him, wide-eyed as if enlivened by her own, sudden happiness. 'Happy, Mr Goode?'

Naturally, he held no such belief about God. Rather, the God he knew had a leaning towards sufferance—certainly did not go in for the frivolities of happiness. Yet, he has chosen the subject for good reason: most unmarried women of a certain age relish the opportunity of speaking about God.

'Indeed Miss Heart,' he continues. 'Though alone happiness does not suffice for it is nigh impossible to be happy in sickness. *Ergo,* Miss Heart, at the very least God did not intend for his flock to be sick.'

'I believe,' says Miss Heart, biting her lower lip, 'I believe…that you have a somewhat childlike fashion of looking at sickness, Mr Goode.'

He laughs once again, relieved that this is the extent of her criticism. 'Children are at least hopeful, are they not?'

Miss Heart looks again to the floor as they cross another vast expanse of pink marble. 'My father recently died.'

'My heartfelt sympathies.'

'I mention it for, though a kind man, he did not think to provide me with an income but left me, in his absence, to deal with his debtors. My aunt and I have been, well, we have been thrown together you might say. She is my only surviving relative and…I hers.'

'There are blessings to be found in one's family.' Another lie.

'It is not an arrangement I should choose, Mr Goode. If such a thing as choice were available to me. However, I find myself suffering alongside my aunt, for it is hard, indeed impossible, to experience happiness when one resides with a sick person. Thus, I would like for my aunt to be Cured, swiftly Cured. If you do not think you are capable of enacting such a thing…' She crosses a hand over her heart and looks into his eye like a rabbit to the bore

72

of a rifle. '…I ask that you leave now so as not to raise my aunt's hopes, or indeed mine.'

You are not a physician, are you?

Jeremiah follows the Miss Heart into the bed chamber where it takes several seconds for his eyes to adjust to the gloom. Drapes are closed, air thick with an overpowering smell of camphor with dust so apparent that it settles on the tongue. A large canopied bed at one end is raised on a platform and brightly illuminated by two enormous gold candelabras.

'You may approach,' says a voice far less feeble than Jeremiah might have imagined for a woman supposedly dying. 'I must see your face.'

Miss Heart exits, silently closing the doors and Jeremiah approaches the bed where a lady—small, almost shrivelled—appears as pale as the pillow she lies upon.

'Come closer,' she says, holding up a pair of spectacles.

'My case, where may I put it please?'

'On the table, then come and stand where I might see you.'

He pushes aside silver brushes and glass perfume bottles, and sets down his case.

'It did not escape notice you did not bow.'

'I could not see you…*Madam*.' If he is to be treated like a lowly servant then he shall behave like one. 'Your chamber is very dark following the gleam of your entrance hall.'

She again raises her spectacles to her face, towards skin that gives off a cadaverous hue. 'Hmm. Not the middling sort. A gentleman I believe. Good teeth. Pleasant voice.' She lowers the spectacles, rests her heavily veined hand upon the damask. 'What in the Lord's name has turned you to drugs?'

'Herbs, madam. I treat for the most part with herbs which I prepare myself.'

'I shall know if you are a fool or not. I know something of medicine. Two years in bed has furnished my mind with many medical theories.'

'I imagine,' he says, brightening at the idea of discussing medical theory. 'You know of Hippocrates?'

73

'You will not impress me with who you know. It is *what* you know not *who* you know as Abe so often told me. Incidentally, I do not confuse eagerness with intelligence. One is for the naïve, the other for the learned.'

He clears his throat. 'Hippocrates was a physician from Ancient Greece. He devised the four humours—'

'Look, I require no lesson in history. There is yellow bile, black bile, phlegm and the other…the other is…'

'Blood.'

'Why of course it is! And I know each person has a season. I flail in the autumn. I have too much black bile. They all agree—and I might add they agree on little else—I am prone to melancholy and to anger. The earth in me makes me melancholic. All hogwash of course! But if one is to understand the language of physicians then you must adopt their peculiar beliefs. But you,' She lifts the spectacles. 'You are not a physician, are you?'

There was some irony to be found in the situation for here he stood at the bedside of an apparently dying woman absorbing insults, taking a gamble on a reward from the rich, when he might be in St Giles insulting his apprentice and gambling with equal odds on payment from the poor.

'By proper, you mean do I speak the language you refer to as hogwash? On occasion I do. But I neither go in for bleeding, nor leeches. I believe in the individual rather than the more rigorous methods of physic. Most importantly I do not believe that to suffer is to heal.'

Reassurance produces a sigh and she places a hand to what remains of the grey hairs upon her head. 'I have been subjected to every Cure you could possibly imagine,' she says, gazing up at the bed's canopy. 'I have seen all sorts. My spirit has been thoroughly insulted. I am told I must be patient. Patient! For what? For death?'

She lapses into coughing. Jeremiah passes the bedpan into which she spits phlegm, a little blood.

'How long have you been bringing up blood?' he asks.

'A year, perhaps more. Not long after my niece came to live with me.'

'I shall fetch my case.'

'Not on the bed. *Not on the bed!* The cover was a wedding present from Abe's mother.'

'You will permit me a little daylight?'

'A little. No more. My eyes cannot take it.'

She cups a hand to her eyes as Jeremiah opens the thick drapes an inch or two.

He opens his mahogany case, opens one or two of the drawers labelled in Latin, relieved he still has something left to give. 'Tell me, tell me how it began.'

'Began? What of how it began? We are nearing the end. Should we not be dealing with that?'

He does not face the old woman, though he does little more than tidy his case, When confiding intimate details most patients—women in particular—found it easier to speak plainly to a man's back. 'It is the way that I progress toward a Cure, madam. It may appear peculiar but I ask that you invest in me what remains of your patience. To Cure is also to understand.'

'More hogwash! One chooses to forget one's ill health.'

'Your age, may I inquire of that?'

She pouts. 'Younger than you think. I am three score year and six on my next birthday. My husband, was much older than me. I kept him young. Nonetheless a ripe age. Is it not?'

'Indeed,' he replies, thinking she looks twice such age. 'And where is your husband now?'

'Dead. Dead these past two years and four months.'

'Grief,' he says quietly, respectively, 'it will send many to their beds in sickness.'

'Grief, for Abe? He loved money more than his wife. His love, it was the exclusive kind.'

Jeremiah closes his eyes, splays his fingers above the stoppers of the bottles and phials. He waits, as he often does, for a sensation to begin, a mild tingling.

'We have no children.'

'I see,' he says. A sensation—a dull ache—emanates from his gut, growing outward and steadily stronger.

'Abe said children would take his money. Said sooner or later one's family is fighting over one's will. That, he said, is what a family amounts to. Grabbing. Greedy penny snatching. His relations were all that way.'

A sharp stab reaches up to his stomach. 'Resentment, regret, these things will disturb the bile.'

'Well, I feel nothing but tired.'

'And what of your friends—do they visit you often?' The ache spreads from his gut to his lungs, forming a tight fiery knot that remains lodged in his throat like a scolding chicken bone.

'What friends? Abe did not have friends. To see them in a synagogue was enough. Friends for a man as rich as Abe were only troublesome: people asked him for money day and night. Day and night. Look, what is this?'

'My personal method, madam,' he says, sounding unnecessarily feeble. 'It requires only your patience.'

His hand falls upon the stopper of a bottle. He opens his eyes, sees that he has chosen angelica, a herb named after its ministering angel. He holds it within the thin striation of light, relieved to find the bottle half-full.

'Pah! Methods! Abe lent money to your kind you know. You gentlemen. The third Earl of Orford, the Fourth Earl of Sandwich. They all needed money. Even the Prince of Wales has his greedy grabbing needs. These families would be nothing without Abe's money.'

'And what of your friends?' he asks, tipping powder into a phial.

'My friends? Look, what relevance is this?'

He faces the bed to find that she still stares at the overhead canopy as if it were posing the question. He approaches, and sits on the coverlet. When she does not object—she seems hardly to have noticed he is there—he touches her cheek with the back of his hand. It is papery and cold. Neglected, he thinks.

'I believe the mind must be in balance with the body,' he says.

His words jolt her as if from a trance. 'There I was,' she says picking up her glasses. 'Not thinking you a quack until now.'

'You may call me what you wish but once Cured you will not care if I am a quack or the King's physician.'

'Well him I hold him in poor regard.'

Jeremiah examines the contents of a phial. 'Half a drachm, mingled with a drachm of treacle with three or four spoonful's of water. Take before you sleep following three hours fasting. Cover yourself well. You will begin to sweat. But by the seventh day you shall be Cured.'

'And you suppose I shall take something without first knowing what it is?'

'Most do,' he says curtly, unable to shed a growing notion of doubt. 'Angelica root powder. Good for gnawing pains of the belly, occasioned by cold. Good for inward disease: pleurisy, other diseases of the lungs, particularly when they come from cold—'

'Cold? I have not got out of bed for two years. How can I be cold?'

'On account of it not being warm in your house.'

'That I have grown used to.'

'We grow used to many things,' he says, taking in the candelabras, four feet tall apiece, making the water in the painting above the bed glitter like diamonds, 'but it does not lessen the objections from the body. I shall return in seven days.'

'Give the drugs to my footman.'

'He is to be trusted to administer them?'

'More than Clara, my niece. The only help she will be in arranging a place in *beit alamin*.'

'*Beit alamin*?'

'A burial ground for my people. My niece wishes me dead, Mr Goode. She thinks I cannot see this. She forgets too easily my reasons for being well again.'

She coughs violently and Jeremiah reaches for the bedpan, holding it whilst the woman spits blood.

'I doubt that to be true,' he says as a dull throb commences in his foot but one he finds strangely easy to ignore.

'Oh, it is true enough! Abe rests in the burial ground at Hoxton.' She wipes her mouth, settles against the pillows, eyes beginning to close. 'There is a place for me next to him, next to both of them. But I am not ready to go yet, not yet...'

He wipes her mouth with his kerchief then closes his case, running a hand across the stoppers to be sure there is nothing he has missed. His aches and pains have diminished now, though the knot in his throat remains tight. He looks to the old woman already asleep and breathing heavily, a slither of spittle escaping from the corner of her lips. He realises he had been afraid to touch her for she had reminded him of somebody, though he cannot think whom. For the first time as an apothecary, he doubts his own cure. Perhaps it is the size of the reward, perhaps the threat of gaol. Whatever the reason, his instinct is obscured by cloud.

Then a clock somewhere in the house tolls the hour and Jeremiah collects his case and departs.

The Dark Angel and a tonic

'My soles are thin, sir. Must we walk again to the Physic Gardens?' bemoans Boswell.

Jeremiah inspects the sole of his shoe. 'A good life can be measured by how much we extend our beings toward helping others, Boswell. We must not give into defeat. Ever.'

Boswell wiggles his eyebrows. 'As you will be extending yourself to that Dark Angel if you set eyes on her again, sir?'

Jeremiah hits the boy across the head. 'I have a patient to Cure and a thousand pounds to earn, as well as continuing to supply you with an education. This, alone, is incentive to get us there. Now, where is my hat?'

A gardener pruning a lavender bed—*snip, snip, snip*—kneels on a piece of cloth, spitting periodically. Jeremiah approaches at a decent pace with no idea how his intentions will morph into words.

'The lady who visits,' he begins.

The gardener says, 'Aye?'

'You know of her?'

Siting back on the heels of his boots, the gardener removes a hat and wipes his brow with the back of his hand. 'Lady?' he repeats, as though unsure of the meaning.

Jeremiah stands as tall as his spine will allow. 'The one who knows much about herbs, who tends to a small plot of garden here. She wears a dark cloak—with a hood.' *The beautiful one.*

The man looks bemused. He squints at the sky. He remains like this for an age so that Jeremiah wonders if he has all but forgotten the question, forgotten a man stands before him raised on his toes.

78

'I said, do you know—'

'I know her.'

'Then pray, has she been here today?'

'No, sir.'

'And do you know where she comes from, in Dorset?' He realises he is speaking with the same contempt that his father had once spoken to these gardeners, and it sours his lips so he adds, 'Please.'

'Our *Praefecrus Horti*, Mr Rand, is the one you must speak with, sir.' The man points to a low red brick building to the west of the garden. 'He gives her seeds, and on occasion she gives seeds to him.'

At this Jeremiah experiences a sense of inadequacy. He looks at the gardener's work. 'You keep this garden very well,' he says, small payment for earlier contempt.

'I do not do so alone, sir. And the lady, Miss Zeldin, she will often tell us if she sees us planting wrong. We did plant our variegated bear's breeches in the sun and Miss Zeldin did tell us to plant it more in shade which we did and it did thrive.'

Jeremiah creases and re-creases the garden membership in his pocket, savouring the exotic sound of Miss Zeldin's name.

'I speak of *Acanthus*, sir,' says the gardener, 'That is the Latin name.'

Jeremiah nods, distracted. *Zel-din. Zel-din.* He claps his hands to enliven his mind as he assembles his thanks.

'You are not the first to ask after her. We thought she was a pickpocketienne at first. Then Mr Rand did tell us to help her if she asked for it. She has been coming these past three years. Some say she has drawn nearly all of these plants.' The gardener laughs. 'I might add, there is not an apothecary who sees her who does not wish he could see her again.'

And so the Dark Angel once more embeds herself in Jeremiah's mind. If not for the gardener (Boswell was nothing to go by) he might believe each appearance to be an apparition for she does not belong amongst the sombre apothecaries and their fledgling apprentices, musing on herbs as if they were already in phials, in no way aligned for appreciating beauty. No, such a woman—any woman for that matter—does not belong in the Physic

Gardens. Though with this particular woman Jeremiah could not discern quite where she belonged.

Within the garden's walled confines (he has never looked at the garden in such a light before), he attempts to complete a sketch of burdock, a plant whose sticky burs he had thrown at his sisters as a child. Little else, however, is accomplished as he acknowledges a rare yet definite craving for female company, something more than the fussing provided by his three sisters. As his quill moves across the page, he begins to give this woman a character, albeit one not dissimilar from his own. She talks fondly of plants. She lives alone. Lives to cure... But the facts of such an exercise are irrelevant for this is the forth time within this walled garden that Jeremiah has not been wholly absorbed by his botanical studies. On the contrary the large, slug-eaten leaves of the burdock plant appear to reveal too much about his present existence.

But then, all of a sudden, he sees *her*. Over by the glasshouses.

'Wait here,' he tells the boy.

'For how long, sir? *Too long and I shall be freezing my baubles off!*' Boswell calls after him stamping his boots.

'*Will that furnish me with a more pleasurable walk home?*'

Jeremiah retraces his steps down the garden's many paths until he comes across the stove house facing the river, in the centre of the garden. The first heated house of its kind, used for cultivating the more exotic plans. Jeremiah approaches its door and hand outstretched raps on the glass.

'Am I interrupting?' he asks heat seeping through the soles of his shoes from the great fire plate beneath the floor.

The *Dark Angel* looks up and smiles. 'Not really. I am drawing Red Valerian,' she says, her voice much deeper than he remembers, somehow... musical.

He stares. Her beauty compels him to stare and he stares hoping to unravel it. He moves closer, wishing to learn something of whatever marvellous formula it had arisen. He smells her rosewater scent and notices a small mole above her lip which gently quivers.

'Valerian,' he says, 'good for improving an anxious state and enhancing sleep.'

She smiles again.

'My name is Jeremiah I.S. Goode. I believe…' A number of beliefs run through his head but none seem appropriate. He believes in the healing power of plants, in a good night's sleep but it seems improbable they are the reasons he has entered the glasshouse. 'I believe you can help me,' he says.

This woman, this Dark Angel, lowers the hood of her cape causing him to take a sharp, audible intake of breath: *so much loose, silken hair and in the bright light of day!*

'Good day, Mr Goode. How do you suppose I can help you?'

He lifts his slackened jaw. Though he spends his days thinking on his feet presently he can think of no other reason for detaining this woman except by mentioning an old hag with an endless staircase.

'I understand,' he begins, 'that you know a great deal about the plants in these gardens.'

Her eyes remain wide either in a state of indignation or trust, he cannot discern which. 'I know them, yes.'

'Better than most.'

'It depends whom you refer to when you say, *most.* You see, Mr Goode, I do not follow the teachings of any particular book or person. I find most men of physic are preoccupied with the abstract. I, on the other hand, believe in the individual over the collective by which I mean the identification of a specific herb to heal a specific condition in a specific circumstance. Whether this herb shall heal or not is as dependent on the individual as the potency of the plant. Do you follow me? I believe in specific remedies for very specific symptoms. It is naturally a given that I believe in Nature's power to restore but it is the specific over the general that I am concerned with and its uses in order to heal.'

It is like listening to the lub-dub beats of his own, presently palpitating heart.

'I have a patient,' he says when finished enthusiastically nodding.

'Most apothecaries do. I believe it is the nature of the trade.'

Humour too! He meets the sparkle in her eyes. 'Well,' he says, 'this particular patient is sixty and six and perhaps shows signs of melancholy.' Though reluctant to ruin this state of euphoria with Mrs Soloman he is driven by this potential meeting of minds. 'She is bedridden. She has a poor appetite and occasionally coughs up blood but complains of no pain from her lungs and there is no hectic fever so consumption has been ruled out. Her pain, what little there is, seems almost to entirely reside in her head. I have, in my *elaboratory*, come up with two, possibly three, herbs I could—'

'Wait a moment.' She crosses to the table and takes a fresh sheaf of paper, a quill and a small pot of red ink. He notices that she does not wear any gloves, that her fingers are slender, though calloused. She makes space on a raised bench near to where they stand, shifting aside seedlings, which hang limply beyond their own pots, weighted by the extent of such rapid and unexpected growth.

'Now,' she says, taking her hair and tying it in a knot at the nape of her neck, Jeremiah watching in a state of awe. 'Tell me all the things you think about her but would never dare speak.'

He laughs. 'There are plenty of which I cannot mention… to a lady.'

'Then forget I am of a different sex. Think of me as a healer like yourself, Mr Goode. Little can offend a person whose mind is fixed upon Curing. Can it not?'

He smiles, moves closer to the bench. 'Well, she is difficult,' he begins.

A fresh sparkle appears in her eyes. 'The sick often are. Usually it is why they are sick.'

'She may be grieving over a dead husband, one it would appear she hated in life.'

'What woman does not hate her husband just a little at times?'

'She has no visitors, though I doubt this to be of relevance.'

'Healing is gained by understanding the person.' She makes notes on a page with extravagant swirls of crimson ink, such an elaborate waste of paper, he thinks, on an embittered old widow, so apparently suited to ill-health. 'Most things are relevant, Mr Goode, loneliness in particular.'

He runs a finger around his collar, recalls his own lonely evenings when Wordsley does not make an appearance, when he hears Boswell and Mary talking somewhere in the house, can occasionally before sleep hear the metrical movements of the boards above his head.

'Go on Mr Goode. Her odour? Her voice, sharp or flat?'

'Rotten apples,' he says, searching for a way to describe the irritation that accompanied her voice. 'These facts, you are certain they are relevant?'

Her brow delicately creases. 'You are an apothecary are you not? I imagined you must know such things.'

In the presence of this woman Jeremiah is no longer sure what he knows for he stands like a choirboy at an altar, mere decoration to this creature's self-assurance. Whether perhaps tiredness allows him to be spoken to this way—*by a woman*—he cannot discern, but in truth he feels emptied of all knowledge: a sudden reckless, freeing feeling and for the first time in his profession as an apothecary he is willing to sit back in his seat like a driver of a carriage who trusts that his horse knows its path home.

After a quantity of questions—obscure even by his standards—the Dark Angel tells him, however, what he already knows, that Mrs Soloman grieves for her dead husband and is not consumptive but suffers from inflammation of the lungs doubtless caused by too many coal fires and a lack of fresh air. It does not matter that he shall now be walking home in darkness. What matters is that he is *reassured*, that he has had the pleasure of listening to this woman speak and the greater pleasure of imagining—amongst other things—her hair falling loose about her naked shoulders. What he does not wish to imagine is leaving.

'But I expect you already knew this,' she is saying.

He confesses that he did, lacing his hands awkwardly behind his back.

'There is something about you, Mr Goode. I am certain that you possess *the gift*.'

'The gift?'

'Why, the gift to heal.'

Mutely, he basks in the warmth of her praise for it must be praise as her lips smile and her eyes are aglow.

'But tell me,' she says leaning forward, 'why do you not act on your beliefs? Why doubt yourself so?'

Had he doubted himself? Why mention the infernal hag if he had not? Had desperation penetrated beneath his fraying coat to his once erodible core of buoyant self-belief? His father would surely be laughing at him. *Offer to pay an apothecary a considerable sum for his Cure and he falls all to pieces!*

'Alas, I do not.'

'Most men do not care for the opinions of a woman. At least not gentlemen of certain standing and certainly not one with his own apprentice.'

'Plants care not if we are man or woman.'

She briefly laughs. 'It is a refreshing change not to be judged as inferior, that is what I am saying.'

Living in St Giles has perhaps eroded such judgement. 'I am told you come here to tend to part of these gardens for your own use.'

'I have tamed a barren corner, yes.' Here eyes narrow as if he were about to take this corner away. She picks up the piece of paper upon which she has written Lady Soloman's symptoms. 'Most relevant is a Cure for loneliness. Friends. Family. She must open her drapes and her windows. She must walk daily, even if only about her bed chamber. She would benefit from a tincture.' She presses her lips together, frowning. 'Please understand this is not my usual habit and I should prefer if it not be spoken about to anybody here… but I happen to have a tonic that shall be of benefit to your patient on my person.' She puts a hand inside her cloak and extracts two bottles. I can only spare one, however. A spoonful is all that is needed, taken thrice daily.'

He feels at once confused and impressed.

'And you must make her understand,' she continues, 'that to get well often requires greater effort than to die. You must tell her that dying can often be a choice. An easier choice.'

Choice. He thinks, what a novel idea.

She says, 'It would help if she could speak about her husband.'

'I shall try,' he says, though does not relish the prospect. 'She is… off-putting at times.'

'Well I do not imagine, Mr Goode,' her eyes lock upon his, 'that you are a man to be easily put off.' She hands him the tonic. For the briefest of moments their fingers touch. Jeremiah's heart seems to expand in chest. 'Now you must excuse me. I must fetch some cuttings to take home.'

'Where is it that you live?' he asks, almost breathless.

'Far from here, in Dorset.'

He cannot let her go so soon.

'I was hoping,' he says—he will later blame weakness for his curiosity, 'that you might permit me a small favour.'

She crosses her arms. 'More?' she says with an encouraging half-smile.

She has no idea! 'I should like you to show me your garden.'

Her head tips. 'As an apothecary you are free to wonder about these garden for it is not my garden but a garden I helped to create.'

'I have a long walk ahead of me. You could help a man to lift his spirits. You will not accompany me on a tour?'

She studies him. 'I have not done so before and… in winter there is little to see…'

She gathers up her skirts. '…So you shall be the first, Mr Goode. Now watch your step.'

In daylight her face alters. She is no longer a closed rosebud, absent of colour but gathers strength from the garden, radiating beauty, a flower in full bloom, as if the very souls of these plants were nourishing her own.

She takes him to an area concealed behind a row of glasshouses and proffers an arm, which she disregards with a turn of the cheek.

'I have divided it into four,' she says, gesturing towards the four aisles leading off a central pear tree, 'The kitchen garden, the medicinal garden, the New World garden and,'—eyes gleam like precious stones, 'some plants that are pleasing to the eye.' She gestures him forwards. 'This was a small favour permitted by Mr Rand.' She points to another bed. 'Foxglove,' she says. 'Both *Digitalis pupurea* and *Digitalis Ianata*.' She gestures to her left. 'It is good for a sickly heart; *Catharanthus roseaus*, effective for carcinoma of the breast; *Fillependula ulmaria*…' He listens to her talk; impressed at the depth of her knowledge and the herbs she has chosen for this small corner.

He asks, 'How is it you know so much?'

'I heal, it is what I do, Mr Goode.'

'Of course.'

'And I am also in the process of writing my own herbal. When finished it will comprise over five hundred herbs from the New World known to Cure disease, complete with a drawing for each entry.'

'You are a better herbalist than I can aspire to be.'

And a woman. You are a woman!

'I did not know it was a competition, Mr Goode.'

'No, no, of course not. Your name, perhaps you could tell me your name?'

'Zeldin, Brigid Zeldin. Named after St Brigid, the patron of babies and printing presses and poets. Poor woman must have had a fine time with all that lot!'

Zeldin, Brigid Zeldin. He lets the name fly about his mind until it settles—nestles—comfortably at the forefront. He takes in Miss Zeldin's garden, each carefully tended bed, accurately divided in accordance with its genera and species. In her small rose garden wild winter roses flower in a plot ingeniously arranged in tiers, cascading at certain points amongst rocks, perennial plants placed in between. He strolls along, taking in plants expertly pruned; climbers carefully secured to the garden's walls and fruit trees draped with expectant nets. After walking much of the garden he deems it entirely systemised with each plant labelled with all its healing properties, a method not observed in the rest of these gardens. The placing of each plant is meticulously considered and beautifully managed. He is reminded of visiting the *Jardins du Roi* in Paris with his father as the personal guest of the Comte de Buffon, a former patient of his father's. Lost amongst the beds he had first conceived how nature might provide the connection between the mortal soul and the miraculous. Possessed of a need to unfurl each petal in order to understand Mother Nature's miracles, he saw for the first time beneath the French sun that nature could be the constant unfolding of God's presence. Standing in this mysterious woman's garden, this declaration washes through him once more as if invigorated, affirmed.

'This area used to be scrub land,' he says, practically jubilant, 'Now the order of the plants, it makes better sense than Mr Linnaeus' system. I can hardly believe what I have seen.'

'Oh, it is not so very different from the rest,' she says nonetheless smiling.

'On the contrary, it is a great deal better, the arrangement far more cohesive.'

The sunlight turns her skin as luminous as the moon.

'There is more to see in the summer months.'

He cannot wait that long. 'Come with me back to London.' But his words are whipped away by a sudden breath of wind.

'If you had come earlier we might have spoken for longer.'

'Not today?'

'No, not today. I must visit a sick lady for whom I have brought the tonic. Then I shall begin my journey home. The lady is with child and a friend of Mr Rand's.'

'You shall visit again, soon, Miss Zeldin?'

She bites her lip. 'I am not certain. I will have completed my final drawing today, I hope. The garden I created here is finished too. Therefore, my job, you might say, is also complete.'

Jeremiah remembers something the gardener had said.

'You have a dog?' he inquires. A dog would at least afford her some protection travelling the long journey home, all alone.

'A dog?'

'The gardener told me you had a black dog.'

'He did, did he? And did he tell you I was also a witch and that I cast spells on those that dared to speak to me?'

Boswell tugs at his sleeve. 'Sir? I can no longer feel my feet.'

Before he can apologise for his apprentice having the constitution of a girl, he is bowing to a billowing cape.

'Who is she, sir?' asks Boswell, as she disappears around the back of the gardeners' cottage.

'She is Brigid Zeldin. And she is… a very pleasant young woman.'

'More than pleasant, sir. I should say touching those diddleys should warm a man's heart from here to Constantinople!'

'I am so very glad you are able to find Cures for your maladies with such ease,' says Jeremiah, snapped out of his reverie. 'I look forward to the day when you apply such ingenious thought to our customers.'

Resisting the urge to whack his apprentice, the subsequent urge is too strong.

'Boswell,' he says, 'wait for me by the exit.'

Our Praefecrus Horti, Mr Rand

Jeremiah lifts his hat. Walking through the perennial quarter, oblivious to the plants, he plans what he must say to Mr Rand. *I would like to share her knowledge.* Too intimate. *I would like some help with a difficult case.* Too needy. *I would like some information for my compendium.* That will do.

His behaviour is at odds with his character. Doubt was something he could have benefitted from in the past. Although somehow, eventually, he had always chosen the right cure. But a thousand pounds had never been the stake and now he finds he would prefer to hand over all his trust to Brigid Zeldin.

He raps upon a low wooden door, to the east of the orangery. He briefly smiles, for the Physic's Garden has always been a place to escape people, not seek them out.

The garden's Praefectus Horti and Daemonstrator of Plants, a man who demonstrates plants to apprentices, explaining their medicinal uses, and arranges many herborizing expeditions, sits at a large desk, the tip of his beard touching the leather desk, a grand tower of paper to one side, books to the other, a haze of pale blue pipe tobacco rising into the air.

'Miss Zeldin,' he muses, after Jeremiah has introduced himself and provided reason for the interruption. 'Miss Brigid Zeldin. A fine young lady whom I furnish from time to time with specimens and likewise she does me. We operate a seed exchange you might say. She has tamed a wild corner of our gardens.'

Jeremiah experiences a swell of silent resentment.

'May I ask,' Mr Rand says, puffing at the pipe that rests at the corner of his mouth, 'what it is you want with her?'

Before Jeremiah's rational, empirical nature can intervene he hears himself explaining, 'I wish to see her again.'

'That, young man,' the older man dips his quill, 'is not something I am able to assist with. Indeed, she is much discussed in these gardens, reported many a time to be an apparition in black. I am willing to discuss why I have allowed a woman to enter these Worshipful Society's gardens on such regular terms, for objections are only to be expected, but I am not at liberty to discuss Miss Zeldin's life as it is lived beyond these four walls. I am right, am I not, in anticipating your next question: where you might find her?'

Jeremiah has no question in the forefront of his mind. He is staring at a picture hanging on the wall. An Amazonian lily. A plant easily confused with the common daffodil. Its scent and its size when seen in the flesh, hinted at its more exotic origins. He had once seen one once in a botanical garden in Paris and had never forgotten it.

'It is not for the reasons you assume,' he says.

'I assume very little. I have only the young lady's privacy at heart.'

At the mention of the word heart, Jeremiah rises from his seat and begins pacing. He loosens the top of his shirt and a surge of frustrated thought rises up through his body lifting his hands to the low ceiling.

'My business is about to be *ruined*.' He slaps a hand against the back of a chair. 'I shall be laying my head in debtor's sponging house in less than a month unless…unless I take drastic measure to save myself… sir.'

He turns his back. Months of acceptance, months of blindly continuing to carve out a living in a parish that is more familiar with death than life, is released like a cork from the neglected contents of its bottle and he slumps, relieved of it, back into his seat. The old man regards him with caution. 'That is the outcome for many an apothecary, good or bad, I'm afraid. A head for plants is, alas, not the same as a head for business.'

'I must still try to save myself. Do you not see?'

'Naturally,' says the daemonstrator, as he puffs out delicate smoke between them. 'But pray tell, what part does Miss Zeldin play in your misfortune?'

Jeremiah picks his hat from the floor, shifts his wig back into place. 'I have been given a chance. One last opportunity to save myself. I understand that what Miss Zeldin does not know about plants, God himself does not know.'

Mr Rand laughs affably enough. 'She has no training in botany. She has taught herself all that she knows but her knowledge indeed appears to be greater than that of any man I have met within these walls.'

'And that is precisely what I need! My patient, she has seen them all, every physician, every apothecary worth his weight in iron. We cannot always know God's will.'

'Perhaps she is beyond Curing.'

Jeremiah shakes his head. 'No. She is melancholic and she does wish to become well which is why she is offering a large reward.'

'I see,' says the daemonstrator, not unkindly.

'If this woman, if Miss Zeldin' Jeremiah continues, 'is who I think she is then I know she can help me return my patient to health.'

In the ensuing silence, where perhaps the daemonstrator ought to be asking who Jeremiah thinks Miss Zeldin to be, the rhythmic motions of a rake upon stony soil mark out the seconds. Alas, it is too late for Jeremiah to rake up his pride to reassemble it around himself again. His entire life swings like an unsteady pendulum before him. Suddenly it seems this one man is able to steady it again. But, naturally, he has spoken too freely. He has spoken as if an important man such as Mr Rand shall forgive him for sounding like a lunatic and he shall not be surprised if his membership to the gardens is quickly revoked.

Mr Rand sighs, sits back in his chair, eyes studying Jeremiah intently. 'Though I do not need to comprehend who has thrown you such a rope I can only hope that it is from an honourable source.'

'Honourable though not perhaps likeable, sir.'

'Then I know how it is to be giving advice for free and herbs to the poor for a penny a bag at the expense of the food upon your own dinner table. I was an apothecary once. I also know how hard it can be to keep the debtors from your door.'

He taps the contents of his pipe into a neat pile upon the edge of his desk as Jeremiah waits for more than mere sympathy.

'Miss Zeldin is completing a herbal.' The pipe is refilled and the daemonstrator's tone brightens. 'She has produced no less than five hundred illustrations that she will then engrave upon copper plate, to be hand-coloured when printed. It shall be a remarkable piece of work. I also agree with the gardeners that what Miss Zeldin does not know about herbs no man does know.'

'Then you must see that she would be the best person for me to consult, given my circumstances.'

'I am afraid not, Mr Goode. You did say Goode?'

Jeremiah nods.

'Mr Goode, if I were to tell every apothecary that knocked on my door where Miss Zeldin could be found there would be a queue from Dorset to London at the poor creature's threshold.'

'So she truly is from Dorset then?'

'And it is a large county, Mr Goode.' Mr Rand sits forward again. 'Look, your family might they not assist you? I must press upon you that difficulties like these are often only temporary if one can adjust one's mind to business.'

Jeremiah shakes his head and shakes away remnants of hope. 'My father,' he says not knowing how he shall politely continue, 'he…is a physician.'

Mr Rand's hum is like an out-of-tune organ. 'I have also come across many a young man living in the shadow of a father, one they wish to prove wrong, or to earn his respect. Friends?'

'They are scarce. Poverty, well, it produces this effect.' He replaces his hat. 'I apologise for taking up your time.'

'Believe me, I comprehend your pride. I likewise understand why you think this woman can help. But Miss Zeldin, from what I can piece together of her life, is…how might I word it?—an unusual botanist. Her spirit is freer than most ladies, her thinking even freer, one might say too free. I fear that such a person might prove dangerous to an eager young man such as you.'

Jeremiah smiles. 'I am not so young and there is little harm left than can befall me.'

'I should say you are twenty eight, twenty nine. Young by my standards. And this is London, Mr Goode. There is always worse.' He pulls at the tail of his beard, eyes dancing, 'as there is likewise better.'

'These, are they from her admirers?' Jeremiah nods towards a pile of envelopes on the edge of the daemonstrator's desk, the top labelled with Miss Zeldin's name.

The daemonstrator packs the envelopes. 'Indeed. Most will be burnt. I do like to burden Miss Zeldin with unnecessary requests.'

Alas, a morning has been wasted, one that would have been better spent climbing the alphabet of his compendium. He has a long walk home. He has shown himself to be an utter fool in the eyes of a respected and respectable man.

'You will not give me her address.'

'No, young man.'

Jeremiah gets up. He kicks Mr Rand's door and rests his forehead against the cool wood. 'She has already furnished me with a tonic. I am a man pleading with you, sir.' He turns back. 'Do you wish for me to fall to my knees, for I will?' He could also throttle the daemonstrator for sitting there, holding back knowledge so unnecessarily. He has one hand on the door handle when Mr Rand speaks again.

'She is from a Catholic village in Dorset. There are not many.'

Jeremiah stands motionless, every shred of his being willing the daemonstrator to go on.

'You did not hear this from me. And do remember, the woman's soul is quite untethered at times.'

Jeremiah turns back. 'Why me? Why am I deserving of such details?'

Mr Rand takes up his quill again, stares at the half-written page before him.

'You have to ask? Should you not be grateful?'

Jeremiah bows his head. 'You have singled me out from all the other apothecaries that have asked and I think that is somewhat deserving of an explanation.'

'An expression of yours brought back a memory. I know of your father, the physician, the eminent Dr Goode, am I correct?'

Jeremiah nods.

'He often visited my shop on the Strand. Over a period of many years, there was no single occasion where he treated me with respect. I waited for a long time for him to venture into these gardens. I thought his seeing me in such a position of authority might serve as my revenge. Then one day he did come.'

'I remember that day.'

'You were that boy accompanying him?'

'Yes, sir.' The mention of his father and he briefly becomes that boy again.

'Then you will understand my reasons for assisting you.'

'Why? When you might avenge my father through me?'

'Not myself.' He dips his quill, 'I am always on the side of the apothecaries. We shall, in time, have are revenge on the physicians for all the distain they hold for us. That I do reverently believe, Mr Goode. Even if it is a hundred years from now.'

Jeremiah thanks Mr Rand and steps outside. It has stopped raining and he is greeted by a plant flowering with a single black flower: *Helleborus niger*, the Christmas rose, rising from a verdant nest, its stamens distinct threads of gold against the solid dark of its petals. It is a plant whose roots prove particularly good in cases of madness and a plant whose petals are all but poisonous.

But the rain has indeed ceased and the gardens appear transformed. With thumbs tucked into his waistcoat pocket, he strides towards the exit, finding his purpose renewed. His shoulders in feel weightless, as if he had cured Mrs Soloman already, as if he had already reached the threshold of the house in a Catholic village belonging to a woman known as the Dark Angel.

Summoned home

The soot blackened dome of St Paul's bulges above London. A large cloud hangs over the distant city, doing nothing to improve Jeremiah's mood as he and his apprentice trek back to St Giles. Soon, he will be back amongst the half-dead of the city, amongst hundreds wrecked by their days, by the cold… another termite returning to its mound. Four weeks are all that remains of his freedom unless, that is, he cures the old woman. But his disposition is perhaps more blighted knowing that he will not see *her* again at the Physic Gardens, that her job there is done.

At Seven Dials a young girl, with familiar eyes, rushes over to clutch at Boswell's arm.

'How dost my buff?'

'Hello Lizzie.'

'How is your wife?'

'What wife?' says Boswell, shaking the girl off.

'Your pretty mute wife or soon she will be!'

'Wife?' asks Jeremiah, eyebrow cocked, as they enter Neal's Yard.

'My sister, sir, is as usual talking no more sense than a dog's arse.'

Not even three o'clock and the sun has already set on the yard, the smoke of somebody's fire hanging like a low mist. Mr Ludwell stands on his threshold smoking his pipe with an expression as substantial as his figure.

'Apprentices—' begins Jeremiah.

'Are not permitted to marry,' finishes Boswell kicking at the cobbles. 'You have told me that many times, sir. Apprentices must go without a woman so that they may better absorb the truer, purer nature of the plants they are studying.'

When repeated back to him Jeremiah can hardly believe he has said such a thing but Mr James had once put it that way, when he was his apprentice.

'The passions of love distract from the purpose of life,' he continues in a tone he hopes is more logical and less puritanical.

'Those being, sir?'

'To serve Boswell. To serve!' Only thirty and one and already he is unwittingly becoming his father.

'Evening, Apothecary Goode,' says Ludwell.

'Good evening, Mr Ludwell.' Whatever the fellow smoked it kept his body in good health; not a flinch did Jeremiah ever feel in his willowy presence.

'Liver is ruled by Jupiter, skin by Saturn, heart by the Sun. But this you must know?'

Jeremiah searches for his key. 'Plants do heal,' he says. 'The *planets* do not, Mr Ludwell.'

'I had always considered you to be imbued with some sense, at least more than Cresley the alchemist, forever bemoaning the reticence of a lump of iron, but here you are telling me it is a mere bag of moonshine that Librans are prone to exhaustion of the nerves...that Taurus is a great recuperative force… You cannot deny that Aries…'

Jeremiah loosens his collar. Culpeper and his, 1655 *Astrological Judgement of Diseases from the Decumbiture of the Sick* remained a knife in his gut. He at last finds his key and pushes it into the lock, escape at least imminent.

'But you must know that Gemini-borne are prone to difficulties with their arms, their lungs, occasionally their shoulders; that those under Cancer are prone to weaknesses of the stomach…'

He closes the shop door. Mary, who must have been waiting in the shop, now stands before *Nicholas Culpepper* gesticulating wildly at Boswell.

'It's your father,' the boy says turning to him.

Jeremiah puts down the drawing of burdock he has been carrying. 'My father?' The words lay thick on his tongue.

'He is very sick,' says Boswell.

Mary nods in an exaggerated fashion. Jeremiah turns his back, resting his elbows on the counter feeling 10 years old again.

'For how long?' he asks softly staring up at the empty apothecary jars, every one representing another victory for his father. When he turns back Mary is holding up three fingers. 'How long has he been sick for, Mary?'

'Three days,' Boswell confirms.

'Mary?' says Jeremiah, 'You answered without reading my lips. Can you hear me Mary?'

Mary looks hesitantly. The boy nods too.

'I did say that her ears were improving with the herbs you have been giving her, sir. She—'

'Mary!' says Jeremiah, 'you can *hear*?'

Mary nods, tentatively.

'This is remarkable! When did this happen?'

'These past six months, sir,' Boswell replies.

'Six months and you did not think to tell me before now?'

'I tried—'

'Six months!' Jeremiah's mind races ahead. 'She took all the herbs I dispensed?' 'She took them like they were your holy water, sir.'

'This is remarkable!'

He heads to his elaboratory, to his desk, where he scatters papers in his haste to gather quill and paper. *Marjoram, apple cider vinegar...*

'Remind me,' he says to Boswell whom he senses staring at him, 'What else has Mary taken?' It is more than remarkable. It is the most miraculous cure he has ever administered!

'Garlic, elder...but your father, sir.'

Jeremiah puts down his quill, wipes a face across his hand as if erasing words. 'Go on,' he says.

'The messenger said that you were to go home on the next coach.'

'What were you told?'

'That he is dying, sir.'

Jeremiah looks through his elebatory window into the yard. Should he feel sad? Relieved? Some solace comes from knowing that his father might be too sick to bother meddling in his business, particularly the business of whom he should marry. With any luck, he might likewise be too sick to chastise him for his chosen profession.

To Boswell he says, 'Pack me some food for the journey. I shall leave at first light.'

'Very well, sir.'

Having made his decision, Jeremiah reaches into his desk drawer and takes out his opium pipe; certain decisions did not rest well with the body.

It does not become a man to be curious

His brother Jasper, the bucket and the scattered meadow flowers. Jasper is dunked. dunked again. His eyes bulge from his childhood face and his skin turns blue. Jeremiah guesses there are ten steps between him and Jasper's body now lying slumped over the bucket but he cannot move, cannot cry.

Unfurling like a baby's hand from a mother's thumb. No longer drowning but delicately sinking. Still, Jeremiah refuses to surrender. Upwards he swims, swimming with vigour against the weight of the inevitable. He keeps his mind to the light, to air, to freedom. He swims as his mouth fills up with water, chest constricting with the force of his strokes. The surface shatters. Then the grip comes as it always does, tightening about his throat, tumbling pain into unknown recesses. Black eyes glare down. He struggles. Submits in the manner of a flapping moth to an oil lamp. And all at once he is sitting up, ripping back the drapes, spilling out of bed, in one long, frenzied, struggle for life.

Come morning, rather than departing for his father's house at Dulwich, Jeremiah decides to visit Chelsea. He had barely slept. By the time he lifts the shiny black knocker in the shape of a gargoyle on Lady Soloman's door, his hands are numb and his ears stung raw by a vengeful wind. If not for the tea leaves, chewed all the way, he might have collapsed like a post horse upon the King's Road.

Boswell stands at his side holding his apothecary case, wearing another of Jasper's cast-off outfits: an oatmeal coat trimmed in pale blue with matching breeches. Rose had given these clothes to Jeremiah, *To smarten your new apprentice,* she had said, omitting to mention that Jasper now sat drawing night and day in his nightshirt. When Boswell had tried the coat on he had declared, *I am a proper ninny now, sir.* And Jeremiah had felt a peculiar sense of pride, an awkward knot lodging in his throat as the boy became transformed. 'A ninny overly concerned with his clothes is also a fool,' he nonetheless pointed out. 'And I shall expect you to work harder as due payment for the cloth.' He will only admit it to himself but he is proud of the boy's transformation.

He knocks again on Lady Soloman's front door.

'Why is it Jews live together, sir?' asks Boswell.

'Perhaps for the same reason little urchins congregate in St Giles.'

'To look after one another, sir?'

'You have answered your own question. Now pull up your stockings and keep your relentless charm beneath your hat. And, besides, are you not also a Jew?'

'My grandfather was, sir.'

'That makes you a little bit of a Jew, does it not?'

'Nah, sir. My mother has to be a Jew and mine was not, sir.'

Jeremiah traces a thumb around the shape of the Dark Angel's tonic in his coat. He knows he shall also have to bite down upon his tongue today. Emancipation from society had done more than undo the strings of his purse and in the presence of Lady Soloman he expects to taste blood.

The Fish—cheeks flushed and the tip of his nose aflame, now appears at the door.

'Ah the tradesman returns!' he says, beckoning them inside with a sniff.

'If you would like a share of the reward, I suggest you cease your insults.'

'A man should not be ashamed of who he is, Jeremiah *IS* Goode!'

'So you do declare yourself to be a fart-catcher then, as is the purpose of all footmen?'

'Fart-catcher?' sings Boswell with a grin.

'You have not heard this spoken of footmen before, Boswell?'

'No, sir.'

'Gad, there are gaps in your education! You see, Boswell, a footman must walk behind the sedan chairs of their employers catching their farts? It is his job.'

Boswell laughs. The Fish hiccups. But watching him stagger up the staircase Jeremiah sees he is too drunk to be greatly bothered by such remarks.

'So this fortune,' Jeremiah asks him, knowing a drunk cannot resist a boast, 'it came from money lending?'

'Money lending and bullion from East Indian and West Indian trades,' replies the Fish.

'Bullion?' whispers Boswell.

'The stuff of coins,' enlarges Jeremiah.

'He made *money*?'

'In theory.'

Continuing up the enormous staircase, Jeremiah cannot imagine getting the shrivelled body of Lady Soloman to descend it, not if he was subjected to live a dozen lives.

'Mr Soloman did arrive in this country from Poland with only the ragged shirt on his back. He became a moneylender. His was the largest counting house in Lombard Street. Amongst other things he would lend money and in his dealings with mankind has been a strict and honest man. He never took advantage of the distresses of a fellow creature.' A finger is pointed towards the skies above and presumably onwards to Mr Soloman. 'He was justly paid every debt he contracted to the uttermost farthing; and in a domestic life proved himself a fond and faithful, loving husband, as well as a steady and sincere friend. Virtuous in every sentiment, he was as unsullied in his reputation as any Christian might wish to be.'

A servant could never resist a boast concerning their employer and the Fish, has his rehearsed for the stage at Drury Lane. But it was entirely unnecessary for every slab of marble served as a salute to Sir Soloman's cleverness. As a supporter of the Tolerance Act, Jeremiah admired most Jews if only for the legal burdens the country imposed upon them. For the most part, religious plurality was nothing more than common sense, providing, that is, the man possessed virtues.

'Do the Solomans have any children?' he asks. Where pictures of family ought to be hanging are landscapes: barren hills and stagnant ponds. A more generous portrait painter might have made something out of Miss Heart's kindness as it hesitated over her plain, wary features.

'Miss Heart is Mrs Soloman's only surviving relative,' says the footman as if anticipating Jeremiah's next thought. 'There have been family differences. But sickness and death they have a habit of bringing people together. Do you not agree?'

Jeremiah looks up at an overhead dome painted with clouds and a pink seraph. On the contrary, in St Giles a person marched in his own solitary battles towards death.

The footman pauses. 'I must warn you,' he says, voice now hushed, 'Her Ladyship is very particular.'

Jeremiah shrugs. 'The dying become prone to certain whims.'

'Oh, it has little to do with her dying, Mr Jeremiah *IS* Goode.'

Jeremiah waits for more but the footman smirks and continues his peculiar waddle, in his restrictive clothing, towards a pair of rosewood doors.

'How should I address your employer?' Jeremiah asks.

'Mrs Soloman, of course. Though I could think of several other names more suiting.'

'But you referred to her as your ladyship.'

'Well this is what Mrs Soloman insists I call her and I am loathe to argue with the person keeping me fed and watered, sir.'

He instructs Jeremiah to wait outside. Jeremiah puts down his case and catches his breath. He notes that the leaves on a nearby plant—more a tree than a plant—have turned yellow perhaps through cold, perhaps through neglect. It is, he decides, more a mausoleum than a home. No wonder the old woman won't venture forth.

Outside the bedchamber Jeremiah stands with his shoulder still twitching. He glances at his apprentice. If the boy, a ragamuffin, can end up in a Palladian mansion dressed as if for a picnic then there might be hope for his own affairs.

'I need a piss, Master.'

'Now?'

'I do hanker after one.'

Afraid the examination will be conducted with his apprentice gripping his baubles, Jeremiah points to a corner of the half-circular landing, to a dying plant in a gilded pot. He snatches the drug case and tells Boswell, 'Hurry'.

But the piss takes an age. The Fish's footsteps fast approach as steam still lifts from an arc of urine. Good Lord, his reward will be forfeited on account of his apprentice having the bladder of a girl! The door draws open. Boswell is still fastening his breaches, sliding across the marble expanse of floor like a duck taking to a frozen pond.

The Fish regards Boswell, suspiciously. 'This way,' he says.

They enter, Boswell still panting, as behind him steam rises from the plant pot.

Mrs Soloman's bedchamber is as dark and as filled by stale air as it was on Jeremiah's previous visit.

'Do I have a new condition? Do I see double of you, Mr Goode?'

'No, madam. This is my assistant, Master Boswell.'

'*You* are giving me the Cure are you not?'

Jeremiah clears his throat. 'I am, madam.'

'Only I might have believed you were giving a boy an opportunity to prattle with his cronies.'

Jeremiah sets down the apothecary case, a weight Boswell has carried all the way from St Giles. He runs his tongue against the jagged edge of a canine.

'I am a man of physic Mrs Soloman. What happens during my treatment shall on no account be spoken of or spread abroad.' Hippocrates again. He could still rely upon Hippocrates.

'Man of physic? You are but a shopkeeper!' An expulsion of air and a finger is lifted towards the door. 'Tell the street urchin to go.'

She subsides into further coughing. Jeremiah lifts her up, offers her a glass. There is nothing of the woman. She is lighter than a pile of feathers. He could crush her bones as one might a sparrow's. Reluctantly—for he would like a second opinion even if that opinion only quantified his own—he signals for Boswell to leave.

'That boy, is he sick?'

'Sick? No, madam. He is possessed of better health than you or I can ever hope for.'

'But the poor, they are always sick.'

'What makes you think he is poor?'

'Why would he put up with you if he were not poor? Anyhow, he did not bow. He gawped.'

He releases her against the pillow. She locates her spectacles on the coverlet and places them over her eyes and inspects him. 'Married?'

'No apprentices are not permitted—'

'Not the boy. You!'

'I am not married, no, madam.'

'Betrothed to be married?'

He sets down his case on the table, opens the drapes a little wider than on his last visit.

'Neither, madam.' Lucy cannot still believe they are engaged. It has been almost two years since she last wrote to him.

'Good!' says the old woman.

He takes out the tincture given to him by the Dark Angel and holds it up to the light. The bottle is three quarters full, dark and glutinous. He dismisses the fact—as he has done many times since—that in a state of awe he had forgotten to ask of its contents.

'Your health—' he is not here to satisfy the inadequate life of a lonely old woman after all—'Is the reason for my visit.'

'I have no health, have you not gathered *that* much?'

He takes a spoon from his case, noticing that his hand shakes. He approaches the bed where, as if used to taking drugs from strange men, Mrs Soloman is already leaning forward, mouth agape like a feeding chick.

'Another poison?' she asks but nonetheless swallows it.

'A blend of herbs to make you well again.'

'Ha! Like the last time. Hear that?' She swallows the spoonful of elixir, turning towards the corer of the room. 'He thinks I have forgotten his last visit!'

Jeremiah squints into the darkness noticing for the first time a figure seated on a chair beside the bed.

'Miss Heart?' he says, surprised by her silent presence. 'I did not see you there.'

'That is on account of her not wishing to be here. She would rather I were dead. But things being what they, I have plenty to arrange before I can die. Things my niece cannot do herself. That much she has adequately proven.'

'We are grateful you have come again Mr Goode.' Miss Heart approaches the bed.

'That is right. You are the one!' says Mrs Soloman.

Clara clears her throat. 'My aunt has faith you can help her.'

This woman can only have faith in her ability to despise. 'My job is to try and I bring a tonic that I believe will assist your aunt greatly,' he says, enthused not so much about assisting Miss Heart's aunt, but imagining the source of his tonic, 'though it would assist if your aunt had a little daylight, some fresh air—'

'Weeds need sunlight. I am not a weed. I shall not be treated thus.'

Jeremiah finds himself smiling at Miss Heart as if they were parents ignoring a child in the throws of a tantrum, though he suspects Miss Heart's smile is more one of an apology, than a genuine smile.

He says, 'I would also like to properly examine your aunt.'

'Of course,' she replies.

'What for?' Mrs Soloman pulls the bedcovers higher.

'To ensure he is treating you with the correct medicine. Aunt. My aunt has not permitted any physicians to examine her yet, Mr Goode.'

'You know why? Because I know my own body, know it better than you do! Is there something wrong with your ears?'

She pulls the bedclothes to her chin.

'Very well,' sighs Jeremiah. 'Then let us proceed this way. Your cough gives you pain?'

'No.'

'Your heart?'

'It beats. Beats fast! And I have a great thirst. I am so tired. I sleep and then feel more tired. I eat but the food slips off my bones. Death eats me when I am not looking. Comes in the night when I dream.' A satisfied expression briefly crosses her face. 'But it won't take me. Not until I am ready.'

'It is important to have things to live for. I am glad,' he says. *Glad*? *He is relieved!*

'You are curious are you not,' says Mrs Soloman. 'I can tell. Well, it does not become a man to be curious.'

'My profession, madam, is one of curiosity. As to your opinion of me, I am here at your service. A Cure does not insist that you favour my character

102

too.' Unlike his father who would attend the bedsides of the sick and dying as a priest might (if he healed it was considered an extra) Jeremiah is not here to adorn, to be liked, to offer reassurance or to seek assurance that his bill should be honoured in any regrettable circumstances. Robert Goode controlled his patients' emotions as if they were puppets but Jeremiah is poorly equipped as a puppeteer. More relevant is his assurance that he does in fact *cure* his patients. However, given the present circumstance, he would gladly exchange something of his father's ability for a little of his own awkwardness.

'May I remind you that if you are not likeable to me you shall not be summoned again?'

'I have gathered as much, madam.' He wipes a hand across his face as though attempting to wipe away doubt. He puts the tincture beside the bed with a firm clout as the withered nutshell upon the pillow continues to stare.

'The tincture must be taken thrice daily,' he says.

'Can you feel his desperation Clara? It seeps out of his skin like badness from a rotted fruit does it not? One can almost touch it.'

'He wishes to help you Aunt.' Miss Heart returns to her chair.

'Hogwash! He wishes to be paid.'

Jeremiah adjusts his wig, tries had to ignore the irritating itch growing beneath it. He wonders if all the other physicians had not failed but given up willingly.

'I shall return in a week,' he says.

'To find me more sick?'

'I do believe, madam, you shall be healed,' he says, jaw uncomfortably clenched as he reminds himself of his belief in Mother Nature and how he believes in the power of plants to cure as much as a waning crescent following a new moon. What he shall struggle to believe, however, is that the world will benefit from having Mrs Soloman in it!

The old woman sighs lengthily. 'You believe, you believe…Anyhow, it has to be soon if you want your money. I give you one month. No more.'

'In usual circumstances a Cure takes as long as it needs.' He barely has a month of freedom left.

'You have had a few days already—during which you failed. Your herbs made me sicker. You are only here on account of Clara. And do not look so concerned, Mr Goode. I am not asking that you completely Cure me of my ills. That will take months though if you meet with success with the staircase

I shall hire you for longer. You understand I am asking only to walk down a staircase? It is not much to ask, to walk down one's staircase—*well, is it?*'

Jeremiah's nods in acquiescence like a Punch and Judy puppet, finding this is all he is capable of at the end of a long and dreary performance.

After Jeremiah packs up his case, he exits the bedchamber and Miss Heart follows him silently down to the receiving hall. It feels as if his entire life pivots upon the outcome of three weeks' time and the fate of a lonely old woman. He shall earn a 1000 pounds, pay off Manners and recommence serving the parish or else be on his way to the Fleet Prison. The Fleet: a place that men entered with nothing and came out with even less, where they perished or returned to gaol through some petty means of survival. The Fleet, in short, marked the end. And yet despite his predicament, despite his present lack of faith in himself (as well as his parish), he spends his time picturing the face of a woman he barely knows: the Dark Angel, and the image provides as much comfort as his own liberty.

'I must apologise,' says Miss Heart, head bent towards her clasped hands.

'You have done nothing wrong,' he tells her.

She fiddles with her kerchief. 'Not directly.'

'For acting as a messenger? Console yourself, Miss Heart. I am here voluntarily. Look, my hands are not chained.'

He holds up his wrists, she smiles, face softening so that two irregular dimples appear, giving sudden character to her plainness. Miss Heart strikes him as a woman used to putting up with others' grievances as if she had learnt to slip away unnoticed into many a darkened corner.

'Do you believe what you have given her will work?' she asks.

Confession rests on his tongue like something tart, something needing to be gotten rid of like a lemon pip.

'I can only hope.'

'*There you are!*' Boswell staggers across the reception hall. '*That took an age!*'

'There is no need to shout,' says Jeremiah, glancing awkwardly at Miss Heart after he notices the footman stumbling behind, even redder in the face than earlier.

'We have been in the cellar, sir,' says Boswell.

'And I can guess what kind of cellar.' Jeremiah turns back to Miss Heart. 'I shall return next week. I am confident that my Cure shall work Miss Heart. Have faith in my methods.' *Albeit the Dark Angel's methods more than his own.*

'Might you return sooner?' she says rather shyly, a blush rising up from her collar. 'I mean if my aunt, well, were to recover quicker than anticipated.'

'If she does you can be sure she will keep me hanging on until the very last minute of the very last day. People who suffer themselves often gain pleasure in inflicting their suffering on others.'

Miss Heart sees him to the door. 'Many have not acted as honourably as yourself, Mr Goode.'

'I have acted as I have been taught by my profession; to treat all patients equally.' He puts on his hat. 'I would, however, prefer to treat Mrs Soloman alone on my next visit. I work best alone, which—' He looks with distain at his apprentice. '—is more than can be said for your footman.'

Behind his apprentice stands the swaying footman as well as a plump woman, he suspects is the cook. She reveals a flash of gums as she smiles. 'Bring this one again. He's plenty fun!' she says, prodding Boswell's arm. 'This place could do with some humour.' The plump red-cheeked woman glares at Miss Heart.

'Mrs Warren, thank you for taking care of Mr Goode's apprentice. You may return to the kitchens now.'

The cook winks at Jeremiah. 'You must have a sense of humour too—to want to Cure the old dragon!'

With which the woman disappeared back into the kitchen again, her laughter echoing along a hidden corridor.

Out on the street Jeremiah whacks his apprentice's over the head. 'Is the old hag not enough without a drunken apprentice to cope with?' He hands Boswell his case. 'The walk, at least, will sober you up. Tell me, does he drink her good stuff?'

'I do not know but I know that he likes to talk.'

'He spoke of?'

'Mrs Soloman. How he wishes her dead.'

'I am certain he is not alone.'

'He says his days are drawn with waiting. Says he hopes to be paid handsomely for his time in service.'

'Doubtless he has his eye on a will. What servant can complain of having too little to do? No doubt he shall be disappointed. Too many servants are surprised by an employer's neglect.' *Many servants and many offspring too, though he shall not be counted among them, for he knows for certain he shall be disinherited. What he requires more is a reprieve yet knows he will never receive it.*

'No will was mentioned, sir. But he did fall asleep for a time and then the cook started asking questions about the drugs given to Mrs Soloman.'

'And you said?'

'That my employer only works with herbs and that the arsenic he stocks for the rats. That shut her up. Then when Mr Farley awoke, he did tell me that Miss Heart was cursed by the Devil.'

'Cursed, how?'

'Cannot have children, sir.'

'And how would the Fish know of such a thing?'

'He did read Mrs Soloman's letters, sir, and one from Miss Heart some years passed saying why she had chosen not to marry. She did not wish to deceive a man into believing she would provide him with a family. She has not the normal womanly Curse. The footman did also say Miss Heart is of uneasy character.'

Who would not be when residing with Mrs Soloman? 'Do not believe the prattle of a Fish, Boswell. Our business is to Cure the old woman.'

Cure her so that he may never set eyes on her again.

'What did you administer her, sir?'

Jeremiah finds he cannot admit his weakness to Boswell. It was one thing to seek a cure from a stranger—albeit a beautiful one—another not to bother inquiring what it contained.

'What would you have given?' he asks instead.

Boswell sniffs. 'From what I heard from her footman, most likely a hefty punch in the face, sir.'

An omen of sorts

'Sir?'

Jeremiah whips back the bed drapes. It is startlingly cold with icicles now hanging on the *inside* of his windows. He is thankful he fell asleep last night wearing all but his shoes. He clutches a vial of laudanum in his fist.

'What is it, Boswell?'

'A customer, sir.'

Jeremiah tucks the empty vial beneath his pillow and casts an eye about for his shoes.

'Go on,' he grunts, inspecting the sole of a shoe worn thin.

'A customer, sir, dying upon the shop floor.'

The first rule of running an apothecary shop is to acknowledge one does not run a hospital, the second to stringently avoid the cost of a burial.

'Go on,' he says, opening the bedchamber door.

'I lay him on his side so that he does not vomit and choke—just as you taught, sir, but … ' Boswell appears pale, wide-eyed.

'Yes?'

'His breath is like a donkey's, sir.'

'Foul breath will not kill a man.' He crouches down and peers beneath the bed, scraping about in the dust for his periwig. *Did the damn thing have legs of its own?*

'But his body convulsed three times, sir. He is surely dying. See for yourself.'

Deciding it unnecessary to wear a wig for a dying man, Jeremiah follows Boswell down to his elaboratory where the air is as stale as a crypt. Later, he must sacrifice comfort to open a window, but not the door; open a door and all manner of vagrants see it as an invitation to take up residence.

'What have you given him?'

'No physick whatsoever, sir. I have spent all the time dragging him inside.' Boswell tips his head. 'I thought you were departing today for Dulwich to visit your father.'

'With a properly dying man on my shop floor it is good fortune I did not.'

Boswell draws back the drape. Jeremiah takes in the comma-shaped curve upon his shop floor. The room appears brighter, the mahogany counter

107

a burnished red. Glancing into the yard Jeremiah sees why. Snow covers the cobbles and is still falling in timid bursts. He crouches to this man blown in by the cold, loosening the buttons at the neck of his chemise. He wears no coat, not even a hat. On his feet rags are tied about his ankles. Left outside and he would barely survive an hour.

'Can you hear me?' Jeremiah presses fingers to the man's pulse, touching skin as cold as granite.

'When I opened the door, he was coughing, sir. I dragged him inside and asked Mary to fetch a blanket for him to lie on. There was a great deal of blood. When he stopped coughing he looked so white I thought him dead.'

Jeremiah says, 'Take hold of his feet.' He takes the man's shoulders and they carry what is left of him into the rear of the shop, Mary holding back the drape. They arrange the man on his side before the hearthrug, a cushion beneath his head. Jeremiah asks Mary to light a fire. The stench is unbearable.

'Why is he sick, sir?'

'Consumption I expect.' He places a hand against the man's chest, grimacing at the space between heartbeats. 'Too early to tell. When you have finished the fire, Mary, fetch him some broth.'

'Humour of the lungs, sir? If there is blood and phlegm you taught—'

'I taught that we do not teach a drowning man to swim but throw him a rope! We are to firstly get his heart beating with some regularity. Broth Mary,' he says to stop the girl fussing over the flames. 'Boswell fetch as many blankets as you can find. Strip all the beds if necessary.'

He looks to the man who is coughing feebly, a thin trail of blood leaking from the corners of his lips. Jeremiah wipes the blood away with his cuff. He removes his coat and places it over the man's chest.

'Do you want to be saved?' he asks, half to himself.

It is perhaps an omen. In four years he has not witnessed a death and now death is blown over the threshold and into his elaboratory. The red curtain that was meant to draw a line between him and disease has finally proven ineffectual.

When Boswell returns with the blankets, Jeremiah wipes a hand over his face and asks, 'Do you recognise him?'

'I have seen him begging. He's from a St Giles cellar, sir.'

He is no longer surprised by whom Boswell knows. But an St Giles cellar is the lowliest place on earth a man might reach whilst still breathing. Doubtless it had an open sewer flowing through the middle, furnished with rats as big as badgers. Yet somehow he must attempt to return the man to this place, either to live or to die.

'The Rookery?' he enquires though one cellar is much the same as any other.

'Aye, sir. He was a watchman once and liked his *Mother's Ruin*. By that I do mean gin, sir.'

'You must go to the Rookery, find someone who will attend to him.' He would go himself but it is easy to lose oneself in the Rookery's warrens and hovels. 'Tell whoever you find that he will be bed-bound for some time, that he needs only a little food and water.'

'There is no money to spare at the Rookery, sir.'

Jeremiah searches his waistcoat pockets.

'It will cost kindness, not much else. Tell them I shall supply all that the man needs.' How he does not know how but as if answering his concerns he finds two pennies in his pocket and gives them to the boy. 'Most people will do much for a penny and there is plenty laudanum to ease his suffering.'

He finds Mary seated before a fire that burns up an old stool. She points at the vagrant.

'He is awake?' Jeremiah half-whispers.

Mary nods.

He crouches down, tells the fellow, 'I shall lift your head so that you may drink. Mary would you help?' How quickly he has grown used to Mary's ability to hear.

Resting a hand against a thick wodge of matted hair, he administers the broth. After several mouthfuls the fellow spits the stuff in Jeremiah's eyes. But there is no blood in the spit and his lips have become pink, no longer blue. This is good. He shall prepare the fellow a tincture of cinnamon bark, dried ginger, boiled potato root and the remainder of the liquorice root. In a few days with some dry clothes he shall doubtless be restored to a drunken beggar again.

Jeremiah asks, 'You are comfortable?'

'Pain,' whispers the fellow, tears washing clean lines through the filth.

'Where?' Jeremiah asks, though he can sense it emanates from the man's heart and spreads over his skin.

'All over. Pain like pins all over.'

Jeremiah takes two vials of laudanum from his desk drawer; doubtless the Navy would have other ways of securing pain relief for its sailors. 'Sit him up, Mary.'

Mary helps as Jeremiah administers the opium. 'Your suffering shall soon cease,' he tells the fellow. 'Watch over him, Mary. Remove the blankets if he gets too warm. There is another vial if needed.' During these moments he thanks God for the poppy flower. He also thanks God for Mary. Gentle, silent Mary with her calming presence, entirely absent of the begrudgingly put-upon nature of other servants. She smiles and it occurs, not for the first time, that Mary might make a good wife. She has done well to put up with him, with chores that lay beyond maid-of-all-work. Three years remain of her apprenticeship and if he is lucky to avoid gaol, it might mean three more years of his maidservant using sweet smiles to gain free produce at the markets. If he made a success of his business it would allow her to blossom, to cook with proper ingredients, to tend to a home worthy of such a title. Boswell, once he is qualified, he is unlikely to hold on to.

'Mary?' he says.

She looks up, her face serene in the firelight, its edges and blemishes smoothed.

'If I do not obtain the two hundred and forty pounds for Manners shortly after Christmas I shall be unable to keep you or Boswell in service for I shall most likely be sent to gaol. Do you understand me, Mary?'

She nods, then looks to the boards. Jeremiah nonetheless feels relieved, finds he has nothing more to say on the subject. After all a man cannot dictate how life shall proceed after his death.

He opens the window a crack and sits at his desk to make a note concerning Mrs Soloman's meals. If she lives without sunlight perhaps she lived without proper sustenance. He has known many a rich woman to subsist on tea and cake alone. But he must put his trust in Miss Heart, trusting that the woman wishes her aunt well. When rid of the fellow on his floor, he will begin testing more herbs, experimenting with a mixture to heal the lungs, guess at the ingredients the Dark Angel's tincture and if he cannot replicate them then he shall produce something of its equal.

He must persuade his heart to be a part of this healing too.

After a time, he puts down his quill and gazes into neglected and overgrown yard. He picks up his quill and begins a letter to his sister to pen his excuses, but after several minutes he finds he has written *Dark Angel* several times across the page.

He gets up from the desk and adds another stool leg to the fire's dwindling flames. The coal man has refused to supply more coal until his account is settled. Only the tradesman with an eye for beauty will keep them in food. Mary sits staring at the man on the floor as if willing his eyes open. Jeremiah wonders, though only briefly, what passes through her mind as she sits there motionless. Perhaps living in this neglected hovel she has grown used to absence. But what other employer would have restored her hearing? Surely he can quell a little of his guilt—guilt that seeps like a miasma into other areas of his life—with a cure well done?

He crouches down. 'Do you have somewhere to go?' he asks. The man stares as if Jeremiah had asked the impossible.

Jeremiah asks, 'Your name?'

'John,' the man rasps. 'John Brown.'

But slips back into sleep, one punctuated by silences during which Jeremiah and Mary hold their breath until the man gasps at the air and they too can resume breathing. Jeremiah realises, perhaps for the first time, that Mrs Soloman is right: death is a presence.

When he returns, Boswell brings into the elaboratory the stench of the streets: the filth and the fried food.

'I found somebody, sir,' he says.

'You did well.'

'His sister, sir. Her husband, he does work at the quays. She has a bed for him and a little food. They live over at the Rookery.'

'You *did* do well,' says Jeremiah, patting the boy's back. 'We shall let him rest here for a few hours.' A feeling of hope for this fellow's life, for his own life, makes him suddenly generous. 'And Boswell, maybe you shall be as lucky when collecting debts as you were in finding this man a bed.'

Tell me about Death

Life is no longer marked by the Gregorian calendar but by how many days until the bailiff next visits. Day and night Jeremiah scratches a quill across the page and little else besides. He fishes from his memory every cure he has ever enacted. You might say his life has become a journey through deep cart ruts that provide no freedom to deviate. Even future visits from Wordsley's he shall see as opportunity to write his compendium by brighter candlelight at White's. At night he writes his compendium on the floor, for it is either candles or coal, and hope comes usually around midnight when, drunk upon letters, his thinking falls beyond reason: for it is then that he believes he shall finish it within a fortnight.

Three blessed weeks until the bailiff has his way, in more ways than one!

A visit to his father is long overdue but there has been no further word from Dulwich which is unsure how to interpret. He has explained to Boswell and Mary that he prefers to ensure his father is properly dying first for the last time he visited he was ushered away at the front door by Violet, 'He's much better now dear brother but mother fears he may take another turn if he were to—', so he had finished Violet's sentence for her with a terse, 'see me' and departed. He does not bother providing Boswell and Mary with the whole explanation.

He looks at the which have been collected from the parish selling the last remaining herbs. Boswell says more shall follow. Thus far, it is not enough to keep the bailiff at bay.

With great effort he has reached Herb Truelove, a herb to expel poisons. Whilst he works, the image of the image of the Dark Angel's face regularly returns, its calm presence offering inspiration. A fire has been lit in his breast and it distracts from misfortune as much as from the cold. He no longer dreams of tall towers and impenetrable walls, places to tether a man's soul but instead awakens with this woman's face freshly imprinted on his mind. It sweetens his breath, drops his twitching shoulders until a splinter or two of life's troubles fractures the vision. But she has not replied to the letter he left at the Physic Gardens under the care of Mr Rand. He wonders what frustrates him the most: fear that he lacks the ability to heal Mrs Soloman, or that he has returned to the Physic Gardens twice looking for a loose-haired

112

woman in a cloak he might never see her again. And now…well, now he feels compelled to compose another.

Dear Madam,

I have written already but received no reply. I apologise for what might appear to be a brief loss of faith but the outcome of this particular Cure lends itself rather heavily to my continued freedom and I do, in turn, most graciously appreciate the advice of a healer who likewise sees Curing as an affect on the whole rather than some partial, temporary occurrence; who favours Mother Nature over the horrors of drugs and regular bleeding. To share my concerns with another apothecary would in addition mean passing on a fortuitous opportunity, for there is no sentiment in trade and one apothecary would as soon as stamp on the shoulders of another than offer his help. Suffice to say that if this patient is healed, then I should gladly share with you any potential benefit that I might reap …

'Never apologise, never explain: the first rules of physic,' or so his father had taught him. Jeremiah falls asleep, quill in hand, and when he opens his eyes Boswell's boots and the aroma of horse shit are level with his head.

'Good morning, sir.'

'Morning shall suffice,' says Jeremiah, standing and scratching voraciously at various parts of his anatomy. He examines his skin for the familiar black specks. He inspects his face in his mother's looking glass given to furnish his new home—a place his father has barred her from visiting— but finds only the usual smears upon the glass.

'Fleas!' he declares. 'I am rife with fleas!'

'From sleeping upon that filthy carpet, sir. My mother used to say—'

'Ah! So there are specific loins from which you emerged?'

'A wit this morning, sir,' says Boswell banging the pestle against the mortar. 'My mother would say itching is a sign of change. I should say you could benefit from some change.'

Jeremiah, stretches his aching limbs, checks the time—not yet six of the clock—and then the other, more insistent, clock starts up: drumming its time to his last march of freedom. 'A sign to change one's clothes no doubt!' he says.

He takes a look at his once impressive black waistcoat, its silver embroidery unravelling and several buttons amiss. The frivolities of fashion are of no further interest to him, how could they be when most in his parish are relieved not to be naked? But if he manages to save himself he shall go to *David Jones* on Monmouth Street to purchase some second-hand clothes, something less funereal. In red perhaps. It shall signify something.

He instructs Boswell to fetch wormwood, some cedar wood too. He tells the boy, 'I shall treat as if for lice. You must do the same and tell Mary too. Now pray, what do you incessantly grind?'

'Mrs Soloman's nutmeg, sir.'

'Grind any more and it shall blow away with your farts. It is to be added to red rose-cakes warmed in vinegar, then heated over a chafing-dish of coals. Light grinding, that is all! Nutmeg shall procure rest and comfort the spirits. It likewise sweetens the breath. Doubtless Mrs Soloman could benefit from some sweetening.'

He checks the time before sitting at his desk. He holds Jasper's paperweight in his hand, turning the smooth glass in his palm as an image of a deformed kitten abruptly obscures his vision. His shoulder lurches as he sees his father's arm flinging the creature onto the muckheap. He sets down Jasper's paperweight. He shakes his head, scratches his ear, attempts to dislodge the thought as the creature lingers a minute longer, dying upon his desktop.

Once the image clears, he rubs his eyes and peers at his accounts. Certain purchases he now regrets: the great hunk of mahogany counter, the alligator from Africa with its leering marble eyes, even this sombre black suit with silver thread brought for a small fortune, not to keep up with the longer fashion in waistcoats but to furnish his insufficient character with dignity. He had not felt equipped at the time, not for any of this. But it was not dignity needed in St Giles. It was herbs. It was time. Patience. Most of all money. His list of debts has become pages long and in the midst of London's worst winter for decades there *was* no money.

He glances down at the names in Boswell's script.

John No Privy, the Rookery

Thomas I.A.M. Poor, the Devil's Rookery

'Boswell?' he asks beckoning the boy with a finger.

Boswell ceases scraping the nutmeg into a jar to peer over his shoulder.

'John no privy? Thomas is poor?' Jeremiah asks him.

Boswell gives his head another scratch. 'Tis what they called themselves, sir.'

'*Tis what they called themselves, sir?*'

Boswell shrugs. 'I was busy getting my letters written down to pay attention to what I was writing.'

Jeremiah sighs. Did it matter? The Rookery was the worse slum in Britain. Half of Ireland was housed inside it: *Little Ireland* or *The Holy Land* people called it. Those living there were as likely to have money as Wordsley a virtuous conscience.

He scratches his leg, his elbow. Itching: such a troublesome infliction. Hard to diagnose for it might mean healing as much as it did nits or fleas.

'Hurry with that wormwood,' he tells the boy. 'Then we shall leave for Chelsea.' 'Am I to come with you, sir?'

'Indeed, I wish to hear your opinions as we walk.' Besides which, he needed somebody to carry his great case, packed for as many eventualities as he could still afford.

By Chelsea, Jeremiah's itching has abated though his flatulence could put a hound to shame. Boswell too appears impressed as he lets out wind with a thunderous echo at Mrs Soloman's bedchamber door.

'Better out than in,' says the boy with a grin.

'Damned wormwood.'

'Change, sir, on that you can depend.'

'No pissing in the plant pots, understand?'

Boswell licks his lips. 'Another bottle of the footman's wine would not go amiss.'

'It is not the footman's wine. Remember that. I, for certain, will not be the one to meet your expenses. Now pass me my case.'

Leaving Boswell outside, knowing he will slide into a place more congenial and warm, Jeremiah enters a chamber partially illuminated by an opened drape. It casts a block of sunlight over the purple damask bed cover, forming a neat square of purple flowers like those—Jeremiah finds himself given to brief fantasy—neatly arranged over a casket.

A smile wavers across Mrs Soloman's lips. 'I am progressing am I not?' she says, looking towards the open drape.

Jeremiah bows. 'We have light. That is certainly an improvement.'

'I persuaded my aunt to let in the day and it has lifted her spirits,' Miss Heart offers, from a chair in the corner. 'Is that not right, Aunt Rachel?'

Against a half-dozen pillows in silk and velvet, Mrs Soloman pulls herself upright. The pillows convey wealth in their quantity, as is the way with pillows. (In St Giles, a luxury is merely to have one's head lifted from the boards.)

'I must insist my niece remain in the room with me. I have known many physicians to take advantage of an old widow and I shall not be one of them. Do not worry, my niece is easily ignored.'

Jeremiah's flinches on behalf of Miss Heart, who remains stoical like a statue impervious to the rain and defecating birds. 'I work better alone but perhaps in Miss Heart's company you will allow me to examine you?'

Mrs Soloman's hands—a collection of bones and veins—weave tightly together upon the damask. 'I am getting better am I not?'

He sets down his case. 'You took all the tonic?'

'Yes and now I require more.'

He looks from Miss Heart to Mrs Soloman. 'It is important I examine you first. If you would prefer privacy then perhaps—'

'Clara is to stay.'

'Very well.' He agrees with reluctance, reaching for the bedcover.

'I improve though I still suffer.' Mrs Soloman keeps the cover retained in her skeletal hands, 'day and night, night and day, Death stands at the end of my bed laughing at me, pointing its finger. Accusing me! And for what? What have I done to deserve its clutches? *What?*'

'Tell me about death,' he says, sitting at her side.

'Death!' Mrs Soloman's jaw muscles palpitate. 'Death comes to you when you are alone. He breaths foul words into your ear, whispers his desires. Wakes you from your most peaceful sleep to offer you his hand. You almost accept it out of… out of loneliness. Out of blessed gratitude. But look at you! You are too young. Too much life in your eyes to know about such things.'

'I know a thing or two about death.'

The old woman falls silent, tears swelling in her eyes, falling along her pale, papery cheeks. Miss Heart passes her a handkerchief and squeezes her aunt's arm.

'Do not fear,' the old woman now says with false cheer, shrugging off her niece. 'Death cannot lure me. My job here is not yet over. Tell him Clara, tell him I cannot die!'

Miss Heart sits back in her chair, smiling with resignation. 'No, Aunt, you cannot die.'

Jeremiah experiences a sensation, like the tip of a feather, along his spine.

'So,' says Mrs Soloman relinquishing her grip on the covers just a little. 'I will settle my husband's affairs and making it to Gates at *Gan Eden* after all.'

'*Gan Eden*?' he inquires.

'Heaven to your people. Jewish Paradise for those who've lived a righteous life, like my Abe. He waits for me there. In heaven and hell there are banquets, you know.'

He teases the cover from her hands saying, 'Banquets indeed.'

'Of course, but in hell they cannot bend their arms to eat the food. Imagine that, Mr Goode! My Abe, ate well. He loved his food. He said there was not a wife in all of England who could plan a meal as well as I.'

Jeremiah's attention is still given to removing Mrs Soloman's bedcover, inch by inch.

'In heaven, yes in heaven, they feed one another. Abe will sure to be eating like a king. He took care of many upon this earth. I expect he shall be fat when I join him. Yes that's it,' She croaks laughter. 'Fat and happy!'

Much improvement upon the miserly man previously mentioned, one who had refused his wife a child.

'Can a lawyer not assist with your husband's affairs?' he says as he slowly, firmly, tugs the cover from the old woman's grip.

'Are you trying to force me into Death's hands more quickly, Mr Goode?'

'Just trying to help. That is all.'

'Help line your purse with coins! It is only I who can arrange Abe's affairs. Only I! Abe was always proud of my ability to arrange such things. Besides.' Mrs Soloman fixes her wide eyes to his hands. 'Your job is to ease my suffering. You have brought it, have you not? The tonic?'

'All in good time.' Only two hours ago had he posted the letter to the Dark Angel requesting more.

He draws back layers of bed linen and encounters a body so frail it barely puts a dent in the mattress. He blows onto his hands and presses them to Mrs Soloman's chest, another to her forehead. He closes his eyes and follows her breath, letting merge with his own.

'What is he doing?'

'Aunt, let Mr Goode do his work.'

'Work? He has all but fallen asleep. I am the one who is sick!'

Jeremiah is oblivious to the women now, rests in a world beyond senses, a world occupied by pain and sentiment. There is a constriction in his lungs, a shortness of breath, a quickening of his heart followed by the overpoweringly sweet smell of rotten apples. Quite suddenly he feels the firm touch of another on his back: fingers digging firmly into the sensitive flesh around his kidneys. He shifts his body, shakes off the sensation and, opening his eyes, asks without pre-thought (for the source of the remark comes from somewhere outside himself), 'How often do you pass urine?'

'Impertinent!'

He looks towards Miss Heart. 'Might you assist?'

Miss Heart blushes but does not respond.

'I go when I need to.' Mrs Soloman tips her chin to the overhead canopy. 'Meaning what?'

'Has the man forgotten how to speak to a lady?'

He too looks up at the bed canopy, not to roll his eyes but to throw up his hands with frustration. 'We are speaking about urine, nothing more. *Urine!*' He turns to Miss Heart. 'Pray, can you help with this?'

'I'm afraid I cannot, Mr Goode.'

In one sharp movement, Jeremiah draws back the bedcovers. Mrs Soloman lifts her knees and Jeremiah catches sight of it.

'Why… ' He wrestles with disbelief. 'Why did you keep this from me?' Blood rapidly drains from his thoughts.

The old woman tilts her head. 'Keep what?' she says.

'Why your foot! Why…did you not mention your *foot* to me?'

'Oh that! It causes me no bother. No bother at all. My heart frequently takes off at a gallop but this, well, it only lays there useless, like a dead fish.'

It is not too late, he thinks, examining three swollen puss-ridden toes, unsure who needs more reassurance, himself or the old woman.

He clears his throat. 'It is not too late for your toes,' he says, unable to tread lightly around the subject for they are the size of dates, *of figs*! This is far more than mere melancholy. It changes everything, I'm afraid.'

'They're *my* toes! Why should it be too late? Too late for what?'

'I mean to say, that left too long,' he glances at Miss Heart, 'they shall turn gangrenous. When that happens your entire body shall be filled by poison and you shall—'

'Hogwash! All hogwash!'

'Aunt Rachael, listen to Mr Goode. He is trying to tell you that if he does not save your toes they shall need to be removed.'

'Hogwash!' Mrs Soloman falls back against the cover. 'A quack! You see that now Clara, I hope? I told you I could not comprehend your insistence in wanting him back again. I am sure you can now see, *he is not the one!*'

Clara blushes. Jeremiah continues to stare at Mrs Soloman's toes.

'Get on with it then! Do you want to save my toes or not? But I tell you this: they do not need saving. My heart suffers. My heart is the thing to need saving. As for my toes they do not cause a drop of distress.'

Jeremiah did not doubt Mrs Soloman's heart needed saving too, but he had put these woes down to grief, down to melancholy, down to living for too long without light, without love. But these toes signified in his experience a need for sweetness. A debilitating need. And Mr James had cured the condition with sugar alone. It offered, however, only temporary improvement. 'Sickness can be like a hungry dog,' his old employer would say, 'Keeps coming back for more!' Yet Jeremiah preferred to treat dis-ease as if the dog were rabid, as if feeding it only drew the inevitable bite nearer.

He sorts through the jars of his apothecary case, selects certain herbs and replacing them again until his gut confirms he holds the right jar in his hand.

'Black Hellebore, twenty grains thereof corrected with half as much cinnamon.' It is, he thinks, the obvious choice.

'What of the tonic?'

'No tonic today. I shall leave syrup of elderberries for your cough, which already seems much improved.'

119

'No tonic?'

'Dis-ease must be unwrapped, Mrs Soloman, as an onion is peeled. Each layer must be given the appropriate Cure, thereby allowing progression to subsequent layers. Eventually… eventually we shall reach the rotten pulp of the problem, on that you can depend.'

This was his theory and it presently kept his mind from desperation. The means along which a cure preceded was from inside to outside, from upper body to lower. But the journey was never as smooth or as obvious as that. Only afterwards did it all make perfect sense.

'Hear him Clara? I sent for you to bring more of what is making me better. I am not a plant. I am not an onion. I am a dying lady! One made briefly well by your Cure. So where is it?'

Given the coach fare he would travel to Dorset that very afternoon. He comprehends the old woman's desperation and likewise her hope. Such emotions explain his own perseverance, but fault lay with his memory for of course he had forgotten like a fool—a lovesick fool—to inquire of the tonic's ingredients, had received no reply from his letters and it would take a week for a second letter to reach Chideock—if indeed Mr Rand had bothered to post it at all, not to mention another week before he hears back and two weeks is too late, even for hope.

Alas, the incessant clock recommences its death march. Then a vision comes, acutely clear; the long husks, crooked, containing yellowish seeds dried to the colour of rust. They are unmistakable. The memory of the stonemason with five gangrenous toes coming back to him too. That's it! In a matter of weeks the lame fellow had walked again!

'This too,' he says, tipping a generous measure of fenugreek seeds into a phial. 'A teaspoon boiled and drank thrice daily.'

Mrs Soloman turns her head away. 'Do you dare to make me sicker?'

'Please trust Mr Goode, Aunt.' Miss Heart's smile is thin.

'Why? He has everything to gain whilst I have everything to lose.'

'Four days of black hellebore, Fenugreek and bilberries,' says Jeremiah closing his case, 'you shall quickly see improvement.' Though with a blackened foot it may still not be quick enough to save him from gaol.

'You are keeping something from me, aside from that tonic. I can feel it.'

120

Surprised that the woman has feelings, he is likewise surprised by her acuity. Perhaps death, like alcohol, could instil understanding beyond the capabilities of its victim.

'Madam, my intention is to heal not trick.'

'So they all say. Now cover me up else I shall perish at the expense of your gawping.'

He replaces layer upon layer of bedding, his mind meandering along alternative routes to Dorset. By boat? As a stowaway? By foot? Branches rap at Mrs Soloman's window, blown by the harsh December gusts. No, he thinks, nigh impossible in such freezing conditions. How, in heaven's name, had he missed such a symptom? This had never happened before. The threat of gaol had, it would seem, robbed him of more than his sleep.

He fastens the lock on his case. 'I shall visit again in a week.'

'*A week?*' Mrs Soloman face closes in on itself. 'But that is an age. I might be dead in a week.'

'The herbs, you understand, they must be given a chance—'

'Bring that tonic! You hear me? It is the only thing to ease my suffering. The only thing!' Mrs Soloman fixes watery eyes upon him. 'Bring it without delay and if I do not I shall find it for myself. Is that understood?'

A sudden downpour

'For your sake,' Jeremiah tells Miss Heart when they are alone in the receiving hall, 'I hope your aunt quickly improves but this foot is certainly a setback and one I, I admit, I had not expected.'

Miss Heart looks away. 'Indeed.'

'I shall return in four days. But the tonic I cannot promise.'

'It would make my aunt immeasurably happy.'

'I realise that, but it shall not, unfortunately, be possible.'

'Happiness must surely, well, it must surely play a part in being Cured, Mr Goode?'

'Happiness is perhaps everything,' he says, thinking of Wordsley who had not experienced a day's sickness in his life. 'Yet happiness can be more elusive to some than good health.'

A long morning and Miss Heart's face draws out the truth like a poultice sucking out poison. Yet, he must resist it and he does so with a long exhalation of air. 'I require your patience, if you please, Miss Heart. Your patience.'

'Then some tea, before your journey Mr Goode?'

He looks about the receiving hall.

'Oh, rest assured, Mr Goode, your apprentice is under the care of my aunt's footman.'

'I see,' he says, not reassured in the slightest. Nevertheless, the offer of tea he cannot refuse. Proper, strong tea.

He removes his hat again. 'Perhaps a small dish.'

The drawing room is a haze of pink marble. Half a dozen chandeliers hang suspended within their individual rainbows. There are several more lifeless landscapes and six long windows that overlook the cemetery. With neither fireplace lit, Jeremiah sits with his hands beneath his thighs attempting to keep warm.

'How do you live in such a place?' he asks.

'I have grown used to it.'

'The cold,' he says, 'I shall never grow used to.'

'You have been very patient with us, Mr Goode.' Miss Heart pours the tea from the edge of her seat. Her shawl slips several times and she shrugs it off as she offers the sugar.

'I only have a month or thereabouts to endure,' he says.

'Of course.'

'And you, Miss Heart, how long must you remain here?'

'Indefinitely,' she says, not meeting his eye.

'Then I expect your feelings toward me must be uncertain?'

She looks up, biting her lower lip. 'My feelings toward... toward you, Mr Goode?'

'I mean to say, that if I do my job to the best of my abilities and your aunt lives longer then, well, I need not speak more plainly, Miss Heart.'

She hands him a cup trembling in its saucer. You believe... you believe that I reside here waiting for my aunt to die?'

He has had enough of disagreeing for one day. 'No, I do not think such a thing. I imagine that she is not an easy woman to reside with, that is all.' He falls back against the back of his chair.

'I could not wish any person dead, no matter who they were or what they had done.' The teapot drips steadily. Jeremiah refolds his arms. 'You must believe me, Mr Goode.' She sets down the pot. He would respond if not for the haze of fuzziness, that intangible thing hovering over her head, something he still cannot place. She now looks at him and with a distinct, yet definite pause before continuing—a pause into which he sees a flicker of someone more capable, someone far stronger than this mild and hesitant niece. 'I wish only…I wish only that my aunt would recover. It is an ending to which I devote many a prayer.'

Jeremiah reinstates his belief that Miss Heart has neither thought a wrong thought nor performed a wrong deed in her life.

'Forgive me,' he says, flicking a piece of his mud from his breeches. 'I have been away from Society for far too long.' She offers some sugar, which he declines, seeing no point in masking the flavour. 'Rest assured, Miss Heart, your prayers are not far from being answered.'

'I do understand how difficult it must be treating my aunt and if not for the… well, the…'

'The reward,' he interjects.

A blush. 'Yes, the reward, Mr Goode.' She stares at a pool of spilt tea.

'And may I ask if you believe I am any closer to it?'

She sets down her cup gently and with practised silence. 'That, unfortunately… is not up… well, it is not up to me to decide the…well, the outcome. What I have noticed is that my aunt's health is not consistently bad. Two months ago she was walking about her bed chamber. Now she does not leave her bed at all. But I am afraid, well, I am afraid I have not been entirely honest with you, Mr Goode.'

He sits taller. Was the reward less than previously stated? Who in their right mind would give away a thousand pounds, after all?

'Pray, continue.'

Miss Heart clutches a hand to her throat as another hand moves to her chest.

'Miss Heart?' He moves around the tea table. Miss Heart pants, her ribs lurch like the gills of a fish. 'Miss Heart?' he says again. He knows he must rip open Miss Heart's bodice but he knows too women of her ilk were never handled in such a manner even when they ceased breathing. But before he can move, she hurries from the room, silk hushing against the marble like a sudden downpour of rain. The door closes. He hears footsteps patter up the staircase, echoing through the vast emptiness of Mrs Soloman's mausoleum. He opens his apothecary case and takes out a small, yet full, vial of laudanum, which he consumes in one gulp. He sits back, waiting for numbness to set in. He had failed to diagnose a gangrenous foot. Failed completely. He looks at the empty vial. Perhaps the stuff is beginning to blunt more than it blunts his pains.

Rest assured, the devil has given up on me

A hollow, desperate cry comes from a baby somewhere in Neal's Yard, as if the creature were startled from a dream concerning its future. Yet despondency is an emotion Jeremiah can ill afford, he thinks as he crosses the yard with Boswell. He has sacrificed many things of late and feelings happen to be the least of such forfeits. Yet the belief remains—for it serves him to hold onto it—that great achievements are measured by the sum of their sacrifices. Thus, healing the sickest, poorest parish in London has certain merits for achievement. Whether his sacrifices amount to anything with Mrs Soloman remains to be seen. One thing he is certain however: she erodes his confidence like rain eating at iron. Yet, a particular idea is hard to ignore: *he would rather Cure an old hag than his father.*

'*Ogh clo, ogh clo,*' cries the Jew, advertising for old clothes.

Jeremiah wipes his boots. 'We have a customer,' he tells Boswell as he peers through the misted glass at two figures. 'Well, let us hope that this time they can read.'

Once inside Boswell drops his apothecary case to the boards.

'You seem to have made yourself at home!' Jeremiah flings his hat at Nicholas Culpeper and widens his eyes at Wordsley who, dressed in mauve and porting lengthy, elaborate frills, sits upon his shop counter.

'Your maid was cold so my footman fetched her some ale.' Wordsley jumps down to rest a hand upon Jeremiah's shoulder. 'She was just writing a note telling me all about Manners, the dun. A nuisance of a fellow by all accounts. What?'

He spills ale from a tankard, along Jeremiah's sleeve. Jeremiah wipes it off, taking in his maid and his apprentice (who is still drunk from Mrs Soloman's wine cellar) and decides they look like two sheep stuck in a bush.

'Manners is my business,' he tells Wordsley, attempting to conceal his growing fear of the bailiff and his wishes. To Mary he says, 'If you are cold you are to use the rest of the sea-coals.' Mary bows her head. 'Now, return to your work.' He glances at Boswell. 'Both of you!'

But nobody moves for there is no work to speak of and Jeremiah pulls back the curtain to his elaboratory and skulks towards his desk.

'*There is to be a winter fayre on the Thames. The water is beginning to seal!*' Wordsley calls after him.

'Ice,' corrects Jeremiah, under his breath, 'the water is beginning to ice.'

He empties his pockets onto his desk top: his pocket watch, an old bent quill, two pennies, his crumpled Physic Garden membership, keys, some wax crumbs, a nutmeg and grater and a rose petal taken from the a winter rose in Brigid's corner (*Brigid, Oh, Brigid!*) of the Physics Gardens. He puts the petal back in his pocket again and makes silent amends with his compendium opened almost meaningfully at Herb Truelove.

It grows in woods and coppices. The leaves or berries are effectual in expelling poisons of all kinds

He looks outside at his neglected garden, shoulder abruptly flinching. Laughter drifts through from the shop. He resents Wordsley's visit, resents that he has reduced his shop to an alehouse and his staff to mere drinking companions. Most of all he resents his friend's unceasing good mood.

Truelove forms a beautiful flower, spread open like a star with a purple head and eight yellow mealy threads of colour. When its leaves wither...

'Me thinks you wish to hang me,' says Wordsley appearing at his side.

'Hang you? There is not enough rope for the two of us. Now what can you want? The hour is too early for gaming.'

'But it is dark enough in here. How do you see to write?'

'With difficulty.'

Wordsley examines the paperweight on Jeremiah's desk, the one given to him by his brother, Jasper, and the only possession he values for it held power to alleviate—just a little—his relentless guilt. Wordsley squints at it, one eye closed. 'Mary tells me that you father is sick.'

Jeremiah shrugs. 'Mary ought to be working.'

'Precisely what she was doing until I asked her to sit with me and wait for your return. She wrote it all down, about your father being sick.' Wordsley's eyes widen like a mad dog's. 'Are you departing for Dulwich soon?'

'No.'

'Why ever not?'

Jeremiah lifts an eyebrow. 'You have turned into one of my sisters overnight?'

Wordsley turns the paperweight around on his palm. 'No.' He peers closer at Jasper's paperweight. 'But I have been reading *The Tatler*.'

Jeremiah tucks in his chin, eyebrow lifted. 'And this is deserving of praise?'

'Not quite, but I see that my rakish behaviour, my thoughtlessness (as others call it) *and* my gambling are no longer à *la mode* either. I am, the magazine, doth tell me, in need of some virtuous qualities. It would seem you are the only virtuous person I know, so here I am to learn.'

'Well, I do not recommend it,' returns Jeremiah.

Wordsley tosses the paperweight then catches it again. 'Last night I gamed with that gentleman. You remember him?'

'You speak of many gentlemen.'

'The one who publishes books?'

Jeremiah looks up. 'Yes, I remember.'

'Well, he know owes me ten pound and is interested in publishing *your book*—though I might have given him a few incorrect facts as to its contents. Anyhow, he wishes to meet with you. I explained to him how I do not understand how you manage it—'

'Manage what?' Jeremiah did not like the way he owes me ten pounds and is interested in publishing your book arose in the same sentence; he does not wish for his compendium to be published as *Wordsley's debt*.

'All this seriousness.' Wordsley takes out a small silver box from his pocket, engraved with his initials and shoves *Nicotiana* plant up an extended nostril. 'I just do not understand how you put up with it.'

'You think me serious for not sitting about like a gossip at a baptism?' Jeremiah knows his friend deserves. It is breeding not character that makes

126

his friend capable of only the most superfluous aspects of survival. Jeremiah sighs. 'A particular patient has made me serious,' he explains.

'You are always serious.' Wordsley steals a look over his shoulder. 'Tell me, you are happy with that young Abigail?'

'Mary? Yes, indeed. Why?'

'She is a fair wench. I could do with a pleasant face brightening my house.'

Jeremiah shakes his head. 'I would not let you have my maid.'

Wordsley tips his chin in the air. 'I am certain this fella will be interested in publishing your book. Though I might have referred to it as a novel rather than a compendium, I do not think it matters a jot. So, you only need to finish it, and then no more of this garret, old friend. Why women hold a peculiar fascination for Grub Street men eludes me. All this writing, to all intents and purposes, is a desperate cry for praise.'

'Praise?'

'Why else would one write if not for praise?'

'To impart knowledge, not seek adoration, Wordsley.' Jeremiah whips Jasper's paperweight from his friend's hands.

'Naturally that is what every writer says but in truth every man seeks adoration. But only some who care to admit it. I tell you this perhaps as *advocatus* to the *diaboli*.'

'Rest assured the Devil gave up on me long ago.' Jeremiah puts down his quill, squeezing a forefinger and thumb into the corners of his eyes.

Wordsley squints at Jeremiah's opened compendium. 'If in alphabetical order you have reached T and are thus nearly done. Are you not?'

'I have reached H: Herb Truelove.'

'Herb Truelove, does it impart such characteristics?'

'It does not. And, besides, true love does not exist.' He turns the leaf of the page. 'It is what animals we refer to as simply the *mating instinct*.'

'Well I am a fool for love and I remember a time when you were too.' Wordsley studies Jeremiah. Jeremiah decides that his friend is truly blinkered by life beyond wealth, certainly unable to fathom the need for a profession or purpose. But Jeremiah cannot so easily dismiss eleven years of uphill struggle. To do so would mean that his life become more frivolous than if he had married Lucy. Meaning would dissolve like sugar in hot water. But perhaps that was the point. Maybe the sweetness mattered and nothing else.

'Do you always dress this way for your customers?' Wordsley asks him, eyeing Jeremiah's black coat.

'What is wrong with my clothes?'

Wordsley steps back, casting an appraising eye over Jeremiah's attire. 'Black, it seems too sombre for a sick bed. I thought that apothecaries wore red velvet gowns with wide Oriental sleeves?'

When the first James was on the throne! Did his friend know so little of his life? 'Please, Wordsley, leave me to my work.' *In peace.*

'Curing this parish is an onerous task. Would you not be better off visiting your father who might, if nothing else, let you inherit some of his patients, now that he is dying?'

'My father thinks me a poor man's physician and nothing more. His patients are wealthy and therefore need to be kept away from my sullied grasp.' Jeremiah looks out towards his yard where a robin, on the window ledge, wrestles with a worm.

'But people alter when dying. He might come round to your…' Wordsley looks about Jeremiah's elaboratory, or what little he can see of it in the dim candlelight. 'To your peculiar plight.'

Jeremiah shakes his head. 'My father despises me. Death is unlikely to change that.'

'You might be surprised.'

'The fact that I won't be *surprised* is why I am not bothering to take a coach to Dulwich, Wordsley.'

'Would you like me to lend you a carriage to get you to Dulwich quicker?'

Jeremiah slams his fist on his desktop. 'No! *I would like to work and in peace!*'

'So shall you be accompanying me to Whites once you have finished your …' Wordsley's nostrils flare theatrically, '*work?*'

'Look, Frederick.' Jeremiah lets out a lengthy sigh. 'I must be sure of a Cure I have administered. A great deal rests upon the outcome of healing this patient. I must succeed or else I am ruined.'

'More rests upon your Cure than a book seller who might make you more famous than Defoe?'

Jeremiah watches the bird still wrestling with his catch.

'I hope so. I sincerely hope so.'

'You won't know until you meet him though, will you?'

'This bookseller, he attends White's?' Jeremiah asks.

'Naturally.' Wordsley lowers his voice. 'And I would be happy to offer you a small loan *in lieu* of publishing your book if you were to attend—forthwith!'

The robin swallows its worm which forms an uncomfortable knot in its throat and now seems to be staring directly at Jeremiah. 'I shall come for a short while.'

'A short while? Surely by now you have learnt the irrelevancy of time when at White's! Worry not. Let us depart with verve. I had forgotten that one must travel London by day as if going into battle.' Wordsley studies Jeremiah. 'By the by, there is something altered my friend in your countenance. If I did not know you as a martyr I would think you had affections for a young woman.'

Jeremiah suspects his own life has become one long gamble as he waits for an answer from a beautiful woman concerning a tonic for a rich lady who may or may not possess the will to be well again. 'What makes you say that?'

'I see a small sign of life in your eye, my friend,' says Wordsley, pointing towards Jeremiah's left eye as they cross the elebatory. 'Yes, of life.'

'I *am* living,' Jeremiah replies, his words flat, like the last drawn-out protestations of a corpse, 'Just not the sort of life you would recognise.'

Do you love her?

After leaving Whites, Jeremiah wonders through the streets of Covent Garden—the Great Square of Venus—a place rife with bawds and bare-breasted whores lurking in piss-splattered alleys; earning their comfort of gin and gaining customers in the manner of a wolf stealing the sickest sheep from the flock.

Jeremiah walks a meandering, drunken path towards the piazza, a place he once visited to purchase his herbs, a place inspired by the Place Royale in Paris. Even at this hour growers unload baskets from carts, the smell of the street sellers' griddles rising into the air. The ground is a wasteland of trodden petals and rotten winter vegetables, scavenged by hungry hands. Before dawn the dealers will arrive followed by the Irish women who distribute the dealers' hundredweights on their heads to the city. It is a relentless struggle: feeding the inhabitants of London; the burden of relentlessness lying heaviest upon the shoulders of market traders and shop owners. And in the centre of this struggle, a tall column—a monument—looming like a misplaced phallus.

Pressing a hand against his coat, Jeremiah feels the outline of a modest win in the lining. He had quickly doubled the sum that Wordsley gave him and though Wordsley would not let Jeremiah repay the loan, it is a comfort to know he can feed his staff for a while longer, pay Manners a little and buy some candle and ink so that he can finish his compendium.

'Hello handsome! Nice curls hanging down from the periwig of yours!'

Jeremiah takes pains to avoid the eyes of the whores wondering around the piazza's edge, their hems lifted, attracting customers with compliments, flaunting their breasts as though selling lumps of cheese. Yet Jeremiah should rather come here rather than St Giles for even a poor man must avoid shitting on his threshold.

Virtue had been discovered, roughly three years ago, strutting outside Mother Winterbottom's house. After tapping her cheek with her fan—the unspoken code of the streetwalkers and the only language concerning fans that Jeremiah properly understood—he had followed her inside. She was recently up from Devon, she said. She was shy, almost prim with clean stockings. Though not a woman to be listed in the *Man of Pleasure's Kalendar* she was nonetheless pretty. With Mrs Winterbottom watching over them, she had said, 'May I take your coat?' and, 'What are your requests, sir?'

'See, lovely girl! You'll have no trouble with her. Honest and wholesome, that's what she is, a rare find. You'll be coming back regular,' confirmed Mrs Winterbottom with a wink. 'You mark my words!'

Even now there remained the traces of a fresh-faced country girl in Virtue's manner. Yet, she was still a whore and like most men of his breeding Jeremiah prefers clear-cut categories. When done here, he will thus not think of Virtue—or any other whore for that matter—until next needing release.

'*Come show me those eyes, such sadness for a fella so handsome!*'

He imagines Virtue's bed, where he will soon lie so why does his mind persistently conjures a narrow room with bars, an over-spilling piss pot and the shrivelled face of Mrs Soloman grimacing like a skull from her pillow!

This life, this City, you shall not rob me of my soul.

His spirit has sunk low. He must be melancholic and should perhaps take suitable herbs to ease his condition but diagnosing oneself is a much harder task that diagnosing another. Certainly, of late he has experienced distance from his actions, something customers had described to him often enough. But he has read *The Anatomy of Melancholy*, knows he should adhere to a healthy diet, sufficient sleep, music and meaningful work, but knows too that this is presently impossible. As for talking the problem with a friend: Wordsley views gaming and whores as the only answer (visiting Virtue he at least takes half of his advice). Yet even if he treats his melancholy how can he ignore the precipice alongside which he walks? Is it not better to keep on with his herbal compendium, to keep journeying in these godforsaken ruts?

White's—why did it have a habit of making him feel worse?

A thought occurs, at once obvious and illuminating. His soul was incomplete; how was it possible to loose something he had yet to seek? Immediately his inner eye fills with *her* image half concealed by a hooded cloak; a woman whose mind excites him as much as her pretty face.

The guard with a compulsive blink sits dozing in the receiving hall, amid portraits of Mother Winterbottom's 'beauties' *en dishabille* hang alongside Mrs Winterbottom, a resplendent figure draped in cerise that falls someway short of her ankles. On her head she ports a wig made from ten heads of human hair imported annually, or so they say, from Paris. Rumour has it, she has surgically restored many a popular girl's maidenhead at the Knightsbridge Clinic, in turn satisfying her more fastidious clients *twice*.

'Any particular girl for you, sir?' asks the doorman.

Jeremiah is already making his way to Virtue's room. He has been mistaken for somebody important. He does not wish to feel important. Not here. He should rather feel invisible here.

A long, constipated groan carries from along the hallway. Crooning and slapping; grown men conversing like children. '*I have been a bad, bad, boy. Punish me. Punish me to make me good again!*' Behind such doors kings behaved no differently to peasants; reduced to their individual fantasies, lost in dressing something commonplace in elaborate guise.

But Jeremiah has indeed an indelible soft spot for sincerity, a category into which Virtue comfortably reside. Ladies of society expected compliments, graceful dancing and a substantial income; matching of expectations quickly pronounced to be love. Whores, on the other hand, did not aspire to such extravagances. They did not, in short, require lies.

He knocks on Virtue's door.

Entering the familiar bedchamber, he is struck by the stink of bodily exchange. The room is much like that of any other whore. A fire shudders in the grate. On the facing wall, a mirror is most conveniently placed and on the table sits a washbasin filled with the remains of previous customers. A good whore needs a full washbasin. Jeremiah has known better rooms, but he has also known plenty worse.

'I've not seen you for some time, Mister Jeremiah. Are you married yet?' asks Virtue, removing his coat and carefully arranging it on a chair.

Watching, to ensure his small purse of winning remains in his pocket, Jeremiah says, 'Alas, I remain too poor for marriage, Virtue.'

She holds his hand. 'Your brilliant, sir,' she runs a finger around the rim of grime, '… it's gone!'

'Sold,' he says, for a moment imagining his grandfather's diamond ring still worn upon his finger, glinting with promise in the firelight. Grandfather Goode: a physician even more formidable than his father, whose ring had been taken to the pawnbroker's along with the crucifix—a gift from his mother—and a pair of silver candlesticks and instead several pound of opium now sat in the drawer of his drug chest in their place.

'What a pity,' Virtue says, lying down beside him. He can feel her eyes studying him, guessing at who he might be to the rest of the world. London is still a novelty to her and her eyes often appear startled, long lashes reaching up to her brows, a dirty splattering of freckles unconcealed by powder. Is she pretty? He cannot truthfully say. Youth, its smoothness, its liveliness makes her so. As to her exact age, well, he prefers not to consider it.

'Peculiar that a man with your handsome face is not yet married,' she says, beginning to undress him.

He refuses to consider, at this hour, the parallel life he might have lived. 'I live an uncommon life,' he says.

Virtue runs a finger across his chest. 'Do you beat a woman senseless?'

'I am not the angry type.'

'Do you share your bed with too many?'

'Neither.'

She removes his breeches. 'Maybe you hate women, despise them. Many do for they do talk about women as wenches, as good for only whoring. They want to lie with me, not take in my face, but to treat me like a stonemason his hammer. But do not fear, Mister. Any secret is safe with Virtue. I am full to the top of my head with untold secrets.'

Secrets being important to Virtue: a glimpse of the personal amongst an act that proved so often the opposite and to those who were cruel she relieved them of their pocket watch.

'If I wanted to confess,' he tells her, 'I would go to church.'

'A Catholic, mister?'

'No, not a Catholic, Virtue.' He watches her eager face waiting to catch hold of a detail, however small. 'But the ring, if you must know, was my grandfather's. He had expectations for me once.'

He lays down and closes his eyes again and Virtue reaches for his hand. 'He was a gentleman like you?' she says.

He sighs. 'More of a gentleman than I could ever hope to be, Virtue. In short, I have been a grand disappointment to my family, a grand disappointment.'

She lies down beside him, strokes the back of his hand as his muscles tightening for a moment until they grow accustomed to affection again.

'How can a man with the gentlest hands I've known have disappointed anyone?'

Jeremiah cannot begin to fathom the complications Virtue must have endured to possess the talent of simplifying a tragedy to a mere sentence. He kisses her nose. 'I am the veritable black sheep of my family, Virtue, and it would seem I am now powerless to do otherwise.'

'A good wife will see you right. I see love in them pretty blue eyes of yours, mister.'

His smile is involuntary. 'What of you Virtue, shall you marry one day?' he asks.

'You are too good for me, mister,' she laughs. 'But there is a carpenter in Devon. He writes to me every month. Tells me that he loves me and I do like that he reassures me. Tis important to be loved. Does this lady write to you, Mister?'

Of late, only his sisters write to him. Lucy had last written two years ago and he had written back asking for more time to consider her request for him to quit his profession as an apothecary. It was hardly a love letter, more a desperate plea to the last link of a former life. He shudders at the memory. 'My sisters write to me occasionally,' he says.

'How many sisters do you have, Mister Jeremiah?'

'Three. Rose, Blanche and Violet. My brother is called Jasper. My mother, you might say, lacked colour in her life.'

Virtue presses his hand against her breast. 'This new love—for I can see there is one, mister, tell me about her.' She sits astride him now.

He feels a pain in his chest and shies from indulging the girl. 'There is not much to tell.'

'When a man touches his nose like that he is either thinking of money or lying. I can keep secrets, mister. Virtue is good at keeping secrets.'

'Virtue, we have talked too much and I did not come here to *talk*.' He pulls the girl forwards and frees her bosoms from the low cut of her dress.

'You are my best customer, Mister, for you do talk to me like I was a woman—'

'Ssh!' he says, kissing her neck. 'I would rather hear I am your best customer for reasons other than talking.'

'As you like, mister!'

Sounds drift in from other parts of the whorehouse, sounds not dissimilar to those of torture. There is a thwack of a driver's whip on the streets below, a clatter of frantic hooves followed by an engulfing silence. Jeremiah listens to his pocket watch ticking from his waistcoat, which Virtue has carefully placed over the back of a chair. It is only in Virtue's bed that the incessant nature of time does not fill him with dread.

'I have known many men, mister.'

Jeremiah opens one eye. Virtue is plaiting her auburn hair. In this light she appears almost beautiful. He says, 'Another subject I should rather avoid.'

'I mean to say, I see certain men that do not care for marriage until they are in love.'

'I was under the misguided belief that coming here meant I saw through the delusions of love.'

'You understand this is not love, Mister, of that I am certain.'

'I do not think this is love, Virtue.'—yet here, in this small room, he presently comes closest to it. 'But tell me, what do you consider love to be.'

'Love cannot be put into words, mister.'

'That's convenient.'

'Love, see, leaves a person no choices.'

'A form of punishment then?'

'Oh, true love not be punishment—though I can show you punishment if you like! I only know that when my carpenter from Devon visits I look in his eye and it is far different to looking in the eye of a customer.'

'Your carpenter must be delighted to hear such comparison.' In the haze of wine, he is half-tempted to ask what she sees in her carpenter's eye. 'So I must look into a woman's eye and find the difference between it and a customer's eye and—*miraculously*!—I am in love?'

'You speak funny, mister, but love is more than that. More than eyes, more than bodies, more than even flesh.'

'Like God? One must believe in him for it to exist?'

'Indeed it may be something similar.'

'In which case I put blame upon my parish. A man cannot live in St Giles and believe in much. Here in the parish of St-Martins-in-the-fields, you are perhaps more fortunate in your connections to the Almighty.'

Besides, he presently has more important things to believe in: namely, saving himself from gaol being one such belief. Four years in St Giles had proven love is for the frivolous, not for those whose burdens were immeasurable heavy.

'You are funny, mister!' Virtue passes him a fresh tankard of ale. 'I think you are making love too complicated, for love is… simple.'

'Perhaps that is it!' He takes several large gulps and hands the tankard back to Virtue to lie down again. 'I am too complicated for love. *Jeremiah I.S. Goode is too complicated for love, God rest his soul.*'

Virtue rests a hand on his chest. 'Complicated you are, mister!'

'*Jeremiah Goode tried hard to love but the act was too simple for his complicated heart. May he inhabit eternity, happily unloved.*'

'Stop your nonsense!'

'Or perhaps there exists something better than love,' he says, closing his eyes, seeing a fleeting vision of the black cape, sweep tenderly over the ground as spent thoughts on love slip silently away. 'Something grander. Something... how does one describe it? Something... unearthly...'

'Now you be teasing! But one day you too *will* know love, of that I am convinced, and when your heart beats as hard as a soldier's drum, you will remember Virtue and you will say, "Blow me, that girl was right!"'

'If such a situation does arise,' he says, 'I shall be sure to find a herb with which to Cure it.'

Jeremiah stares at a large crack running the width of the ceiling. If Virtue were his wife perhaps the earlier incident would require an apology.

Reading his thoughts, Virtue says, 'Am I loosing my way with you, mister?'

'I have much on my mind.'

'Something troubling you, Mister Jeremiah?'

'She is beautiful,' he says.

'Do you love her?'

'I barely know her.'

'Love between strangers can be the best kind of love,' Virtue says with a knowing smile.

'It is? Well, I find it disagreeable.'

'But you do not see her looking ugly in the morning. You do not see her lift up her skirts to piss in a pot. You do not see her shake with snoring.'

He laughs. 'I do not see her at all. Lay down a while, Virtue.'

'Tell me, do you love her?'

He draws in a deep breath. 'I barely know her.'

'Do you see her often?'

'I have only seen her but a handful of times.'

'Perhaps you like her more through not knowing her.'

'Perhaps.'

Jeremiah closes his eyes, begins to drift. A walled garden. The scent of lavender, of roses...

'You must seek her out, mister. Bring her to live with you. Just as my carpenter is going to do to me one day.'

'I doubt,' he says, softly, 'she will want to see me again.'

'Did you insult her?'

'I expect so.'

'You? A gentleman!'

He opens one eye. 'I expect you are familiar with my better side, Virtue.'

He had, in not so many words, accused a woman who had kindly helped him of being a witch. Berore he had spoken to the daemonstrator, he had seen her—the Dark Angel—again in the glasshouse. He had approached and confessed, one more like a lovesick fool—his admiration for her garden. She kept her back turned as he spoke and when he had finished sloughing words she told him quietly, 'Please go.'

Virtue toys with a lock of his hair. 'Oh, mister! Customers who call the most are the ones to insult me the most. They do not understand their desire, that is all. You need to tell her that you love her, all women like to hear that.'

'Having a woman in my thoughts does not constitute love, Virtue.'

'But you must *tell* her that you love her for when she knows your feelings it will change everything. I may not know much about nothing, mister, but I know about love.'

As this is where he comes closest to love, he closes his eyes again and drifts. When he wakes Virtue is sleeping beside him: mouth open, eyelashes quivering. He is torn between the urge to kiss and the urge to lecture about finding proper employment. Tell her that cleaning floors is good and honest money. But like most of this city, hypocrisy comes easier. He covers her with linen and deposits a half crown on the table, between the pile of letters—no doubt from the Devon carpenter—and three fish bladder sheaths, none used by him; a whore, after all, charges for her time, not her successes.

Once outside he walks along Chick Lane towards St Giles, his thoughts traversing from his compendium, to writing all he knows on Hoarhound, to Mrs Soloman's cure. Virtue's attentions (despite the forsaken act) have been restorative, his *fidentia* revived by a little affection. Now he sees that he must trust he can cure the old woman, alone. He shall see this sudden loss of faith in his own abilities as something that needs to be overcome, like the tic in his wretched shoulder. *Physician heal thyself*!

He walks on and as he approaches Seven Dials he senses a shadow, a presence beside him, senses it as if it were his own shadow or a tangible prophecy. Somehow this presence seems to belong to him.

Then, pray tell, what qualifies you to write such a book?

'Is your novel any good?' asks Wordsley, gazing at the reflection of himself in the back of a teaspoon. They are seated before a fire at White's. It is noon and has just begun snowing. Wordsley has been here since the previous night's gaming and wears a richly embroidered waistcoat, splattered with gemstones, sparkling like the Lord Mayor's firework display.

Jeremiah stretches out his legs. Hunched up with cold for so many days his body needs to unfurl. He is slightly ashamed, however, at the state of his stockings.

'Compendium,' he says, 'I am writing a herbal compendium.'

'Ah.' Wordsley breathes onto the spoon, hanging it from his nose. 'I told the bookseller you were writing a romance novel.'

'Do you know a damn thing about my life?'

'Not much,' says Wordsley, 'but you see I would not want this fellow to think me a complete liar. So, is it good, this book?'

'It will be, when finished.'

'Excellent!'

Wordsley begins pacing the room, spoon hung from his nose. There are thankfully no witnesses, other than a discreet servant beside the door, now examining a tray of bottles with some intensity. Jeremiah prefers White's this way. In daylight the salon appears feminine—though not a woman never sets foot inside the place—yet by oil lamp, with men shouting their bets and booing their losses, it becomes a place of intense masculinity, of vivre and occasional misery.

There it is: this longing for the feminine again.

He takes another sip of his hot chocolate, enjoying the sensation of it gliding along his throat, heating up his belly. He rests a hand on the compendium, half-completed, upon his lap where it sits like a faithful pet.

'My ambition had been to write a botany book,' he confesses once Wordsley has completed a circuit of the room without dropping the spoon.

Ambition is perhaps too aggressive a word for something intended to be beautiful but he had intended to prove his father wrong; show he had not simply gone to St Giles and *disappeared*.

'Then write a book about plants,' says Wordsley.

Jeremiah shakes his head, exhaling his flaws. 'Linnaeus published *Systema Naturae* and there is nothing to be added to it.' The trouble with botany books: they gave discernable truths which no one could dispute.

Wordsley crouches level with Jeremiah's chair, his face powder emphasising the redness of his eyes. 'My friend, as a gentleman you must hold onto self-belief. Do you hear me? Without self-belief you have no right to call yourself a gentleman.'

Jeremiah does not need Wordsley, of all people, to lecture him. 'I no longer care what I appear to be.'

'But you must. A gentleman must remain king of his world. At *all* times. The best then follows merrily.'

Ignorance, Jeremiah decides, is bliss only for those truly immersed in it and, for those who must observe it, it is nothing but painful.

'Where is this fellow?' he asks.

It is the third visit to White's they have made in search of the elusive Mr Jacobs, the bookseller and, naturally, Jeremiah is beginning to suspect it is a ruse to get him to game.

Wordsley points his silver spoon. 'Ah, he comes now! Now, remember self-belief shall make you king.'

A short, rotund man approaches their table. His grey beards stick out at the sides giving the illusion he has the whiskers of a twitchy-nosed rabbit. He smiles loosing both eyes within ample flesh.

'My esteemed friend Jeremiah Goode.' Wordsley gestures, with a degree of silliness.

'Good day.' Jeremiah responds, bowing.

'Presently, his business does poorly but what person commences writing for any reason other than desperation?' Wordsley grins at Jeremiah. A weight settles across Jeremiah's shoulders and he smiles back as though this action were part of an apology.

'However,' says Wordsley slapping his back. 'It is a difficulty that a selling a good book can nonetheless rectify. Now do excuse me for I spot a willing victim. I mean to say there is another punter and the gaming table beckons. Goode, what numbers do you say?'

'Hazard?' Jeremiah inquires, glancing hesitantly at the bookseller as if his every move might come under judgement.

'Hazard, why ever not?' says Wordsley.

'Then seven as main, with a chance of five,' he offers.

'Always dependable. Though as an aside,' says Wordsley, cupping a hand to his mouth, 'my esteemed friend is not always so obvious.'

Jacobs sits the other side of the fire and signals for Jeremiah to be seated too, though he has already taken Jeremiah's chair.

'Tell me,' the bookseller says, his plump legs swinging back and forth like those of a child, 'this novel? What is it about?'

'Well…it is in fact, a… well, a compendium, sir.'

'*What did you say?*' asks the bookseller, pinching his nose between thumb and forefinger.

'A compendium of herbs.'

The bookseller's legs cease swinging. He pulls at his whiskers and glances about the room as if to ward off tedium. 'A compendium,' he sighs as if Jeremiah had said *disaster*. 'Then, pray tell, what qualifies you to write such this com-pen-di-um?'

'Very little,' sits on the tip of Jeremiah's tongue. 'I trained for seven years as an apothecary,' he says instead. 'I have managed my own shop for four.'

'A shop? Where is your shop?'

'St Giles-in-the-fields.'

'And you believe there are people willing to buy a book from an apothecary practising in such a place?'

'I believe so,' he says, with surprising fluency.

'I see. I see. This… compendium is it complete?'

If he were a different man he could continue his lie, say that by the end of the month it shall be complete. But Jeremiah has lost the ability to make his life appear seamlessly whole to others. Cracks running from foot to toe are now too obvious for disguise. Besides, *complete* is a word that recently rests uneasily on his tongue.

'Not yet,' he says. 'It shall be finished, however, by spring or the early part of summer.' *If I am still a free man by then.*

'Summer?'

'There are certain specimens I still need to collect that cannot—'

'Yes, yes, but your friend described your need to publish as rather urgent.'

'The urgency is money, sir. If you might advance me a sum *in lieu* of—'

'Gracious. That is not how it works, Mr Goode. Not how it works at all.'

Jeremiah sags deeper in his seat, tucking his holey stockings beneath the chair.

'A book is an object most can ill afford. I do not sell books as a baker sells buns, though indeed I wish that I did. No, the usual means for publishing a book is for the author to contribute to the costs of printing. Do we understand one another, Mr Goode?'

On the ceiling Jeremiah notes Cupid, a bow and arrow in his hand. He imagines it aimed directly at the centre of Jacobs' brow to injure rather than incite love.

'Now if the book were to be a masterpiece, on the other hand, of the likes never before seen in this country—we represent Defoe, you understand— then in such circumstance I would indeed be happy to offer in advance a small sum in the expectation, you understand, the return shall be plentiful. But as your book happens to be a…?'

'Compendium.'

'Yes a compendium, well in such circumstance this arrangement remains doubtful.' Jacobs pinches his nose again then slaps both thighs. 'Let us converse again in the autumn, Mr Goode. By then you shall perhaps know if you are to be a genius or another, let us say, Grubb Street failure.'

Prison cares nothing for genius.

'There are,' continues the bookseller stroking his whiskers. 'Other such herbals I believe. What makes yours unique?'

He wants to mention his unique methods, that too many times to count he has been proven right by instinct, by a vision, by the patient's pain mirrored in his own all too receptive body. He wants to override the general sense he is more commonplace than exceptional.

He takes a deep breath. 'It will, when finished, contain over five hundred herbs from the New World known to Cure disease. Along with a description of its uses, each will be faithfully replicated upon the page.'

'I see,' says Jacobs. 'Certainly, that does sound very thorough.'

Too caught up in his own feelings of inadequacy he ignores that he has just described the Dark Angel's herbal, described a compendium he might hope to complete in 10 years not two weeks!

The bookseller hands Jeremiah his calling card.

'The autumn,' he says, moving his mouth about as if chewing on toffee, taking in Jeremiah's wig, his frayed waistcoat, the tips of his soiled and much stained shoes. 'I shall perhaps hear from you again in the autumn. If it is good, better than good, a work of some genius, you need not go to another bookseller. There are seventy or so of us booksellers in London and most waste more paper than they sell. I take risk on certainties, Mr Goode, and I pay handsomely for the copyrights. If I publish your herbal then you are certain to attain success. Good day to you, and I hope to see you before too long in my shop in Fleet Street, a convenient premise adjacent to the Printshops.'

Jeremiah mutters his thanks and watches the leporine bookseller scurry away. The autumn is a distant place. By then he is likely be incarcerated in Manners' house or more formally imprisoned in the Fleet. Following, there would be little hope of re-establishing himself as anything other than a beggar. He has thus just wasted yet more minutes of his freedom.

'So, have you joined Grub Street?' Wordsley asks joining him, spilling wine on the carpet.

Jeremiah removes his wig and scratches his head. 'It is not a membership one gains in haste.'

'Why ever not?'

As usual Jeremiah finds it hard discerning where his friend's gift of sociability ended and sincerity began.

'Surely he must comprehend your role as saint in your parish? Perhaps you need someone else to document your rising. There are plenty more booksellers, some less rabbit-like I suspect.'

Jeremiah shrugs, presently unable to find humour in the disaster that is unfolding in the shape of his life. 'No doubt he would rather have the novel you had mentioned,' he says.

Wordsley belches. 'There is always another book you might write. *The Complete Book of Martyrs*. What do you say, Goode?'

Jeremiah sits forwards and slips a few handfuls of coals into his pocket for later. 'It may appear to you as martyrdom but for me it is a path I have had no choice but to take.'

'Nonsense!' Wordsley takes some ham, folds it and then squashes the entire piece between his lips. 'Now I have news of something else,' he says, providing flashes of pig's flesh, 'a thing to brighten your spirits.'

'Nothing but a visit from the Lord himself would do that.'

'I am having a ball in a week's time. No masks, only fanciful dress.' More wine drips down the front of Wordsley's waistcoat, amongst his jewel-crusted hide. 'Lucy Aldridge is invited. You shall come? It shall go on for days and I have enough champagne to sink the HMS Merlin!'

Jeremiah thrusts a penny for the hot chocolate into Wordsley's waistcoat, glad, for a change, to be the one surreptitiously handing over coins.

'If I am not by then in prison,' he says.

'My friend,' replies Wordsley, 'are you not there already?'

I heal, it is what I do.

By the time Jeremiah leaves White's, snow is falling heavily. Not yet four of the clock and lamps are already lit forming a row of yellow-tinged halos the length of Chesterfield Street. The absence of people gives the impression that in the space of an hour London has abruptly died.

Jeremiah tucks his half-finished compendium inside his waistcoat and pulls up his collar. He walks past the many shops and their protruding signs: the Civet Cat for the perfumers, the lock of hair for the perruquiers, the beaver sitting primly above the hatter's shop...

At the junction of Curzon Street, he senses someone is following him, as if another's shadow falls in time with his step. He walks faster, unsettled, wonders if it is a pickpocket or a whore. Manners, the bailiff, perhaps. He turns expecting to find the bulk of the debt collector ready to taunt, but finds only a lamp lighter, body pressed against the post as he stretches up to the gas. Otherwise, the street is deserted. His shoulder jerks towards his ear—once, twice, a third time—and he presses on.

Resolutely, he decides against stopping at Virtue's boarding house. It will only prolong the inevitable cold awaiting him back home. Besides, he has his compendium to write. After prolonged work he shall drink valerian tea in the hope he shall fall asleep in a bedchamber where icy stalactites grow at the windows as long as walrus tusks.

Slush soon soaks through his shoes to his stockings. Gentlemen's shoes are not made for this weather: the heels became treacherous and the leather is cut too low at the sides and where the bailiff has taken his silver buckles the front gapes open, flapping like a pair of lost wings. Riding boots—two pairs—have been sold to the clothes shop on Mammoth Street along with his overcoat and three tricorne hats. At the time it had been summer, the streets steaming, a vengeful cold so hard to imagine. If he manages to save himself then he will buy the whole lot back and several more pairs of shoes.

Wordsley's words come back to him then: *Are you not already there?*

Was he? Was money, not profession, the principle of life? Had poverty indeed imprisoned him without the need for bars? If St Giles had taught him one thing, it was the difficulty in surviving one day into the next and it presently applied to him as much as the rest of the parish. Yet the truth was he had never felt more alive. It was, he suspected, the closest he had come to experiencing God's grace. Each day becomes a matter of faith. In society one's beliefs were blunted by fashion, by wine, by pointless chatter. Contact with the divine became a formality, depth of feeling suffocated as a tight corset squeezed air out of a rich lady's lungs. To Wordsley he would thus return the question. 'Are *you* not there already?'

He reaches Neal's Yard, as brightly lit as always, his own shop cast in near darkness. He blows into his hands and continues northwards.

The truth was that cravings for new coats and scented gloves were invariably brief. As for spending money for money's sake, he has little need; he could live without late nights at the gaming tables or the attentions of Virtue. He could live without most things except purpose; the great abyss of meaninglessness he most feared. A life stripped bare revealed what was truly relevant, what was not. A life of service, surely that is all a man can aspire to?

Then he hears her voice like a correction to his thoughts: *I heal, it is what I do.* There are, of course, other needs aside from a man's profession but they are needs he has grown accustomed to living without. But lately, this Dark Angel, this stranger, crops up in his thoughts with the regularity of the penny post. His heart lurches each time and as her voice trails away a hollow, hungry space spreads outwards like a dark inkblot upon the page.

I have to see you again.

I have to.

Beneath a box at the entrance to the Rookery sits a man almost hidden amongst a pile of cloth, swaddled in blankets, face in patches blackened by cold. His eyes narrow and he flinches as Jeremiah approaches.

'I'm looking for Joseph Cook,' says Jeremiah, glancing up at the rotting wood covering the windows above; windows not boarded up on account of the window tax—nobody paid tax here—but because broken glass did little to keep out the cold.

'Cook?' croaks the man. 'Cook is up them stairs.'

Jeremiah pauses. 'What do you know of the fellow?'

'He was sick. Now lives with his sister.' The man wheezes laughter from a pair of lungs close to collapse, 'Cook, he can play a good game of Gleek.'

Jeremiah lifts his hat, takes the rickety stairs, careful to avoid missing treads and an assortment of empty gin bottles. At the top he steps over a woman, sleeping. He wonders if she is still alive and by instinct crouches down to rest a hand upon her shoulder whereupon the woman shivers violently. He then notices the baby pressed against her chest, its cheeks covered in grime, its lips tinged blue.

'I have nothing left for you to take,' she whispers.

Jeremiah pulls out a penny from his waistcoat. 'Please,' he says, as the woman looks up, fear stretching her expression into a grimace. 'Have this.'

Her red and filthy fingers uncurl as she takes the penny and places it inside her mouth, lips clamping quickly shut.

'God bless you,' he tells her but the words feeling insubstantial: a mere excuse. But what else can he offer? In a few days, if not sooner, they shall both be made corpses by the cold, if the baby was not one already.

A door opens further along the unlit passageway. 'Who goes there?'

Jeremiah stands and squints towards the voice. 'It is I, madam, Jeremiah Goode.'

145

A woman who barely reaches his chest, wearing a man's coat and a ripped blanket wrapped around her shoulders, rushes forwards. 'Well I be glad!' she says. 'Jeremiah I.S. Goode, the Apot'cry. Come in! Come in!'

He follows the woman into a dark room, where the stale air settles on the tongue like a sediment.

'We are in bed,' says the woman though it is barely five of the clock. 'We were coming to visit you once Joseph was properly well. He is nearly recovered now. He was my ma's healthiest son and shall be again by the look of it! Well I never the Apot'cry himself.'

'I am glad of this news,' says Jeremiah his eyes now adjusting to the dark so that he can see he stands in a room barely nine foot by nine.

'News? It is a blessed miracle! He has not worked since his wife died. Fell into the comfort of gin. The Devil took hold of his senses. It happens to the good on occasion or so my ma often said. The good fall just as hard as the bad. But now he's not touched a drop for 2 weeks and next week shall start work at the quays as a snuffle-hunter on account of my husband putting in a good word. How glad we all are for your presence in this parish. How very, very glad Mister Apot'cry!'

Jeremiah feels a glow in his chest, of pride, of joy, he cannot precisely define it. 'Tell Joseph to visit my shop so I might see him in good health for myself.'

The woman grins. 'Tell him yourself for he lies at your feet!'

Sure enough at his feet lie two men side by side on a straw mattress and Jeremiah can just make out the whites of their eyes.

'My husband and my brother, the bed's big enough for three,' says the sister, 'and there are no lice for I shake it out weekly. You were lucky we were not sleeping for when they both start snoring I cannot hear my own heart.'

'Joseph?' says Jeremiah.

He waits as a man emerges from the dark to stand a foot or so above his head. He takes hold of Jeremiah and pulls him forwards, gripping him as he sobs silently onto his shoulder so that Jeremiah can do little other than keep himself upright.

'You saved me from perishing.' The man begins to weep.

'You saved yourself.' As usual Jeremiah is surprised by the sense of reverence for life. 'And I hear you saved yourself from gin too.'

146

The man shakes his head. 'But for my life I have only you to thank, Master Apot'cry.'

'He is nothing but a saint!' declares the man's sister.

Jeremiah senses something more is required of him, more than the penny in his waistcoat pocket. He clears his throat.

'God has given us but one body. We must care for it as a mother cares for her child. We must resist the temptations the Devil throws in our paths, for with health one can aspire to…' He searches for a fitting end; both hands turned heaven-bound like a bishop at his altar as three faceless figures continue to stare at him. All that remained was his health, yet here he was lonely, poor and for the most part cold. He had meant to say that in good health one can weave life's tapestry with efficiency, but that would be impertinent. 'With health,' he says, looking for inspiration to the faint moonlight entering the boards at the windows, 'With health one can aspire to…being better and…and… and to taking action. Forthright, determined action!'

He is given a brief round of applause. Certainly, the clergy had never offered its calling. To preach required a degree of certainty.

'Come and see me at the shop,' he says, patting Joseph Cook's back. He takes another two pennies from his waistcoat and presses them into the fellow's hands. 'I have plenty of tonics to keep up your strength at the quays.'

'You are too kind, Master Apot'cry.'

'Nothing but a saint!' declares his sister, who plants a sloppy kiss on his cheek. 'A saint in our very own parish!'

'A saint requires saintly ways, Madam,' he tells her, 'and I, alas, possess very few.'

'A saint never recognises the saint in himself. Am I not right Joe?'

'As always, sister.'

Before leaving the Rookery Jeremiah places his coat across the sleeping mother and child. Shivering at least indicates the mother is still alive.

Elation, however, as he walks the streets of St Giles, is soon replaced by despair. What good was it attempting to bestow health upon the poor when their lives were so wretched? Without money was health not an expensive adornment? Of course, Wordsley was right: poverty imprisoned, but regarding his own poverty was it not a matter of finding the right lock for the right key? Certainly, honouring his father's dying wish to marry the 'Aldridge girl' was one such convenient lock. But to finish his compendium in 2 weeks before the bailiff returned required not the right lock or the right key but a blessed miracle and in St Giles the only miracles began and ended in the shop of Jeremiah I.S. Goode.

Which left Mrs Soloman.

Another week has passed and he has still not received a reply to the letter he had entrusted to Mr Rand requesting the contents of the tonic from the Dark Angel. He has few concerns making a substitute tonic but he needs to persuade Mrs Soloman to relinquish some of her stubbornness; she would test a second tonic against the previous, of that he had no doubt. If the House of Lords had granted him a profession over a trade, some 30 years past, allowing apothecaries by law to prescribe and dispense medicine, then might Mrs Soloman show him respect too? He could participate in an anatomical discussion as well as any barber yet had chosen to put his faith in plants; the removal of body parts he left to the likes of his father who viewed a body (and so much else!) according to its lines of severance. Yet why must his mind keep returning to this Dark Angel—a woman whose name he does not even know? Perhaps it is doubt in his ability to cure a woman of wealth that he must fight and nothing more.

Snow falls across Neal's Yard forming an almost yellow haze. Jeremiah's tracks are quickly covered. *A thousand pounds.* Enough to pay off his debts and relieve him of his rent for an entire decade! With a 1000 pounds there could be more Joseph Cooks; more people who might pick out the brighter threads of hope amongst the dim weave of their pitiful lives. With a 1000 pounds he might remain a free man and treat many more of this parish.

He might even pursue a Dark Angel from Dorset.

'Not usual to see you out after dark, Mr Apothecary,' says an cloying voice to his right.

Jeremiah turns. 'I am still permitted to carry out my business.'

Manners rushes forwards. He grabs each of Jeremiah's shoulders with force and throws him against the astronomer's shop front, whose drapes are unfortunately drawn.

'I have some business for you too, Mister Apothecary.' Manners presses his face against Jeremiah's nose and his knee against Jeremiah's groin. 'Some business that might benefit us both?'

'How so?' Jeremiah manages.

'I have needs just like the next man.'

Jeremiah closes his eyes against the foulness of the bailiff's breath. 'Let me go, for God's sake,' he says, to which the bailiff squashes Jeremiah's nose and digs his knee harder into his groin.

'God? Ha! He cares nothing for you. Now shut your hole!' says Manners, eyes wildly gleaming, 'or I shall have to shut it for you.' He lunges forwards and kisses Jeremiah mouth, his tongue forcing a passage through Jeremiah's lips. Next Manners' hand works its way down his breeches and Jeremiah hears himself yelp. 'Don't like that, Apothecary?'

'If you don't get—' Jeremiah wrestles against Manners whose strength, he imagines, is one of the reasons for his position.

'You will what?'

Manners hand squeezes his ballocks. Jeremiah thrusts his own knee towards Manners' groin and successfully hitting his goal, leaves the bum bailiff gripping his baubles and moaning that the next time he won't be so gentle with Jeremiah. Jeremiah lets himself into his shop and quickly locks it again. It seems the world is crowding in on him and unless he cures Mrs Soloman he is done for.

Waiting for an angel

Following several hours of necessary, though not entirely effective, escape into his compendium (the vision of *her* face apparently impervious to any form of distraction) Jeremiah has reached lavender. Though several gaps remain under 'H', he anticipates lavender being a somewhat easier herb to recall.

The flowers seeped in wine are efficacious for those troubled with the wind or colic, if the places be bathed therewith...

He scratches his arm, lifts his periwig—an object he wears now for warmth rather than formality—then enthusiastically scratches his head.

With fennel, asparagus roots and a little cinnamon it is good for giddiness of the brain. To gargle is good for toothache.

It flowers at the end of June, beginning of July.

He lets his quill fall to the desktop. Not a single wretched drawing of lavender in his possession. He has scrambled about his elaboratory on his knees looking for one (across a floor that Mary has yet to clean) and though it is a flower so commonplace as to be found in every garden of England, a flower with a scent every man in England is familiar with, he must copy it from Linnaeus' book! Perhaps he could omit the drawing or copy a petal from memory. He knew well enough what the plant was capable of. Yet a compendium without a complete set of drawings was but a body without an integral soul. With 2 weeks, rather *thirteen* blessed days remaining of his freedom, there was no time left for fussing over perfection.

He scratches his thigh.

If he could hold onto freedom he might finish the compendium by autumn; spend the summer roaming through the fields and forests of Kent and Sussex seeking specimens. Yet his thoughts do not stretch to the summer for long for he is quickly brought back as a swallow is bought back from wherever it went in the winter: to this perpetual flight in the present.

'Itching again, sir?'

He all too easily forgets about the boy.

'Itching is the least of my concerns.'

'Change is coming, sir. On that you can rely.'

'Change is part of life. It requires no great mastery to predict it. And in life, Boswell, you would do well to remember, one can rely on very little.'

'God's mercy, sir. Some might call it God's Grace?'

'The mercy of God,' says Jeremiah, unable to help laughing, 'Is the thing a poor man dreams of when he cannot afford the comfort of a chocolate.'

He wonders what the boy has been doing all morning. Writing love letters to Mary no doubt.

'You shall be collecting debts this afternoon,' he says sternly. Even captains of sinking ships and their sailors cannot sit letting waves wreck the stern.'

'Mr Manners visited when you went abroad, sir.'

'And you did not think to tell me this sooner?'

'I forgot, sir. He said you will go to his sponging house before you are tried at court and sent to gaol.'

'How considerate.'

'He says it is not too late to pay your debts when you are looked up at his sponging house.'

'If I am not able to raise the money as a free man what hope have I of doing so as a prisoner?' Debts whilst locked up by Manners were perhaps the least of his worries.

Boswell falls silent. Jeremiah turns back to his compendium, racks his mind for any experiences involving lavender. There was once a girl he had treated for persistent fainting fits—not in the Rookery but in one of the other slums. It was a condition Mr James, his old employer, might have called giddiness of the brain. He had treated her with lavender, horehound, fennel and asparagus roots and a little cinnamon and she had recovered quickly and 2 years later he had been invited to her wedding. He had declined the invitation: weddings always brought with them a sense of guilt.

'My mother would say you were waiting for an angel,' Boswell says, beginning to sweep the floor.

'An angel indeed.'

'She was a Catholic, sir. I think they are more given to believing in angels.'

'I see.'

'Her father was a Jew. She said being both a Catholic and a Jew had made religion a little confusing for her. She said that she did not know if Christ was coming or going.'

'I imagine that could be confusing.'

'When she died, sir, and I went to live with my grandfather—he was the Jew that I fetched drugs for—he did know I was suffering grief for my mother and he said my mother was the sort of woman that would be turned into an angel in the afterlife, though he said he wasn't personally given to believing in such things. Often, I think of her watching me like rays shining down from the Sun, and I think, well, I think that she is responsible for me working with you, sir.'

'Poetic. And how might she be responsible?' says Jeremiah commencing a sketch of lavender from memory, only half-listening to the boy.

151

'A ragamuffin like me becoming an apprentice! Such a thing would have given my family a bellyache from laughter. How could I have become an apothecary without an angel, sir?'

'You are not an apothecary,' he reminds the boy, 'or not yet at least.'

For a time Boswell continues sweeping. Jeremiah commences a lavender petal from memory. The bells of St Giles' church begin ringing a familiar melody.

'Some in this parish say that you are an angel, sir,' Boswell almost whispers. 'The Apot'cry Angel they call you. Although the women will say the *handsome* Apot'cry Angel.'

'Misguided fools.'

'I know that you only speak like that for my sake but are deep down happy to hear such things.'

'I am?' Silence was needed for work. Comforting silence.

'Angels, you see, sir, do not always have a pair of wings.'

Jeremiah puts down his pen and pinches the bridge of his nose. 'There are no angels in this parish, Boswell. That much I know. If your grandfather spoke of angels it was to keep you from despair. I am not given to such deceit. I accept my fate and that it is for the most part godless.' His breath fogs in the coldness of his elaboratory. 'Next week I shall begin arranging my affairs, inform this wreck of a building's landlord of our impending departure.'

There is a pause into which the reverend would add something hopeful and uplifting but once more he sees the Dark Angel's face and is distracted by the feeling in his chest, in his belly and other places besides. Besides, he is not up to sermons today.

'What of Mrs Soloman, sir?'

'A rich diet, or one tending toward sweetness, might produce gangrene as much as an injury. Either way, I shall recommend salad, some greens and roots with only a little meat, plenty broth and soup. I shall ask Miss Heart to apply daily compresses of horsetail and arnica to help heal the tissue. Though onions applied to the flesh will quickly instil healing and stir up the blood, but I am doubtful I can persuade Mrs Soloman of such measures.' He sighs. 'But it will not heal in a month. Thus, she is as close to walking as I am to flying with or without my great pair of angel's wings!'

The boy continues to sweep.

By virtue of his circumstances, by the error of his ways, he can consider himself no more an angel than Boswell is a genius. He turns back to his desk and there on the wall, flickering in and out of existence, he sees the illusion of a rainbow. Red, orange, yellow, all the colours. He runs his hand over it. He passes his hand before the window to breath up the pattern of fractured light unable to detect its origin.

The truth is he is abandoning his ship, letting his half-baked apprentice and mute maid struggle in torrid waters. The thought brings a short sharp pain to his chest. When he looks up the rainbow has gone.

She can be immensely stubborn

Miss Heart stands, a splash of lemon, on the shop floor blinking like a mole emerging from its darkened burrow.

'I hope that I have not called at an inconvenient time,' she says fiddling with the strings of a hat.

'Time we have plenty of,' says Jeremiah with a nod toward the bailiff's new note attached to the door, one informing his customers that the shop will soon be closing, which, naturally, they could not read. He turns to Boswell who has followed behind with his broom and a bucket of sand, about to buff the floor. 'Fetch Miss Heart something to drink,' he says, 'I am sure she needs warming after her journey.'

'No, it is a brief visit.' Miss Heart looks to her gloves. 'I have come, well, as you might have imagined, I have come…about my aunt.'

Jeremiah's jaw clenches and unclenches. 'But of course. Pray continue.'

'You see she is out of bed and has, well, she has managed to walk to her bed chamber fireplace, unaided.'

'That is good news!'

'Yes, it is. In fact Aunt Rachael has been walking, well she has been walking daily. You can imagine, well, you can imagine my sense of relief.'

'Your aunt's relief too. But… her foot,' he adds tentatively, 'it does not cause her any trouble?'

'No. What I mean to say is, she does not, and has not complained. I have changed the dressing on several occasion and the sores, well the sores appear to be healing. I hope…I do hope you shall soon, come and see… see my aunt for yourself.'

'Naturally.'

Miss Heart revives both dimples with a smile. 'It seems, well, it seems that you have created a miracle, Mr Goode.'

If he survives this catastrophe he shall create a 'Miracle Chart', place a score upon it every time he hears these words. They are words that revive his spirits but do nothing to settle his debts. 'I am very glad, Miss Heart.'

'I must, however, apologise,' Miss Heart goes on, examining her gloves with some intensity so Jeremiah notes a small, out of places stain on one of the fingers of her glove, a smear that is incongruent to Miss Heart's otherwise pristine appearance. He wills her not to shame them both by mentioning her little outburst. He cannot blame the woman for expressing her emotions. After prolonged time in Mrs Soloman's company even the strongest would be forgiven for crumbling like dust.

'Apologise, Miss Heart?' he says with some reluctance. 'Whatever for?'

She presses her lips together. 'Although my aunt is, you might say she is quite happy…'

Her story surely does not end here! 'Go on Miss Heart.'

'…there is, another, difficulty.'

When is there not? 'Of what nature, Miss Heart?'

'She demands the elixir—the tonic—the one you so kindly, well, so kindly brought on your second visit. She has finished the last bottle and believes that her cough has worsened again. She claims—rather frequently claims—that if she cannot breath she cannot, alas, walk.'

'And has it worsened?'

'I am not certain but I expect, well, I expect that wanting the tonic has more to do with my aunt's stubbornness, Mr Goode. She does not like to be refused a thing.'

He rubs the whiskers on his chin. 'Healing is a complicated affair, Miss Heart.' *Too complicated by far in Mrs Soloman's case.* 'What may work one week will not work the next. But its progress is in a forward direction only. I should prefer that your aunt continue with what herbs I administered to her on my last visit. She must give them time. In my experience I have found that drugs Cure with immediacy but not efficiency, herbs on the other hand take time but exert a more lasting power.'

He speaks of time as if it were his friend, as if he had plenty to spare.

Miss Heart wrings her hands. 'I am sure you can appreciate Mr Goode, she can be immensely stubborn.'

Amongst many other things. 'Then permit me to administer another herb for her cough but the rest of the herbs she must continue taking until I next visit.'

'I thank you for your kindness but…' She pauses and Jeremiah imagines this woman's life filled with many 'buts', 'I do sincerely feel the tonic would be more greatly received.'

He rests clasps hands atop his periwig. 'I'm afraid it shall not be possible.'

'I…I do not, well, I do comprehend you, Mr Goode.'

'Healing progresses in certain direction, Miss Heart.' He scans his shelves and takes down some marshmallow leaf for the cough. He cannot say why but he is driven to the truth with this woman. Perhaps it is her plain, unassuming face, the palpable kindness, the sense that she requires nothing for herself. 'Please,' he says, handing over a bag of herbs, gaining control of a tongue loosened by a life in St Giles, 'I must be trusted Miss Heart to carry out my job. I intend to Cure your aunt and you must do your utmost to reassure her of my methods, reassure her that a worsening of symptoms is quite common before improvement. Let me be the one to heal, if you please.'

Miss Heart bites her lower lip. That haze again, he thinks, like the small almost imperceptible blemish on her glove, an intangible flaw that seems to hover like a heat haze over her character.

'Alas, I am not a patient nurse, Mr Goode.'

'Oh, I doubt that to be true—'

'It is! Sickness,…well, it irritates me. A shameful thing to admit but there it is.' He finds it is hard to imagine anything other than himself irritating this woman. 'So you see, I would like my aunt to be Cured quickly for her sake as well as mine.'

He strums his fingers on the counter, another bout of honesty creeping up on him like an irritating tickle to the throat. 'Miss Heart, I am afraid I may have not been entirely truthful myself.' He rubs a hand across his face. 'And as honesty is, I feel, a thing with which you are intimately acquainted'— his sighs is louder than intended—'a confession is due.'

'Oh really Mr Goode, there is, well, there is no need—'

'There is every need,'—his mind now travels alternate routes of persuasion. 'The tonic that I gave your aunt on my second visit comes from a woman who lives in Dorset. A herbal healer.'

'Dorset,' Miss Heart shakes her head. 'I see, or at least shall try to.'

'I obtained it from her at the Physic Gardens where she no longer visits and I am afraid I do not presently possess the money to make a journey to Dorset to obtain more. Foolishly, I do not know what the tonic comprises. Call me a fraud and I shall, of course, understand if you wish to dismiss me.' He holds her eyes, doubt a little alleviated when she places a hand across her chest in line with her heart. Of course! She protects it—*from him*!

'I see,' she says again.

'I can only put my actions down to a simple loss of faith.'

'Well, it took a great deal of persuasion for my aunt to, well, for her to come round to your methods, Mr Goode. If she learns that you…well, she might not be quite so willing to… willing to trust you again.'

He bows his head thinking that when she is of good health she will find no reason to judge the person who cured her. 'I understand,' he says, relieved the woman does not at least cry but misplaced or otherwise, guilt brings with it a concession. 'I do not know the exact place where this woman lives but if you inquire at the Physic Gardens at Chelsea, they perhaps can help.'

Discrete smugness crosses Miss Heart's face. 'That will not be necessary,' she says, her voice altered. 'As I have explained, sickness irritates me. What you do for my aunt, you thus also do for me. I shall try to convince her that a change of heart is for the best.' She reaches into the folds of her skirts and pulls out a purse.

She continues to smile. 'I do not think you would have taken such action unless you saw fit to do so. If it is an advance on your reward that you require…My aunt is frugal, she does not agree to something being purchased unless it is firstly received—she sees herself as, well, custodian to my uncle's fortune and I am, as I explained to you, not an independent woman—but… well, I do not uphold all of my aunt's beliefs despite her being my benefactor.'

'Perhaps, though, for the duration of this Cure you might uphold some of mine.' He should not be taking money, of any amount, from a woman of such little means. This was not how he meant to take from the rich to give to the poor.

Miss Heart places several coins on the counter. 'It is not much, rather not as much as you deserve.'

He bows his head, wary of meeting the same strength in her eye that has suddenly overcome her voice. 'I shall travel immediately to the gardens to learn of her whereabouts,' he says.

'Please, Mr Goode, I require no further details concerning your trip and my aunt, well… she need not learn about it either. But another visit at your earliest convenience is all that we—how shall I put it?—require.'

Jeremiah takes the coins, conciliating his actions with the thought that they come from Mrs Soloman (not a penny-counting husband as is the case with most of the ladies he once served on The Strand) yet he bows with absolute gratitude. But as he watches the woman negotiate the ice, walking as she (at times) speaks—in hesitant spurts—he finds he is unable to decide whether she brings out the very best in him or the very worst.

'Perhaps you are right,' he says turning to Boswell.

'Sir?'

'Perhaps all this itching shall amount to something.'

'Sir?' says Boswell smacking his lips.

'Mrs Soloman is walking. Sheer force of will is doubtless responsible but nonetheless the woman walks!' He stabs a fist in the air. 'The wind of change doth blow in our direction Boswell!' He peers at the boy whose jaw is quite distorted. 'What in God's name are you doing with your mouth?'

'My tooth, sir, it hurts.'

'Oil of cloves applied hourly. Now, toothache, let me see, is that not a sign of something…?'

And whistling he returns to his desk where he stacks the last of his coins into several neat, small piles: a little for coal, for food, a little to keep the bailiff at bay and just enough remaining for a coach fare to Dorset. When he looks up again the rainbow is fully restored to the wall.

A Desperate Plea

By the time Jeremiah reaches the Chelsea Physic Gardens it is raining: plump, intermittent drops like intervals of pigeon turd. Not here for the usual reasons, he stands at the entrance for a minute or two, as if he deposited from the sky, summoning the verve to enter.

He scans the gardens but, not surprisingly, finds no sign of a dark cloak or a Dark Angel and so crosses a muddied path to Mr Rand's office. Once Mr Rand has identified him through the purple haze of tobacco smoke—he says, 'You are here again, young man. What is you want this time?'

Jeremiah eye rests upon the desk. 'You did not post my letter, sir.'

The daemonstrator follows his gaze. 'I was waiting to give it to Miss Zeldin in person.'

'But her work here is finished. But you know this!' Jeremiah reaches forwards and picks up his letter only to find the first letter he had written placed beneath. 'Why? Why, did you not post my letters?'

Mr Rand rises from his chair. 'You must compose yourself, Mr Good,' he says. 'This sort of behaviour will not do anybody any good.'

'Compose myself? I am loosing my life and with it my mind and I am thwarted when…' He sees Mr Rand's frightened expression reflecting his own. He watches the way his pipe visibly shakes in his hands causing the smoke to zigzag at his side. He clears his throat, attempting to speak more calmly, to undue his actions, 'I am thwarted when I need to see Miss Zeldin again. I need to see her, sir. You must comprehend this need.'

'And I have told you that if I gave out her address to every man that asked there would be a queue from her door all the way to London. Was I not generous enough with you?'

'No, no you were not, sir. Would you have been visiting every village in Dorset?' His voice matches the daemonstrator's in force and volume.

But the daemonstrator shakes his head. 'I told you that it was a Catholic village. I was more than generous in my response. Look young man, I am acting in Miss Zeldin's best interest. Can you not see that?'

'My life hangs in the balance and you are playing games with me.'

'That is not so, young man. Not so at all. I am protecting Miss Zeldin.'

Jeremiah bangs a fist on Mr Rand's desk, lifting the pile of letters he now knows is reserved for the Dark Angel—no doubt dozens more struggling apothecaries like himself seeking their salvation. 'I will never tell that it came from you. *Never.* But you must help me, sir. You simply, must. I cannot live another day feeling this terrible pain in my chest.'

At this, the deamonstrator falls into his seat. 'I understand your sentiments, better than most, young man.' How could he understand the yearning that gripped Jeremiah's heart. 'Miss Zeldin is a creature unlike no other.'

Jeremiah breaths deeply. 'She can assist me, I know she can.'

There is a lengthy pause which Jeremiah's sister Rose would call *the angel's moment,* when he sweeps overhead and deposits here blessings.

'But it did not come from me, is that quite clear?' says Mr Rand.

'I beg your pardon, sir?'

'Miss Zeldin's address, it did not come from me—understood?'

'Quite clearly, sir!'

'Chideock. A village not far from the sea. A place once occupied by Catholic martyrs, or to I'm lead to believe. Take these with you,' he says, reaching for the pile of letters and holding them out to Jeremiah. 'I am certain she will find amusement in most.'

Jeremiah takes the pile of letters. 'Pray tell, are there many apothecaries that seek out her superior knowledge?'

Mr Rand shakes his head, appearing crestfallen. 'No, most of them are only foolish enough to request her hand in marriage. If this is what you seek, I warn you that convention is not what Miss Zeldin strives for. No, not at all.'

'Thank you, sir,' says Jeremiah, not wishing to further contemplate Miss Zeldin's marriage proposals. 'I shall be indebted to you for eternity.'

The daemonstrator brightens a little. He puffs for a moment on his pipe. 'As I have often said to my children, life is a question of balance. We must have some pain amongst the pleasure, in order to appreciate the merit of the latter. I for one believe that, in balance, our lives hold equal measure of good and bad.'

If Mr Rand ever felt inclined to test the simplicity of his theory, he should take a look at the poverty-stricken in St Giles: bad luck was often meted for a lifetime.

'That said, I have a good feeling about your situation,' the deamonstrator goes on, 'You see, Miss Zeldin spoke to me about you, briefly. She seemed to think you had a certain gift, one that she likewise possesses: a gift for Curing. Rather surprisingly, there are not many apothecaries who possess such a thing, most have either an interest in plants or money but rarely both.'

Without Miss Zeldin's appraisal, Jeremiah would have believed himself to fit into one of these category, not recognising that his love of botany had morphed into something more significant, but then, a man without a mirror can often be surprised by his own reflection. 'But use your gift wisely, young man. With it, I am certain you shall free yourself from debt. And when such time arises I will be here acknowledging your tenacity, a thing that has arisen despite, it would seem, a complete lacking in paternal decency. Go forth! Do what you must do to save yourself and, if you please,'—if not for the smoke, Jeremiah is certain he would detect a blush now spreading across the deamonstrator's cheeks, 'Please give Miss Zeldin my best regards.'

'I will indeed, sir. And…' Jeremiah bows his head, 'thank you for your kindness. I am—'

'Eternally grateful! I know, I know. Now, go! Your destiny, I am quite certain, awaits you.'

A sweetheart?

On the 20th day of December Jeremiah sets out westwards in search of an elixir of unknown contents. He has chosen to travel on the coldest day of the year thus far, a day when he ought to be travelling to Dulwich to see his sick father, to eat Christmas pyes of chopped tongues, beef suet, eggs, currants and spices and attend church at day break for an uninspired sermon given by Reverend Alcock. His father, still alive and grumbling with no further decline in health (according to Rose's last letter), had requested the family assemble for the occasion and, for the first time in many years, wishes to include his eldest son. Doubtless the dullard reverend of Camberwell had advised it. Before departing for Dorset, Jeremiah had, however, written his regret at not being able to attend, stating an urgent need to travel. Posting the letter in the city's drop-box, he felt only relief. Perhaps, after all, there was only so much buzzing against plate glass a bluebottle fly could do before flying in another direction altogether.

Forward motion in a public coach subsequently gives Jeremiah the sense he is achieving something. He experiences this perpetual movement in a box—for it can hardly be deemed a *journey*—seated in near darkness: the windows boarded up. Coach travellers, they say, prefer it this way but the air is fetid with flies—*in the middle of this cold spell*—looping circles above a dog's back. Milk drips from a mother's bare—engorged, infected—breast onto the sleeping face of her child. A young man drinks from a bottle: supping and belching; leg outstretched in a state of decomposition providing, yet further fodder for the flies. The dog by his feet presses its teeth into its anus, looking up every now and again gums drawn back, its mind set upon its arse. When it comes to the rawness, the nearness of human existence, nothing comes closer than a public coach.

In the inadequate light, Jeremiah distracts himself with a book by David Hume given to him by Wordsley. God, according to the philosopher, was a complex idea formed from simple ideas. Ideas, Hume writes, are caused by simple impressions. After a struggle, Jeremiah ceases to read. All riddles. Philosophy, he has always said, is for men who have little purpose, who find merit in translating life's muddles into abstract, unfounded terms. What they needed was more experience of life. It came as no surprise that Wordsley enjoyed Hume. He had no reason to know that the Almighty's involvement was nominal (as nominal as that of the banker's involvement in a game of hazard). Wordsley in short had little need for God. But then it is perhaps Jeremiah's unwillingness to wait patiently with upturned palms for God's (unwarranted) mercy that is precisely the cause of his predicament.

This 1000 pounds' reward that has been dangled in front of his eyes: must he consider it God's mercy, an angel's pity: one last chance, or another street leading nowhere; further punishment for a lifetime spent disobeying his father, seeking a profession that had brought his family nothing but embarrassment? If indeed it was a trick, and the reward was to remain beyond an apothecary's reach, then he would prove fate the cause, not his actions. After all, did God not help those who sought help for themselves? Did God not show his mercy upon those who put another's needs before their own? Naturally, he sees where failure might lurk: convincing Mrs Soloman, not only of the merits of recovery, but that there was better company to be had than that of opportunistic physicians. He needed a cure for loneliness as much as for sickness and with her great distrust of her niece, there seemed no remedy close at hand. He must thus focus attention on the physic, whilst drawing a line at moving into the mausoleum himself. Upon his return and, dependent on Mrs Soloman's improvement, he shall administer more of the tonic whose ingredients he had forgotten to enquire about. Logic for perhaps the first time in his adult life has, it seemed, abandoned him.

After some time and with the book open upon his, lap, Jeremiah falls asleep. Despite the surroundings his dreams are convivial even, one might say, arousing, that is, concerning a woman with a black cape and the comeliest of eyes …

The first stop is the *Coach and Horses Inn*, Chiswick, where a young fellow (with rotting gums), assigned the jobs of polishing tankards, imparts the news that a snowstorm is approaching.

'Travel now and there is no knowing when you shall return,' he says in the inspired way that overcomes people when speaking about the weather.

Jeremiah sips his ale, shrugs, for he it is a risk he must take. Has no choice but to take.

'You should travel by boat,' the fellow says, spitting on the silver. 'I have heard no stories of the sea freezing.'

'Along a Thames that is already frozen?' says Jeremiah. 'The ships carrying coal cannot make it through such thick ice. The river's only use now is for the Winter Fayre.'

It moreover resembles a cemetery, ships' masts deeply imbedded in ice like eschewed headstones.

When the coach sets off again there is only one other passenger: a plump woman with a frost-face: ravished by smallpox scars. She grips a bundle of clothing on her lap. She nods several times at Jeremiah. He nods back.

He travels light; rather, he has forgotten a change of clothes. A change of clothing had seemed an extravagance. As a child his mother had said, 'Indigo must you do everything today? Do you believe you shall expire by the morrow?' But it had more to do with the insubstantial nature of past and future than impatience. He had learnt with age the present was solidly there, significant and reassuring. He only spoke of future matters out of duty, not seriousness. To plan ahead seemed as believable as when a child cried, 'Let's imagine!' Though it saved him from worry, when presented with a problem—as in the form of Manners—he flailed like a drunk tossed unexpectedly into deep waters. The art of planning one's life, he had learnt, could not be acquired overnight.

Ladies, he knew, thought a great deal about the morrow, striking off the days until they were married. He had been expected to remember past conversations and spill his own past (not to mention his future) like a travelling seller exhibiting wares. It made him feel unwanted in the here and now. Prostitutes were different, living from one encounter to the next just as he had attempted to live (however meagre an existence) from one successful cure to the other. Whores he understood.

Several miles of coughing and the woman tells him, 'I have had the cough now for a year.'

It is as if they know by instinct.

He has no apothecary case, only four vials of laudanum wrapped in the folds of his coat. It does not escape attention that the woman ceases to cough when engaged in talk.

'You are travelling to where?' he enquires.

'Southampton. I am going to see my daughter. She is sick so I must take care of her for she is having her third child. She was bedridden for her last two births two months early and spent extra lying-in. When the blood comes they send her to bed. Her husband, he is a respected a silversmith for gentry folk. He is her second husband. The first died when they were married but a year. They are common law married—jumped backwards over a broom, or whatever the custom be now, my daughter thereby keeping her property from her first husband. Her work is in a millinery shop. But she jumped the broom in Chiswick where I live with my husband whose work is in a printing factory. Filthy hands. Ink never comes off! He is my second husband too, the first died drunk in the street. There was no property, naturally. My son-in-law has relations by the sea so my daughter moved to be near them. I try not to feel any bitter but I do miss her. She is my only daughter. Six sons you see. All grown men! I visit my grandchildren, often you understand for one day I shall be gone and I wish for them to remember my face. I say it is important to know the past, where you have sprung from. My husband, ill-natured at times, says if our sex is set upon a thing we cannot be turned from our resolutions. Do you not agree?'

She does not wait—does not wait for the breath to enter her lungs before continuing, which he suspects part explains the troublesome cough. After he has learnt the ages and names of all her grandchildren, the name of

163

her son-in-laws hound, Jeremiah deems the barking cough to be infinitely preferable. On and on the woman prattles about her life, deadening his thoughts so that when she asks, 'What is your reason for going abroad?' He hardly has space in his head left to respond.

'A sweetheart?' she suggests.

He scratches his head, not because there is an itch (mercifully his itching remains in London), but because he must enliven a mind that fell asleep a little past Chiswick. 'I am searching for a herb,' he says. 'A herb—an elixir—to heal someone who is sick.'

The woman laughs. He leaves her to her coughing. After a time the coachman opens the flap admitting a gale and a flurry of snow, making it clear why travellers prefer boarded-up windows. 'Next inn, all must change! All must change!'

'I change here for Southampton,' says the woman with a wink. 'And you? Will you find your Cure around here?'

'No, madam.' He raises his hat. 'Not here.'

The prospect of another adventure is lost somewhere between London and Shaftesbury. Twelve hours of travel renders Jeremiah's back stiff, his stomach pitifully empty. The driver exceeds his 15 miles a day. Before reaching the coach house the Cleveland Bays stumble so frequently that at the last turnpike Jeremiah fears they might collapse in their harnesses.

But eventually he is standing at last and ordering ale, finding the dialect strangely altered so that he understands only half of what is being said to him. The Mitre Inn is a place awkwardly attached to the east end of the town's church. He gathers he must remain here until first light when the next coach leaves. He is heading to Seatown—a village just a few miles from Chideock—a journey that involves several more stagecoaches and wagons. Without money for a bed—not if he is to catch another coach back to London—he must sit and sup his ale by the window. He would like to lie a while, ease his spine. Twelve hours on a wooden bench, jarring in and out of potholes, have all but broken it. He would like to eat, but the inn is out of food. So he sits at the window, fear of being robbed keeping him upright, counting sheep on the common as ale and half a vial of laudanum steadily quell his aches and pains.

They leave at first light. Four others occupy the coach: an old man, a younger man and two much younger women who look like sisters. Jeremiah amuses himself translating their conversations into an English he comprehends. After a time his entertainment falls silent and each person avoids the other's eye with dedication. One of the sisters has an uncomfortable pain in her uterus. Jeremiah wills it away. The horses proceed steadily; the wheels running in deep ruts etched a foot or more into the road, the pace of seven or eight miles an hour frequently hampered by drovers with their leisurely hogs. Yet occasionally good, clean air wafts inside, that of earth and wet grass; smells whose subtleties do not survive London's smoke.

An escaped slave

At the next inn Jeremiah picks up a newspaper and learns that a black horse fifteen hands and a bay mare fourteen hands have gone missing. The press gangs have been very brisk along the shore collecting seamen. In the next paragraph he learns that John Ablet received the death sentence for stealing a horse from Thomas Sutton but was afterwards reprieved but an 'ancient gentlewoman' of 72 years from West Sussex, with an estate worth £300 per annum, has defended herself against the extremity of cold weather and taken to bed in an honourable way with a young fellow of 23 years from Cumbria. The news from London concerns only sheep. Farmers are watching their sheep in pastures around Paddington dressed in soldier's habits with muskets and bayonets, hoping to catch villains who had been skinning their sheep alive. His Majesty promises a £50 reward. He is about to close the newspaper and ask the serving girl for some vegetables and hock of ham when another notice catches his eye:

A Negro, aged about 19 years, belonging to Capt. Edw Archer ran away from Bell Wharf, having on a plush cap with black fur, a dk waistcoat & old breeches, branded on his left breast with EA. Head shaved. Whoever returns him to Lloyd's Coffee House in Lombard St shall have a guinea reward & charges.

He knows of Captain Archer, an old patient of his father who had lost an arm in the War of the Spanish Succession.

'Tell me,' he says when the girl takes his order, 'how far to Chideock?'

'Chideock? It be more than seventy mile is Chideock.' She appears to assess his clothes, even his filthy buckle-less shoes. She says, 'I have a sister that lives in Lyme Regis.'

'How long will it take?'

'I would not know. I have not visited my sister for twenty years.'

Jeremiah eats his vegetables, studying the snow. His nurse once said God had assigned each child a snowflake at birth. Though he doubts the individuality of snowflakes—surely God was too busy for such trivial undertakings—he enjoys picking out patterns upon the plate glass, watching them disappear again as if they had never existed.

Examining the body during his dissections with Mr James had attuned him to the depth of God's creations. Much of what he observed was encased so that the pumping, contracting and ticking were kept hidden. God preferred to deceive with simplicity: in a sheet of fallen snow, in a swan gliding effortlessly across a lake so that only an enquiring mind might discern the complicated patterns that held snow together; realise that effortless swimming was the result of effortful flapping; that life could be taken for how it was or examined closer in order to understand the immeasurable complexity of its beauty. It required not so much effort of will but fervent pursuit of knowledge, never trusting what one saw but to believe instead that *everything* held more than the eye was able to observe. It made him wonder at times how far God had taken such an idea.

His thoughts return to his compendium—the love of his life or at least the only love he had committed to but, alas, had refused to commit to him. There was hope (blessed hope!) that Mrs Soloman's money would allow him to finish it. Yet, the pressings of time were inescapable. A man called Manners marked out his days as a jockey marked the last few furlongs of a race against a horse's flank. Used to striding to his own peculiar rhythms, he does not perform well under duress. If anything, it made him sleep more.

Locked up in Manners' home he might still cure Mrs Soloman, even finish his compendium before the trial commences, but that assumes that Manners will provide paper and ink. It assumed, therefore, too much. This was the difficulty when considering one's future; it invariably involved the deluded belief in assumptions. Thus, Jeremiah's preference is for what lies before him, what he can *see,* though presently, his view is like that from the window—obliterated by snow.

He takes several drops of laudanum.

M for money. M for Mrs Soloman. M for madness.

But he would take no further risk. Miss Zeldin had to become his accomplice. Together they could heal an old woman. He does not doubt she will assist. *I heal, it is what I do.*

'Did you want bread, mister?'

He brings himself back to the inn, looks up at the young wench staring at him, her teeth hanging over her lower lip as if if an attempt to quell something surprising. 'S'not very fresh.'

He takes the chunk of bread, its texture like brick. 'Tell me,' he says, 'what time will the coach be leaving?'

'There are no more coaches today or tomorrow, sir. They say there will not be another until January.'

'*January*? January is but a week away!'

'Aye, mister. The roads are *trek-eer-ous*. One horse coming from London has broken its leg on the ice sending the coach tumbling so that the driver was squashed to his death.'

He stabs at a solitary green potato with the two-pronged fork. 'What of coaches returning to London?'

'None mister for the gale is travelling east. We have rooms upstairs. Shall I be preparing one?'

'At what cost?'

He regrets asking as she takes in his clothing, eyes coming to rest on his waistcoat, which—fraying or not—makes him stand out like a high priest at a Quakers' meet house. He wonders if he should tell her about the abscess on her neck—that she tries to hide with a shawl—that it should be lanced, that she should drink red clover tea to purify her blood.

'Three shillings for the room,' she says, arms tightly crossing over her chest. 'That is if you want it all night.'

'Too much. Let me talk with the landlord?'

'He's away for Christ's Mass.'

'Then I shall just rest here a while.' He looks about, does not find so much as a cushion as comfort. 'I shall pay you for some firewood. By tomorrow I expect conditions shall be improved.'

'As you wish,' says the girl, taking too much pride in the power temporarily granted her. 'I shall fetch you a blanket.'

Jeremiah dreams of walking through fields of skinned sheep, pouring raging oceans of blood. He wakes to finds the fire is out. He gets up from the three chairs he earlier arranged into bed and looks up at the full moon. His pocket watch says past five of the clock. The snow has ceased falling. All is still and smooth and white, the trees and bushes stooped awkwardly under their new weight. Beyond these laden trees lies the curve of a lane, leading, beckoning.

As he looks for a means to light the fire, a thought occurs—such a thought may even seem obvious to a man who lacked patience, whose life is presently marching to the distant throb of time—of course, he must walk! He must be halfway there already. On account of Miss Heart's kindness, he has a small sum with which to stop at inns, besides, walking he enjoys. Walking shall clear his head, leave space for Mrs Soloman's cure and for the ethereal and encouraging image of Miss Zeldin.

Finding the key in the door's lock, he opens it and is immediately rendered motionless by cold. He shuffles round to the stable yard through thick snow and stirs a horse from its sleep. He finds sacking, some string and makes coverings for his shoes. He finds another sack into which he cuts holes for his head and arms. This he places it over his head, scattering his shoulders with oats. The horse snorts through his nostrils.

'A fine sight I am, I know,' Jeremiah replies.

He looks across the valley where the sun is beginning to rise. Then he proceeds in the opposite direction, snowflakes hanging briefly on his lashes. Slowly, deftly with his odd-shaped feet, he begins a slow crunch westward.

The saint of childhood fears

When eventually the sun rises it transforms the world from something commonplace into a scene fit for archangels. A row of snow-covered trees tunnels overhead like a sugared cavern and the path in the sunlight glistens as though diamond dusted. Yet tiredness creeps up on Jeremiah, permeating every ounce of his body like a sickness. He wipes snow from a tree stump to sit awhile, sitting stranded in a place far beyond cold.

Looking about he can see there is neither house nor church. It is Christmas and he has only mile upon mile of snow for company. He considers a prayer. It has been a while since he last prayed. Perhaps, his mother was right. Perhaps, St Giles has turned him into a heathen. He used to pray: selfishly and childlike: *make me clever, make me brave*. If he passes a church he shall stop, go inside and fall remorsefully to his knees.

He closes his eyes.

The Lord is my shepherd, I shall not want. Though I walk through the valley of the shadow of death…

He opens his eyes, looks up at the solid white sky. 'Comfort,' he says aloud, 'The Lord is my comfort. Eh? *My comfort!*'

There she is! Miss Zeldin: smiling, holding up a basket filled with flowers: daffodils, tulips—the hopeful flowers of spring.

'*Wait. I require your help!*' he calls to her.

But she lifts her hood and disappears, covered as easily as a footprint left in the newly fallen snow.

He inspects the sacking on his feet. Where wet shoes once provided a layer of warmth they now add to the chill in his bones. Yet he feels toes beneath the leather—numb yet mercifully still attached to his body. With more effort that he has perhaps summoned in his entire life, he sets off along what might be a lane or a field or even a river for there is no discerning what lies beneath the unblemished landscape as he walks and walks and walks and walks…

St Giles was a nobleman, the saint of childhood fears. He dispensed of his riches in order to live at one with nature and converse intimately with God. Throughout his life he restored the sick to health and took care of the poor. He understood nature. Perhaps, thinks Jeremiah, to understand nature was to understand God. Perhaps placing one's faith in nature was akin to placing faith in God. Perhaps, it was simply a form of prayer.

Jeremiah laughs. His body moves as if of its own accord. Left, right, left, right, harms freely swinging. He has heard of people marching in their sleep but a body doing so whilst awake seems absurd. He is a mere passenger to his body's motions, its desires.

His mind roams too; there was a time when he had considered nature at odds with God's grace. Nature was selfish, concerned with one's ability to thrive. Grace on the other hand was accepting, patient and infinitely kind. Yet somehow—and he had not yet got this straight in his mind—grace was deceptive like the swan gliding effortlessly across the pond; that is beneath the surface there was more to it, a kind of enduring resolve. Thus far, any effort on his part had not amounted to the blessing of God's grace, except perhaps for his methods of healing (though he is not entirely certain of this fact either). Nonetheless he remains hopeful, hopeful he might one day become a deserving recipient. After all, belief in divine intercession must, at the very least, require hope.

He stops, cups a hand over his eyes. Smoke curls from the chimneystack, the sun barely a slither now hovers above a distant hill. On the horizon he makes out a low building, hugged by thick snow. When he eventually reaches it he kicks at the door with his knee, afraid if he wraps upon it with his hands his bones will shatter like ice.

A young farmer's wife, cheeks scrubbed red by the elements, opens the door. She stands for a moment staring mutely. Attempting to greet her, Jeremiah finds his own tongue struck equally numb.

'John? John? Come hither.'

'What is it Molly?'

'There's a man right frozen stiff at our door!'

'Then kick him inside, woman.'

He is led inside, ducking beneath low beams into a scullery, following mile upon mile of whiteness the intensity of colours appears unreal, like a theatre's stage. A red-headed man, with cheeks as bright as his wife's, sits on a chair before the fireplace, a tabby cat curled like a comma of new life upon his lap.

'Where are you from?' he asks.

'London,' Jeremiah replies, tongue loosening, perhaps melting, a little.

'You have you walked from where?'

'I cannot precisely say.'

'I shall fetch some dry clothes,' the woman says, leaving the room.

Jeremiah stands in the centre of the room, dripping upon the flagstones.

'Where are you headed?'

'Chideock.'

'In this weather?'

'Yes, in this weather.'

'Stand closer to the fire. Warm your bones awhile.'

Jeremiah does so and his body descends into a thaw. Pain, previously suppressed by numbness, grips his entire body so that his fists form knitted shapes at his sides and like a baby, newly born into this world, he finds himself drawn into life with astonishing agony.

'These should fit you,' says the wife, returning and placing some clothes on the back of a chair.

'Fetch him some food, Molly. Hungry?'

Jeremiah finds his body has not yet regained enough mastery to proceed with a nod.

The farmer points at a chair. 'Course the man's hungry. Sit down, man, sit.'

Jeremiah wishes he could curl up like the cat on the hearth mat, like an unborn infant cupped by the safety of its mother's womb: loved, reassured, without concern for his future. Instead, he sits there speechless and in pain on the edge of an un-cushioned chair.

The wife puts a pan on the stove and then kneels at his feet to untie the sacking.

'I have lost sheep with coats a foot thick this winter,' the farmer is saying. 'And you—*you ass*—think you can walk through these parts dressed like the mayor on parade day?'

With his feet removed from his shoes, the wife still seated at his feet attempts to dry Jeremiah's stockings. The pain, at first excruciating, subsides into regular throbbing.

'You have no snow in London?' the man persists. 'London, be it the great indoor city?'

'Stop it John! Stop it! Let the fellow be. Can't you see he is nearly turned blue with cold? Stop your chiding!'

'I am testing, that is all.'

'Testing for what?'

'Testing if the man be an idiot.'

'Look at his shoes John,' She holds up his sodden shoe for the farmer to inspect. 'His waistcoat. I have seen Mr Ellis wear one similar. Now John, where does the Bible say that in offering our help to a stranger we must chide him? You must ask the Lord's pardon in your prayers tonight or expect his wrath.'

171

'Hell woman! A man can amuse himself at his own fireside can he not? Besides the man wears a sack for a coat.'

Jeremiah parts his blistered lips. 'My name is Jeremiah Indigo Samuel Goode and I am travelling to find a herb to heal a sick lady.' A shot of pain uncurls both fists completely. 'I am an apothecary.'

'*I am an apothecary*! What will it say on your stone: *an apothecary who froze to death. A man who ought to know better.*'

'Dress now,' says the wife, frowning at her husband. She gets up and pats the pile of clothes. 'I shall give you some privacy. Let him dress, John.'

Once the wife has left, the farmer throws the cat on the floor and stands.

'My wife,' he says, 'she believes in helping folk. She has not left this village her whole life. Now see I know how folk think so let you be warned, I have a musket. I shall shoot you dead before you get to that field.' He points to the window. 'Then I shall bury you in a ditch where you'll have no stone except those in the earth.'

'I am not here to rob you.'

'My wife belongs to me.'

'I do not wish for your wife.'

'So damn thee, get dressed! '

While Jeremiah undresses, removing the sack, struggling with his waistcoat buttons, the man stirs the stew on the stove.

'No horses in London?' he asks.

'The coach cannot pass on account of the snow.'

'The coach never passes through here. Travel a mile as the crow flies to the inn and you shall find where the coach stops.'

Jeremiah removes his stockings, discovering toes as red as winterberries. He says, 'I had not realised I had so strayed so far.'

The farmer laughs. 'Not used to straying? A good little sheep are thee?' He laughs, turning his back, stirring the stew on the stove with a clatter. 'You must wait for the snow to thaw. No hope of a coach till then.'

Jeremiah puts on what he assumes is the farmer's nightgown for it smells of another man's sweat. 'I cannot wait,' he says. 'I must seek a Cure for a patient.'

'You shall have work here. Plenty animals to tend to.' He pours the stew into a bowl, splashing it upon the floor, where the cat eagerly laps it up. 'Plenty cows to milk.' He laughs again, though his laugh is more of a grunt than a proper laugh. 'Plenty here to keep thee busy. We shall see it as God sent us an angel.' He laughs and hands Jeremiah the bowl. 'When the weather turns and the blessed snow thaws there will be more work in the fields. A man does not walk from London to Chideock unless he is desperate. When you get back to London you can send my wife one of those jars. Them ones in blue and white, with the pictures of angels and flowers on them. She would like that. I shall give it to her for her birthday.'

Jeremiah takes the warm bowl, a small shudder passing through him. 'I cannot stay here.'

'Ney? Then you'll be arriving at Heaven's Gate and no place else if you catch your death with cold.'

'I shall not die,' says Jeremiah sipping the soup, burning his lips.

'Why so sure of yourself? It be the coldest winter we have known and we have known plenty and you think you will merrily dance through the middle of it?'

Jeremiah wipes his lips on the nightgown's sleeve. 'It is not my time. Every man knows his time when it comes close and this is not mine.' Death he daily battled, death he was used to putting off.

'Then I say you do not know God. Knowing when we are to die we should sooner give up.' This last part is seemingly addressed to the cat.

'It is not my time,' affirms Jeremiah, picturing the swan, the tiny ripples it makes moving through the surface. There is more to this walk, more than an encounter with Death of that he is certain.

'Then hear what I say.' The farmer stares at him. 'I say do not provoke the Lord.'

*

An empty vial of laudanum sits a few inches from Jeremiah's nose. He gets up, in a series of effortful actions, grimacing, shuffling in search of his shoes. His toes are swollen but no more painful than the rest of his body. He looks about for the sacking, cannot find it and sits down to wait for his mind to catch up with his body, snatches of last night's dream slowing his actions. *A black horse, the beast submitting to his control running through a field of poppies,*

Jasper at his side, Jasper smiling. There is no doubt it was a dream; in waking life Jasper never smiled, nor could he run.

Then he sees, besides where the farmer had sat, a pair of boots. He picks one up and measures it against his foot. He listens. The house is silent aside from a chunk of snow sliding from the roof to the ground and startling the cat. With a quick glance over his shoulder he puts both the boots on. They are sturdy, heavy boots built for mud and for snow. Lacing them, he wonders: *what would my Father think if he could see me now?*

No longer Indigo

A mile of snow compares to 10 miles without. Jeremiah drags the farmer's boots through drifts that reach knee high. To distract from the weight of his thoughts he conjures his sisters: pious Rose, outspoken Blanche and Violet fluttering with her insubstantial ways, each of them compelled by their relentless curiosity when it came to their eldest brother. He thinks of Lucy Aldridge, her silliness, her prettiness, her love of luxury. Such comfort is repellent to him now—unless, that is, it concerned writing implements or candles. He imagines his apprentice and maid huddled for warmth in the attic, Mary resting against Boswell's chest listening to his heart. He knows perseverance will one day make Boswell a fine apothecary though it is doubtful whether he will be there to witness it. And Mary, well Mary shall not always have the protection afforded by her beauty.

He passes several inns on a road upon which he trips on stiffened, buried ruts made by a thousand carts. Stumbling towards the setting sun, he believes he walks westwards. He passes villages—four of them—where he finds neither horse nor a solitary beast. By nightfall, he is walking holding out his hand as though some invisible creature grasped at it. There is little solace to be found in solitude, not here amongst the white nothingness. Eventually a vile hunger breaks through, stabbing relentlessly at his gut.

After an unknown quantity of time he reaches the King's Head. He pushes open the hefty door to enter a small room with a singular table where several men are gathered, sheaf of papers set before them. They appear to be conversing about farming. One says, 'I do diggy vor dree hours.' Another, 'Dree, when I be bricken all day!' They fall silent to regard Jeremiah's meandering route to the fireside. Two men laugh. After so much silence even the sound of their supping gullets is too much to bear.

But taking a corner seat, Jeremiah settles hesitantly beneath their stares like a wasp beneath the hand about to strike it, and a young girl, no more than 12, comes to take his order from the bill of fare. He orders wild duck, some parsnips.

'There is a back parlour,' she says, quietly, though all men now stare openly. 'It is quieter there.'

Hobbling behind the girl, he is shown to a small panelled room overlooking a valley, filled like a basin with white flour. There is a fire, a long table and two benches and another chair before the fire draped with a rug. It comes as close to Heaven as a man might wish. Promising to return quickly with his food, the girl hovers for a moment by the door, wrapping a lock of hair around her finger. Another time and he might have complimented her on her manner, on her long black hair, but Miss Zeldin now occupies his thoughts just as the Sun occupies the skies, obscured only momentarily behind cloud.

'Thank you,' he says instead, and turns away before the girl can pass judgement on the colour of his eyes.

After she has gone, he takes off his boots and settles before the fire, feet stinging as they thaw on the hearth. How quickly a man's needs can change. To exist with warm fingers and toes seems almost too much to aspire to.

'There will not be another coach for a week or more, sir,' says the girl when she returns with his duck, still twirling her locks about her finger. 'We have a room prepared upstairs.'

'There is more comfort here than to be found in a bed chamber.'

She bites her lower lip. 'How long shall you be staying here?'

'I shall be here for one night only,' he says. 'I shall be gone by daybreak.'

The girl bows her head. Behind her hangs a picture of a Negro, a man as black as coal, watching him as if his gaze held power to align thoughts.

'Tell me,' he asks calling her back, 'Am I far from Chideock?'

'I do not know of such a place, sir.'

'Then I am far. What county is this?'

'Dorset, sir.'

'Then I am not so far. The coach heading west, does it stop here?'

'Every Tuesday and Thursday.'

In stumbling blindly through the snow he has done better than he imagined. The girl leaves him and within minutes he is sleeping, food cooling rapidly upon the table.

His dreams are not so convivial. He walks through fields, snow pulling his feet to the earth until one enormous pull and his entire body drops through ice, through the obliterating whiteness. *Splash!* He thrashes about, body naked, the surface above beckoning, all light and liquidity, inevitability all but shunned as he starts to swim. At what point the pair of hands reach down he can never be sure, but it is at a point where his mind breaks free of all tranquillity and the black eyes reflect back his fear as he braces himself, waits for the breath to be squeezed out of him as it always is, and…and this time there is a small alteration in the sequence of events and past his face floats a solitary white feather, gently descending, its spine slightly curved like that of a newly born infant. Alone in a field, naked yet unbothered, he now feels conjoined to the landscape and thinks, with some lucidity, that being here is not a mistake after all but something of an honour…

It is not the first time Jeremiah has spent all night in a chair but it is the first time he has done so sober and without the aid of laudanum. In most of his dreams he will walk. By morning he will feel exhausted. He will eat cold duck and then wearing a farmer's boots, a chemise over his coat, he will set off with the sun rising behind him like a great ball of agony.

Jeremiah watches the snow for a time, finding it hard to discern if it is falling or rising. He stops to eat the rest of his bread beneath an old oak. He takes a few drops of laudanum from his last phial. He sits awhile with his mother. She is sewing, wearing a smile of pleasant composure. Jasper sits at her side, resting his head upon her shoulder.

'We were at first only concerned by his crippled foot,' says his mother. 'There seemed to be nothing amiss with his mind.'

'What do you remember of the cats?' Jeremiah asks her.

'Black, grey, ginger,' says Jasper.

'Father strangled the runt. You remember that day, Mother?' Jeremiah kneels before her. 'At the stables? Do you recall it?'

'I remember a wheelchair was not going to be adequate,' Anne Goode replies, patting Jasper's hand. 'After that day it was so much more than a foot. His head suffered. I do admit. But it is all such a long time ago now. The past is like a lily growing from the bottom of a pond, Indigo. Eventually it bursts through into the light. Does it not? And lilies, they do so flower—do they not? Jasper has his drawings to occupy him now and is most content when drawing. And you, what of your own happiness?'

'The cat, what happened to it?' he persists, clinging to his memories.

'Your father's love, it never came easily. His nature, well, it is to give to strangers over family.' Her laugh is polite, crisp. 'A little like you perhaps, Indigo dear? No?'

'*Jeremiah*. I am no longer Indigo,' he says.

'Of course, it all happened afterwards. Afterwards you told us all you were not to be called Jeremiah, you said it so… frequently. It was as if, well, we were quite surprised that Jasper lived, though what sort of life can it be for him really?'

'Black dog,' says Jasper, 'Black dog.'

'Such a charming girl.' His mother inspects her sewing, holding it up to the snow.

'Who, Mother?'

'That girl.'

'Which girl?'

'You know which one.'

'Lucy?'

'No, that it is not her name. I am certain it is something else.'

A gust of wind blows for a moment, scattering the illusion of both Jasper and his mother into tiny pieces no larger than snowflakes. Sensing that the wind is warning him, Jeremiah picks himself off his knees. He finishes the last of his bread and sets off again, staggering into the gale. Walking, he imagines himself a boy attached to a generous paper kite, skirting across valleys his mind on the tips of its toes.

Afterwards.

He had sat on the opposite side of his father's desk, the gas lamp burning in a green glass shade, casting his father's face in sickly light. A book lay open: an arm stripped of skin, its muscles painted the palest, most delicate of pinks.

Ashamed.

The word he remembers most. That and, 'Take it boy!' as the cane thrashed at his bare backside over and over. 'Take it! *Take it!*'

Crime and befitting punishment, boy.

Pain is a slippery fish the mind cannot grip for long. There were regular lashings, how severe it is impossible to recall; the words he remembers now more than pain. The terrible, terrible words.

You tried to drown him. In a bucket. You committed the unforgivable sin of attempting to take the life of your brother. Your own brother!

Slowly, from his father's words he pieced together the events. Scattered flowers, followed by anger then drowning. *Drowning.* It became his most vivid memory, and remained so. Yet he sees the events from a distance, as if from above. It is not his hands gripping Jasper's neck, pushing him beneath the water, but a distant Indigo. A child forgotten, lost to an immutable past, bound up as if in hard, unforgiving rock.

Dying can often be a choice

Endless fields and Jeremiah comes to a stream. He tests the ice with his foot. It feels solid enough. He steps across, feet sliding away from him. If he makes it across, he tells himself, *God will carry me to her threshold.* At the far bank the ice lets off a crack like a pistol shot and he heaves himself onto the bank just in time, and a limp willow branch moans at his weight. Turning back he catches shards of ice separating and slowly sinking leaving behind a black, coffin-shaped hole.

Every once in a while, perhaps at intervals of a mile or so—distances have become immeasurable—Jeremiah feels the urge to lay his body in the snow. Whilst his intelligent mind knows this is courting death, the more gullible side believes it shall revive him. He becomes thus two people: one pleading, like a spoilt child to have its way, 'Just for a moment, a short nap. *Please.*' Whilst the other offers logic and reasons, 'Do you wish to perish? Sleeping in this temperature you will last but an hour. Keep going until the next village or you will make an even bigger fool of yourself…'

For the first time he senses he is two discrete people. There again perhaps he is neither. Both, after all, address him as 'You'. And why does one of these people—these strangers—wish him dead? Was death therefore a choice? What had Miss Zeldin said? *You must tell her that dying can often be a choice. An easier choice.* His father had once spoken frequently of how a patient's speed of recovery directly related to the amount they paid their physician: the greater the bill the quicker the cure. Thus, he needs to find a way to encourage Mrs Soloman to live, to make her believe not only that she can be cured but that she *needed* to be cured. He remembers his words to the farmer. What made him so certain it was not his time to die? Will? Something more substantial? Faith? Hope? An enduring—though unsubstantiated—belief in God's grace?

His head a muddle of unanswered questions, he pauses for a piss, carving intricate patterns of deep yellow upon the snow. He says his name aloud, snow deadening the words.

Jeremiah I.S. Goode

Is Good.

Good.

He takes several drops too many of laudanum.

Fastening his breeches (with immense difficulty), he turns his mind to the architecture of a plan, one that has him marching across England in search of a tonic. Rather than Mrs Soloman and her cure, his thoughts hover over Brigid like a low mist hugging a field. He considers her beauty, its ungraspable nature. Yet, walking through a canvas of white, it is her beauty that he paints upon it, that anchors his thoughts as if this whole farcical plan—plan was perhaps too rational a word—but as if it were simply a means of reaching her and nothing else besides.

Beauty had entranced him from a young age. His first encounter came from his nurse—employed as an act of kindness—she was Cook's niece. Unlike most women Mrs Goode had nothing to fear from her husband's appreciation of female staff. She knew of his mistress. She knew all too well about his lack of affection. Yet five children, constant calling on friends as well as church, proved adequate distraction. Besides, the daughter of a wealthy man of business fell under no illusions regarding the fidelities of marriage. What surprised Jeremiah, however, was her lack of regret. A portrait of her painted before marriage hung in the salon. It might well have been a painting of their nurse. Both had long dark curls, dancing green eyes and a complexion, more French than British. It was a painting his mother referred to, not unkindly, as, 'The Girl' as is perhaps she had shed her youthful skin in the form of Nurse Abbott. He sees the same disregard for beauty in Miss Zeldin. Imagines her looks are only made relevant by those she encounters, the people—like himself—who cannot help but stare. As for his own beauty, it seemed to belong to the past, to Indigo: a young man able to indulge in the beauty of botany, not spend his days duelling with death.

Indigo, a boy with ambitions towards botany. Indigo, the other side of Jeremiah.

The other *you*.

Always several steps ahead

He walks straight Roman roads, tracks that curl like grass snakes between narrow strips of fields. So much space! In London one could uphold the misguided belief that there was good reason for people living on top of one another. Out here it seemed absurd, as if London were a ditch that masses had tumbled into *en route* to someplace finer.

On the low-lying icier parts he has to pick himself off his backside. On one particular fall a stag wanders past, pausing to stare, its polished antlers casting lengthy ravines across the snow. He trots off as if he had lived in snowy conditions his entire life. Nature, thinks Jeremiah, is always one-step ahead.

When he rests against a tree, closing his eyes to encounter the brilliance of pain, the silence is absolute. The snow has ceased falling. Even the birds have given up singing. Yet, silence only serves to emphasise his pain. Having spent these past 11 years offering patients a cure for their pain, it seems remarkable a bag of herbs had sufficed. He cannot imagine his own pain abating, not with a ton of the stuff—though more laudanum might do the trick, but the remainder sits in a drawer in his elaboratory waiting to be sold to those who lack the money to pay for it. But self-pity must be dispensed with. He must stay focused upon his journey, on his destination, on the tonic a certain Miss Zeldin will furnish him with.

Seatown 5 miles

He had passed this finger-post several times already. He is walking circles. He cups a hand over his eyes trying find a light—*or any sign of human life*—but finds neither light nor chimney to break up the speckled view. The snow is falling faster now. He can barely see a foot ahead. It occurs with ominous certainty that if he is to survive through the night—*a space of time that presently seems eternal*—he must keep moving or else be buried alive.

He wonders what is happening beneath the flesh. He pictures his labouring heart, its ventricles squeezing the blood, the opening of tiny valves that let blood pass through to the atria and which receive it willingly, before squeezing it out again. Life: one long, undetected squeeze. And from somewhere: the spark of life to keep it all going.

Mr James, his old employer, would say, 'Most gentlemen know more of the construction of their carriage than they do their own bodies.' Frequently lament that, 'If only men knew the delicate, refined piece of mechanics assigned to them they would act as a responsible guardian before, well, before it is too late.' Mr James had no desire to understand the wretchedness of a man's soul or how it drove him ever closer to destruction. He only acknowledged that men and women gave their bodies the attention they gave to a hanging at the Tyburn gallows only when it went awry. Rich or poor were no different. But physical pain was the great leveller. Death's prospect altered all, earning the reverence that ought to be given to the body in life.

Plants of course were different for they discreetly withered and died. Bodies, they rotted for an age, rotting from inside to out, amid much vomit and puss. Until the head—having spent a lifetime ignoring the body—became suddenly consumed by it.

He stops, sits down in the snow. Perhaps he could lie down, just for a moment.

There are rumours

'Where are you from?'
   'London.'
   'Where are you going?'
He searches his mind but finds the answer lost.

'Do you hear me?'

'Miss Zeldin?' he finally says, as if posing a question, to the man tugging at his sleeve.

'Then Chideock is where you are going,' the man says, 'Get up off the ground.'

Jeremiah tries to oblige but finds he cannot move. His body had given up the fifth—or was it the sixth?—time he had passed the sign to Seatown.

'Get up I say!' A man's beard spumes from beneath his snow-laden hat and a pair of hands lift him out of the snow. 'Mount my horse. Can you manage it?'

Jeremiah staggers, shivering uncontrollably. 'I shall try,' he whispers.

'You are lucky,' the man tells him as Jeremiah makes a fool of himself with the stirrup. 'Chideock lies over that hill. Indeed you are lucky I am travelling your way on a night like tonight. We physicians, alas, must travel in all weather.'

Having mounted the horse with a series of near misses, Jeremiah grips the pommel with an agonising grasp.

'Miss Zeldin,' says this physician, 'has few visitors. What brings you to her door?'

Fate.

The beard tips nearer. 'My inquiry is one of concern for her, that is all.'

'I am looking for a Cure…for a patient…I believe Miss Zeldin can assist.' 'You are a physician from London?'

'An apothecary.'

They begin travelling up the hill; Jeremiah's eyes start to close, his mind lulled by the horse's swaying gait.

'There are rumours,' the physician shouts through a sudden, thick crescendo of snow and wind, 'Myself, I take little heed. *Come on ol' girl!* But rumours are rife in a place like Chideock.' The horse slips on some ice though quickly resumes an unsteady plod. 'Her brother visits from time to time. He is from London. You said you were from London?'

Jeremiah attempts to nod, lids barely open.

'From time to time my path crosses with Miss Zeldin. She might deliver at a village birth and I might attend the patient of the new born

182

for some reason or other. You know of course that she is a healer whose gifts are rare?'

Jeremiah fails to respond, all his strength given to remaining upright. Parts of his body seeming to disappear, as if he is trying to balance a head upon a pair of somebody else's shoulders and, with so much downward motion surrounding him, he has the impression he is steadily floating upwards.

You nearly perished

Brigid Zeldin was sitting sewing a torn petticoat at her fireside when Dr Faversham had banged on her door. Lost in thought, planning a future that was, to all intents and purpose, beyond such order, she had not heard boots crunching through the snow as the physician guided—half-dragged—the apothecary to her door. The man was consumed by fever. Any other night, and she might have entrusted him to Dr. Faversham and his wife but not tonight for tonight was her dead brother's birthday and melancholy, seeking a distraction, reached out to them. Yet it was not the fever that Brigid Zeldin felt she could conquer so much as something veiled by the cerulean blue of the apothecary's eyes; a hollow wretchedness, haunting despite its familiarity. Thus, she welcomed Jeremiah Goode into her home and the physician carried him upstairs to the chamber where her elder brother slept on his infrequent visits, and Brigid Zeldin spent the night on the floor, awoken occasionally by the names expelled from the man's dreams as his fever pitched and pitched again.

The following day he continued to wrestle with fire, closed eyelashes fluttering like nervous wings as she moped his brow and fed him bitter tonics and teas. The rest of the time she spent in silent prayer. Then, a remarkable thing happened, whilst tending to this man whose face when sleeping resembled something of the divine: time lost all meaning. Hours swam by effortlessly, chores, her other patients, falling by the wayside. For the first time since arriving in Chideock, Brigid Zeldin felt she was where she was supposed to be, that nothing—*nothing*—else mattered aside from healing this stranger.

Darkness, warmth and bursts of intolerable pain. Then an angel's voice touches his ears like the warmest of sunlight.

'You have been very sick. Dr Faversham brought you here.'

Brought him where? Heaven? Hell? A debt collector's sponging house?

'You nearly perished.'

How had such relief been avoided?

'Rest, for you are safe now.'

An absurd thought...

When he comes round, Jeremiah realises two things instantaneously. Firstly someone—most likely the footman—is trying to poison Mrs Soloman and, secondly, he is in a stranger's bed entirely naked.

He looks about the room as it performs a series of arthritic ticks. A fuming pot somewhere in the room wafts lavender up his nose. It is a small room. If he stood up and stretched out his arms they would reach the uneven wattle and daub. Little gives way its owner: a chair, a small chest of rough pine and a stool. No pictures, only what appears to be his periwig hooked over a candlestick on the mantel. The muslin hung above the window billows inwards and beyond a chorus of birds blithely sings; otherwise there is silence: no street sellers, no church bells, no carriage wheels sparking over cobbles, only the blissful sighs of Mother Nature.

Some time later he hears footfalls travel up the staircase. A latch lifts and the door draws back and the face, that has proven a pleasant distraction throughout the hardest of times, is there, smiling at him.

'I am relieved to see that you are awake,' she says, entering with a tea tray.

Jeremiah tries to sit up, tries to speak—to offer up some form of apology—but finds he can do little more than return a smile.

'Your fever broke last night,' she says, setting down the tray. 'I had began to think it never would. You have been immensely sick.'

'How long have I been ...' *In this bed naked?*

'Five days.' She follows his gaze towards the window. 'The snow lies three feet thick beyond these walls. Wagons will not be leaving Seatown for a week or more. So, until the roads become passable again you must remain my patient. I have brought you some broth and tonic.'

'Thank you.'

'There is no need to thank me. Healing is what I do. Besides, I am not in the habit of turning a dying man out into a field in the midst of winter.' He watches her movements as she draws back the muslin at the window, graceful, caring. 'Though I must say, I cannot imagine what possessed a man to walk from London in such weather.'

My reason is you! I came to see that smile, to hear your melodious voice, as creamy as thick chocolate. Oh how irrelevant reason is suddenly rendered!

He sits straighter and, clearing his throat, offers, 'There is a patient—'

'There is no need for an explanation as soon as you open your eyes, Mr Goode.' 'You remember me!'

'I meet a lot of people at the Physic Gardens but in time, yes, your name came back to me, in time.'

He pulls the bedclothes higher. 'You undressed me?'

'I did. You were buried alive and drenched to the bones. Dr Faversham saw only your boots. What, pray, did you expect me to do?'

He shrugs with defeat and perhaps a sense of shame as she passes the broth.

'Be careful, the soup is hot. I shall fetch your tonic.' She crosses back to the chest and pours the contents of a bottle into a dish. He gazes—with considerable longing given his condition—at the curve of her full waist; the slope of her shoulders. His eye is drawn to the length of her neck, the delicateness of her earlobes.

She is here. She is really here.

'A few more days of bed rest and tonics and you shall soon be fit to travel again.'

He accepts the dish, bringing it to his nose, imagining how many times Miss Zeldin's lips have touched this very rim.

'Rosemary, lavender, peppermint, mullein and thyme,' she tells him.

'There is something else besides,' he says.

'Black pepper and garlic. Together they work to reduce fever. You fought against the fever for five days and nights. I have never seen a person thrash about so much under fever's hold.'

'Garlic?'

'Garlic adds fuel to the fire, Mr Goode, to burn up the last of fever's flames.'

185

'But it can likewise extenuate melancholy.'

'And are you melancholic?'

Have his actions been those of a man of stable disposition?

He slurps his broth. 'Not presently.'

'The window, shall I leave it open for you?'

'Yes,' he says, giving not a thought to the window. 'But you will stay awhile?'

She takes the finished bowl of broth. 'I have neglected my duties for too many days so have plenty to do and you shall sleep peacefully now that your dreams are less fitful.'

She knows of his dreams.

'The elixir, the one that you gave me when we first met—'

'Shh now, Mr Goode. There will be plenty of time later.'

Deeper needs

Jeremiah is next awoken by the urge to urinate. He drops both feet to the floor and peers beneath the bed. *No piss pot.* He stands, too quickly. His vision blackens and he has to sit for a time recovering his sight. After finding his clothes, neatly folded on a chair and his periwig—entirely bald on one side and hanging over a candlestick—he dresses in the farmer's nightshirt (the periwig he cannot abide even in good health) and descends a narrow, tightly curved staircase towards the sound of cluttering. He presses both hands to the walls to steady his gait. Halfway down he hears a man's voice—deep and sonorous—followed by Miss Zeldin's more melodious tone. He rubs a hand through his hair, trips, rights himself and takes the rest of the stairs at a slow shuffle, the farmer's boots freely dispensing mud.

This recovery from illness—did it not bear resemblance to infancy?

The parlour smells of burnt evergreen, ink and dried herbs. What appears to be a large drug chest is lit up on one side by columns of light streaming through two latticed windows. Upon the table in the centre of the room sits a sheaf of papers, proud like a flat-topped mountain—*Miss Zeldin's herbal*. Rather than envy at this sign of industry and completion, however, Jeremiah experiences only admiration, the sort given (he fears) to the things one admires but cannot accomplish oneself.

'Mr Goode, you are up!'

Miss Zeldin holds back a drape to a doorway leading to the rear of the cottage. Her hair hangs loosely over both shoulders. She wears (he cannot help noticing) a burgundy mantau with a stomacher intricately embroidered in tiny red flowers and laced with red ribbons.

'I had not expected you to get out of bed so soon.'

'You are alone?' he asks, drawing his eye from her the frill of her stomacher.

'Indeed.' She wipes both hands along the apron at her waist. 'I am preparing your tonic in the scullery. You may watch if you like.'

'I heard voices,' he says, following, wondering how to delicately bring up the matter of the piss pot.

'Clattering, Mr Goode,' she says, holding back the drape. 'You heard clattering.'

The back room moreover resembles an elaboratory rather than a scullery. A row of four-gallon carboys sits on a shelf above a long table. Above, strings of poppy-heads, chamomile, centaury, sage and mint dry in neatly tied in bunches. An array of Delft jars adorns the shelves of the dresser, bright blue and white in the sunlight and, next to this, is another chest much like the one in the parlour, drawers neatly labelled. A magnificent copper pestle and mortar sits on a scrubbed table top and on another counter sit the ubiquitous scales of his profession—polished to a high sheen. All around the room are scattered phials and labelled boxes in different shades of wood. Finally, his eye comes to rest on the hearth, to the bulb and pipe of a great copper still protruding, twisting snake-like in the nearby condenser, slotting inside—it would seem—quite perfectly.

Miss Zeldin holds up a bottle to the light as she fills it with liquid.

'My patient,' he says, regarding the cooking pans, wondering if he might discreetly borrow one to relieve himself in. 'Has been concealing a symptom from me.'

She glances at him. 'Most do and usually from themselves.'

'She has an almost gangrenous foot…but she no longer coughs and spits blood, thanks to your tonic. Mercifully, she need only be well enough to descend her staircase, an event that shall—*praise the Lord*—precipitate receipt of a handsome reward and—'

'Reward, Mr Goode?' She looks at him now with narrowed eyes.

'Indeed. My patient is a difficult woman. She refuses to part with a penny until the feat of descending a staircase has been accomplished. Until learning of her blackened foot I had deemed it a fairly straightforward case. But Lord she is difficult.'

A drop of spilt tonic runs along Brigid Zeldin's thumb and she licks it off. 'Lazarus was a difficult patient.' She casts him a furtive glance. 'But it did not deter Christ's willingness.'

'With another of your tonics, Miss Zeldin, I do not doubt my patient will heal and quickly too.' He picks up a pair of tongs, inadvertently testing their grip. 'My patient's problem is moreover one of stubbornness. But with your tonic and only your tonic, I might add, the woman believes herself halfway toward being Cured, if not two thirds of the way. But she is shrewd. That I know. If I do not have an exact replica of your tonics, I fear she would have kept a sample to test this new one against, despite whatever I may produce in my elaboratory to equal it. If there was no money involved I would have given up like the string of previous apothecaries and physicians.' Desperation leaves little room for the subtler shades of impropriety, those greyer areas between goodness and what is truly bad but then... 'But then I have fewer choices than most at my disposal.'

She wipes the bottle's neck with her apron and places it upon the table.

'Stubbornness, Mr Goode, is an unwanted blemish upon a person's character.' 'That is just the sting of it, Miss Zeldin.' He runs a hand through his hair. 'She has dismissed every physician seen, including the king's physician. In two years, she tells me, not one has come close to providing a Cure.'

'I am sure a man with his own *elaboratory* is able to produce his own Cure. This tonic, I am afraid, is yours and yours alone. You must regain your strength or else you shall leave here and fall immediately sick again.'

'Elaboratory,' he glances at his enormous boots, 'is a word I use to impress my apprentice, that is all.'

'And impressing is important to you?'

He clears his throat. 'A man of my means has little inclination towards impressing, Miss Zeldin.' *Until now.* 'But for the sake of my apprentice I like to dress something commonplace for it serves as subtle encouragement.'

188

He looks outside and sees a log shelter behind which he can relieve himself. Until he does so he is unable to think clearly about any subject. He edges closer to the door.

'I should not have provided you with a tonic when we first met at the Physic Gardens, Mr Goode. I have experienced more than one sleepless night on account of my carelessness.' She regards him side-stepping across the scullery like a crab with a frown. 'I have always prided myself on administering herbs to the individual, treating every person as unique. I am writing my own herbal for that very reason. Other herbals I find too preoccupied with the general.'

'I whole heartedly agree, but I hold similar beliefs and, I believe, can relay my patient's symptoms with some degree of accuracy.'

She sets the tonic down. Two red spots have appeared on her cheeks. 'Mr Goode, I must tell you something.' He feels compelled for some reason to smile. 'I served my apprenticeship—if you can call it that—with my maternal grandmother in Ireland. I am not governed by any guild. As to whom I serve, I am summoned either at births or when the sick can no longer afford or put trust in their physicians. The rest of the time I am blamed for crops failing and all manner of disaster. Even my herb garden apparently flourishes at the expense of the villagers'.' Her voice begins to tremble and she turns her back to stare out of the window. 'So you see, Mr Goode, I cannot allow myself the luxury of making mistakes. Diligence is the only means I have at my disposal for protecting my reputation.' She turns to face him. 'It was wrong of me to provide you with the tonic and I must apologise if you have journeyed here under any false assumptions.'

He reaches for the door handle. Outside, icy snow meets his knees. The air is crisp and cold and calmingly pure. He takes deep lungfuls of the stuff before relieving himself behind the log shelter; urine the colour of clove honey steaming and pitting the snow. He looks up at the clear blue sky and feels the sun warming his cheeks. She will come round, he thinks.

She will come round.

As he collects firewood, clattering resumes in the scullery and he begins whistling a tune, one he has not sung since childhood.

Arms laden with firewood, he crosses back to the scullery and hears a sound, like that of a stiff brush scraping over the ground, that appears to come from the low-lying brick construction on the far side of the garden. He is halfway there when Brigid calls his name.

'*Mr Goode?*'

He sinks into a drift and decides that following this winter he never wants to set eyes on snow again; shall hibernate at the first sign of a snowflake.

'*Where are you going, Mr Goode? I am making some tea.*'

He looks to the new brick building, wondering how she had afforded these constructions. He turns back, sees her standing on the threshold to the cottage, shading her eyes from the sun.

'*That building is for my animals,*' she says.

'*A sound in your barn,*' he yells back, '*I thought...*' What did he think? If it was an intruder did he imagine he would strike the fellow? And how nimble at such a task did he think he would be, given his weakened state or, for that matter, any state? '*I thought I should take a look,*' he nonetheless says; a look he could surely manage.

'*It is a barn full of animals, Mr Goode. Nothing more.*'

A rat, though unpleasant, might only require a thwack with a shovel.

'*Mr Goode, animals make many sounds. Please come inside.*'

He turns, traipses back to the door, abandoning the notion of demonstrating his chivalry. He dips once more, thigh deep, into what seems to be a muckheap and sends logs spilling from his arms towards Brigid's feet.

'I heard someone in your barn,' he says, freeing his legs as Brigid stoops to collect spilt logs.

'A goat and a horse,' she says, shaking her head. 'That is all you heard. There was no need for more logs, Mr Goode. You are not here to wait on me. Come inside or you shall catch your death from cold.'

'I thought I could assist—'

'There is no need. Really no need.' She relieves him of the remaining logs. 'I am used to doing things myself. My way.' Her eyes have turned as hard as flint. 'And it would greatly assist me if you would not interfere.'

I harassed Mr Rand

Seated before an inglenook on a cushioned chair, Jeremiah cradles a bowl of chamomile tea. The stone seats either side of the hearth are scattered with layers of drying herbs. Above the mantel hang further herbs in neatly tied bunches. Some flowers—white winter roses—are arranged on the table next to the yard-tall stack of paper and adjacent to this is an easel and a shelf of expensive looking inks in crimson, jade and indigo. The cabinet along the facing wall has three-dozen labelled drawers (he has counted them) and is much like the one in his elaboratory. Suffice to say it is a room that offers reassurance. He stretches out his legs. Knowledge. Order. Though he does not trust these things implicitly, they bring the same comfort that he suspects his customers experience when they step over the threshold of his shop: the comfort of *hope*.

He offered to attend to the fire but was quickly rebuked and now watches as Brigid expertly assembles a neat pile of logs into a pyramid. She sits back on her heels. When the smoke trails upwards, she brushes her hands together, satisfied.

'My father used to say I was good at building fires.' She looks at him, half-smiling as flames begin to dance. 'He was a man not usually given to compliments.'

'I fear it is a characteristic given to most fathers.'

She does not laugh, nor even smile. 'Now, I think you are ready for some proper sustenance, are you not?'

With which she quickly disappears into the scullery. Restored by the chamomile tea, Jeremiah gets up and wonders around the small parlour. He takes in an exquisitely drawn *Centranthus ruber*—red valerian—on the table-top easel. He reads the page atop the stack of papers. *A Complete Herbal containing five hundred plants taken from life and used in the practice of the physick.* He picks up her quill, brings the feathers to his nose and inhales something of its scent.

'Some tea, from India. The food is coming.' Brigid returns and deposits a tray on the table. She unlocks the rosewood tea caddy and adds two spoonfuls to the pot. 'Breaking one's fast is important, and no more important than following a sickness.'

He puts down the quill, trying to comprehend where in the day they have reached and says, for want of something better, 'Do you have a maid?'

'No, Mr Goode. I do not.'

'Let me—'

'I need no help. As I have already said, I do things my own way. Besides, you have not travelled all this way to assist me, Mr Goode. Callers rarely do. Now excuse me whilst I shall fetch bread and some goat's cheese.'

She exits the room again, skirts dragging effortlessly over well-worn flagstones. This time she is gone so long he imagines it is to milk the aforementioned goat. A door opens and closes. A blackbird sings as if with forced merriment. He crosses to a bookshelf and selects a copy of Peter Schoeffer's *Latin Herbarius*. He leafs through its pages thinking, *callers rarely do*. What *callers*? And what did they *want*? More clattering and Brigid sweeps back in, cheeks slapped red by the cold, her hair now a little dishevelled. She sets down a plate of bread and one of cheese and lays out the knives and plates.

'Please, Mr Goode, sit down.'

He sits facing her and accepts a plate of food and when he presses the soft cheese between the bread finds that it is still warm, that its creaminess dissolves on the tongue.

She pours the tea. 'Do you like it?'

He nods. 'You produce all your own food?'

She sets down the pot. 'Not all, Mr Goode. Even islands rely on the sea to be deemed islands. It's enough to know I would not starve if abandoned.'

Abandoned, he thinks, a strange choice of words. 'How long have you lived like this?'

'You mean alone? Seven years. Next you will want to know *why* I live alone.'

He remembers Mr Rand's words: she is, at times, quite untethered, Mr Goode. 'No,' he says. 'I would like to know how you spend your days.'

She hands him a napkin, unfolds another for herself and places it across her lap. 'You must know by now that I heal.'

'I mean to say, what it is you do when you are not healing?'

She smiles. 'As you can see for yourself, Mr Goode, I do not have a maid. I thus spend my time tending to my house, tending to my garden—when it is not hidden by snow that is, and the remainder is spent making tinctures and tonics and bags of dried herbs which I sell to the parish and occasionally on market days at the nearby towns. It leaves little time for much else.'

'Callers: they come to you to be… Cured?'

192

She studies his face then pushes a stray piece of hair behind her ear. 'Villagers call when their fear of death is greater than their fear of me. They do not come here for my friendship, if that is what you mean. Eight martyrs were once put to death in Chideock for their Catholic faith. This is not a place of sentiment, Mr Goode. It is a place of great distrust.' She frowns. 'You are from London?'

'Yes,' he says, tracing a knot in the wood of the table with his thumb. 'A few miles east of Chelsea.'

'Many people speak to me at the gardens but I travel up for as short a time as possible and usually have little time to converse.'

'It is a long journey.'

She removes a spot of something from her plate. 'I travel on horseback, Mr Goode. The journey takes two days either way. I do not like London and if it were not for my herbal I would never have reason to visit. I do not understand how people live in such a place.'

'Necessity,' he says, pushing aside an image of Brigid Zeldin sitting unconventionally astride her horse. 'And little else besides.'

She nods assertively. In her eyes he sees other colours, like those beneath the black on a magpie's wing, colours seen in the best and brightest lights. 'But of course, most would rather follow one another like sheep into a ditch than ask why.' She cuts off some cheese, spreading it with her head tilted to the side. 'They should rather not form their own opinions but rely on the opinions of others. Do you not agree?' She looks up and holds his eye so that with certain shame he recalls his unintentional insult concerning a black dog. 'But you do not strike me as such a person, Mr Goode. I like when a person strives to be true to their own beliefs. It is thus difficult to see why you came here.' She looks at him carefully. 'How did you know where to find me?'

'I harassed Mr Rand.'

Her laughter is deep. It takes him by surprise. 'Mr Rand is usually the one to do the harassing. I must congratulate you! Are you usually of such a persuasive nature?'

'On occasion.' His eyes fall to the table top. 'When my need is great.'

'A bold statement.'

'Being in great debt I expect has perhaps made me bolder.' He also expects this relinquishing of pride to hurt and is surprised by the lack of pain. 'In recent years I have made many mistakes, Miss Zeldin. You might say I do not consider the consequences of my life properly. But—' He sighs. '—though I may not have a head for business my intentions are always honourable and an honourable way to pay off my debts has found its way across the threshold of my shop.' He flattens his hands on the table top. 'But I heal the poor, Miss Zeldin. I am not, I fear, equipped for treating those with money.'

'There is little difference between the body of a rich person and a poor person, is there not?'

'The other difficulty is that my… methods seem to have failed me recently.'

'How so?'

He should not be speaking so weakly to a woman, least not one he admires. 'I did not detect her blackened and rotted foot. Had not an iota of suspicion about it.'

'Come Mr Goode. It is not your fault that your patient kept a symptom from you surely?'

He runs a hand through his hair. 'But a patient withholding information has never previously effected my ability to Cure, Miss Zeldin.'

She sighs. 'In order to help you, Mr Goode, I would need to see your patient and as I do not intend to go to London for some time I am afraid I cannot do so. As I think I have already explained, I must know a patient's mind as well as their body. In other words I need to see them with my own eyes.'

'The reward,'—He picks dirt from a nail—'shall save me from debtor's prison and I shall also have enough to spare to pay handsomely for any help.'

'Money has little to do with it. It is understanding the sickness, it is understanding the nature of a person.'

Her opinion is indeed akin to examining himself in a looking glass. He knows what he says to be true as he knows the blemishes on the back of his hand and yet the reasons that make him believe her to be a kindred spirit are the very reasons she will not help him.

'Mr Goode, are you sweating?'

He dabs at his brow with his cuff. 'I am just glad I have found you, that is all.'

She twists her cup in its saucer. 'I must explain something to you, Mr Goode. My patron saint is Brigid. She was from Kildare, where my mother was raised. I was born on February 1st, her feast day. Saint Brigid offered her virginity to God. She told the man who wished to marry her to go to the woods behind her house where he would find a virtuous maiden to marry. The man did as she said. She healed a leper who afterwards vowed to serve her. When people—and there were many—wanted to marry her, she blinded herself to avoid such a fate.' He places her cup on the table, folds her hands neatly before her. 'I heal, Mr Goode. It is what I do.'

He has spent enough time in the company of whores to understand not all women required wedlock. 'I need to heal a patient, Miss Zeldin.' He speaks slowly, reminds himself that he has never been refused a thing before, not by a woman. 'And I believe you are the person to help.'

'And I have told you, I cannot properly heal without seeing the person first and with my own eyes.' She begins collecting the plates, returning them to the tray, the clattering at odds with the peace of the room.

'I can offer you a place to stay.'

'To stay? But I have no urgent need to travel to London. The last of my drawings is complete. I am sorry that your journey has been wasted, Mr Goode. I cannot help you further. I am sorry.'

He pushes back his chair. 'Whatever I say will not change you mind? I can go into great detail concerning my patient's complaints. You might be surprised at my observations, at the similarities with your own. Will you at least try to assist me?'

She shakes her head, stacking the rest of the crockery. 'I have made my decision, Mr Goode.'

'Then provide me with the same elixir as before. That is not much to ask. Is it?'

She studies him. He runs his hands through his hair. 'Tell me, Mr Goode, why out of all the apothecaries in London, why a woman from Dorset?'

He briefly laughs, glancing at a portrait of an innocent-looking young boy hanging behind Brigid's head as he attempts to tame a tongue which wishes to announce: *Because I have never met anyone quite like you before. Never!* 'I think it has to do with the reputation you have…in Chelsea,' he says.

'Mr Rand has furnished me with a reputation, has he?'

'In that he described you as knowledgeable and a fine transcriber of nature.'

She laughs. 'Mr Rand thinks he can make money from me, that is all.'

'Make money how?' he asks, experiencing a sudden surge of anger towards the daemonstrator.

'He has offered to find a bookseller for my herbal. He has said it will sell many copies across the country. I have told him the herbal is for my use and my use alone, for when I am old and my memory no longer serves me. When I am dead, then he may do with it as he pleases. You see I believe in people, not books, Mr Goode.' She collects the tray. 'Perhaps there is another at the Gardens whom you may ask for help.'

'There is no sentiment in trade, Miss Zeldin, especially not in one filled with as many quacks as there are plants. If I ask another then he is the one to whom my patient will be giving her reward. But please understand my patient only wishes for *your* tonic. If I do not therefore acquire it I am done for.'

She crosses the room with the tray, pausing at the drape 'Mr Goode, please save your persuasion for your patient and put your faith in your gift to heal. To continue this request is to only insult both of us.'

He crosses the room, hands held between his head. 'What if I tell you my so called *gift* appears to have diminished since a great deal of money is involved.?'

'Oh *please*, Mr Goode!'

The crockery begins to rattle as her arms contend with the strain of holding the tray. 'I am no longer sure what exactly it is you require from me but if it is my reputation then I am afraid, Mr Goode, I cannot part with it.'

'Come to London.'

'Mr Goode, many a lesser man becomes attached to his nurse but I had thought better of you.'

He draws back the drape for her, defeated.

Why this woman?

Later, as Brigid pours tea, Jeremiah finds he cannot bring himself to meet her eye for fear of finding disappointment there. The sun casts the parlour in fragile light. The air is filled with the scent of burning pine. He acknowledges whatever contentment he found here, it must soon come to an end.

On the table sits Brigid's herbal, piled high, awakening him yet again to the insufficiency of his own efforts. Distance gives one's life certain clarity and looking to Brigid Zeldin's herbal he sees that if he were to work day and night he could not hope to finish his own efforts by spring or even summer; sees that the only salvation lies upon the bony shoulders of Mrs Soloman. Though he cannot say exactly why, he suspects this shrivelled apple core of a woman holds more power to destroy him than he has ability to heal her. He also has little inclination now to try.

'It is a pity you won't publish it.' He gestures at the paper, selects a sheaf: white archangel: a flower otherwise known as dead nettles and adds sincerely, 'It is very good.'

'A pity for whom?'

He looks up. Her expression is one of composure, doubtless worn for villagers when summoned to their bedsides: weary with unappreciated duty. 'Well, Mr Rand—'

'Mr Rand! He is worse than my elder brother. What these men cannot bear is a woman having a mind of her own, having a mind to do what they fear to do themselves. It is utterly inexplicable to them that in a woman lies a capability and intellect to match their own.'

Anger dulls the shine in her eyes. She bites her lower lip and Jeremiah is burdened with a desire to kiss her, can feel the anticipation of the kiss, feel it as though it were his answer to *everything*.

'Do you know women must make a secret of learning as if it were a lameness, Mr Goode?'

Of women and learning he admittedly knows little. 'I understand your resentment. My father possesses a similar view toward my abilities.'

She tips her head. Her features soften. 'Relationships between fathers and sons are often fraught.' She passes him a tea dish. 'I am sure he means well.'

'Not my father. He cannot accept that at four and thirty I have my own merits. He is a physician. According to him only the members of the Royal College of Physicians know a thing about physic. Apothecaries, well, they are the lowliest.'

Brigid rests her hand momentarily over his. 'I see he has caused you much anguish.'

'I had thought…' he touches the flesh, which had just touched hers. 'I had thought I might impress him before he dies but he is sick and I am heading toward gaol.'

'How would you impress him?'

He smiles at the realisation. 'By writing a book, a herbal. Something, I suspect, he is unable to do himself. Receiving constant adoration from dying patients leaves him little time for such endeavours, though he has spoken of it often. But,' he sighs, 'it appears I shall be attempting to finish my efforts whilst in prison. And my father… well he shall be proven right about both my abilities as well as my choice of profession.'

She holds his eyes. 'To my mind we are all builders of our own prisons, Mr Goode.'

He shakes his head. 'If I had built the Fleet, rest assured, I would have thought to include a means of escape.'

'I mean to say we all hold memories and feelings that imprison us until, that is, we learn how to set ourselves free.'

Why this particular woman? Of all the women in the country, why one who speaks in these strange tongues? He has never felt such longing nor such fury and frustration. As for impressing her, he would not know where to begin.

'You spoke the name Jasper many times when you were sick.' She pours him more tea. 'Is this your father?'

He smiles at the thought of Jasper. 'No, Jasper is my brother.' He runs a hand over his face. 'I am not welcome in my father's home, not until now, not until he is dying. But my brother lives at home for he is not capable of living elsewhere.'

She assesses something in the air above his head. 'Your father wishes for you to heal him, I expect.'

It is not a question. Nonetheless, he shakes his head. 'Not the eminent Robert Goode.'

'You may be surprised. Dying changes everyone. Some even become desperate enough to seek out the advice of a witch.'

Did she just wink? He cannot be sure.

'My father believes in bloodletting and amputation, not in the power of herbs, Miss Zeldin. But at times—' He stares into the roaring flames. 'At times, you know, I find his hatred almost a comfort.'

A muscle in Brigid's upper lip twitches. She recovers the anomaly with a smile and returns the teapot to the tray. 'In the absence of love, it is often easier to punish one's self, to view a father's faults as one's own. Now you must excuse me Mr Goode. I have to attend to many things. My work here is never done.' She looks towards the fireplace, an almost imperceptible sadness crossing her features. 'But please rest for it shall hasten your return to health.'

She could suggest that he swim to France and he would presently consider it. 'And what of your own gaol?' he asks.

She pauses and addressing the curtain, says, 'I am half-French. My father, for all his simplicities, understood the Enlightenment better than most. From an early age I gathered that God's divine punishment is not absolute but a choice. I believe in reason over doctrine and in knowledge over religious servitude. The miracle, I found myself aspiring to, was that of Mother Nature. My father, alas, never recovered from my distaste for the Catholic faith, for my upholding a belief in intellectual superiority. If I were a son then perhaps it might have been different. Perhaps then he might respect my idea that humankind is only another species of animal and as such we cannot be certain of a privileged position in Nature. It is a thing we must earn and for me the process of earning has been intricately entwined with understanding. The more I understand Mother Nature, the more I have been able to understand myself. Religion of the organized kind, however, continues to elude and Catholicism, well, I find it particularly unreasonable. Yet intellectualisation of the differences between Christian ideologies I must say interests me more than bloody battles. I do occasionally attend church: the surroundings comfort me. Yet ultimately, I remain a deist, Mr Goode. Christ to me is a moral teacher and not a creator of abstract miracles. It is reasonable enough to assume a supreme being exists, that I do admit. What is not so reasonable is assuming that the Supreme Being interferes in the daily creation of one's life. What I am trying to say is that insofar as religion and many other beliefs are concerned, my mind no longer possesses the power to imprison me; any punishment which I perceive to be doled out by God is moreover the result of my own doing. I apologise if this is at odds with you own believes and offends you in any way.'

'No,' he replies, his own beliefs being simple by comparison: the God he was familiar with dished out regular and doubtless deserved punishment and every once in a while took pity on him, moreover resembling a relationship he had once had with his nursemaid. Since living in St Giles, however, he had come to doubt the existence of God altogether. 'On the contrary,' he says, 'I admire your beliefs, Miss Zeldin, and rest assured... you could never offend me.'

God's Grace, if such a thing exists

Jeremiah reads the book Brigid brought earlier to his bedside: Linnaeus's *Systema Naturae*. Goethe once described Linnaeus as the most influential man he knew aside from Spinoza and Shakespeare. Linnaeus's book appeals to Jeremiah's, often unmet, desire for orderliness: Kingdoms divided into phyla, further divided into classes, into orders, families, genera and at the apex: species; Linnaeus's scheme, based on the structural similarities of different organisms: a work of genius. Life, with all is complications, could be neatly classified.

When not reading he sleeps—peacefully sleeps, at intervals drinking broths and bitter tonics. Contentedly, he lies in Brigid's bed, or sits at her fireside drinking tea, eagerly awaiting the time when she will appear. The idea of writing his compendium seems suddenly absurd, as if it were a peculiar punishment dreamed up by some former self to pass the time. And though he reads, it is Brigid's presence not plants that occupy the vacant aspects of his soul. A thousand times she could enter a room and a thousand times he would be no less pleased to see her: composed, beautiful, emanating grace as spring blossom gives off scent and her voice, when she instructs, when she reprimands, is just as pleasing and, though she might regard him as if he were an unidentifiable creature crawled out of a small hole, he still delights in it, regarding her every action with awe as she carefully and precisely administers her cures, from time to time receiving the reward of a cool hand placed upon his brow or arm, whereupon his bones soften beneath.

Once or twice, when she has stood not a yard from the bed, he becomes quietly and uncomfortably aroused, lying back grinning asininely, wishing the bedclothes were thicker, bringing to mind Mrs Soloman and her footman and other, similarly off-putting, thoughts.

He does not think about laudanum at all.

Concerns about the old hag's tonic and whether he shall obtain it have also become insignificant, like fallen leaves whose destiny is to settle, rot. His contentment defies every disturbance. Thus, he recuperates at leisure, existing in a dream-like state between the comforting trills of Brigid's tea trays. London, St Giles, barely form a blot on his internal landscape as he experiences a constant and healing dose of happiness. Indeed *happiness.*

They sit at the table together. Jeremiah reads Linnaeus' book as Brigid Zeldin paints a flower: bluebell: the flower of humility as the world beyond recedes like a dark nightmare bleached pale by daylight.

'I apologise for the tawdriness of the crockery,' she says, gesturing to the tray at her elbow.

He watches her shawl as it slips from her shoulders, then takes in the green porcelain dishes with their bright yellow flowers; he can barely recall the pattern on his own crockery.

'My older brother's wife sends me her old sets.' She sets down her pen and releases the scent of tea from the caddy. 'She imagines I spend my days drinking tea and little else besides. She likes to shop for useless things. It lies beyond her comprehension that one's purpose in life might be more relevant.'

'I shall write to her and explain that you spend your days drinking tea with strangers who are *extremely* sick.'

She smiles but quickly turns her attention to stirring the pot.

He clears his throat, asks, 'Your brother, he visits often?'

'He calls to advise me on how I should be conducting my life from time to time.'

'He is your patron?'

'My patron?' The teapot lid drops with a clatter. 'For Conrad to give money would mean he condoned the way I live my life, Mr Goode.' She retrieves the teapot lid, rubbing her neck. 'My brother could never do that. I am fortunate enough not to be dependent on my brother, nor any man. Exchange of services, is that not the way the world operates?'

He nods towards a small oil beside the cabinet, the only painting not of a flower or herb. 'Is that your brother?'

'It is my half-brother.'

'He also lives in Dorset?'

'He is dead.'

Jeremiah's chest prickles with grief. 'I am sorry for your loss.'

Brigid busies herself with pouring the tea.

'Be reassured,' he says, thinking of Jasper—'worse things in this life can befall a person than death.'

'I sense you are feeling much stronger today, Mr Goode?'

'I am.'

'Then I shall inquire in the village when the next coach will be leaving Seatown.'

A hollow sensation spreads outwards from his gut. He should have perhaps avoided the subject of her brother.

'Though I must say,' she adds brushing aside something on the table, 'there does not seem to be much of a thaw, thus far. You may still need to remain here for a few days longer. It has been pleasant having your company. You are not like the usual gentlemen I come across.'

A compliment! He twists his tea dish in its saucer. 'Perhaps a few more days will provide time for me to live up to your ideals.'

'Concerning what?'

'About the world being made up of exchange of services.'

'That is not entirely your fault. I have more than once refused your offers of help. Sometimes we take, other times we give.'

He bows his head. 'Thank you.'

'I have told you once and shall tell you again. I heal, Mr Goode, tis what I do, and as such there is no need to keep thanking me.'

'You have made a better business out of doing it than I, Miss Zeldin.'

'Oh, I am not so sure I would call it a business. I rely on the kindness of others. Rather, when it comes to money I get swept along by what my mother called God's grace.' Her eyes glint a little. 'I take it you are familiar with such a notion?'

There are two perfectly shaped squares of light in her eyes now, like entrances to someplace else, someplace finer. 'Perhaps,' he says, running a hand over his unshaven face.

'But I doubtless talk too romantically about the earning of one's living but grace is the word that comes to mind. If I have to be thankful for something then it is surely grace.'

Jeremiah suspects God's grace is the reason that writing his compendium has become so arduous. His frustration at transcribing his methods has taken on a form of its own to produce a kind of anti-herbal. This alternate herbal, grown out of alternate methods, perhaps encapsulates his life. Thus grace, though it helps cure his patients, brings with it the unquantifiable which, however hard he tries, do not form the basis of a book.

A spider suddenly drops from its web snatching sharply at its thread with trust. 'I believe I might experience what you speak of… when I Cure a patient,' he says. Three sisters have taught that keeping thoughts private spared one from ridicule and for a moment he holds his breath, waiting.

Brigid leans forwards. 'In what way, Mr Goode?'

He inhales deeply. 'When I Cure my patients, Miss Zeldin.'

'Go on.'

He struggles: having never spoken this aloud before. 'I experience my patient's pain beneath my… own skin …' He pauses, striving for the best way to describe it, takes a big gulp of tea. 'For at time their sickness becomes mine,' he says. Her smile encourages and he leans closer. 'You might say, Miss Zeldin, I become their sickness in order that I might Cure it.'

'The sounds remarkable, Mr Goode.'

He sits taller, finding himself driven to more remarkableness, buoyed by a peculiar infantile willingness. 'For a short time I understand what it is… to be at one with everything… to understand and converse with nature with apparent ease. When it happens I enter God's favour, of that I am certain.' His pride is now hanging shamelessly out like a shirttail from a pair of breeches. 'In the process of healing I gain God's own view of a person and their dis-ease. It allows me to Cure them.' A magpie squawks but otherwise the world does not come to an abrupt end on account of his revelation.

'You surprise me, Mr Goode.' She stirs her tea dish, spoon ringing a triumphant *ting-ting-ting* against the porcelain. 'My own method of questioning a patient seems quite primitive by comparison.' She gazes towards a window, open a little. 'I have often thought that the Supreme Being must believe irreverently in order and beauty—nature existing by way of example of this.' Her eyes widen and fix intently upon his. 'Then, if one's life becomes indistinguishable from God's intended harmony then one might suppose one is being carried by God's Grace, as part of some divine scheme. Free will is relinquished—for a time—so that one is supported as if by a pair of angel's wings, until one possesses the means of fully supporting one's self. That is my interpretation of God's Grace, though I can see it is not quite so explicit or indeed meaningful as your own experience, Mr Goode.'

He finds he is unable to contribute anything more on the subject of grace, can hardly come to terms with his own frankness. He mumbles, 'You have always lived alone?'

Brigid's expression alters. The tea dish rattles in its saucer. 'The question again arises! Next you will want to know if I am lonely. Well, I am not and never have been. I find solace in my own company for it is only in solitude does one become familiar with the language of one's soul. Does that satisfy your curiosity?'

He looks up at the spider spinning its web on the ceiling, dropping to the wall to anchor its web with dexterous faith. He had not meant to offend. A little impulsively, perhaps, he had wanted to know everything of her life. Others' lives were usually of no interest, even, at times, his patients' lives. But with Brigid he wanted to *know* in order to understand, in order to possess her. Most certainly he knew she was wise, equipped to express thoughts and sentiments of import better than he. Yet despite his admiration, his desire is a burden: to presume more from the person who had saved one's life showed only the utmost ingratitude. His desire, therefore, must be concealed like a puss-ridden boil in order to bask in Brigid Zeldin's attentions, however temporary.

'I apologise. You make me curious, that is all—' Then he buckles forward, clutching his chest. He attempts to move but the pain strikes for a second and third time so that he cannot breathe for fear of provoking it.

'What is it?' says Brigid.

'I…' He cannot say more but continues holding his heart, agony screeching, high-pitched and inharmonious. Then she is kneeling beside him and such is the pain he feels he shall never move nor breathe again.

'Is it your heart?' She places her hand over his. 'Can you breathe?'

He grits his teeth, tries to speak, his eyes fixed ahead at the painting of Brigid's young brother on the wall, the brother who had not survived beyond infanthood. He knows that the pain does not belong to him. How else has he lived except guided by this instinct? This is not *his* agony but *hers*.

'Tell me,' he manages, speaking through bright streaks of suffering, 'Tell me the circumstance of your brother's death.'

Brigid Zeldin abruptly stands and exits the room, taking his pain with her.

Tayo

Jeremiah opens his eyes, breathless, drenched in sweat. It takes many deep breaths and the sight of a full moon to bring him back.

Why did the dream of Jasper have to follow me here?

In search of water—he has found the water in Chideock as passable as any beer in London—he takes the stairs to the scullery, sores on his feet catching on the rough texture of the boards. He can smell bread baking. Perhaps it is not so late. He draws back the curtain to find Brigid with a brown-skinned man who ports a mop of frizzy black hair, wearing a cassock, belted at the waist by a rope.

'Mr Goode, it is late,' says Brigid. She steps forwards, gesturing towards the Negro. 'This is Tayo. He brings no threat.'

The man takes several steps back, wide-eyed, unblinking.

'Tayo is from the Igbo people.' Brigid sets down a knife. 'He is from the Kingdom of Nri, believed to be one of the oldest kingdoms in Africa. He is also a healer, Mr Goode. Much like ourselves.'

'What in God's name is he doing in your scullery, Miss Zeldin?'

Brigid smiles thinly. 'Tayo was bound for the Americas, Mr Goode, but his ship sank not far from Southampton. He escaped, swimming through the iciest seas. Eventually, he arrived at my door. As you know, I am not in the habit of turning away a person in need.' She brushes her hands together. 'I am pleased now that you too have eventually met, however. Any form of deceit does not sit well with my character, though I hope you can appreciate, Mr Goode, that I was protecting both of you.'

The Negro remains in the shadows. Thirst quite forgotten, Jeremiah keeps his eyes to the fellow. 'When did he arrive?'

'Last winter.' Brigid's lips now flatten into an impatient line. 'That at least was the time when his ship sank.'

'Last *winter*?'

She nods at the Negro who exits the room by the garden door.

'Mr Goode?' she says taking another step towards him. 'Be not afraid.'

Betrayal, loss, murder are the thoughts foremost in Jeremiah's mind, not fear. 'This is unexpected,' he says, 'Very unexpected.'

'Life is full of the unexpected,' she tells him, 'But if one looks hard enough there is usually some good to be found in the unexpected.' She picks up the knife and begins slicing some bread. 'Tayo is teaching me Igbo, Mr Goode. It is one of hundreds of languages spoken in his country and to think we have but a few languages spoken in England.'

In his silence, he strives to comprehend.

'Perhaps, Mr Goode,' she says regarding him, knife poised, 'you should return to your bed.'

'He lives here, Miss Zeldin, with *you*?'

'Indeed. In my barn.'

'*In your barn*?' Does she feel shame? Guilt? If only he could perceive more than his own disappointment. 'But he is a Negro, Miss Zeldin.' He slumps against the dresser. '*A Negro*.'

'Goodness, Mr Goode, you are sounding a great deal like my brother. Coming from London I imagined you might not fear the unfamiliar. I see, however, that my assumptions are wrong.'

'I know of plenty of Negros, Miss Zeldin, all employed as servants.' She holds the knife in line with his heart. 'They do not live companionably with a woman, *at least not one of fair skin*!'

'Please do not raise your voice at me, Mr Goode. If you must know, and it is not any of your business to know, Tayo tends to my garden as payment for his keep. It is far too large for me to manage alone. And the barn that he sleeps in he has built with his own hands.'

'You are living companionably with a Negro? Can you not see this goes way beyond the realm of impropriety? It is downright *wrong*!'

Brigid puts the slices of bread on a plate with trembling fingers.

'Wrong?' she says. 'If you are interested in what is *wrong*, Mr Goode, I ask you this. Back in his village in Africa, Tayo was a witch doctor, a position that is one of chaplain and physician and not without political importance. But the British people decided that the Africans did not live as they did and thus had no right to freedom. In the name of greed they destroyed whole villages, braking up families and taking men, women and children alike. They did this in the name of money and profit, Mr Goode. If you believe that a man who has spent his life healing others, or any African for that matter, deserves to spend his days in slavery for no other reason that existing, then…' She stabs the knife in the loaf again. '…Then you are not whom I imagined you to be.'

Was he ever such a person? His arms hang at his sides. His thoughts tumble over one another like drunkards into a steep-sided ditch.

'Negros,' he says, barely above a whisper, struggling to gain a voice of authority, 'they are nor like you or me.'

'Oh, I do not count myself amongst you and your kind, Mr Goode. But I must say I had considered you different. I had thought your position made you more accepting of… of humankind.' She presses her thumb against the surface of the butter, imprinting it. 'Now I see I was wrong. The villagers know nothing of Tayo. If they did, they would return him immediately to Southampton where he would likely lose his life crossing the high seas. It is a treacherous journey. I am told only ten survive out of every one hundred shipped to the West Indies. So if your intention is to confide—'

'I have no intentions.' He pushes his hair back from a brow now damp with sweat. 'I am for God's sake concerned for your safety, that is all.'

'I am safe, Mr Goode. Much safer than before Tayo arrived. Plenty come to my cottage to taunt the *witch*, to leave their carcasses of rotting animals on my threshold. Now I have Tayo to frighten them off and lately … lately, I have been left quite alone.'

He tries to set himself on Brigid's side, not the villagers', but convention offers the far safer net. 'Then I am not certain the situation is entirely legal.' When had he been bothered about the Law before? 'In fact you would do well to take some legal redress on the matter. I can help rectify the situation for you, Miss Zeldin. If Tayo has in any way threatened—'

The dish falls to the floor with a clatter, somehow the butter remains inside. 'If defending another's life is illegal then I have no interest in your laws. As to rectifying *my* situation I should say that you would do better to firstly rectify your own!' She retrieves the butter dish and begins spreading the bread with efficient swipes. 'You are a free man Mr Goode, free to sleep wherever you should choose.' She picks up the plate. 'Now if you please, I must take Tayo his bread.'

We are all free

Under usual circumstances, not that any of this could be looked upon as *usual,* Jeremiah would take a brisk walk. Walking would clear his head; throw up the more obvious solutions. But the snow is thick and his body has not yet recovered its strength, so he sits at Brigid's fireside, though it is has long since extinguished and Brigid nowhere to be heard, and recalls every plant he knows in alphabetical order—*oh, the comfort of order*—so that by the time he has reached hound's tongue he is deep into sleep.

A field full of poppies, of blood red heads. He walks arm in arm with his father, toward distant blue skies and lone clouds, seagulls skimming the surface of the day. After a time they come to a hill, so steep they tear at bunches of grass in order to climb it. At the peak a view of London, a comforting latticework of houses spiked by dozens of church steeples with the great, grey, hump of St Paul's bulging heavenwards.

The hill slopes more gently on this side. The grass is shorter, dabbed thoughtlessly here and there with daisies and buttercups. In the distance waits a woman dressed in gleaming white, carrying a parasol.

'Lucy!' says his father triumphantly so that Jeremiah can tell he is smiling. 'Lucy Aldridge!'

Jeremiah wills his feet to move, vaguely aware he inhabits a dream.

'You shall learn what to do,' says his father, 'you have plenty of time. Do what is right and redeem yourself.'

But Jeremiah is sliding back down the other side of the hill, sliding on his buttocks, sliding so fast over the earth his teeth rattle in his head.

When Jeremiah opens his eyes, he checks his teeth. The plate glass at the windows rattles. As for his teeth, they are thankfully fine. Brigid sits close by, writing by candlelight.

'I am most thankful to you for bringing me back from the dead,' he says, tiredness catching and slowing his words. 'Most thankful.'

Shadows alter her features as she looks up from the page. 'View it as a symbolic death, Mr Goode.'

'I shall,' he says, restraint still slumbering. 'You must know, I am reluctant to leave.'

She licks her lips, eyes darting between his face and the fire. 'You might see your recovery as a birth: the phoenix rising out of the flames and out of the ashes.' She gestures towards the fire, now lit. 'In a day or so you will be less reluctant about leaving for you will be properly well again. Sickness has a way of renewing the world. It gives us eyes that see without the dust of sin so that we can fully appreciate God's beauty.'

He wipes sleep from his eyes. Dust or no dust he has no trouble appreciating this woman's beauty. 'I walked half way across the country to be here... with you, Miss Zeldin.'

'Mercifully you shall have an easier journey home.' She brings the end of the quill to her lips.

He turns away to the hearth, to more passionate flames. 'I do not wish to leave, Miss Zeldin.'

'An apothecary has obligations. Does he not?' she adds. 'Obligations that cannot be so easily set aside.'

'In truth it would be immeasurably easy.' *Then I should be able to spend my days in your company.* 'These days I am an apothecary in name alone. It seems, well, it seems life has got the better of me, Miss Zeldin.'

She stretches out her legs in a gesture of uninhibited relaxation. 'You are still healing, Mr Goode. In Africa, when a man has fever, they dig him a grave. They tie a cockerel to his left foot. The villagers light candles to conjure up spirits in order to heal him. He remains here for seven days after which time they believe him reborn. A rebirth. We have much to learn from the Africans. Do you not agree?'

It comes back with the force of a whore's slap. 'Where is he?'

'Who?'

'The…African?'

'In my barn. Actually, I have been thinking that Tayo might administer you a healing. If, that is, you might relinquish a little of your fear.'

He stands knocking his head on a low beam. 'Miss Zeldin, in the good Lord's name what are you thinking?'

'Thinking?'

'Keeping this African in your barn?'

'Mr Goode. Tayo's belief is that we are all haunted by demons within our own souls. He believes in the practice of exorcism and a proper rebirth. He has carried out plenty in Africa and healed many of their burdens. It is Tayo's belief that sickness resides as much in the head as much as it does in the—'

'Stop this infernal gibberish!' He grips the sides of his head. 'Hand the fellow back to Southampton or set him free.' He paces the small confines of the room: six steps from end to the other. 'What are you thinking keeping him here? The man is making a mockery of you. Can you not see that? Can you not see he takes advantage of your kindness?' A yard or so away from her face he stops, holds her eyes, searches for reason but what he finds in the shine of her sloe-coloured eyes is the reflection of his own face, distorted and fearful. Turning away he says, 'You would do well to be rid of him, Miss Zeldin.'

In the bedchamber upstairs he collects his coat and his wig and returns to the parlour to ask for his purse. Brigid retrieves it from a drawer. After assessing its weight he is told of an inn in Seatown. Directions are given.

'I advise you not to travel any further until the weather improves, Mr Goode.'

'You will not listen to sense?'

She is unbolting the door, tightening her shawl. 'We are all free. It is the best and most cursed gift God has given us, Mr Goode.'

As she pulls the door open, frozen wood protests over the flagstones, Jeremiah inhales rosewater scent for the last time. A tug, like an invisible thread, pulls at his chest and his subsequent actions seem not to belong to him, as though he must wrench his body free from its desire.

'Walk far and it shall be at your peril,' she tells him.

He tightens his neck scarf. 'Rather this kind of peril than that found at the hands of a Negro!'

He sets off briskly into the night, along a path Tayo has recently cleared. Cold air hits his chest and suddenly and violently he coughs up a cup's worth of phlegm. Afterwards, he stands straighter, lighter, as if he had rid himself of all that was rotten and festering inside. With fragile limbs he presses on, eyes fixed upon miles upon mile of open fields, lit up by a new moon.

At the bend in the road he turns back to his sanctuary. The door is closed but he make out a face at the window, a face that cares enough to regard him. Little does he know Miss Zeldin can see no more than the light of the fire and her own face reflected in the glass.

Love is but a reflection of oneself in the looking glass

Brigid Zeldin asks Tayo to follow Jeremiah to Seatown. Neither man travels far. Cold, exhausted Jeremiah collapses not 300 yards from the gate of Brigid's cottage. In Tayo's arms he is carried back to Brigid's cottage. Afraid his fever might return, Brigid sits by his bedside, mopping his brow, conversing at length, shedding words as though shedding dead, unwanted layers of herself.

'In my memories,' she says, 'I see my reflection in the stream, the twisted reflection of anguish upon my face... Thankfully I have come to learn guilt can often come from being put upon too greatly by others. Guilt can be a form of hopelessness, turned inwards... I pause to remind myself of the rain. It rained heavily that day, unnaturally so, in great obliterating sheets... The rain pressed my clothes tightly to my skin. It drowned the sound of crying. I realised much later, of course, that reflections only happen when the sun shines... That alone provided the comfort I need.' She holds his hand tightly. 'I did not kill him, Mr Goode. Whatever they might say. I did *not* kill him.'

He wants to say, 'Of course not,' but exhaustion smothers his efforts and he returns to a pleasant dream, one in which Brigid's face is full of sunshine again.

Swimming. Nothing more to it. Swimming was how it had all begun: weightless in the warmest of wombs. Water the essence of life. Purity washing away grime. Diluting sin. Weightless. An untarnished conscience. Clarity. Oh, forgiving light, blessed light. What uninhibited ease. He moves through these waters with surprising grace. These hands now support, carry, lift him up, cradling him, like his nurse's own arms. Up, up, up toward the light, to where drops of the sun's rays leach through the surface. And here now: beyond the still, calm surface. Breathing air. Breathing life. Alive. Damn it! Alive!

At some point during the night, Jeremiah opens his eyelids and, in the moonlight, finds Brigid holding a hand to his brow.

'There is nothing I cannot survive in order to be with you,' he says. 'Come to London with me.'

'I do not care for London,' she replies, gaily but gently.

'Then I shall make you fall in love with it!'

'You are full of romance. Life does not anchor the romantic for long. You will soon be adrift amongst impracticalities. Romance is of the surface of life, a feather floating on a rough and troubled sea.'

'I am already adrift. I love you Brigid.' Three words that make a space in his heart, which he can sooner stop than cease kissing her which he does, holding her cheeks and pressing his lips to hers as if the future of civilisation depended upon it. In a shamelessly quivering voice, he declares, 'I love you, I love *you*,' kissing her nose, her brow, her cheeks, expressing in his passion over and over again in his astonishment.

Love was not then reserved for poets, or for clergymen when speaking about God. Men who had lost everything of importance could be reborn in love, surrendering to its grasp, renewed by its steady embrace. His entire existence had been accumulating towards this moment; as if all the sorrow, all the pain, the manifold disasters were necessary in order for the ecstasy of this one blissful moment to exist.

But after declaring his love there follows a pause—no laughter—but a pause.

'I might indeed learn to love you,' she says, 'but I believe relationships between men and women to be fraught with difficulties.'

'*Fraught?*' he says, as an owl's cry taunts beyond the window. 'What do you mean *fraught*? That you prefer a life without *this*? That your ungrateful patients are enough?' A thought occurs: like most unmarried women her love is exclusively God's, despite what she says. (The African he refuses to consider.)

But rather than acknowledge his questions she sighs, resentfully so, and it is worse than any ridicule. Ecstasy departs, draining the blood from his face. His heart plummets to his gut so that he lies, bereft, upon the pillow.

'You see I do not believe in such a thing as true love. Love is but a reflection of oneself in the looking glass.' A finger traces a pattern over his chest and he imagines her nail gorging his flesh, reaching inside for his heart and squashing its life force. 'To begin with we see only our best, our most noblest selves but after a time we see only the bad. Tayo says relationships are like the meeting of two trees. At first we examine the leaves, the texture of one another's bark. We offer up our approval, but once stripped bare we find there are few differences, a slight difference in shade, that is all. Then after a time we resent being exposed, but by then it is too late. We see our lovers in this raw state and we resent it without realising...' She pauses, her eyes glassy and distant. 'Without realising we share it. Eventually, both lovers wants to cut the other down. Destroy them. You see, we all have something to hide. Is it not better to leave one's bark firmly in place, Mr Goode?'

He clears his throat. 'I counter that with what Plato says when he speaks of humans split into two by the gods, how they can never be happy until unified.' He pauses, tries to align his thoughts; hardly unable to believe he had uttered such a thing, simultaneously grateful for a subject he had once considered redundant—that of philosophy. 'You are ashamed about what you spoke of concerning your brother?' he adds. 'I shall never mention it again.'

'Ashamed? Why should I feel any *shame*? I thought I explained that whatever guilt I may have experienced at my brother's death it was but an accident. Where is the shame in an accident, Mr Goode?'

'The African?' He would find the culprit who wished to imbue his life with misery. 'He does not want me staying here? Is that it? He prefers to be the man of this house? Is that the reason you will not return my love?'

'Tayo has no say in the lovers that I take.'

His breath catches on the harshness of her words; *lovers* spoken with such ease, as if it were the most natural thing in the world for an unmarried woman to take *lovers*.

'And this is my house. Not Tayo's, nor any man's. And perhaps I am not the one who has something to hide.'

He pulls her neck towards him and kisses her neck. 'I hide, insufficiently, only my desire.' She has gorged his flesh so that his heart bleeds upon the bedclothes yet his desire is still buoyant and so, it would appear, is Brigid's for abruptly she kisses him, her tongue urgently seeking his.

'Undress,' he instructs, pulling away from her embrace.

'You are sick,' she says, smiling, nonetheless removing her apron.

'And I have made a miraculous recovery!' And he watches as she removes her garments by the light of the moon, slowly, so that he takes in the soft curves of her bosom, her generous hips. He lifts up the bedclothes, asks that she undresses him, which she does with equal slowness and care. Then, lying in the narrow bed together, they cling to one another's flesh like the two halves of a fragile shell buoyed in a storm-irked ocean. Jeremiah, acknowledges he has never lain so contentedly—so nakedly—next to a woman before, knows too, he is exactly where he is meant to be.

'I have found you,' he whispers.

'We have found each other.'

And as his body thaws into hers, he is no longer sure where her pleasure ends and his begins, for bodies and minds deliquesce into something of a stupor. Holding Brigid in his arms, it is quite clear they are more than the sum of their fragile parts. They are unified, made whole. With some certainty he knows no further hardships can befall him, not now he has Brigid.

Dr Jessop's visit

Brigid's head rests against the dent in Jeremiah's chest. He watches her hand furl around his. He watches the flickering movements of her eyelids and wonders what dreams take place beyond the veil of flesh. He would like to possess her again. Several more times in fact. This snow, it could last a lifetime and not be long enough and, still, he has no urge for laudanum.

When he next opens his eyes he lies in the narrow bed alone, buttocks exposed and hanging over the edge. Voices carry from the parlour beneath. He dresses quickly, spending an age searching for a lost stocking. Then he takes the stairs and partway down pauses at the sound of a man's voice. A quivering sensation starts between his ribs. This time he has recovered enough strength to speak to the Africa, speak like an Englishman: with forthright civility then return him to Southampton and set him adrift to the Colonies.

'Ah, here is the patient now!'

Jeremiah stands before a man with an uncontrollable mass of white beard, a man not black but distinctly white. He wears a green coat, the colour of envy. He smiles—or perhaps leers—waiting for Jeremiah to recognise him.

Brigid steps forwards, hands clasped behind her back as if concealing something. 'Dr Faversham came to inquire whether you would like to join him and Dr Jessop in Dr Jessop's carriage travelling to London. They are leaving the day after the morrow.'

'We have had news the roads are passable,' says the intruder. 'Temperatures have increased. This sunshine will last at least until the new moon or thereabouts. We shall manage the ice well enough. I am quite certain of it.'

A physician—*who else!*—sent to torment him!

'I shall make my own way back,' he says. He stares at the toe protruding through his stockings like a child who must sulk to be properly understood.

Brigid approaches. 'I have answered on your behalf, Mr Goode. I must travel that day, to Lyme Regis. It would be convenient if we departed together. Besides, is it not better to travel in a carriage than a coach to London?'

'A fine carriage, I might add,' says the physician. 'Healthy young horses. We need only make two or three stops on the entire journey.'

Jeremiah is rendered mute.

'My friend intends to leave for London at daybreak,' Dr Faversham is saying, 'Dr Jessop, you understand, has a house in Clapham Village, though his driver would not mind venturing across the river. I imagine your customers must be missing you.'

Should he suspect collusion? 'My apprentice,' he says, 'is able to tend to my shop in my absence.'

'Wednesday morning then.' The physician puts on his hat. 'And I must remark that you have made a significant recovery. I expect Miss Zeldin has been an excellent sick-nurse.'

'I heal with herbs, not nursing,' corrects Miss Zeldin with a tolerant smile.

'Yes indeed and I should like to see your wonderful garden for myself one day. I have heard many tales of your marvellous herbs. Such an undertaking. It is a wonder you manage it when so much of your time is given to attending births and deaths.' He pauses, rubbing his hands together, glancing at Jeremiah with a smile. 'Miss Zeldin fills in the little gaps which I leave in the village. A solitary physician, alas, is only capable of so much.'

His laugh is cordial but beneath lies a hopefulness that bothers Jeremiah. He watches as the physician takes Brigid's hand. Watches it hang laxly in his grip as he plants it with a kiss, the froth of his beard pressing for an interminable time to her flesh. He experiences a stab in his chest, not solely on account of the kiss but at Dr Faversham's patience, a thing to be so obvious as to be palpable.

'Well, good day to you both. I shall call again on Friday. You shall find Dr Jessop convivial enough. I believe you mentioned your father was a physician in London?'

'I have no idea what I said in a state of delirium.'

'Indeed, indeed.' The physician fumbles with the front door lock. 'Well Dr Jessop is an eminent physician, present at the births of the Duchess of Devonshire's brothers. He is well acquainted with most of London's physicians. Perhaps he knows of your father.'

'My father is dying,' says Jeremiah, wishing this man might soon join him.

'A pity, but rest assured I have seen many a fellows including yourself brought back from their deathbed.' Dr Feversham lifts his hat. 'Good day to you, Mr Goode.'

Jeremiah sinks into a chair. Brigid sees the physician out. Once the door is closed she looks at him sternly.

'You were ungracious, and to a man who saved your life.'

'Do you hasten my departure?'

'You must realise you cannot remain here.'

He shakes his head, gets up and reaches for her waist. 'What if I do not?'

'I heal, it is what I do,' she tells him gently but urgently, 'I cannot exist to satisfy the needs of a man, not any man.'

But she kisses him and he kisses her back. What follows is not the predictable, comfortable passion he has with whores in which release is its aim. It is raw, undiluted, animalistic; a passion that draws him closer to Nature. To God. With one hand he lifts the hems of her many her skirts, with the other he unfastens his breaches. With his body pressed to hers there is no sense of an ending, but of moments in which a part of his self is given, ceaselessly. For this woman he would be born a thousand times. Endure a thousand agonising births. He would be happy to exist as her lover and nothing besides.

'The physician is a menace,' he tells her. 'I wish to remain here, to forget this world ever existed.'

She presses a finger to his lips. 'Shhh,' she says, 'this world cannot forget you.'

And she kisses him with a hunger, using her tongue and he closes his eyes and sees only the brilliance of pure blinding light.

Why should healing stop at medicine?

Despite the threat of Dr Faversham, Jeremiah continues his convalescence in a state of bliss, in which Dr Faversham's friend's carriage and the blanketed world beyond the cottage once more disappear. He is permitted to read Brigid's herbal. He marvels at her perceptions: some obvious (though often absent from his own notes) whilst others he acknowledges with a desire to test them.

'Rosemary oil rubbed across a balding head does encourage hair to grow?' he asks, curiously.

'If loss of hair is not a condition suffered by both parents, indeed. I have found plenty of women whose hair re-grows after childbirth, or men who are grieving, or struck by hard times who lose their hair and likewise regain it.'

She lays some bread and cheese on the table. 'Tayo wishes to treat you.'

His attention returns to rosemary, how when applied to the veins it could make a man merry.

'Tayo, Mr Goode, wishes to treat you.'

This time, he looks up, frowning. 'I heard you the first time.'

'Please, Mr Goode—Jeremiah—he only wishes to ensure you are reborn without sin. Those were your words, were they not? That you felt reborn in love?'

'Words spoken when lying together hold different meaning to those spoken in the parlour.'

'You know much more of lying with women than I know of lying with men.' 'I think you are *not* ignorant of what it is to lie with a man.'

She takes the drawing of rosemary from him and returns it to its proper place in her herbal. 'I offer you help,' she says. 'That is all.'

'Indeed that is all you wish to offer me I know. But tell me, does a woman protecting a slave needs more help than a man in search of an elixir?'

'I protect a man—a human being—not a slave.' She throws her hands to the air. 'How in God's name do you profess to Curing the misfortunate when you are so ignorant of the world in which they reside?'

Her anger arouses him, creates a yearning like a deep crevice running through the centre of him. 'I would hardly consider myself ignorant, Miss Zeldin.'

'No? Then you ought to know that for most life is a struggle. Why should healing stop at medicine? What of those that are tortured, abused in the most inhuman ways? You are stubborn. Too stubborn for your own good, *Mr Goode*! When you returned to confess your folly three nights ago saying that you would do anything to make me happy, I told you about the pain I saw in your own soul. I confided that I wished to help you. That I could Cure you properly. But it seems you would rather remain in this state of ignorance and blindness. Tell me, how do you expect to Cure others when you are helpless to heal your own suffering? To forgive you must surely know that you must firstly forgive yourself. No?'

'I consented to your help, not a Negro's.' Perhaps Mr Rand's analysis was easier to revert too. Indeed, the woman was quite untethered.

'You are stubborn! That I am certain is why your father banished you.' She picks up her herbal and places it on top the drug chest. 'Stubbornness!'

If it was stubbornness then he had inherited it. He rests his face in his palms. 'I wish to be with you Brigid,' he looks up. 'Not healed by you. Is that so hard to understand?'

'You have no idea about love!' She begins clearing the drug chest, removing bags of herbs from drawers and tipping them out, stray pieces falling to the flagstones. 'And you cannot see what is in your best interest.'

'My only interest is you.'

'There is most certainly a reason God has given you a stubborn old woman to Cure!' She tosses more loose herbs to the floor. 'No, at least, you can see how irritating you can be!'

He crosses the room and takes a drawer from her hand, for only when immersed in their passion does she cease mentioning the infernal, omnipresent African.

'Is that why has God has sent me you?' He kisses the end of her nose. 'So I can see what the power of my stubbornness can secure?'

'You think lying with me makes me forget why you are here?'

'No, I know exactly why I am here.' He kisses her and she does not resist. He kisses the length of her neck. 'So that you can entirely consume me.'

Unless we have healed ourselves

Later this morning Jeremiah must travel with Dr Faversham to London, to the part-dismantled web awaiting him there. For more than a week Brigid has risen early to feed her animals, leaving him to his dreams: some convivial, others uplifting, in which the African looks on, no longer wishing him dead. But this morning Jeremiah wishes to think only of Brigid sleeping nestled in his arms, her dark hair fanned across his chest, her breath a steady comfort. He remembers what he had told her before they slept—gallantly so—that if the worst snowstorm of the century could not keep him at bay nothing could.

He pushes his body against the crevices of her body. When she opens her eyes he says, 'I will live companionably with the Negro. I shall do whatsoever makes you happy.'

'Live where?' Her voice is as light as petals, half seeped in dreams.

'Here, with you and Tayo.' He cannot help dispense the Negro's name as if it were a bitter pip to be gotten rid of. 'In time,' he says, 'we shall learn to ignore one another.'

She sits up, arches her back so that he cannot help stare at the fullness of her breasts, the soft mound of her belly. 'No, you must return to your life.' She pulls back the covers and crosses the room to her clothes. 'And I shall return to mine.' She crouches over the piss pot. 'Solitude is necessary for the good health of my soul.'

'You are not living in solitude,' he says flatly. 'You are living with *him*.'

'As much as you are living with your apprentice.'

'But the Negro is a slave.'

She finishes dressing in silence and goes outside to do what she had to do with the animals. He lies in bed, staring up at the beams. What awaits him? A business that is the property of a debt collector? A dying father whom will no doubt offer help if he marries a woman he does not love? Or the unforgiving bars of a gaol cell? He wonders where he might be now if he had become a physician and married Lucy Aldridge. Doubtless rich with a brace of children and a heart free from this miserable ache.

Once dressed, he sits at the table in the parlour unable to bring the broth to his lips. Brigid places a parcel wrapped in brown paper beside him.

'For your journey—the goat's cheese that you like.'

'Thank you,' he says, unable to imagine liking anything ever again. 'I have something else,' she says.

He looks up, hopefully.

'I have decided I cannot stand between you and gaol.' She places two bottles before him. 'Tincture 1 and Tincture 2. The first tincture is the same as I have already given. Your patient must only take the second bottle once she has finished the first. I have added some fenugreek for the gangrenous foot. I have never known it to fail.'

'I no longer care if the woman lives or dies,' he says with sudden frankness.

'Then if you would prefer not to have—'

He grasps her wrist. 'Come with me. I have a room. A bedchamber you can call your own. We need not live like man and wife. We can Cure the sick. We can Cure the blessed rich. Brigid, *I love you!*'

She shakes off his hand. 'Love should not diminish one's responsibilities. God's love does not, after all, exclude. People may exclude but never God.'

'Responsibilities?' He laughs. 'In a village where they blame you for crops failing?'

'Mr Goode!'

'And the sting of it is they think you a witch for all your help! For all that you do, this is the thanks they give you.'

She shakes her head, turning away from him.

'Or,' he continues ranting, 'lest we forget the African, who I assume is another of your responsibilities?' He presses a hand to his heart. 'Eh?'

'Please, Mr Goode!'

'You deny what I say?'

'Let us not fight.'

'Then come to London with me.'

'I cannot come.' She turns to face him, tears in her eyes. 'But I have a message, from Tayo.'

'For heavens sake!'

'He wishes to see you, before you depart.'

'I asked you come to London with me and still you speak of your infernal African?'

'I wish for you to meet Tayo.'

She must know he would do anything. He crosses his arms and does not meet her eye.

'Unless we have healed ourselves, Mr Goode, we are not capable of healing others.'

'You have healed me, have you not?'

'I have healed your body. Now your head and your heart must likewise heal.'

The Exorcism

The three of them stand in a triangle in the parlour, in the small space between the table and the front wall. Tayo stands, clutching a long stick, a great mass of black hair adding a foot or so to his height. He removes his boots so that he stands barefoot, the bones of his feet standing out like the roots of a tree. He has, Jeremiah notes, incredibly long toes.

'He has promised not to kill you,' Brigid says with a smile.

Tayo leans forward to whisper something in Brigid's ear. He regards Jeremiah, with eyes of burnished amber. Rather than absorb their surroundings, they appear to emit immense luminosity.

'He says that you must sit down,' says Brigid, pulling out a chair for him. 'And that you must close both of your eyes. I shall be in the scullery.'

Jeremiah runs a hand around his neck. 'You are leaving us?'

She glances at the slave and back again. 'Tayo will not harm you, Mr Goode.'

Tayo smiles, revealing large teeth as white as a rhino's horn. He moves in front of the chair, kneeling to place his hands on Jeremiah's shoulder uncomfortably close to his neck. Then, using his thumb and forefinger he closes Jeremiah's eyes.

So, this is what length men speak of when they refer to the extent of their love for a woman.

His breathing soon becomes shallow as the African beats a stick against the flagstones, chanting and clucking. Images come to mind; vibrant, lucid images...of his childhood, of Stony House cast in brilliant sunlight; the scent of straw, the clatter of shod hooves over cobbles and then everything dims and a crack of thunder reverberates through him.

The African's chanting reaches frenzied pitches. His hands force Jeremiah back against the chair. Air is expelled from his body as an image rises up in Jeremiah's mind.

He stands some distance away from the stables, from a bucket, observes his own petrified reflection. A figure—his father, teeth gritted—is bent over the bucket, retrieving a slumped figure from the water. He examines the face, lifts the body to his chest as he cries, 'Oh Lord Jesus, forgive me!'

Jeremiah falls forwards. The African catches him.

He looks down at his own hands. He holds bunches of wild flowers, some without heads: poppies and daisies and some vibrant yet poisonous foxglove. The rain falls sharply against his flesh and the flowers wilt as around his feet puddles begin to form.

The African emits a final howl and Jeremiah opens his eyes. A large pair of hands are gipping his neck. 'Father,' his thoughts plead, '*What did you do?*' And a pair of pink palms retreat and the mound of the African's hair falls upon his lap.

Jeremiah scrambles out of the seat and around the other side of the table. 'Brigid?' he calls. 'Brigid?'

She appears from the scullery just as the African drops to the floor.

'He had explained this might happen,' she says drying her hands on a cloth, 'he has taken something out of you and must wait for his own body to be rid of it. Our bodies are capable of containing much hurt, more than we can possibly imagine. Despite what you thought, the pain that you observed in me was not my pain but your own, Mr Goode. Now you must release it.'

Jeremiah lightly kicks the African's side. 'He is feigning sleep!'

'He will recover. Leave him be. You must leave now.' Her eyes dart to the window. 'Dr Jessop's carriage is fast approaching.'

He collects the tonics, the package of food and his hat, feeling nimble, as though lifting objects that were lighter than expected, as if his arms were rising in an exaggerated fashion like a puppet's.

Brigid is already at the door. 'We shall never experience contentment in this world unless we abide with Nature, Mr Goode.'

He holds her cheek, taking in every detail of her face, committing it to memory, every crease, every blemish. 'I wish only to abide with you, Brigid.'

'Nature, she will show you those small, encouraging moments of grace. Not I.' And she pulls away, patting his hands like a mother to a child, and he knows his heart shall never be vulnerable again. 'You have a talent for healing,' she says, 'an inner knowing. It is your gift. It is your grace. Please remember that.'

He shakes his head. 'This grace brings me nothing but pain.'

But she is pushing him outside as he steps over a dead bird—a blackbird—and into the gardens. He stands a moment gazing at splashes of colour breaking through the melted snow: patches of green, strips of mud along the road, mistakes upon an artist's perfect canvas, this great thawing unforeseen eventuality.

Dr Jessop's carriage pulled by two bays draws up beyond the gate and Dr Faversham dismounts the steps, lifting his hat at Jeremiah.

He turns back to Brigid. 'Abide with me, not with Nature.'

'We can never abandon Nature, Mr Goode. Remember too, reflections in water happen only when the sun shines.' Then she kicks the dead bird from the step and retreats into her cottage and Jeremiah is left for a moment straddling two worlds. before, feeling unbearably light, he walks in the direction of Dr Jessop's carriage.

Thus, Jeremiah's love affair ends with a dull journey in which two doctors speak of the merits of Claudius Amyand's successful appendectomy, the quality of French roads, moving onto other topics the reserve of the serious-minded and Jeremiah, in his confinement, gazes out at the landscape, at the great conquered land lying between himself and his beloved and inwardly weeps, acknowledging that a whore in Covent Garden had foreseen it all.

Money is made easily at the docks

The parish of St Giles-in-the-fields is ankle deep in slush, crossing the road akin to wading through marshland. Some good has come of it though: the near absence of beggars, though Jeremiah suspects few have survived the freezing nights. He walks, greeting those that he recognises with a nod, hats a mere luxury in this part of town. Yet he finds the general disregard for appearance, for disguises and façades, reassuring. No gentlemanly manners. No professional courtesy. Just the ability to walk, chest a little puffed up with pride: porting the cloth of the eternally wretched. He strolls past children who ought to be working who instead play in slush. He shall miss their: 'Mister Potticary, spare a penny?' He shall miss the drunkards tumbling out of the *The Angel Inn*, the shopkeepers chasing thieves down Bowl Alley. For this is St Giles, a place in a perpetual state of decay; a place not attempting to be anything other than what it is: his home.

He walks for a time, past the Mass-house where the solitary priest resides, past the site of the demolished leper hospital—St Giles the patron saint of the lepers—and along Grape Street, which once ran alongside the hospital's vineyard. The stench alters from one street to the next. Was it any wonder the Great Plague had started in a parish where the miasmas were so strong as to be visible? He heads towards St Giles' Circus, happy to stretch his legs following a lengthy final journey from Chichester. And, despite the persistent ache in his heart, he relishes the happiness in returning home.

Passing the houses of the Huguenots, the silk weavers, the French Protestant refugee escaping King Louis' persecution, he lifts his hat to several of his patients standing out on the streets. As outcasts of different kinds, they understand one another. Hardworking, they are rarely seen from daybreak to lamplight.

He is told by one, 'There's a hanging at Tyburn Master Apot'cry. They'll bring the man to a St Giles Bowl in the hour. Will you watch?'

'Not today.' Mother Proctor's Pews and hangings at the Tyburn Tree provided poor entertainment for a man dealing with his own tyranny. 'What did he do?'

'Pilfering.'

'The usual crime.'

No, he is not in the mood for witnessing a convicted man. He presses on, passing The Rookery crammed into a small space between Great Russell Street and Seven Dials. He salutes several Irish costermongers loitering in a doorway.

'Spring,' says one with a painful toe, 'won't be long now.'

He taps his hat. 'No, not long,' he agrees—*for some*.

'We know what is occurring,' says another, gin bottle lifted. 'We shan't let them get to you, Apot'cry.'

Either the bailiff's notice had done its job or this was the insightfulness of Mother's Ruin. In response, he salutes and moves on.

Reaching Neal's Yard, he stands for a moment, regarding his shop, gazing at the peeling paint, the windows thick with soot. Certain letters are peeling off so that the sign instead of *Jeremiah I.S. Goode* it barely reads: *miah I S ood*. Shabby! Forlorn! A rejected façade! Doubtless even the poorest were deterred from buying a cure from such a place. Standing 10 yards back it is as if he stares into an empty abyss, albeit a familiar abyss.

'Sorry place!'

A hand slaps his back.

'Mrs Marzio has her eye on it, though. Says it will do nicely for her girls. Says her gentlemen customers need a quiet, out-of-the-way-place for their visitors to come. We like quiet, out of the way places, do we not, Mr Apothecary?'

Jeremiah shrugs off the debt collector's hand. 'Tell Mrs Marizio she shall have to wait.' He stops to read the new notice on the door.

Apothecary Shop to be sold with counters
& Mortar and all things there unto
Belonging. Enquire of Mr Manners

Inside he startles Boswell dozing with his head on the counter.

'Mrs Marzio will have to wait until I'm dead!' says Jeremiah beneath his breath as he removes his hat.

'Sir?' says the boy wiping drool from his face.

'The bailiff is following me,' he explains. 'Such a welcoming surprise!'

The shop door is thrown open. 'My, my we have come down in the world Master Apot'cry,' says the debt collector, sneering. 'Holes in thy stockings, boots of a peasant and, if I may say, that hat of yours has seen better days.'

Jeremiah removes his hat.

'And a periwig gone bald. My, my Master Apot'cry!' Manners licks his palms, flattens his russet-coloured hair. 'You are a sight.'

'What do you want?' Jeremiah asks.

'I urge thee to guess!' the debt collector says, sidestepping towards the skeleton. 'But I am surprised you have to ask! But seeing as you do, a dish of tea would not go amiss.' He wraps an arm across the skeleton's clavicle bone. 'He bears a striking resemblance to you, this bony creature. Does he not?'

'We can ill-afford tea,' Jeremiah says, tossing his hat on the skeleton's head and drawing back the curtain. 'As a matter of fact we call ill-afford *a thing*.'

'Now every gentleman has a secret stash of tea in their possession that I do know,' prattles Manners, oozing a trail behind him. 'Something locked up in his tea caddy somewhere. Come on Master Apot'cry. A cup of tea would do me well.'

Jeremiah flicks through the letters on his desk, picking them up and examining their seals. He hopes Mary has hidden the tea caddy as ordered. 'I am not *every* gentleman,' he says. The debt collector is scowling at his botany books. 'Do you have no other clients to bother? A week remains before my debts are due.'

226

'*Clients*, how sorry-isticated.' Manners gazes at himself in the small, round looking glass, fingering the boil on the end of his nose. '*My clients*! Look how sorry-isticated I am!' He sucks in his cheeks. '*Gimme* some of that white face powder worn by gentleman and I believe I could pass for one of your kind Master Apot'cry! Handsome object: that glass.' He takes the looking glass from the wall and turns it over. 'Handsome object that would look mighty fine on my wall.'

Jeremiah slits open a letter with a paper knife, his knuckles turned pale. 'The glass was a present from my mother.'

'Well I never had a glass afore.' Manners tucks the looking glass under his arm. 'Much obliged. Any more treasure to be found here?' He points to Jeremiah's paperweight. 'What is it?'

'A glass paperweight.'

'Seeing as you have no use for paper now—'

'I have plenty of use!'

But the debt collector snatches the paperweight from Jeremiah's compendium and examines it. 'Pretty thing,' he says, and tosses it into the air and catches it again.

'Put it back!'

'Else what?'

'It was a gift from my brother. I order you to put it back!'

'Now, now Master Apot'cry. Your gifts are my gifts and soon your freedom—' Manners' eyebrows wiggle threateningly now, 'as well as your body shall be in my possession.'

'*Sir?*' says Boswell, standing at the curtains with the light behind, so that he appears to be surrounded by a halo.

'What is it, Boswell?'

'I have the money for Mr Manners, sir.'

'Not now,' he tells the boy whose thoughts must be still adrift in dreamland.

Boswell steps closer. 'Shall I give it to him, sir?'

Wishing the boy would return to sleep, Jeremiah waves him away and makes a grab for the paperweight but Manners is too quick and conceals it behind his back.

'Must be valuable this paper-weighter. I like valuable objects.'

'It is of sentimental value alone.' Jeremiah makes another grab but as he does so the looking glass tucked beneath Manners' hands crashes to the floor, scattering blue jagged shards across the boards.

'*Here!*' Boswell stands between them, now holding out three large pouches bulging with coins to the debt collector.

'What's this? Money you were thinking of keeping from me Master Apot'cry?' asks the dun.

Boswell nods in a conspiratorial fashion at Jeremiah. 'One hundred and fifty pounds,' he declares.

Manners adjusts his stance, crunching glass underfoot. 'A hundred pound shy of your debt! Why didn't you say? You might have kept your mother's glass. Seven years' bad luck and I shall never see my pretty little face hanging in my home.' He grabs the purses and puts shoves them down his trousers. 'The paper-weighter I'll not be bothering with.' He crunches over the shards of glass. 'One more week, Master Apot'cry. One more week until the rest is due!' He blows Jeremiah a kiss and exits the shop.

'Well?' says Jeremiah once the shop door has slammed.

'The parish, sir, had heard about your circumstance as well as a few of the women of Covent Garden and they made a collection for you, sir. It seems that you are popular!'

Jeremiah scratches his head. 'You told them all I was going to debtors' prison?'

'No, sir. The fellow who you took in when he was frozen half to death on your threshold listened to you speaking to Mary. He heard you speak of gaol. He collected this on your behalf. Some came from the men at the port, where he works. A woman called Virtue, also knows of your circumstances apparently and did make a collection from the Covent Garden *nuns*. The rest came from the parish. Pennies from people who never got the chance to pay you, sir.' Boswell clasps his hands before him a look of smug satisfaction on his face.

'But a penny from the whole parish would not amount to such a sum.'

'Money is made easily at the docks, sir. I should say John Brown filched some of the goods and sold them again. It happens a fair amount amongst snuffle hunters.'

'Marvellous! I am paying off my debts with stolen goods!'

Boswell pulls a flat-lipped smile. 'Your opium, sir, did that not also come from the Pool?'

'Is that any concern of yours?'

'No, sir, only you did say it came from the East India Company, where it was to be used to treat sailors on their long voyages to the Orient but you said that the poor of the parish did need it more than the sailors. Are you not the poor of the parish too, sir?'

It was a dreadful habit: confessing to the boy when drunken. 'One hundred and fifty pounds,' he half-sighs. '*One hundred and fifty!*' It was pointless, after all, to let the pleasure of the moment pass him by. He falls to his seat. 'One hundred and fifty pounds. Quite *extraordinarius!*'

'Us Jews do have a way with money like you said, sir.'

'You had little to do with it. Besides there is little of the Jew left in you. Jews are clever. But speaking of Jews, how fares Mrs Soloman?' He looks at Wordsley's invitation. 'Are you bursting to tell me how the old woman jogs up and down her staircase thrice daily?'

Boswell hangs his head.

'Boswell, why the molly act?'

'Miss Heart did call and was disappointed, sir, to find you went abroad.'

Mary enters the room carrying a handful of coal, literally one handful.

'Good day Mary,' he says, increasing the pitch of his voice. Mary smiles back. She looks fuller about the face, he thinks. Radiant. 'Boswell has been explaining the luck he has with money—being a Jew. How fortunate for us gentiles to be in such proximity to a fellow swimming in such good fortune, do you not agree Mary?'

Mary tilts her head at Boswell who appears older recently, with his frown and drawn-in lips.

'Miss Heart,' says Boswell. 'Did visit when you away.'

'I am sure that was a pleasure for you.' Jeremiah laces his hands behind his head. 'Continue.'

'She said she had thought you would be making a twice weekly call at her home.'

'When hell freezes!'

'She said that if you didn't visit before a certain date she will think you are no longer able to Cure her aunt.'

'Mercy! What date?'

Freckles on the boy's face clump together like pollen, trapped in his scowl.

'Come on you clever Jew.'

'It be…well, it be today, sir. Methinks.'

Jeremiah dismisses Boswell and rearranges his desk. He cannot consider a coach journey, not today. He must familiarise himself again with the scantiness of his compendium and try hard not to make comparisons with Brigid's. A break from it all has renewed his belief he can finish it and he has reached Lovage: a herb that digests humours, a herb to provoke a woman's menses. When distilled the water relieves quinsy. It also removes spots or freckles from the face. Culpepper says the herb is under the sign of Taurus and of good use when Saturn offends the throat, which as far as Jeremiah is concerned is absurd. But nonsense is what he must fight against if he is to ever make a sense of his theories!

He takes off his sorry periwig, puts his feet up on his desk and looks about. After the simple decoration and meticulous order of Miss Zeldin's cottage, he is surprised at the clutter in his elaboratory. He had previously vowed to a love of order. There are the heftier tools of his profession: the distillation apparatus, the grinding implements and the pill-making equipment (that has frankly never worked) at odds with the intricate gold ceiling and the mouldings on the walls—installed by the mercer who had occupied the shop before him: shop keepers being an ostentatious sort. Serving his sentence in debtor's prison, the mercer had plenty of time to contemplate the folly of his fondness for gold leaf, as Jeremiah would have time to contemplate a love of nature over money and a presiding inability to say 'no' to the poor. As to the mess of this elaboratory, it was surely a sorry depiction of the greater mess residing in his soul.

Yet feelings of inadequacy are paled by a perpetual longing for Miss Zeldin. These feelings far outweigh any fear for his future, feelings seem to flourish with every moment he is separated from her. The sensation is part way between a blow to the chest and hysterical wonderment. And he must—*must*—force himself to believe in the biggest miracle of all, believe that his love shall somehow, by some means, be returned. It is a prospect that inspires him much more than saving himself from gaol.

Several hours later the shop bell rings and Boswell drags his booted feet back to the shop. Mary continues hovering around his desk like a dragonfly over a meadow stream.

'Yes Mary?' he says, rereading the invitation from Wordsley. A ball and no masks required!

Mary hands him a note. He reads it slowly, having trouble deciphering her script. He looks up.

'Am I to understand the money I gave to you before I left, whilst enough to cover most of your debts with the sellers, was not enough to encourage them to continue our accounts?'

Mary nods solemnly.

'It would seem Boswell holds the purse strings in our residence, not I.' What little remains from Miss Heart's money he intends to spend on coaches to and fro Chelsea, having suffered enough blisters to last a lifetime.

Mary shrugs, studying her fingernail.

'The meaning of your shrug, Mary?'

Mary bites her nail.

'The dolt!' Still grasping Mary's note, Jeremiah pulls back the drape and lurches into his shop. 'Boswell, you are a damned fool! You gave the entire sum to that wretched…ah, Miss Heart. Good day to you!'

A sickness in her blessed heart

Miss Heart stands on the far side of the counter, smile rapidly falling.

Boswell clears his throat. 'Miss Heart came here concerned you had not replied to her letter, sir.'

'Thank you, Boswell. Your letter,' says Jeremiah holding up the fistful of papers in his hand. 'I was coming to it.' He draws back the elaboratory curtain. 'Please enter my study, Miss Heart.'

He kicks shards of the looking glass out of the way and pulls out a chair for Miss Heart to sit upon, brushing off loose fenugreek seeds from the seat. He sits down facing her, crossing his legs to hide the holes in his stockings. For the first time in more than a week his shoulder performs a vicious and observable flinch.

'Tell me, ' he says, a hand pressing down upon his shoulder, 'how does your aunt fair?'

'She is improving,' says Miss Heart, tightening her lips.

Jeremiah digs his hands into the lining of his coat, which he has not had the opportunity or the inclination (considering the cold) to remove. 'Improving that is good but we need her to keep walking.' *Down her great staircase.*

'She would very much like the…well, the tonic again.'

'Indeed, I have the remedy to her troubles,' he says, holding up one of Miss Zeldin's vials, passion once again responsible for him not asking Miss Zeldin what it contains.

Dimples return to Miss Heart's wan cheeks. Her hand flattens against her already flattened chest. 'I am as relieved as my aunt will be!'

He checks the bottle is marked with 'Tonic 1' and hands it to her.

'She walks daily?' he inquires.

'Yes and accomplishes it very well. I do not believe it shall be long before she can attempt her staircase.'

'That is good news!' *Though not good enough to reach a heart so bereft.*

'You shall visit…soon? I ask on account that I am going to Bath tomorrow to take the waters and would like to know that my aunt is cared for in my absence.'

'I shall be able to visit tomorrow,' he says with as much enthusiasm as he can muster.

'Thank you, Mr Goode.' She glances about. 'I must say this is an interesting room.'

'One day I shall get around to tidying it.' Either he or the debt collector.

'My father used to preserve birds. His working room was much like your own. His need to see things stuffed, well, it fascinated me as a child.'

'I embalm no animals here. Though one might be forgiven for thinking my apprentice in a permanent state of preservation.'

Another blush rises. 'I saw the note on your door.'

'The debt collector's insistence.'

Miss Heart's smile is so kind that for a moment he imagines she sees the precipice alongside which he teeters. Her lips struggle as if to say something unsayable.

232

'You have an impressive collection of books, Mr Goode.' she says into the chasm.

'Botany and herbal books.'

She acknowledges the pile of pages upon his desk. 'And…and you are writing one yourself?'

'Trying hard to distil my knowledge, Miss Heart,' he says, turning away from the pulp that comprised his efforts. 'And it in turn is trying me.'

She briefly smiles and swiftly turns and he follows her back into the shop where she pauses at the counter.

'Oh, one last thing, Mr Goode, I have a friend who has been… you understand… married for a time and is still… well, she is still without child. The doctors have examined her and believe it shall never be possible for her to have a child at all and it struck me that perhaps there are…' Cheeks give way to flame.

'Ways of ensuring conception? Naturally, Miss Heart! There are many herbs to help increase its likelihood.' Jeremiah climbs a ladder, selects a gallipot. 'As with most herbal remedies, however, time is as much a part of the process as…' He stumbles over *lying together*, fine for whores, too intimate for the delicate substance of a lady's ear. 'Red clover, nettles and raspberry leaves, half ounce of each infused for four hours in a tea, Miss Heart. How long has your friend been seeking a remedy for her condition?'

Miss Heart peers up at the alligator. 'Oh…I am not certain. She travels regularly to take the Bath waters, however.' The flush returns. 'She is a determined sort, beneath…'—Such interest toward a gallipot of dandelion leaves—'Well, beneath her shyness that is.'

'A pound of each Boswell,' says Jeremiah handing his apprentice two gallipots. 'To be drunk thrice daily, Miss Heart.'

'The woman's dimples sink deeper with pleasure. 'Thank you, Mr Goode. Oh, I almost forgot! Cook requires some arsenic, for the rats.'

'Arsenic, very well.' He decants the last into a bag.

'What must I owe you?'

'You have been generous enough already,' he says, his eye caught by movement in the yard. 'Boswell shall attend to you.'

He kisses the back of Miss Heart's hand and steps outside, heading towards the shadows, with any luck closer to the person who has been following his tail like a shadow for weeks. He approaches slowly.

'*The Potticary!*'

'Who goes?' he says, skin bouncing off his bones.

'Your old patient, Mister Potticary!' says a tattered woman, stepping out of the shadows, clutching a bundle of rags to her chest.

'I kept it!' she says, extending a bundle for Jeremiah to inspect. 'It's a boy.'

He peers at the wrinkled face child, sleeping and a surprising picture of health.

'I am glad to hear it.' And he was. 'Very glad,' he affirms.

'Enough gin and he sleeps all night—in a drawer beneath the bed. Not a customer has noticed him. That is, not yet but do not know what I shall do when he gets too big for his drawer.'

Something portentous needs to be said. He can think of nothing other than warning the woman not to get herself with child again but not in the mood for pointing out the obvious like some thick, leather-skinned vicar, he decides it is morning of things to be glad about.

'I wish you well, madam.'

'Do you have children Mister Potticary?'

'No,' he says, and fearing the direction of travel quickly adds, 'And no wife either.'

'That pretty young thing, she is not your wife?'

Mary's looks are for the most part lost on him lately. 'You speak of my maid?'

In place of what ought to be soft feminine laughter, the woman cackles and wheezes and narrows her eyes at his shop. 'Did you put that bun in her belly?'

Affirmation of his suspicions is quickly shrugged and a proclamation offered, one that might serve as a homily. 'My maid was an orphan. She can read and write. There are some institutions that can benefit a young—'

'Good day, Mr Goode!'

'Good day,' he replies, as Miss Heart turns a corner of Neal's Yard, clutching her herbs.

'Bless me! Is there a woman who don't have the eyes for thee around here?'

'That lady did call about her sick relative.'

'And my last job was a nun!'

'We were speaking of homes for orphans, madam.' Either that or she must leave the child in a rich parish where it would be farmed out to the countryside to be fed.

The whore is grinning. 'That one has a sickness in her blessed heart for thee I dare say.'

Jeremiah raises his eyes to the small, almost peculiar shaped space of sky above the Yard. Hope, he thinks, is no more or less blinding than the effects of gin. 'I hear there is to open a foundling hospital in Coram's Fields.'

'You misunderstand me indeed. No one is going decide for me, Mister Potticary. This one will be different. Special. Mothers have that sense about their children. He's my twelfth so I should know and the rest were all a waste of nine bleeding months. But this one—I was thinking something grand like William, or George after our king.' She strokes the sleeping child. 'This one has special things coming to him Mister Potticary. You wait and see.'

Jeremiah takes a deep breath of dismal London air. He pats the baby's head. '*Waiting,* alas, I cannot guarantee.'

He bows and strides back across the yard, past the astronomer's shop where Mr Ludwell stands in the doorway, smoking his pipe.

'Day and night she comes to watch you, Mr Goode. That street woman watches your shop, like the moon watching this Earth.'

Jeremiah takes in forlorn expression on Mr Ludwell's shoulder. 'You will not see her again around here,' he offers, adding, 'Are you quite all right, Mr Ludwell?'

'Indeed. All things must die. Death is written in the stars since the day we are born. And with Pluto's convergence on Saturn—'

'I beg pardon?' Jeremiah says, unable to read any ill-health in the man's body.

'I shall be dead afore winter is through. As soon as Saturn enters the fray, which it always does, I shall be off beyond the celestial bodies o'er our heads. In the end, Saturn one can depend upon, if nothing else, Mr Goode. If nothing else. Death and Saturn one can depend upon.'

235

He senses the man's loneliness. But loneliness is a luxury for most of this parish, and, not in the mood for a proceeding lecture on the wrath of Saturn and the forbearance of Uranus, he enters his shop. In truth, he has had enough of Neal's Yard for an afternoon. Nonetheless 5 days away and situations have improved: 150 pounds of his debt paid off by the parish; Mrs Soloman walking to the top of her staircase and Miss Heart and Mrs Soloman happy on account of Miss Zeldin's tonic. Perhaps all that what required for his life to proceed with a modicum of success was his absence.

'Miss Heart's money, sir,' says Boswell as Jeremiah enters the shop. He hands across the counter a handful of gold coins. 'I bit each one and they all be honest, sir. Aren't you happy, sir? Five pound for two ha'penny bag of herbs. That's a profit to speak of! A generous woman be Miss Heart!'

'Having just been to Dorset in temperatures that would freeze a donkey's baubles for the woman's aunt, I believe it is the least I deserve.' His thoughts are occupied elsewhere. 'Now this time do not give it away. Give it to Mary for food, before we all starve.'

Jeremiah returns to his elaboratory. He's no fool. Rather, his three sisters have enlightened him on the subject of women and their ways. He is being bought like a carcass at market, but for what purpose he cannot determine. After all, there is a reward out for curing the old hag. But something else constricts his thoughts, like the gaols in one's head Miss Zeldin spoke about, like the prison once constructed by his father in which he must become a physician or else marry Lucy Aldridge.

He checks his pocket watch—an hour remaining of daylight (if the light in St Giles at any hour could be called daylight). Sitting at his desk he is troubled momentarily by the thought—the memory—of a kitten, something odd about its legs. The image fades and he opens the rest of his post. Wordsley's ball is next Saturday. Several bills from druggists, one from his persistent tailor and Mr Doodle the periwig maker who says he will take back Jeremiah's balding wig to reduce his bill. He scans through an old letter from Miss Heart discussing her aunt's improving health, the cold weather and wishing him a pleasant Hanukkah. The letter from his mother he reads with more care.

My Dearest Indigo,

After Christ's Mass your father was taken gravely ill. Dr Carmichael is not certain he shall stay much longer on this Earth. Suffice to say your father has dismissed his physician. We have all urged him to reconsider his actions and summon him back, or at the very least employ another for we fear that he suffers needlessly, but he is resolute and after much provocation has made a request: that you attend to him in his extremity, dear Indigo. I ask that you Please come urgently. See this as an opportunity to make amends. Come quickly and bring with you Anything that might alleviate his suffering.

Your loving,
Mother

Doubtless the only thing he is capable of doing to ease his father's suffering is to agree to marry Lucy Aldridge. Though perhaps there is something else. He brushes soot from his apothecary case, takes the key from his waistcoat and opens the drawer where the opium is still stored, distilled by Boswell in small vials and labelled in irregular script, 'Laudanum'. He takes the remaining bottles (several having been dispensed at the Rookery to the hopeless) and places them carefully inside his case.

In the direction of humiliation

The next morning by six Jeremiah sits at the dining table breaking his fast 2 hours early with bread and a small glass of beer. He misses butter. He misses cheese. He misses cold roast beef. Even a herring or two might brighten the loathing he has for crust after crust. One thing brings cheer: at least Mary has ceased forcing peasemeal, oatmeal, or any other Scottish food upon him.

He watches her blacken the grate. Today must have been washday; her hands are red and raw. He will offer her some horse chestnut before he leaves, to ward off the inevitable chilblains.

He dresses in his best coat—last worn to White's, stiff from a burgundy stain across one sleeve—and with his purse concealed in his breeches out of sight from the highwaymen, he is ready to depart for Dulwich. Having made a profession out of battling death with a carving knife, Jeremiah does

237

not expect his father to give up easily, anticipates several more callings to his bedside and plenty more bouts of ridicule. No doubt his mother had panicked when sending for him. Panic had always been something she still excelled at.

Boswell is stooped like an old man, cleaning the shop floor with a broken broom and a bucket full of sand. 'Going to see Mrs Soloman, sir?'

'No, my sick father.' Jeremiah sets down his case on the counter.

'About time, sir, if you do not mind me saying.'

'I shall take slippery elm and some horehound for his cough.'

'There is no horehound left.'

'Then some sage, there must be some sage and some peppermint too.'

'How about some lungwort, sir?'

'I have taught you well.' Though the newly distilled laudanum his father will appreciate more. Jeremiah dispensed the stuff freely at death but even at this juncture he had difficulty in believing in death's certainty. Death he preferred to see as punishment meted out by God for those who gave up easily, not something preordained or decided. The God who left souls to starve on the streets did not fret over such details. Nature intended life to be long. The instinct every man held in his breast was to live, not to suffer. Not to die.

Boswell hands him the packets, which he places in two inner pockets of his coat. He wonders whether his father will consume them, whether he cares whether he does or does not. Whether his father shall subsequently live or die he likewise dismisses along with the notion that to heal one's heart ought to be involved. His father had long ago destroyed any fond feelings in his son.

'On no account,' he tells Boswell, 'shall Manners enter this shop.'

The boy nods. He has shadows beneath his eyes. Recently, he has appeared older than his years. Perhaps he has more understanding of the situation than Jeremiah allows even himself to grasp.

'Look,' he says, in a tone of greater reassurance. 'look what miracles we have accomplished thus far!'

Boswell looks up but, perhaps seeing something amiss in Jeremiah's eye, quickly looks down again.

'Let us think of Manners as no more than a sickness in need of a Cure.'

'Aye,' says Boswell, buffing the counter with his sleeve. 'Shall I be collecting your debts while you are gone, sir?'

'You shall be doing little else. But take so much as a penny for yourself and I shall hear of it.'

Boswell's smooth skin unreadily frowns. 'Without this shop, sir I have no home. It does me no good to thieve from you, sir.'

It is obvious the boy is not considering pilfering but Jeremiah is struck by the boy's earnestness, by an outlook that does not belong in St Giles.

'You are the man of the house in my absence,' he says, 'You must take care of my elaboratory, of my domestic affairs.'

'Yes, sir.'

'So that one day perhaps this shall be yours.' A ridiculous sentiment for surely he saw his life expanding to accommodate more than his servants.

'I see, sir'

He attempts to loosen the boy's frown with a smile. 'And remember, Boswell…' 'Sir?'

'To be beholden to your wife upstairs!'

Boswell kicks the counter. 'She's not my wife—I tell thee! We work under this same roof, that is all, and I know you would not have me work at all should Mary become more than a maid to me. An apprentice must remain pure of mind and I want to be a good apprentice, sir and only a good apprentice so that I may one day serve, as you do, the people of St Giles for they are my people too.'

The boy wipes something invisible from his nose.

'Looking at you now,' says Jeremiah. 'I might mistake *you* for the angel around here.' Chiding formed the foundation of their relationship and was achieved with far more comfort than seriousness. 'Too bad, that I have seen you outside this shop.' He flicks the boy's head. 'And know *thee not to be of celestial origins!*'

He hands Boswell the keys to the drug cabinet and the shop door. Mary enters with a small parcel of food, which she hands Jeremiah. At Boswell she smiles sweetly.

'I shall not be gone long,' Jeremiah tells her raising his voice, wondering if Mary has yet adjusted to hearing his voice, wondering how can he leave a ship he must keep afloat? 'My father comprises tough mule hide. I have no

doubt he will live another fifty years. If Miss Heart happens to call tell her…
I shall visit her aunt upon my return. And above all guard my notes with
your life or I shall never complete my compendium.'

'I do not think that Mr Manners can read, sir,' says Boswell. 'He told me
that his employer, the bailiff, writes his notes.'

'Small blessings.'

Mary taps Boswell's shoulder. Her eyes look to his, heavy lidded
adoration.

Understanding Mary's subsequent swipe through the air Boswell says,
'Mary wants to write something for you, sir?'

Despite his impatience, Jeremiah nevertheless hands Mary a quill.
She writes slowly, the tip of her tongue pushed between lips as she etches
uncertain letters across the page.

'Names of sisters?' Jeremiah reads after she hands him the sheaf, 'They are
Violet, Rose and Blanche,' he tells her, unable to fathom Mary's need to know
such details. 'My brother is Jasper. I was christened with the name Indigo.'

Mary smiles, grabs hold of the quill again. She draws, as a child might
draw, the half-circles that comprise a rainbow.

Jeremiah laughs, concealing, he hopes, his embarrassment. 'My mother
longed for some colour in her life,' he says. *Who could blame her, married
to his father?* 'Fortunately,' he adds, 'I have left her familial rainbow. I am
Jeremiah now, not Indigo.'

Mary places a hand over lips, takes the quill again and draws a 'J' on the
page with a question mark.

'Jeremiah is my middle name. Also my grandfather's name.'

Boswell says, 'So Indigo is a colour?'

'Indigo is the colour blue. The very same colour your backside will be if
you mention this again.' Jeremiah puts on his hat. 'Now guard this shop with
your life. For it is all the worth I have left in the world.'

'I will…Indigo…sir.'

Mary makes the shape of a rainbow with her hands, still smiling.

Jeremiah turns his back and hurriedly departs. One of the worse mistakes
a man could make was divulging personal information to one's servants.

He opens his shop door, prepared for further humiliation. Without tact,
his father shall ridicule apothecaries as, 'Dispensers of drugs. Grocers, nothing

more, nothing less!' He shall remind Jeremiah that he will inherit *not a thing*, end his sermon by emphasising that becoming the most eminent physician-surgeon in the country did not come about by believing in *quackery*. Before leaving, Jeremiah will deposit his herbs at his bedside and depart feeling a little as if he had been dragged to Dulwich by his ankles.

But he is cheered by the prospect of seeing his three sisters and Jasper. He will enjoy being the centre of their attention, watching the smiles on their faces. He will spend time alone with his brother, dispensing certain herbs, easing his relentless guilt. He will consider asking his mother for a clandestine loan; will find too many excuses not to and in the end will find pride the best silencer. When he returns home he shall, for a few days, feel like a great coward.

Of course, his father might show respect to his son if he did not return like the prodigal son. They might converse as one man to another if he did not arrive filthy and smelling of the public coach. He might impress his father with his knowledge if he was not so rusty in the art of conversation, so easily drunk on wine. He might, in short, be treated as a man if he brought more than inferiority to the table. If he arrived in his own carriage with his purse full of gold, his father might regard him more than a thing to be ignored and wholly resented. But until such times, he must pull up his collar and go forth in the direction of humiliation.

He checks the laudanum is secure in his case and at the last moment rushes back to his elaboratory for his compendium, which he places on top of the vials. Then, holes in his stockings and mere pennies in his pocket he sets off for Dulwich too caught up in medicinal remedies to realise that he journeys with an open, earnest heart, that since Dorset, since Brigid, or even Tayo, resentment for his father has dissolved like a sugar pill in water. 'After exorcism,' said Brigid, 'comes deliverance.'

His sisters

Jeremiah boards the stagecoach from Gracechurch Street and gets off at the Crown Inn at Dulwich where his three sisters flock to inspect him.

'Look how thin you have got!'

'He forgets to eat, or else his maid forgets to feed him.'

'Look at those curls beneath his wig! Indigo, you need to shave your head!'

'Why is he dressed all in black?'

'He wears nothing but black these days!'

'He looks to be in mourning.'

'Perhaps he is mourning. Indigo, are you in mourning?'

'Of course he's not in mourning. He's an apothecary. They dress that way.'

'Why Father does not dress in black!'

'Father is not an apothecary, Blanche.'

'An apothecary, is that so very different from a physician?'

'So,' says Jeremiah, 'If you wish to know how I am fairing after several hours of travel in a filthy public coach, I am fine aside that is from the intolerable pain in my legs, my spine and my head.' Already, they were at the junction between apothecary and physician minutes after he had alighted at Dulwich.

'A month from now,' says Rose, taking his arm and leading him across the road. 'And we shall have you as fat as Cook's cat.'

'That may very well be but on the morrow I shall be returning to London.'

Faces alter, resettle and resume their natural expressions of curiosity softened by a ceaseless naivety.

'But you know that Father is terribly sick. You must know that,' says Violet squinting in the sunlight.

'More terribly sick than last week, Violet?'

'Much more,' says Blanche.

'So you *must* stay longer,' says Rose. She leans towards his ear as they approach the family's coach and four. 'Forgive him as God surely forgives you, Indigo.'

The diatribe is familiar. It is as if each sister has been given a script before his arrival and Rose, the oldest, will always be the first to include God.

'Remember,' she says settling like a swan on her eggs beside him in the carriage, 'he is dying and we have a God-bound duty to forgive the dying.'

Jeremiah looks out of the window towards the oak-lined avenue of Cox's Walk: the long, dark tunnel that leads to the house of his childhood. Unlike most tunnels, however, the light at the end remains burnt out.

'Should the dying likewise forgive?' Blanche, the youngest, the one most used to speaking her mind, the one most like her eldest brother.

'The dying,' he tells her, 'do very little else but die.'

'And will you watch?'

'I am here to prolong Father's life, Blanche, by whatever means possible. I have not come as an observer.'

Violet, the most beautiful and the most stubborn, crosses her arms. 'Well you would have done better to have come sooner!'

He stretches an arm and taps his sister's nose forgetting that Violet—that all three of his sisters—are grown women now. 'Whatever I do it is never good enough for you, dear Violet.' In fact, now they are grown, he is more driven to chiding them. 'I have to earn a living,' he professes. 'As men of little means must occasionally do so.'

Violet chin tilts towards the roof of the carriage. She sits, like his two other sisters, amongst mounds of linen, superfluous silk and froths of lace, accustomed to spending her time travelling in a padded carriage between drawing rooms. He envies them their ignorance.

'You do not seem to be taking Father's sickness with any seriousness.'

'If I were to believe in the seriousness of sickness, dear Violet, I might never rise in the morning. I would certainly not believe myself capable of enacting a Cure.'

'Do you believe in the life of the soul beyond the body?' asks Blanche.

He sits back, pondering the question, one he frequently chooses to ignore. 'Yes, I suppose in truth I do.'

'Then you must believe in ghosts?'

'I believe in ghosts who are sometimes confused with the living.'

'Living ghosts?'

'Lost souls.'

'Why are they lost? What is their purpose on earth if they are already dead?'

'I confess I do not know the answer. Perhaps to teach the living a lesson? Perhaps to learn? Perhaps even to help.'

'God forgive him,' whispers Rose performing the sign of the cross.

'Help the living?' says Blanche, 'But what help can the dead give to us, dear brother?'

'Perhaps they know not how to help themselves.'

'Blanche, there are no lost souls roaming this earth!' Violet says, turning on him with a warning glare.

'Come to St Giles,' he tells her, 'I shall show you plenty living-dead, enough to make you believe in the after-life existing on Earth.'

'I do not understand,' says Blanche.

'Stop upsetting her,' cries Violet.

'For heaven's sake Blanche is a grown woman. There are things of this world that it would do you no harm to know. To be fed, to be alive, not to be dying, you are luckier than most. Every day I leave my shop and meet children whose bones show through their clothes, who must work ten, eleven, twelve hours a day by the most unimaginable means to earn their crust. I see girls your age with children and no money to feed them. Entire families who must sleep in one insufficient bed in the clothes they are sewn into for the entire winter. This should not upset you, Violet; it should make you immeasurably grateful. Whilst you worry what pin to wear with what dress, what gloves fit with what cape, a woman your age somewhere in the most abysmal slums in London is afraid to close her eyes in case she never opens them again.'

Rose silently sobs. Violet clucks her tongue like a chicken.

'Do you speak of angels, Indigo, when you speak of lost souls,' asks Blanche.

Jeremiah smiles. 'I am not romantic enough to uphold a belief in angels, dear Blanche. As for Heaven I am not certain I go in for it either. Living in Hell has altered my opinions of the hereafter. Besides there is too much to preoccupy me in this life.'

'If Mother could hear you! Your lack of reverence she would find shameful.' Rose dabs her tears and performs the sign of the cross several times.

Blanche taps his knee with a conspiratorial smile. '"Do not be afraid," the angel says.'

'Shameful!' says Violet. 'You suffer in St Giles for your arrogance brother and your arrogance alone and because of your arrogance you cannot see that this is so.'

'What a veritable riddle my life has become!' He laughs too loudly before becoming quickly serious again. 'But then my name within this family has been *shame* for as long as I can remember and there seems to be little I can do about it. But tell me, Blanche, why are you preoccupied with the life of the soul? Is it that you fear for father's soul?'

Blanche's hangs her head.

'You do?' he asks, with ill-concealed amusement.

'Indigo!' warns Violet.

'Father has saved many lives,' Jeremiah tells her, with some reluctance. 'He is assured his place with God, of that you can depend.'

Blanche looks out of the window as the carriage wheels crunch over the gravel drive to Hall Court. She says, 'It is not father's soul I am concerned for.'

Death shall not reconcile us

In the Goode dining room, the mouldings on the duck-egg blue walls give the impression of being seated in a piece of Wedgwood pottery. A pair of elaborate chandeliers is reflected in a long sombre stretch of mahogany table: a present from the King of Denmark and Norway who had visited England in an attempt to marry his son to King George II's daughter, but more used to a secluded life, had fallen sick and was attended and promptly bled by the *eminent* Doctor Robert Goode. It is a room that appears quite perfect, until occasional bursts of sunlight cast the air as a frenzy of restless specks like fragments of its inhabitants' minds. In one corner a black and gold chinoiserie screen conceals a chamber pot behind which guests relieve themselves during the long meals over which Robert Goode had once presided, not as paid employer but as a man of considerable wealth.

Today the room is filled with the aroma of a suckling pig, an animal that sits in the centre of the table, an apple stuffed in its surprised jaw. Large bowls of potatoes steam in pots and swim in butter gravy. Jeremiah sits quietly salivating, resisting the urge to swipe a potato from the bowl and plop it into his mouth. After months of pease soup he is famished.

'We met Indigo from the coaching inn Father,' announces Rose, sitting to her father's left, to whom her eyes regularly dart.

'Apothecaries?' says Robert Goode, head lolling towards his soup bowl as he slurps from his spoon, 'they like to travel this way?'

Jeremiah slices through the blushed, roasted flesh, shoulders hunched. 'On occasion, Father.'

'It is to be expected, apothecaries being mere drug dispensers to the physicians. Pretensions toward physic, that is the art of the apothecary. But rest assured physicians are the ones to carry out God's work, least with any ability or dignity.'

'The poor, do they not deserve to be well too, Father?'

Robert Goode turns to his wife. 'What is he doing at our table, Mrs Goode? Who invited him?'

'If you remember, Mr Goode, you did request to see your eldest son again.'

'Then you must also remember an earlier wish that I had forbidden him to enter this house *ever* again!'

Anne Goode's eyes silently plead for civility. She clasps her hands before her as if in prayer. 'You have been very ill,' she says. 'You did request many times to see Indigo your…first born.'

'I did?'

'Many times, Mr Goode. You said you would like to make amends. You said that death was too final an act and that no decent play should even end in such a manner.'

'You did, you did!' Jasper cries, grappling with his cutlery as if he had never previously held such items. '*You did!*'

Jeremiah smiles. His brother smiles back and thoughts surface as they always do: *What did I do to you?*

'The ranting of a man in the midst of fever are to be ignored, Mrs Goode. Have I not told you this many a time afore?'

'Indeed Mr Goode but Dr Green did say it was more than mere fever, Mr Goode.'

'I have been working too hard. That is all. I need rest, recuperation, and I shall be out healing patients again as I ought. No man should neglect his duties for long and no man is less forgiven for neglecting his duties than a physician.'

Anne Goode turns to her eldest son an earnest hand pressed to her breast. 'Please Indigo, pass the potatoes.'

Jeremiah passes them as he studies his father whose attention is now given to his bowl of soup as if there were live, wriggling creatures within it that must be killed. Robert Goode, the great and eminent physician (degree from Cambridge, Royal College of Physicians, Company of Barber-Surgeons), a man whose philosophies went beyond Descartes and a follower of Stahl, a man who advocated blood-letting at every opportunity, sits at his dining table steadily dribbling. 'This,' he had told Jeremiah frequently, taking out his case of brass blood letting devices: the tourniquet, the stick gripped to dilate a patient's veins and the red and white pole much advertised by Barbers, 'This, forms the backbone upon which the flesh of medicine hangs. No bloodletting: no Cure!' When it came to administering drugs, Doctor Robert Goode adhered to Hoffman's beliefs: preferring sedatives and irritating stimulants. Otherwise at all other opportunities he freely sliced the body open or else amputated. A lower leg he could remove in less than three minutes. For many years Jeremiah had tried admiring this man.

'Are you attending church?' asks Anne Goode, as her husband falls into rhythmic slurps.

'Rarely, Mother.'

'Pray tell, why ever not?'

Jeremiah drops a potato into his mouth, wipes his mouth on the back of his hand. 'On the Sabbath I like to sleep.'

'Sleep? St Giles-in-the-fields, is it not a God-fearing parish?'

Jasper scores the armrests of his high backed wheelchair with his knife, staring at the ceiling. He regards the air with curiosity so that Jeremiah wonders whether he sees severed family ties streaming upon invisible currents.

Jeremiah helps himself to more potatoes, piling his plate high: his hunger fortunately lying beyond guilt. 'There is plenty to fear in my parish, Mother, but as to whether people fear God...' He pushes a piece of meat into his mouth with his fingers, licks the grease from beneath overgrown, blackened fingernails whilst his mother looks on wide-eyed, horrified, '... well that I cannot say.'

His mother blinks back something into the recesses of her soul. Her voice cracks. She clear her throat and begins again. 'You speak like a heathen. I can barely believe my own ears.' She whispers, 'My own son. Is it common for those living in London to live so... so irregularly?'

'Secularly and lamentably conspicuous. Believe me, Mother, I could tell far worse. Last week a father cut off his son's leg after he was hit by a carriage.' He rips flesh from the bone. 'They could not afford the surgeon's bill.'

Anne Goode stares at the ornate swirls on the ceiling above her head. Her gaze flicks towards her husband, still intent on his soup. 'Your thoughts have become corrupted,' she says. 'I fear for my own son for he now possesses the mind of a common heathen!'

'He teases,' says Violet throwing Jeremiah a glare. 'That is all, Mama.'

'I do not tease, Violet. Poor people are expected to live without proper protection from the law as they are expected to live without medicine when sick. If they suffer some form of abuse then they must put up with it. If the crime they commit involves a rich person, however, they will be quickly punished but if they are dying then they must simply do so without inconvenience. What the rich do not know, what they do not want to see, is that the poor suffer through no fault of their own. They suffer simply because they are born.'

'Stop upsetting your mother,' says Robert Goode.

'Tease, tease, tease!' says Jasper knocking his wine glass to the floor, a lurid stain spreading across the cloth. '*Tease is what we do when the juice runs dry. Tease is what we do when we just can't cry.*'

His mother summons the maid, who she instructs to strip the table. Enlivened by her ability to ward off this descent into calamity, by the fact a clean table cloth usually does the trick, she turns her attention to Jeremiah. 'St Giles has altered you,' she says, her tone hushed. 'I fear you are not the Indigo I remember but have become a man whose origins are quite unfamiliar.'

'You are perhaps right,' he replies.

'Your manner is brusquer. Besides which you are looking too thin, far too thin.'

'On account of eating too little.'

'The Lord answers our every need if we only surrender ourselves to his will.'

'Doubtless I have surrendered to something.'

'You must seek His salvation.'

'St Giles, Mama, is a place of lost souls,' whispers Blanche.

'Do not encourage him, Blanche!'

'But it is true, Mama. Indigo's parish is befallen by poverty, which makes the parishioners believe themselves to be neglected by God and they have relinquished all belief in Salvation. Is that not right, dear Brother?'

Jeremiah casts a look to his father still slurping then he presses a finger to his lip. 'Perhaps,' he says. 'But let us not speak of it now, Blanche.'

'*Tick-tock, tick-tock. Time never stops*,' says Jasper, thumping his knife against the now cloth-less table.

'Who gave that boy cutlery? And wine! What does the boy want with wine?' His father points a finger at Jasper. 'And since when has he started eating at *this* table?'

Jeremiah takes several mouthfuls from his own glass, watching as his mother wrestles the knife from Jasper's clasp. Of course he is not a boy but a man of one and thirty trapped for all his days in the mind of a child.

Jeremiah wipes his mouth. 'I have brought some herbs for you, Father.'

'What for?' his father grunts.

'A combination I have found effective in the treatment of consumption.'

'Why? Why would I want something you had to offer? Have I been rendered a lunatic by sickness?'

Jeremiah takes a deep breath, a hand moves involuntarily to the stem of his wine glass. 'I believe I can return you to health again, Father, to you former self.' He sounds unconvincing even to himself. How can he cure when his heart is not committed?

His father narrows his eyes. 'You have harmed this family enough. Caused enough agony. You are but a great storm thrashing through our lives! Leave us be I tell you!'

The silence is absolute so that the recklessly swirling dust specks can almost be heard. Nobody moves. A log hisses upon the fire. A candle drips upon the unblemished cloth. Jeremiah forgets to breathe.

After an eternity, Robert Goode sets down his soup spoon and raises himself up on his knuckles. 'You have done more harm than a lifetime can cure, Indigo Samuel Jeremiah Goode. I ought to have disowned you long ago. Instead I gave you a chance of redemption. And what did you do? Decline all opportunity to restore respectability to this family with a suitable marriage, shaming us all over again! And now you dare to drink wine and eat food at our table. If father's had rights to transport their sons I would have put you on a ship bound to the America Colonies long ago!'

He falls back against his chair, head lolling to one side. Rose rushes forwards to wipe soup from his beard as Robert Goode makes growling sounds. Rose fusses for a time and all the while the tall mantle clock ticks on and on like a death march.

But Jeremiah is at least drunk again. He sets down his cutlery and lets his mind seek escape. He recollects recipes, a particular recipe—one he had never used—involving a human brain; a medicinal substance used by ancient Egyptians, recorded in the *Papyrus Ebers*. This *Golden Water* involved beating to a pulp the brain of a man who had met with a violent death. Tile flowers, peony, betony, black cherries, lavender and lily, yes lily, added in equal measure. He forgets, in the fug of wine, the point to such a tonic…

'What do you have to say for yourself?' his father is saying.

He clears his throat says, 'Death shall not reconcile us then, Father.' This released as a statement free from emphasis as much as of hatred. 'I do not love Lucy, not as lovers love one another.'

'Love?' his father's brows hang low over his eyes, '*Love*? What does love matter anyway but to stable boys?'

Anne Goode clears her throat. 'Snow is soon on its way, so I hear.'

'Snow, Mama?' Rose retreats to her seat.

'That's right, coming from the west.'

'Surely it shall be milder by the time it reaches Dulwich, Mama?'

'Stable boys look for meaning behind procreation.' His father picks up his spoon. 'But gentlemen understand the true purpose behind wedlock. You, you understand nothing of it. You not only show a total disregard for your family but indeed any regard toward convention whatsoever!' Expulsions of air rack Robert Goode's body. The spoon sinks into his soup. Rose offers some wine but he shoos her away with a flick of the wrist. 'How long Mrs Goode?' he asks.

'Mr Goode?'

'How long is he to remain here?'

'Well…' begins his mother pressing a hand to her heart.

'I said *how long*, Mrs Goode?'

Jeremiah looks to the pool of blood on his plate, swirling amongst the meat.

Anne Goode clasps a hand to her throat. 'Indigo has come…well he has come—'

'I shall depart after lunch, Mother. I shall leave some herbs before I go.'

'Leave nothing!' Robert Goode lapses into a choking fit that renders him too weak to resist further help. Aided by two house maids, Rose lifts him from his seat and helps carry his frail body from the room, each footfall accompanied by the thwack of a cane and with each strike Jeremiah's shoulder performs another, more violent flinch.

'He means no harm,' says his mother as the ticking of the cane fades. 'He is very sick.'

'He ought to be in bed,' says Jeremiah, relishing the difference in the air, now that his father is absent.

His mother dabs her nose with her kerchief. 'I wanted us to have this dinner together for I fear it might be the last.' A smile lifts his her lips. She brightens. 'Did you see how Jasper has been getting along well with his cutlery, Indigo?'

Jeremiah looks to the scored armrests and to his brother now squashing a potato with the back of his soupspoon. 'When did he last go abroad?'

A look passes between Violet and his mother.

'I ask when did he last leave this house, Mother?'

'We—not any one of us—possesses the strength to push his chair,' says Violet.

'Could Collins not assist? Does Jasper not attend church?'

Jasper whacks the arms of his chair with his fists. 'Church,' he says, 'church, church is for birds. Birds with beaks.'

'In church he talks too much,' says Violet.

'Silence disturbs him,' says Rose.

Jasper continues squashing his potato with the back of his spoon.

'He brought father grave humiliation,' amends Blanche. She leans towards him. 'He dashed to the altar during one of the reverend's dulls sermons, ranting about the Ten Commandments and why Moses wore a dress and not breeches,' She pulls a flat smile, as if it is the only way by which she can control her speech and says, 'He has not been allowed out since then.'

'When was this?' Jeremiah takes in Jasper's pale skin, his neglected hair hanging mid-way along his spine, tied hastily in a forlorn-looking tail. He shakes his head.

'A year ago.' Violet bites her lip. 'Perhaps longer.'

'Mother?' asks Jeremiah.

'I…I was not aware it had been that long.'

Jasper and a litter of cats

The entrance to his brother's bedchamber on the ground floor is hidden in panelling behind the staircase. From the corner of the house it overlooks the lawns and a large spruce: a tree that is little altered since their childhood. In the distance, above woodland, is the chapel tower of Dulwich College: a school for poor scholars, it's peak replicated many times upon Jasper's walls amongst other drawings: churches, cathedrals, ruined abbeys, mansions, monuments, all faithfully replicated to the last gargoyle. Certain of them are drawn from different angles or broken down into their constituent parts. But all, without exception, are drawn in black ink. Not a smidgeon of colour to be found.

Jasper, who is sitting in his chair gazing out at the window, turns when Jeremiah enters. Jeremiah senses the usual emptiness in his brother's head; happiness in particular an alien emotion. Prone to violent fits of temper, Jasper is more familiar with scowling, screeching or howling like a hound, but when it comes to expressing love or joy he seems to inhabit a persistent state of apathy.

'No smile for your brother?' Jeremiah teases, unable to alter his character even for his brother but any chiding will be recompensed with it a pound of herbs on these too infrequent and often furtive visits home. 'No brotherly embrace?' he asks.

Jasper taps his lip impatiently with a forefinger.

'I take that to be your "no".' Jeremiah examines some fresh drawings: recognises parish church, the Langley's house, St Paul's cathedral: five different drawings of its dome. 'I thought we should take some air,' he says.

'You may walk or I shall push you in your chair. Perhaps you should like to draw something?'

Jasper at last acknowledges him, nodding with exaggerated child-like nods.

'I see there is not a picture of the coach house on your walls.' No pictures either of this house, but then what prisoner wishes to pay reverence to his gaol?

Jasper shakes his head again. As always, searching beyond the blankness is akin to seeking scratches in a solid marble surface. Yet, as always, Jeremiah sees his own features faithfully copied: the same dark curls, blue eyes and thick lashes: the image, or so they are told, of their maternal grandmother. Was it any wonder his father's hatred had turned towards Jasper?

In the yard Collins—now an old man—wears a chemise, sleeves rolled, despite the frost still lying on the ground. He drops a sheaf of straw and salutes, veins and sinew proud upon his forearms.

'Master Goode,' he says, with a firm but discreet nod of the head. He is not pleased to see Jeremiah, cannot bring himself round to trust him again even after all these years.

'I have a new job for you,' Jeremiah tells him once various pleasantries have been exchanged. 'Jasper is to receive fresh air twice a day. He is also to attend church. You must lift him in the landau. Are you able?'

'Aye, sir,' says Collins, with a thin smile.

'And if there is a particular place that he wishes to draw, you must take him there.'

Collins wipes his brow with the back of his hand. 'Very well, sir.'

Jeremiah senses a change in the man's attitude towards him. No doubt Collins expects him to become head of the household now. What he cannot know is Jeremiah would as sooner sell his own teeth than step into Dulwich Society.

Jasper draws whilst Jeremiah sits on an upturned bucket, tilting his face towards the sun. Jeremiah believes wholeheartedly in the miraculous power of sunlight, even weak winter sunlight. He has seen bow-legged children walk with legs straightened after recommending mothers to take their offspring out of their hovels and into the light. He has seen the elderly regain the use of stiffened limbs after a good and constant dose and people of all ages rekindle an appetite of food. He has also found it to be a good cure-all for melancholy, as good as *chase-devil*, as good a cure as lying with a whore once was. However, there are many things that Mr James taught him which he must administer with care for fear of a recommendation to Bedlam yet his views on sunlight he has never been afraid to preach. The sun cures, of this he has no doubt.

Jasper draws in silence, absorbed as each dash upon the page is assigned to memory so that later he will reproduce the building with fanatic faith. Yet only buildings interest his brother and buildings alone, not the prettiness of a flowers or the unpredictable mass of a person's body. His studies encompass only the inanimate. Never the living.

After a time, Jeremiah yawns, pulls his coat together and stretches horizontally across two bales of rough straw. Later today he must visit Lucy to pay his respects to her father, humble himself before her obvious beauty. Staring up at the mounds of cloud above his head, he can already feel the expectations of Dulwich Society pressing into his bones.

'What do you remember?' he asks.

Jasper glances up, then quickly back at the page.

'Do you remember any of it? Did a splash of water alter you so completely?'

No doubt his mother is right: St Giles had loosened his tongue. 'Very well,' he says, 'Answer me this. Was it my fault?'

In the pause he can make out the grinding of a horse's jaw and the pounding of the blood in his ears. He cups his face in his hands.

'Cat!' says Jasper a smile crossing his lips.

'I apologise.'

Jeremiah follows his brother's gaze to the stable cat: black, nimble, clever-looking. The creature presses its body against Jeremiah's legs. He absentmindedly strokes her fur, running his fingers through the dusty coat. Jasper stretches his hand out and the cat twirls in and out of his legs, inert on the step of the wheelchair.

When they were children, he remembers at once, they had once found a litter of cats in a stable; a fat tabby amongst the mass of writhing fur. His sisters, their dresses spread out across the dusty straw, had selected their favourites, named them: Blackie, Tiger, Fluff—commonplace names. Jeremiah guessed which one would consume the most rats. Then the clap of hands scattered his sisters like pheasants at a pistol shot as Robert Goode stood silhouetted at the stable door. He examined the cats, stooping low to select the smallest like a vulture swiping its pray, choosing the one that Blanche moments before had named Tiny. He picked it up by the end of its insufficient tail. As his father left the stable with it, Jeremiah saw that it had but two limbs. Later, he found the creature on the muckheap, a raven avidly pecking out the remains of its eyes. Jeremiah flailed his arms at the bird then picked up a stick and prodded the spaces where the cat's limbs ought to be. It was still breathing.

Opening his eyes, Jeremiah is relieved to find Jasper sitting very upright in his wheelchair. He sits inert aside from the frantic scratching of quill upon page. The yard remains cast in a tint of red light as his eyes to adjust. He waits for his mind to pick apart memories from life; sifting them like chaff from grain, though which represents the chaff and which the grain he cannot always be sure. He knows only one thing: losing his grip upon the present always unsettles him.

'Why do you not come and live with me, Jasper? There is a room you can use as your own.'

His brother kicks the cat in the gut.

'Let me arrange my affairs. In one year from now you can come and live in St Giles. From a room in the attic it is possible to glimpse dozens of rooftops and spires. You could accompany me to the Physic Garden. I could teach you about plants, how to draw them. You might work with me in my shop.'

Jasper frowns.

'Would you not like that, my brother?'

Jasper shakes his head.

'You will not let me show you something of life beyond the walls of this garden?'

Jasper shakes his head more vigorously this time and unable to determine where his guilt ends and love begins, Jeremiah can do little other than abandon the subject. It is perhaps too late for amends and, occasionally, he fears he might read more into his brother than is even there.

'You are right. I can barely keep two servants. If I am sent to debtors' prison—well, there will be no home to speak of.'

'Prison,' repeats Jasper, kicking the cat, sending him scampering.

'This, dear brother, this home…' Jeremiah gestures towards the grey house looming behind and perched some way up the hill. 'This life of leisure serves as padding from the sharpness of existence lying beyond these boundary walls. Father believed I was to grasp at opportunities presented to me, not shun them like some over-indulged child. But it is too late now. So far am I down the scraggly path to Hell that I could not hoist myself up even if both arms were comprised of iron. As children we do not know our own fortunes. As adults we preoccupy ourselves with finding them again, but I am certain that we end our days searching…' He talks waiting for Jasper to meet his eye, but when Jasper eventually looks up, he cups his chin in his palm. A stranger looking at the two men might be forgiven for thinking he was listening to Jeremiah. But he knows better than to wait for a reply, least one of any sense. He talks as if speaking to the looking glass. Invariably Jasper's eyes reflect Jeremiah's misgivings, his errors—there are plenty—and sometimes he feels the distance between him and his self-contained brother is not so great after all.

'But why do I tell you this?' he says stretching out, 'we each have our own woes to alone surmount. Every man is given by God that which he is able to withstand. It would seem he has not come up with a new means of testing our faith, though I for one wish that he would.'

The sun slips behind a cloud, leaving winter in its wake.

'No more Lampblack ink?'

Jasper shakes his head. Jeremiah ruffles his brother's lank hair, looking at the image of the coach house almost complete aside from the plants.

'Then that is perhaps enough for one day.' Jeremiah gets up, loosens the brake on the chair. 'Life is not living without ink, is it not?' He turns Jasper towards the house. 'I used to feel the same about plants before—'

Abruptly, the stable cat cuts across their path so that Jeremiah has to sharply turn the chair to avoid hitting the creature.

'Cat!' says Jasper in delight. 'Cat, cat, cat!'

'Cat!' Jeremiah replies but for a brief moment he sees not the cat but an image of Brigid Zeldin, cape billowing. He shakes his head and the cat disappears beneath a stable door and he pushes Jasper towards home.

A chance to redeem yourself

Before supper, Jeremiah makes the visit he knows he must make. Lucy Aldridge sits on a chaise longue sniffing a small bouquet of flowers, black fabric stark against her pale flesh which is draped here and there with pearls. She smiles, sweetly, head tilted to flatter her features. An English rose. Her entire purpose to be admired.

'Mr Goode!' she remains seated extending her hand, angling her head and forcing him to kneel before her in order to kiss it. 'How lovely of you to come.'

He emphasises that he has come to express his regret at the death of her father. She dabs her nose. 'A pity you could not come earlier.'

'Forgive me.' He drops to a footstool. 'Your mother, how is she?'

'Taking the waters at Bath. She will be happier knowing you have called. You are still…working?'

'For my sins.'

'You have heard about George?' Her forehead puckers as if snagged by a fine thread.

'I hear very little these days.'

'You are funny, Mr Goode. Well, George wishes to travel to the Americas to work for Uncle's shipping company. He is terribly determined you know.'

'Then I am certain he will meet with success in the Americas.' There is only so much concern he can muster for a brother now worth several hundred thousand, whose pomposity anyhow shielded him from most of life's adversities.

'The Americas are wretched! Besides Papa's wished for George to oversee his estates. There is nobody else. Least nobody we can trust.'

'Nobody,' he says, hopelessness creeping into his tone.

'You understand we require someone we can *implicitly* trust.'

'Your sisters?'

'Neither is married but that is another story entirely. Of course, it would require a well-bred, modest man. One not afraid of…well,' Her mouth wrestles with the word, '…work.'

He regards her cautiously. 'I am certain your family will only attract such gentlemen.'

'Flattery was always your *forté*, Mr Goode.' She plucks off the last petal from a daisy. 'But it is a pity that you have become so terribly…ambitious. I do not remember you being so.'

She blushes yet it is all too obvious: she is the cat, he the disadvantaged mouse. 'You impart lustre to something quite dull, Miss Aldridge. I have a trade, nothing more, but I cannot abandon it.'

Abandon: as if his shop was a ship and he its captain.

Lucy leans forwards, her eyes glowing a bright, clandestine amber. 'Well, Mr Goode, that might not be entirely necessary. I have my own income now as well as…' Her gaze momentarily drops to the floor in an affectation of coyness, coy not coming naturally to a woman half of Society now revered '…my dowry.'

Four years have passed since they last met. *Four years!* Without doubt she remains beautiful but with a beauty that reminds him of a pretty vase; an empty vessel occasionally made more attractive by its adornments. He sits on his heels partly dumfounded as Lucy crosses the room to perch at the harpsichord.

'You did not reply to my last letter.'

Shame is unexpected. 'I have been busy, I apologise.'

'We are all busy, Mr Goode,' she says, commencing a piece by Haydn. 'But does that give us permission to neglect those that are close to us?'

'Granted,' he unwillingly agrees. He sits before Lucy, a failure. Yet despite the threat of gaol, the loss of everything earned over 11 years he still cannot bring himself to accept her proposal for underlying his stubbornness is the most enormous need to declare, LUCY, I AM IN LOVE WITH ANOTHER!

She finishes her piece on the harpsichord and returns to the chaise longue, head provocatively tipped. 'Stay for supper, Indigo.'

'I am expected back home.' He stares vacantly at her décolletage, at the seven familiarly feckless freckles as he considers what he knows he ought not to consider. It would be easy. He could recommence where he left off. Year upon year society only stagnated. He could forget that he had seen more disease than Lucy would see in a 100 lives; forget all the people he had known living no better than rats; forget this instinct to diagnose, to cure, to help the unfortunate. In time he might even forget that a life without plants was one without meaning, or that a beautiful woman living in deepest Dorset enthralled him.

Lucy picks plucks the petals from her posy. 'When George told me that he wanted to work for our uncle, I said that it did not matter what a gentleman did, so long as it is done well. Do you not agree, Mr Goode?'

She mocks him. She has heard of his failures in St Giles. She is the cat holding up the mouse by the tip of its tail. He runs his eyes along her bosom and her excessive skirts, coming to rest on the tip of one slipper.

'Alas, I do not agree, Miss Aldridge,' he says, thinking how she has changed, how her life in society had replaced any remaining tenderness in her with the shallowness of greed.

'No?' She fans herself with the flowers. 'A terrible pity.'

He looks out of the stone mullion windows where he can see the maze, the orangery beyond. In a leaden sky a lone gull is swept up by currents towards London. Towards freedom.

'Sometimes purpose is thrust upon one,' he says, surprised at how incapable he sounds.

'So dramatic, Mr Goode. The trouble is—' She leans forwards, tickles the end of his nose with the flowers so that he wonders whether such a woman knows the meaning of *trouble*. 'The trouble is you have become so terribly serious!' Her laughter ridiculously high-pitched, scratches at his ears.

'Serious?'

'Yes, serious! But now you are here, Mr Goode, perhaps you might enlighten me about a lotion I wish to purchase. I am told all the apothecary shops in London are selling it. They say it is guaranteed to preserve one's beauty indefinitely. Not *Persian Handkerchief* but something infinitely more effective. How tired I am of wearing *Ceruse*. Oh, its taste is so bitter it nauseates me so.'

'The main ingredient is lead,' he tells her, fearing this to be yet another trap.

'I see you do not go in for it. But then your handsomeness, Mr Goode, is something that ought never to be concealed.' She sighs loudly, falling back on the couch, fanning her face, tinged with colour that is not derived from any apothecary's lotion . 'Such a terrible pity.'

If one's feelings are entirely absent

'Indigo you are covered in mud. Even your hat is muddied!'

'Leave my hat be. Mud will not harm a man.'

'We heard you called upon Lucy Aldridge,' says Violet.

He removes the sacking from his shoes. 'You know being watched is too much for a grown man to bear.'

'Grown?' Violet slouches over the banister. 'Surely not?'

'Lucy, how is she faring?' asks Rose, helping to remove his coat.

'As well as to be expected.'

'Grief much alleviated by her enhanced income?'

'Violet!' says Rose, shooting her a glare. 'You must learn not to tarnish another with your brush.'

Jeremiah throws the soiled sacking to the floor. He has had enough of Lucy for a day, perhaps a lifetime.

'Shall you marry her, Indigo?'

'Never. Why do you ask, Blanche?'

'Mama and Mrs Aldridge were talking outside church. A suitable match they said.'

'You imagined it,' says Rose, 'In heaven's name why would Lucy Aldridge consider a proposal from Indigo when he has kept her waiting for too long? Besides, I hear there is another courting her.'

'None as unique as our Indigo! I am certain of what I heard, but of more importance to our brother is that Lucy bores him.'

'Bores him!' says Violet, 'Bores him, on fifteen hundred a year? Really Blanche. And you would do well to remember we must honour our parents, Blanche. We are all duty bound to secure good marriages, even Indigo, though perhaps he has forgotten such a thing living where he lives.'

Blanche looks at him with indignity flaming her cheeks. 'Or perhaps Indigo has received less generous attentions from father than us.'

Jeremiah nods, smiling as Blanche as always defends him.

'Besides, not everyone places income over feeling, Violet.'

'Feelings are nothing but troublesome,' says Rose.

'Not,' interrupts Jeremiah, 'if one's feelings are entirely absent to begin with. But enough! I must see father before I depart.'

'Depart? For London? So soon?' says Blanche, gripping his arm.

260

'I have a sick patient to treat who may, if I manage to Cure her, earn me a great deal of necessary money.'

'There!' says Violet, 'Jeremiah only professes to have high morals when it suits him. He is as much motivated by money as the next.'

A vision of gaol occurs and Jeremiah cannot defend himself. He cannot mention this possible fate to his sisters. He cannot confirm that he is a bigger failure in business than they conceive him to be in love.

'I am Jeremiah,' he tells them flatly, 'Not Indigo. I left his infernal familial rainbow long ago!'

Still time to repent

Rose takes his arm and whisks him up the staircase; past disagreeable glares from the paintings of past relatives, and along the creaking corridor to his father's bedchamber. 'He has taken a turn for the worse,' she says.

'No doubt I am the cause.'

'Please Indigo, see it as your chance of redemption?' she whispers, urging him inside. 'A God-given last opportunity.'

Several candles illuminate the room and the shadows flicker and stretch. The drapes are drawn aside from one window flung obtusely open. Jeremiah would expect no less from a man who administered icy baths to strengthen his children's livers, who made them sleep in unheated rooms without bedpan or thick blankets in the midst of winter. Jeremiah's baths are these days carried out in scolding hot waters as a rare concession to household comfort. As to the lack of warmth in his own home, he shall never grow used to it.

Crossing the Aubusson rug, a present from the French Ambassador (whose gangrenous toes his father had once sliced off in their entirety) he notices his mother before the open window, head bent to her sewing. Sunlight catches the silver in her hair. His father is propped up in bed reading a book. Jeremiah approaches, hands clasped behind his back as he attempts to cloak himself—*arm himself*—with a profession, however insignificant his father may deem it.

'What do you want?' Robert Goode asks, not looking up. 'Have you not a shop you must manage?'

'Few enter my shop these days for it has been a cold winter. Most of St Giles are now starving. I attend to as many as I can.'

'Poverty is like the plague. It spreads too quickly.'

His father always did possess the skill of seeing straight to a problem.

'I came here, Father,' Jeremiah looks at his well-worn shoes, 'to Cure you.'

'Your mother wanted you here.'

His father reads the Bible. He is not a man given to reading scripture. Perhaps, he is dying after all.

Jeremiah looks towards the rug. 'Because you remain my father.'

'In name alone. So say what you must and then leave.'

'I have asked for Collins to help with Jasper's chair. It would benefit him greatly to go abroad.'

A small, irrelevant cloud of dust is sent into the air as his father slams his book shut.

'One son shaming me, is that not enough?'

'Jasper possesses a love of architecture. He has a need—'

'His damn' needs are that of a baby. What does a baby remember of its teeth cutting? Your brother will die remembering precious nothing of his life.'

Jeremiah thinks of Jasper's drawings, the intricate details, how he remembers them all, year after year.

'And before you say it: he has a mind for buildings, but rest assured it accommodates little else. Your mother has spent days seeking his affections. Wasted days for Jasper thinks only of architecture. Is that not right. Mrs Goode?'

'Indeed, Mr Goode,' his mother replies, stabbing at the fabric with her needle.

'Jasper cares only for his own needs. The rest of the world might not exist. But for Jasper's faults we know where to apportion blame.' He chokes. Jeremiah offers tea but is waved away.

'I brought these,' he says, holding up the herbs, 'Lung-wort for the shortness of breath and—'

'Keep your damned herbs!'

'You are taking a physician's drug?'

'I am being bled by Doctor Littleton. Or was.'

The methods of one physician were much the same as the next. 'How frequently?'

'Daily.'

Then this is the reason why his father appears weak. 'Too often,' he says. 'You are too weak to be bled.' Bleeding, failed all in the end for physicians took from the body the very thing it needed to thrive.

'Did I ask your advice?'

Jeremiah glances from his father to his mother, knows he shall only rile his father's blood if he stays. 'I must leave for London.'

'That's right. Get back to your quackery. You are an upstart who cares nothing for abstract book-learning, that much you have demonstrated.'

'I must leave to see a patient of some wealth in Chelsea.'

'If she has wealth, what would she want seeking the advice of an apothecary over a physician?' His father slaps his hand against the cover of his Bible. 'An apothecary's role is to dispense drugs to physicians? Nothing more. You have as much knowledge and right to heal as a witch.'

How many times has he been told this and yet he still stands here like a fly buzzing relentlessly against a windowpane that never gives.

'Physicians have failed this lady,' he says, tone more than a little provocative. But despite his father's sickness, something presses him to say more. 'As you know I do not go in for fashionable pills, those containing arsenic and mercury. Cure operates through understanding the individual, through understanding the nature of plants. Modern methods treat the disease, not the person. If modern physic concentrated its efforts less on the capabilities of a drug and more on the patient's maladies then sicknesses might be Cured.'

'Your father has talked enough.' His mother sets down her sewing and approaches the bed. 'He must rest now. Leave him be, Indigo.'

'Mrs Goode, I have not finished,' his father says shaking his sagging, sallow face, 'A person employs an apothecary over a physician on account...' He coughs, splutters, '...on account of not having the guineas. As to who seeks the advice of an apothecary: only the poor or the gullible. In the kingdom of the blind, the man with sight is king, as you perhaps are aware of living in St Giles. No doubt it has given you self-importance but I can tell you this, none is due! Now, I know what death is and I know I am dying though it is a fact to be kept from your sisters. Thus you have little time left in which to repent. Do you hear?'

Jeremiah bows his head to where a thin slither of daylight cuts across the boards. 'Repent?'

'That is what I said.'

'You will forgive me, Father?' His voice cracks theatrically like a boy's. A grown man who cannot look up for fear of meeting the ridicule in his father's eye.

'If your actions demonstrate your desire to repent, yes, I am.'

Jeremiah waits for the world to make sense again. Are the burdens of his father's disappointments not great immovable rocks after all? How long he has waited to hear such words.

'Mrs Aldridge is concerned for her estate,' his father continues. 'She requires someone to run the land, to oversee collection of rent. They require a man they can trust.'

'But I know nothing of running an estate.'

'You will learn. As the husband of the Aldridge girl you will have plenty of time. And, from what I understand, there is money enough to allow for mistakes.'

Jeremiah tugs at his cuffs. 'You still wish for me to marry Lucy, after all this time?'

'It is not a wish, more an order. My physician gives me a month to live. Might I die and leave one capable son upon this earth?'

Jeremiah draws himself tall. In his mind's eye he sees a prison cell, its bars, hears the clank of heavy keys turning in locks. 'You will give me the opportunity to consider your offer?'

His father's eyes slip shut. 'You have until you leave.'

Aged five or thereabouts, Jeremiah assembles into piles his collection of wild flowers collected from the meadow. Jasper hobbles about the yard, his deformed foot causing him to frequently stumble and fall. Quickly tiring of playing alone, he snatches a handful of Jeremiah's flowers and tramples them underfoot laughing as he does so. Incensed, Jeremiah takes hold of Jasper's neck and forces his face into the bucket. He holds him beneath the surface until the boy ceases struggling. Afterwards, lungs squeezed empty of air, the wet-faced Jasper is rendered an idiot, his brain all but dead, reduced to a never-ending state of infancy.

This was a story repeated to Jeremiah with such frequency that he had formed vivid images of it. Like stained-glass pictures in church windows, the stories remain ever present. Unlike other childhood memories, however, he sees himself enacting these atrocities as if from a distance. It is not his bare hands about a boy's neck but a stranger's. He observes as if he were the audience. Briefly, he sees his fearful face reflected in the water. He cannot—and he has tried ceaselessly—begin placing himself in the boots of this angry young boy. But this is the story repeated in the Goode family, amongst themselves, never—you understand—to outsiders.

When it became clear Jasper was not going to recover, beatings were dished out daily to Jeremiah. By the time he left for the Royal College of St. Peter in Westminster School, they diminished to monthly. Back home between terms, the whippings resumed their ferocity, according to his father's whim. If Jasper misbehaved, Jeremiah was to blame. If a patient had not paid a bill, it was Jeremiah who suffered. Much of his youth had thus been spent standing, arse battered and bruised. But the responses of a child to the cruelties of a parent are often the same: in time Jeremiah learned to appease. What child, after all, does not harbour a secret wish to gratify his father? He bore his cape of guilt, was eventually shaped by it, so that eventually Robert Goode's two sons became crippled by different means.

Downstairs, on the table in the receiving hall, Jeremiah deposits two packets of herbs and a tincture with a note as to their uses. He then slips out of the door; walking the garden path with the sense that every step adds years to his age, so that by the time he reaches Dulwich Wood he is once more a man of a score and eight again.

His Father's Deathbed

Rose stands, arms tightly crossed, on the threshold of Stony Hall. 'Where have you been? Father, he has taken another turn for the worse.'

Jeremiah tosses his deformed hat and balding wig somewhat defiantly at a chair. 'Doubtless my presence caused it.'

'Go to him quickly, Indigo.'

The bedchamber is as Jeremiah left aside from Reverend Alcock. He appears from the shadows—a small man with a large belly and round, smooth face—and takes Jeremiah's hands. Given the smile, they might just have recently finished a game of croquet, one in which the reverend had won.

'God bless you child!'

Jeremiah smiles at the reverend's crucifix rather than his mask and thanks him for his vigils at his father's bedside. His mother sees the reverend out to the passageway from speaking in low whispers; the door left respectfully ajar for death before she returns to her sewing.

His father turns to face him with eyes deeply excavated hollows, his beard grey and sparse. At the corners of his mouth saliva congeals in lumps.

Father?' says Jeremiah leaning over the bed.

'Indigo,' says his father, attempting to lift a hand from the bedcovers.

Jeremiah places his hand over his. 'There is something else I have brought something else to alleviate your suffering, Father.'

'I told you…I want nothing you have to give.'

'Not even some Laudanum?'

His father's lips flicker into a smile. 'I see you have come round to my methodology.'

'I would prefer to administer a tonic but—'

His father lifts a hand from the bedcover. 'But the opium is all I require.'

Jeremiah picks his case from the floor and sets it on the chair.

'Where is your physician?'

'I have dismissed him. He wanted to use Mr Cox's purgative waters. I believe in drugs, not water.'

Jeremiah shakes a phial of laudanum. 'Mr Cox?'

'He has sunk a well in his garden. Calls it Dulwich Wells. The Green Man tavern, south of the village, is now a place of healing. The fool that he is! You know,' his father's face takes on a dreamy expression, 'I hear music.'

'Music, Father?'

'Sad but beautiful music: violins, the piano. Reverend Alcock says it is God's way of easing one's suffering.'

'And does it, ease yours?'

A crow squawks from beyond the window and they both turn towards the drawn drapes.

'No,' says his father, 'but it distracts.'

'That is often enough.' Jeremiah sets down the laudanum phial. He feels older, older than his years even. 'I would like to examine you, if you would permit me?'

His father grunts. 'If you must.'

Jeremiah places a hand on his father's heart, the other across his brow. He closes his eyes and inhales deeply. He waits. But in the space where he feels a patient's pain at the very least discomfort he feels nothing, as if... as if his father were already dead.

'You are finished?'

Jeremiah removes his hands. 'Yes, Father.'

'I am dying, am I not?'

'Nonsense.' Jeremiah busies himself with his case, 'You have a heart as strong as an ox.'

His father's head shakes in slow contortions. 'No. My heart is...torn asunder.'

'Sit forwards.' Jeremiah places a hand behind his father's head and administers the laudanum. He has not had need to take a solitary drop since returning from Dorset; love, it seemed, could overcome even pain. He felt the ills of others only briefly now, as if he had found a way to let pain—his own included—pass through him on its path.

He waits with a piss pot on his lap, awaiting the inevitable. Before long his father's breath becomes rapid. His body crumples over the edge of the bed and Jeremiah is there, with the pot. Wiping away vomit from his father's mouth, he resettles his head on the pillow.

'Hearts can mend,' he says, dispensing with the pot.

His father shakes his head. 'Not hearts poisoned by grief.'

'Grief?'

'Grief is much the same as guilt. Both sit in the heart and rot like a foul summer humour.' His father's eyes are red and small. 'Converse with me Indigo. I prefer it to the music. Talk to me about your days. Tell me how you spend your days.'

Jeremiah scratches his head. 'My days?' he says. *Well, I wake up beside the fire. I write for it stops me thinking about the absence of any customers and the sick of the parish I should be attending to and then between every dip of the quill I see her face; her eyes, her lips...*

'Well,' he begins as a knot like an unforgiving fist forms in his throat. He gets up, prods a log in the fire with the poker as a stopper is forced over the opened vial of emotion. He then crosses back to the bed.

'I am writing a compendium,' he says, arranging the bedcovers.

His father's jaw falls slack, 'About what?' his father's eyes have become so vacant Jeremiah cannot tell if it is scorn or genuine interest that drives him.

'Plants and their healing properties,' he says, his tone too light, insubstantial, like a meadow reed blown this way and that.

His father does not appear to have heard, turns his head as if regarding a pleasant scene, one taking place on the far side of the bed. His smile fades and his eyes half-close. 'As a boy you liked the Physic Garden at Chelsea... *why does God not provide each plant with a set of instructions?* you asked me eagerly. You would have made a good physician—if you weren't so stubborn. Tell me, you enjoy healing the sick of your parish?'

'Enjoyment is irrelevant. I ease the parishioners' suffering. But it is also a job for the politicians. What these people need is medicine for free but, alas, I am not the one to continue providing it.'

'Ach, but we all suffer. Man suffers...not only in sickness. It is our responsibility to...find a way to see past our suffering.'

Jeremiah's hands hesitate over the pages of his life, 'I have brought... my compendium with me.'

His father looks at him, hatred rising in his eyes, swirling like mulch. 'What of my own suffering, shall you ease *that*? You have come to give your answer, have you not?' He coughs, wheezes as though drawing his last breath and Jeremiah holds his compendium to his chest like a shield. Eventually, his father speaks. 'The Aldridge girl?' he says, 'What shall you do?'

*

His mother is waiting outside. She embraces him. Her shoulders seem bonier, her hair a little greyer, yet her scent is reassuringly familiar: that of violets and tea leaves. Jeremiah will remember it all his life.

'Your father is comfortable?' she asks.

'I have given him enough opium to make him so, Mother.'

'Thank you, dear.'

He takes her arm and thinks how she appears to grow smaller on every visit.

'It is what I wanted to do several weeks ago,' he says.

'I understand but it is stubbornness.' She brushes her hand against his cheek, 'It is a Goode family trait. You have been crying?'

'Tears of relief,' he lies, 'That is all.'

'You are a good man,' she says patting his arm. 'God knows your willingness to serve.'

Lucy Aldridge is old news

After lunch Jeremiah returns to the bedchamber where he finds his father still sleeping. Perhaps, he had miscalculated the dose. He takes out the first page in his compendium: Aconitum, the wolf's bane, a plant capable—if used in wrong dose—of destroying life. At lower doses it paralyses and numbs nerves to excruciating pain. He begins reading aloud but after Adder's Tongue and Agrimony, his throat becomes parched and he sets down his herbal.

'Call me once Father wakes,' he tells his mother.

'He looks happier,' she says, looking up from her needlework, 'even in his sleep. Something you have said must have made him so.'

Downstairs, he follows the sound of his sisters. When he enters the large though sparsely furnished salon (spending his easily earned money was not a favourite preoccupation of his father, not unless entirely necessary) they cease speaking, regarding him with obvious curiosity as he crosses to a chair by the window.

'We think you are in love!' declares Blanche.

'We have decided there is something altered in you,' affirms Violet.

Jeremiah belches: a gut used to vegetables and beans does not fare well with duck. He sits on his father's chair, the most elaborate piece of furniture in the salon. 'I can guess whom this concerns.' He shall keep the news—his weakness—from them for as long as he can. In his father's company wisdom and strength had departed when most needed.

Blanche, full of vivacity says, 'Lucy Aldridge is old news. When is there going to be another sister for tea and tattle?'

'If you are to be the head of this household, Blanche believes you ought to be married,' says Violet.

His neck scarf feels tight about his neck and he tugs it loose. 'Old news,' he says, 'I wish that it were.'

'But surely there is someone you love? Every man has a love, does he not?'

A break in the clouds sends shafts of sunlight obliquely through the salon. Awash with light Jeremiah might reveal a little of himself. It is all his sisters crave: to share his thoughts; it is a womanly trait after all. Besides, they shall learn the truth sooner or later from their father.

'There is a certain lady,' he says.

'I knew it! Who?' shrieks Blanche. 'Is she from the village? Who Indigo? *Do tell us*!'

He smiles, examining the buttons on his waistcoat. 'She lives in Dorset.'

'Where in Dorset?'

'In a village where martyrs once lived then died for their beliefs, as martyrs are wont to do.'

'We do not care about the martyrs! Is she coming to London to be with you?'

'If I can find a way, aye.'

'Is she beautiful?'

'More beautiful than you can imagine. And clever too.'

'When you shall you marry her?'

He scowls. 'Marry?'

'You are teasing us,' says Violet. 'Do stop!'

'Beyond Dulwich, love does not always end in marriage, Violet.' He considers Lucy, the promise to his father, but lets this thought go.

'If your beloved is God-fearing?' says Rose, hands clasped before her as if in prayer. 'A lady of faith will wish to marry the man she loves. She is an Anglican?'

He holds his cup up to the light. It is so fine it seems almost possible to see through it to the green of the meadow beyond.

'A Christian once, but not of our kind.'

'A Catholic?' says Blanche, the one most connected to his thoughts. 'Catholic women long to be confined to a nunnery. It is why they refuse marriage. Oh poor, poor Indigo! Do you love her, dear brother?'

He smiles but remains silent. Virtue was right to say it is so much more than a word.

'We have just heard news Lucy Aldridge is engaged!' says Violet suddenly getting up and moving to the harpsichord.

Jeremiah turns to her sharply. 'You know this for certain?'

'Yes indeed,' says Violet, tinkering on a key, 'She sent a letter, not an hour ago. She is to marry her officer this spring. She could not prattle enough about the irrelevancies of the fellow: his broad shoulders, his thick mop of hair. I daresay she would do better with a puppy than a husband.'

He examines a fingernail with mock interest. 'Does Father know?'

'We have only just heard. But Father is never interested in village news,' says Blanche. 'You must remember that he cares little for the details of our lives, more so now that he is sick.'

'Blanche!'

'It's true, Rose!'

A shiver spreads from Jeremiah's head and along his spine. 'Well, this particular news he might care to know.'

'Well, I care to know about this new love of yours. Is she like Lucy? They say certain men fall for the same kind of woman over and over.'

Jeremiah thinks of his earlier weakness; his undying need to please the one person impervious to his efforts. 'I will marry Lucy,' he had said, as if already at the altar giving away his freedom for a fortune. He shakes his head, bringing himself back to the sanctity of the present. 'No, she is nothing like Lucy, Blanche. One is fair, the other dark; one as natural as the other is contrived.' He sighs, finding he can breathe a little freer now. 'Two very different people.'

'What does it mean, contrived?'

'The opposite of you, sweet Blanche.' He softly pinches his youngest sister's cheek. 'She is the goodness of Nature herself. Whatever she does or says is done because it is right. Her compass points only toward good.'

'Toward *Goode*? You are a wit!' says Violet, playing a flat key on the harpsichord.

'Then she is perfect for you,' says Blanche. 'Of course she shall come to London!'

'Alas, she has responsibilities,' he says, straightening his cuff, reminding himself that, if nothing else, the Negro is his reason for being at peace with his father.

'Then you must become her responsibility, brother dearest?' Blanche sits on a stool before him. 'Do you read one another poetry? Do you sit on riverbanks beneath the moonlight? Oh Indigo! When shall you bring this angel for a visit? Please say it shall be soon.'

He smiles. 'That shall depend on how deserving you are of your brother's company.' He sets down his tea bowl and crosses to the full-length windows, staring at the last patches of snow on the grass. How many days had he spent roaming this meadow in search of one particular flower or another, the threat of his father's beatings never far from his thoughts? Indeed, plants had been his escape for as long as he could remember.

Blanche sighs. 'We shall all be exceptionally deserving.'

'Jasper?' he says, turning back to the room, eyes dazzled by low winter sunlight, tired now of their chatter. 'Where is he?'

'He is terribly sad,' says Violet, closing the lid of the harpsichord. 'He feels our sadness though fails to comprehend it.'

'He begins drawing more intensely, day and night,' says Rose, 'Even mother cannot pacify him. He has become a statue that draws.'

Jeremiah looks at his sisters arranged about the room like delicate pieces of pastel furniture. They understood little of the world beyond the salons of Dulwich. Yet it was not their fault. They read: Rose books on religion and philosophy; Blanche books on politics but the people within the covers were no more real to them than the characters in a novel, perhaps less so. Not fitting with convention, Jasper for the most part eluded them.

'Why have you not told Jasper Father is sick?' he asks.

'They were afraid he might want to see Papa and upset him,' says Blanche.

'Of course,' says Jeremiah, his shoulder flinching, the sentence summing up his and his brother's childhood and how it had revolved around *not upsetting their father* until their father was the one to sufficiently upset them all. And now he has come to enact the unspoken role assigned him: to ensure

272

that his father passes from this life to the next without upset. Accused of near-murder almost his entire life he shall thus prove his father's character assessment to be true.

'What is the matter with your shoulder?' asks Violet.

'I wish that I knew.'

'Surely you of all people can do something to stop it jerking?'

Jeremiah smiles at Blanche. 'I can Cure most things it would seem other than my own maladies.' Perhaps this too is a lie, though the itch has at least abated. To itch, some say, is to meet one's cure.

Blanche pushes her arm through his. 'I think our brother suffers from love sickness,' she says rolling her eyes at her sisters, 'Oh yes! Our dear brother is in love!'

He wants only to see you

Jasper is in his usual seat before the window, head bent over St Paul's cathedral, in the foreground the River Thames. He looks up at Jeremiah, face ashen, grave, yet still appearing 10 or 15 years shy of his age.

Jasper looks up at him then quickly away again. On the table is a plate of uneaten meat.

'The herbs I bring, you must drink them. I have brought more. I shall bring them regularly now.'

He may have lost his self-possession, his verve, when it came to curing a rich old woman but his own brother he shall never give up on.

'You are eating?'

Jasper continues to draw, his hand making sweeping, confident dashes across the page, at odds with his sulking, child-like expression, pausing only momentarily to shake his head at the question. Jeremiah looks to the drawing part of which has been painted: new red brick buildings beneath the towering bulb of St Paul's. At the water's edge, before the old timber constructions of the docks, boats are moored without sails so as not to obscure the view of the gold barge passing by, red-and-blue flags streaming through the air. Other boats are drawn carelessly as if Jasper resented any deviation from the neatness of bricks and mortar, of straight edged-timbers.

All without exception, including the smaller boats and water taxis haggling for views, are absent of people.

Jeremiah recollects the day of the picture. His father had taken the family to see the procession at Southwark on Lord Mayor's Day. He had not invited Jeremiah for he had already been paid off, excommunicated, living in a state of invisibility in St Giles-in-the-fields. His shop had recently opened. Word had spread that a lunatic was offering drugs to the parish on account. People queued, the line extending, at one time, the width of Neal's Yard. Men with only one leg, women with shoals of children: all waiting patiently for his services. Jeremiah had looked at them believing this popularity to be a measure of his success. He had told the druggist as much when presenting him his third order of medicine in a week: 'I am giving the parish what it has longed for: proper medical attention.' He had bragged and the druggist had laughed. 'Anyone would think you were giving them a Cure for free!' And amid this lavish philanthropy he had been too busy for Lord Mayor's Day.

He looks closer at the picture, slowly coming to life in colour. 'What is it?' he asks, pointing to a black shape in the water.

'No touch,' says Jasper.

Jeremiah peers closer. A frailly drawn figure floats face down in the water. Not unusual to see a body floating in the Thames it was, however, unheard of to see a person in any of Jasper's pictures.

'You saw a dead body on Lord Mayor's day?'

Jasper nods, waiting, pen lifted. Jeremiah rests a hand on the boy's shoulder. Grief, like a swell of pain, rises up from his gullet and lodges in his throat. He opens his eyes.

'You are concerned for Father?'

Jasper nods rapidly.

'You would like to visit his chamber?'

Having thrown his pen aside, Jasper already waits at the door like a hound before a hare hunt.

'Indigo!' says his mother, catching sight of Jasper, her expression fixed with fear. 'What can you want?'

'Jasper,' Jeremiah gestures his brother forwards, 'wishes to see his father.'

'*He* wishes?' His mother's eyes dart towards the bed. 'Father sleeps. Bring Jasper another time. Return him now to his room, Indigo.'

'I am awake, Mrs Goode.'

They all three turn to the bed, his mother immediately rising and crossing to the bed to stand protectively at her husband's side.

Jeremiah tugs at Jasper's sleeve. 'I have brought Jasper to see you,' he says. 'I hope you do not object, Father.'

'Jasper? What can he want?'

Jasper stands at the foot of the bed, wide-eyed at the slowly disintegrating, almost inconspicuous shape of his father.

'He wants only to see you.'

'Very well. He has done so.'

Jasper glances at Jeremiah. His brother winces. Perhaps his understanding is only a little skewed, after all.

'Get out,' his father says.

Jasper rushes to the door.

'Jasper?' calls out Jeremiah but it is too late: his brother has fled the room.

'I shall return to administer more opium,' Jeremiah says, concealing his disgust with duty. 'You shall not suffer further.'

'We are both grateful,' says his mother. 'Your father has slept more soundly than he has for many months.' She pats her husband's hand.

Jeremiah bows his head, turns to leave as his father mutters something. Jeremiah turns back to the bed. His father's eyes have closed. 'Father?'

His mother looks up, fear now turned to sadness. 'He says it is not his fault.'

'Not whose fault, Mother?'

But his mother says nothing more, nor does she meet his eye again. She shrugs, looking back to his father, to the half-formed smile on his lips.

'Father?'

'Go now,' urges his mother, 'leave him to sleep in peace.'

He examines his feelings

Blue sky and scudding cloud, a meadow strewn with flowers. Jeremiah looks down at the water's surface: rippling, black. No hands to strangle him, no

Negro to despise him, but if he stares hard enough he sees his own reflection: the reflection of a horrified child. He pulls himself quickly upright. It is not a stream but a bucket. A stable bucket. Flowers are trampled about him: oxeye daisies, snake's head fritillary, devil's bit scabious—to name but a few. He rubs the back of his neck, hunched over the empty bucket as rain splatters the back of his neck.

Jeremiah wakes to hear Brigid's voice as if she were there in the room with him, 'Remember, reflections in water only happen when the sun shines Mr Goode.' Then he falls back to sleep, a pleasant sleep in which Mary has cooked a large dish of trout and they share the delicate pink flesh in the dining room above the apothecary shop. His sisters and Jasper are there: laughing and raising glasses whilst at Jeremiah's side a familiar presence provides comfort. Then, obeying the logic of dreams, he is next beside a stream and her voice says, 'See how the rain dimples the surface!' Turning to see her, however, he hears another voice, 'He has passed, Indigo. He has passed.'

He opens his eyes to find his mother's face, appearing elongated by the burning candle in her hand.

It was raining that day. A heavy unforgiving downpour.

'He died peacefully,' says his mother.

'At twenty minutes past three of the clock.'

'What?' he says, wiping his eyes.

'Your father died at twenty minutes past three of the clock.' His mother looks satisfied, as though this was the important part, as if they had gathered earlier to place bets on the time.

When she leaves, Jeremiah gets out of bed. Once dressed, he is unsure what to do next. There has never been a death so close. Doubtless, certain etiquette must be assented to, but as etiquette is often at odds without what he would do naturally, he remains for a time at the end of the bed, sitting motionless in the dark. He examines his feelings, prodding them as he would a customer with complaints of a pain in the gut. He opens the drapes. Dawn is breaking over the meadow and the forest beyond. Red skies, angels cry. He seeks appropriate memories, tests them for sincerity. He had once assisted his father in amputating a gangrenous finger. Though the part he played had been minimal—passing of instruments, folding back a bloodied cuff—he had not fainted, nor had he been called *a girl or a damned molly*.

Is he head of the Goode household now?

His stomach aches. There is a small (though unlikely) possibility he might be rich. Surely immoral to think this so soon? Then he hears in his head his father, as though he stood beside him: *Are you a man or a molly?* And then glancing at his part-finished compendium on the dresser, he straightens his back and marches forth in search of some etiquette.

The family stands around the bed of Robert Goode. Reverend Alcock reads solemn prayers and blesses the body. His father's face sags as if his chin had already departed for heaven. Jeremiah remains somewhat surprised at how small his father's body appears, small, almost humble-looking. When living he had appeared twice such dimensions. He tries to imprint a memory that shall one day be relevant.

As Jasper toys with the bedcover, exposing one of his father's feet, Jeremiah is struck by the shape of his father's toes, how they appear identical to his own: forming a neat row of diminishing heights from first to last with the toe nail on the little toe so tiny it appears absent. *We have the same feet.* Jasper turns to him and he is unsure if he has spoken the absurdity aloud.

'Amen,' whispers the vicar.

'What of your own peace, Master Goode?'

Jeremiah sits in the darkest corner as they drink tea in the salon: staccato sentences punctuated by the crashing of teacups onto saucers.

'A man who has done so much good,' says the Reverend who often would preach, *Mend your clothes or never expect to mend your lives*, or on the subject of children, *Break his will now, and his soul shall live, and he will bless you to all eternity* whilst consuming great quantities of wine and cake at the expense of his parish. He was a man with much in common with his father.

'Indeed, Mr Goode did live for his patients,' replies Anne Goode, continuing to stare at a small hole in the carpet.

Jeremiah looks to the family portrait above the fireplace: an informal arrangement beneath an oak, commissioned many years ago by a fashionable French painter; arrogant as such men were wont to be. Jasper, a baby, sits upon his mother's knee, dressed as a girl. The sisters sit beside him on the bench in various shades of froth and lace. Blanche, not more than four or five, holds to her chest a china doll dressed in royal blue. She extends it towards Jeremiah who stares at this doll from a standing position at one end of the bench, dressed, to all intents and purposes, like a giant canary in yellow breeches and matching coat. He had been wearing faun on the day. The artist had treated him with distain after he suggested another oak tree where the meadow flowers were more varied and prettier.

'I look for light,' said the painter. 'Not flowers!'

'My son has a fondness for flowers,' mocked his father.

'*C'est vrai?*' Then you shall look *très joli aussi* when I am finished!'

At the other end of the bench, just beyond the oak, his father leant against a stick. Aloof, sombre, dressed all in grey, his face turned towards the house as if keen to dissociate himself from the disarray of family. His expression, as always, was one of utmost gravity.

This gravity remained his father's demeanour throughout their childhood. On the occasions he had taken Jeremiah to the coffee houses to meet his patients, he had become almost unrecognisable: laughing affably, offering his distinguished patients utterances overwrought with kindness. To any casual observer he might have appeared sincere. Money had metamorphosed his character from tyrant into trusted confidant. Yet, tyranny was reserved for his family, who refused to mirror his professional life. He was exemplary, could they not be exemplary too? One son displayed a propensity for obscure choices whilst the other had proven ostensibly indestructible. In the end pretending neither one existed had been the only way to improve his standing in the wider community.

'What of you young man? Shall you be returning to the family home?'

Jeremiah beaks free of his reverie to stare at the vicar.

'No,' he says looking quickly and somewhat quizzically at his mother. 'I have my own…responsibilities now Reverend. Not to the scale of my father's but…' He trails off, unwilling to divulge his difficulties; vicars were inclined to give off an outward appearance of capability when being little more than vessels for passing troubles over to a higher source.

'We shall be fine here. I have my girls to take care of me,' says Mrs Goode, with a thin smile.

'Ah, yes, the girls!' says the vicar with excessive exuberance. 'Mr Goode, I presume, made suitable arrangements for their future?'

'Indeed,' says Mrs Goode. 'They shall all be provided with adequate dowries.'

Blanche sniffs loudly and objectionably.

Jeremiah stands. 'Reverend, may I speak with you a moment—in private?'

Opening his father's study, Jeremiah soon realises he has chosen the wrong room for conversation with the parson. Nevertheless, Reverend Alcock is shuffling closely behind and he can do little other than enter.

'Please,' he says, gesturing to the chair, the same chair he had regularly bent over to receive beatings; beatings that cut and bruised, that had moulded his memory to his father's designs.

The room comprises dark, cheerless wood like a husk to his father's character. Books, concerning physic, are locked away behind glass. Jeremiah sits at his father's desk feeling small, irrelevant.

'He despised me,' he says, staring out at the window, at the clock face on the small tower by the stable yard. 'And for me most of my adult life.'

The vicar palpates the muscles of his jaw as his brow corrugates. 'I was aware of some difficulties. The dying, you understand, like to confess.'

Along one side of the meadow, where the field dips down sharply, the chalk upon which London rests is exposed. Jeremiah had once run through these fields, eyes closed, arms spread and fallen off the edge of the verge into the orchard. The shock was worse than the injury, but lying on his back, chalk crumbling beneath his nails, he spotted the purplish red flower of a thyme broomrape; a plant he had spent years looking for. It was worth every bruise and he later thanked God in church. Reminded of it now he realises it was that God's grace and plants first formed an association. Grace, he wonders now, must it always follow a fall?

'I understand you like flowers,' the reverend begins again, as if unsure how to untangle Jeremiah's confession.

'My passion is plants.' A lie. His passions now resided, not in mere vegetation, but in a lonely cottage in Dorset. 'But I do not wish to speak about flowers. I want you to understand that I prefer…not to know what my father confessed to you.' He had anticipated a confession. His shoulder flinches up to his ear as if anticipating the thwack of his father's cane and guilt, as always, presses down upon his shoulders. Another flinch. Then in the distance, a distinct pounding of a drum like a frenzied heartbeat, a life force, a force as powerful as love.

Life. See! You cannot take that from me!

The reverend brings his hands, clasped as if in prayer, to his lips. 'That is your decision. To make as you see fit.'

'I wish him peace.' A lone gull retreats, slowly, resolutely towards London. 'That is all.'

The reverend picks a speck of something invisible from his cassock. 'And what of your own peace, Master Goode?'

Following the incident Jeremiah is unable to properly recall, Jasper spent several weeks in bed, his crippled leg now of little significance. In time, he became the boy in the downstairs room, and for many years, Jeremiah has not a solitary memory of his brother. Eventually, the boy disowned the world as it had disowned him. He created instead his own world: one that comprised straight, unassailable lines: pictures in which perfection was still possible.

Last pages

The coach travelling to London is empty aside from a man with a gash on his arm. He reminds Jeremiah of Jesus; the Jesus pictured in church with unkempt hair, a beard and glistening, knowing eyes.

'Might I assist?' Jeremiah asks.

'If thee are not concerned by blood,' says the man, already unfolding the rag wrapped about his arm, exposing a long cut, deep, fortunately narrow enough to avoid amputation.

'What caused it?' Jeremiah opens his case.

'My wife.'

'You wife?' Jeremiah lifts his brow. 'Then I shall not ask what provoked it.'

The fellow smiles, sucking in air through his teeth, loosing the serenity of Christ. 'I am a man that drinks too much,' he says. 'My wife says she would prefer it if I were to think not drink.'

'One does not necessarily accompany the other.' Jeremiah selects burnet ointment. 'You need your arm for work?'

The man laughs. 'What man does not need their arm for work?'

Jeremiah kneels before him and applies the ointment in gentle dabs, noting the fellow's breath, fetid with alcohol. 'You must rest for a few days or it will not heal quickly.'

'Rest? How is a man to rest with a family of nine?'

Jeremiah looks up. 'You would prefer to lose your arm?'

The man tips back his head and lapses into silence as Jeremiah takes out a bandage, one scrubbed so efficiently by Mary there remains only the faintest mottle of blood. He applies it then sits back, staring out at the open back of the coach.

'You are a good man,' the fellow says.

Jeremiah sighs. 'So I am told.'

'There are few of your sort in this world.'

'I imagine God cannot be cruel to his flock too often.'

The fellow shakes his head. 'I think you know that deep down it is a blessing.'

In time Jeremiah is rocked asleep. He has been awake since three of the clock, then foolishly staying for the reading of his father's will. The lawyer: a man who spoke with his head tipped to control a stutter, declared, 'In..in… in…Indigo Jeremiah Samuel G…G…Goode is not to benefit from Robert Samuel's Goode's w…w…will.' True to his father's word, Jeremiah would not receive *a farthing*. He had departed soon afterwards amongst an outbreak of wailing from his sisters, unable to discern the greater upset: father's death or his own misfortune.

Opening his eyes he is back amid cluttered streets. He stretches then stoops for his apothecary case. The lid is open. Inspecting its contents he finds it all but empty: no compendium, not a solitary bottle of herbs, only

281

two small vials of laudanum. A solitary page flutters up from the floor, catches on a breeze and floats out of the back of the coach, the half-finished image of lavender drifting up, to be quickly lost to London fog.

The staircase at the eleventh hour

Mrs Soloman walks across her landing resembling a crane fly in the last throws of its death, one dressed for a ball. Legs skitter across marble, as if an indiscernible breeze disturbs her trajectory. Her head, its few scraps of hair, are concealed by an eschewed periwig. Eyebrows painted on too high make her appear in a state of constant surprise, and with several fabric moles adorning heavily rouged cheek, she resembles a code in need of deciphering. She wears a pale pink gown, her feet are bare, one foot still uncomfortably blackened, yet the skin, Jeremiah notes with some relief, is shiny with newness.

He offers her his arm to the old woman who barely reaches his chest.

'Leave me be!' she screeches. 'If I must walk down my staircase I must do so unaided!'

He steps back breathing in the incense lingering on his clothes. Earlier that morning he had attended church: the Catholic church of St Anselm and St Caecilia at Lincoln's Inn Fields. Brigid had disowned her Catholic faith but inside the unassuming building he imagines himself closer to her. He liked the smell of frankincense, the Latin solemnity. He was half-tempted to confess, this church appearing more inclined to forgiveness that his own, but he remembered Brigid's words, 'The Catholic church forgives but drowns you in guilt.' But what would he confess to? Ineptitude? An insufficient memory when it came to details of his childhood? Drowning, he'd had enough of.

He considered Brigid's belief: one surmised as a belief in nature. He respected her views about God not intervening in the intricacies of daily creation. It quelled disgruntlement in a God who regarded certain parishes as more deserving than others, but what he failed to grasp was Brigid's belief in punishment being self-inflicted and therefore separate from God. Did she thus believe in God's grace and not his wrath? How then did he justify his own existence when it seemed to be God's wrath in perpetual action?

The sermon produced something more than the usual boredom. Afterwards he had stared up at the altar, at Christ being removed from the cross. Stained glass cast his skin in a rainbow of light. Following Wordsley's ball—which he would attend out of duty—and with the money he was to receive from curing Mrs Soloman, he would journey to Chideock. Here he would lay his life bare before the woman of his every waking thought, offer the idea that somehow, by some means, their lives might become irrevocably intertwined.

But such a future hung on the outcome of one woman descending her staircase. One embittered hag and 33 stairs. Without her reward it was debtor's prison; a partially paid of debt was still a debt to a man like Manners. And after gaol Jeremiah would be unable to furnish his love with so much as a compliment.

'Fetch me a chair!'

The footman rushes off and drags a heavy gilt chair into the centre of the landing. Mrs Soloman sits, leaning back against two embroidered stags locked in combat.

'I had forgotten how tiring walking can be,' she says, making a show of wiping her brow with the back of her hand. 'I am beginning to wonder why people bother with it.'

Having walked that morning from St Giles, ankle-deep in slush, the last of Miss Heart's money having been spent on travelling to Dulwich and back, Jeremiah is inclined to agree. 'May I suggest you save your wonder for after you have succeeded in your quest?'

'Or perhaps her ladyship has had enough for one day?' says the Fish, puffing out his cheeks, doubtless ready for a glass of his employer's best wine. Jeremiah wishes to kick him in the shin for his insouciance.

Mrs Soloman wags her finger at him. 'No! I have said I shall do it today and so I shall. Today I feel well. I only wish Clara were here. She would have something sensible to say, something encouraging. Rushing off to take the Bath waters for Heaven knows what reason. Now, move the chair Farley. I am ready to begin again.'

'You have done well thus far,' says Jeremiah.

'Be quiet with your flattery Mr Goode. You think I can't see through your act?'

Aside from the money, in truth Jeremiah hardly cares if this woman lives or dies.

Miss Zeldin had said that in order to heal, one's intentions must be honourable. As far as Mrs Soloman is concerned, his intentions remain as honourable as those of a whore abiding in a monastery; any shame absent.

'When we first moved here,' she pants as she takes another slow shuffle forward, 'I had imagined these rooms full of children.' An arm sweeps above her head so that she almost falls over. Jeremiah and the Fish dart forwards. 'Get off! Both of you!' She takes two more small steps, reaches the banister where she launches forwards, gripping it so that her body leans obliquely. 'But the rooms remained empty, even of guests.'

'But there are many happy memories,' says the Fish.

'There are?'

The Fish slithers closer. 'Mr Soloman loved you very much, your ladyship.'

'Abe liked someone at his side. That was all. A woman that required affection or even kindness would have slowed him down in his relentless march toward accomplishment. He did not require beauty for beauty's sake, for there was no one he needed to impress.' She pauses, one foot hovering over the first stair as she gazes up at the clouds painted on the ceiling. 'So he married me. I was not even a Jew but it was my loyalty he favoured. I have often wondered whether he died not knowing the colour of my eyes.'

Jeremiah clears his throat. 'One is green, the other brown.'

'I beg your pardon?' Mrs Soloman turns on him sharply, holding up spectacles, hanging from a chain, to her eyes.

'One,' says Jeremiah, 'is distinctly brown, the other green with gold flecks close to the pupil.'

She presses her hand to her heart. 'You surprise me, Mr Goode. A whole lifetime and only my mother has passed comment on the incongruity. Perhaps Clara is right after all, perhaps there is more to you than one sees with one's eye.'

Jeremiah bows.

'But,' she says, lifting her foot again, 'the ones with the comeliest faces—you are doubtless aware of your own eyes—are to be trusted the least. I told

Clara as much but the girl gets set upon a thing. Perhaps...' She lowers her other foot onto the stair, 'Perhaps you will prove an exception, Mr Goode.'

'Perhaps,' he says, little interested in what Clara has set her mind upon.

'But thus far,' she squints at him, 'you do not strike me as someone exceptional.

Not exceptional at all.'

The spectacles swing on a chain about Mrs Soloman's neck. She laughs. It is a scornful laugh: the laugh of a wicked woman given too much power. She takes another step forwards. If she were a crane fly he would have trampled her underfoot by now. Instead he must stand here, fist pressed against his lips, as seven years of training and four years of running an apothecary shop culminate in one miserable hag and 33 stairs.

With so much marble it is as cold on this staircase as outside on the streets. Jeremiah stares out of the large oval window where snow is blown in reckless swirls. He wonders what Mrs Soloman will do when she reaches the bottom. Forty or fifty people would occupy a space of this size in St Giles and here resides one old lady barely living at all. But perhaps he has more in common with Mrs Soloman than he cares to acknowledge: a life away from the prattle of society; only a servant and his eschewed opinions of the world for company...

'Tell me Mr Goode, have you calculated it yet?'

'Calculated what, madam?'

'How much money you are to receive from each stair?'

A muscle spasms in his shoulder. 'Keen to see that my Cure has worked, the only calculations made are in what I have administered you.'

'Hogwash! You are here for the money. Don't tell me otherwise.'

Jeremiah shame is real. When first moving to St Giles he had vowed only to cure not to judge. Had desperation eroded this belief so thoroughly? Was he becoming more like his father: treating the rich with smug insincerity in order to fatten his purse. But there was something else: the suspicion something more was required of him. He cannot fathom it but can only sense it, tightening around him like a bandage to its wound.

Yet Brigid's success, not his own, has them gathered at the top of the staircase. He expects he could have achieved the same, given time, given peace of mind. Nonetheless he nearly lost his life in curing the old woman and thus, by some means, he must enjoy the descent, enjoy it as if watching the last furlong of a race whose outcome was assured. For Mrs Soloman has 31 stairs to go and if insults were anything to go by, strength of character alone will carry her to the bottom.

The sermon this morning had, with timely relevance, been about God's intervention at the eleventh hour, how faith needed to be tested to be proven. Life, in short, required plenty patience. Customers regularly tested Jeremiah's patience. Happy when healing, he would be happier still if they offered their bodies up mutely. His father on the other hand exuberantly about the weather, political affairs, etc. attempting to distract from his plans to amputate. For Jeremiah, talk unless it involved diet, sleep or exercise, came between him and the cure. Looking at Mrs Soloman now, toe hovering over a stair, he wonders why people could not be more like plants: gracious, silent.

This then must be the eleventh hour: the moment before his redemption, the last hour of his suffering. There was no compendium. Manners was unwilling to alter the terms of his demands and the parish remained too poor to pay him. Therefore his entire salvation lies in the hands, or rather legs, of one miserable woman and her ridiculous staircase.

'Farley, fetch a chair for me when I reach the bottom.'

The bottom. These words were like a melody to his ears. He allows himself to imagine what it might feel like receiving the reward: akin to running through a meadow, arms outstretched, feet barely touching the grass. He fears what such an unburdening might do to him: turn him into a body removed of its bones! And what would he spend the money on? Free herbs for the poor of St Giles? Or a shop in the Strand where the rich and their physicians could come to buy their tinctures and tonics and in turn supplement free herbs for the poor?

'What are you smiling at?' Mrs Soloman snaps him from his reverie.

'Your achievements thus far, madam.'

The old woman takes another four stairs and pauses, eyes closed. 'Why are you not married?'

Brigid Zeldin appears in his thoughts, as she so often is. 'We have spoke of this before, madam. I am not, I suspect, suited to marriage for I can happily abide my own company.'

Yet he abides Miss Zeldin's.

'Well somebody must abide it! My niece, you know, she has few desires of her own.'

'I am certain you underestimate Miss Heart.'

'On the contrary. When she leaves a room it can easily go unnoticed. In fact when she enters a room it is as if someone just left. Could you not benefit from such a woman?'

He shakes his head as though an insect were caught in his ear. 'Benefit?'

'Yes, could your home not benefit if nothing else from a vase of flowers carefully arranged or a new sampler before the hearth? Think carefully about what I am saying.'

'I have no vases, madam, not even any coal. I am not in a position to offer a wife much.' He pulls his coat together. 'May I ask the nature of your enquiry?'

'The plain ones often turn out to be of most benefit, Mr Goode,' says Mrs Soloman, trampling on her niece's life as though it were an old carpet. 'Abe was in habit of telling me this. A companion one can converse with, he would say, is of more benefit than vanity and pride. One needs, particularly at your age, a sweet nature. Whether one can go as far as to describe Clara as sweet in marriage remains to be seen, but she is agreeable in all ways and is, one might say, quite rational. Anyhow, once you have your reward you shall be, I expect, in more of a *position*.'

'My reward, madam, shall be spent on my debts, on furnishing and keeping a shop or two.'

'You forget Clara shall have her own wealth, that she is heir to all this?' She wobbles for an instant, her arms waving overhead like a Turkish dancer's. Jeremiah lunges for her arm. No matter how much he wishes to tumble the old hag to the bottom, there stood only 29 steps between him and recompense.

'You shall hardly know she is there,' she continues to rant, shaking him off. 'She is no more or less trouble than a wall covering. Imagine her as an expensive flock. She would cause you even less trouble. No trouble at all.'

Jeremiah falls silent; a sense of dread rises from his gut and causes him to sweat.

'Mrs Soloman,' he says, loosening his collar, 'Please understand, I cannot marry your niece.'

'*Why ever not?* Oh perhaps I shall not bother with these stairs after all. I shall wait for the new London Hospital to be finished. It will, you understand, be the first to welcome my people. Yes, I shall go there to die instead!'

She falls silent. Jeremiah presses a knuckle to his lip. He finds he has nothing to say. A clock ticks. Then, mercifully, miraculously, Mrs Soloman continues her descent. Perhaps it was a mere whim, one that showed, however distorted, some depth of feeling towards her niece. In gratitude for the acceptance of his decline, Jeremiah passes the time counting his blessings. Remarkably, with each stair closer to his salvation he finds something new to be thankful for. By stair 27 he is praising the astronomer in Neal's Yard for the time he lent Jeremiah a candle, and by stair thirty he is so elated he sings silent praise to Farley the Fish and their fortuitous meeting at *The George Inn* in Southwark. How miraculous fate could be! How slight the hand of God! And how wondrous that in such dark weaves he could still entwine the most brilliant of gold thread!

At stair 31 Mrs Soloman pauses, both hands gripping the banister.

'My niece,' she whispers. 'Marry her and this reward shall be yours.'

Jeremiah hands rests upon the banister. He finds he cannot move, like Punch the puppet at the end of a long performance.

'I do not comprehend,' he says, though he fears he understands completely.

'I said, marry my niece then the thousand pounds shall be yours!'

I believe he is baring his soul

He now remembers who Mrs Soloman had reminded him of, on his very first visit: his father. He stands before her trying to defend principles surrendered at his father's deathbed but in the end he had not even able to defend whom he chose to love. He had, of course, agreed to marry Lucy Aldridge. Rendered a child, bent out of shape by guilt—fashioned or otherwise—he had given himself up to a final act of appeasement.

He says, 'I should prefer to offer my services free of charge for I cannot marry your niece Mrs Soloman.'

'You turn your nose up at a thousand pounds?'

Jeremiah looks to the fish propped up against the chair, a blush dappling his sallow skin. He knew, thinks Jeremiah, *he knew*. 'I have honoured our agreement and in fact gone far beyond the dictates of duty. I ask, therefore, that you to do the same, madam.'

'*Madam, madam, madam.* One more step that is all that remains.' Her arched brow lifts higher. 'One more step.'

Jeremiah sinks down to sit on the last stair, the great slab of marble standing between him and so much. A hollow sensation opens up inside: an emptiness that he imagines to be the space of Mrs Soloman's womb; a space she was attempting to fill with a rashly assembled family. Even he must impose limits on what he is willing to cure.

'I do not love your niece,' he says flatly.

'Pah! More money than an apothecary might see in ten years and you turn it down on account of love? You, a gentile!'

'Madam, of all the blessings in my life I most value, I am presently most thankful for my liberty. I likewise believe wholeheartedly… ' She glares at him but it is his father's sharp eyes and scathing mouth he sees now. 'In the liberty of making up my own mind,' he continues with unsteady forthrightness, 'particularly when it comes to whom I choose to marry.'

Mrs Soloman lifts her chin. 'So say many men living in debtor's prison! But have it your way. I shall return to my bedchamber. Farley, lend me your arm.'

'Wait!'

Mrs Soloman glares harder at him, a slither of saliva escaping her lips. He takes a deep breath. Lets his face rest a moment in his damp upturned palms. Was the Lord extending a drowning man an oar? He tries to think. Had he refused Lucy to be given a second chance with Miss Heart? Did he—a gentleman plagued by misfortune—have the luxury of choice concerning matrimony? Perhaps, his father was right. Perhaps love, after all, was the pastime of stable boys, of lamplighters and he was just another self-indulgent participant.

He looks up at his tormentor. 'Prove to yourself you can do this,' he says. 'Take a step into your own receiving hall. It is a magnificent house. It deserves your presence, does it not?' His heart beats hard, but with life not with fear. When had curing been about guineas? It had been about achievement, both his own and his patients'. It had been about success. 'Do not let your disappointment in me ruin your accomplishment. I shall not take the thousand pounds but one more step and you shall know you are for the best part Cured.' And though it might not be his cure that his brought them this far, he would have reached this point, eventually, by his own peculiar methods and he almost feels entitled to rejoice in Brigid's cure as if... as if it were his own.

The old woman regards him with a discerning stare. 'She is right, my niece. You are not like the rest. There is something honourable about you.'

He bows in gratitude, or perhaps to ingratiate himself: he cannot give up now.

'My son died when he was but two years old, Mr Goode. He lies with Abe in Hoxton. It seems I am entitled to a proper family only in death. My husband was willing to convert to Anglicanism for his son.' She sighs. 'Ah, but my wretched body tells me it won't be long now but, *aye-yie-yie* without an heir it shall be too soon for Abe. He wanted an heir you understand. Something I could not provide for him.' Her eyes hold his. 'Until now.'

'I recall you telling me that your husband did not want children,' he says.

'He did not want other people's children, Mr Goode. I did not want to spill the details of my misfortune to you. Pride can do more than send a person into hiding. I suspect in my case it has kept me alive. You see, Abe did not want Clara occupying our nursery, though my sister would not have objected. No, Abe wanted his own child, but after Daniel there were no more children. Too little time.' She lifts her finger. 'You would do well to marry her, Mr Goode. This house needs youth. It needs children. I strongly urge you to do so before it is too late, too lat for you as well.'

He says, 'It must have grieved you greatly to lose your son. I am sorry to hear of this.'

'Sorry! Why is everyone always sorry for someone else's loss? It does not help. Not one bit!' Her eye glistens with unshed tears. 'You answering "yes", now that shall help.'

He takes a deep breath but speaking words is like pulling strings from his heart. 'There is someone else—another that I love.'

Mrs Soloman turns to her footman. '*What* is he saying?'

The fish smirks. 'I believe he is baring his soul, your Ladyship.'

'Well tell him to stop!'

'If I married your niece it would not be beneficial to either Miss Heart or myself,' he says. 'I ask therefore that you pay my expenses: the coach fares and the herbs and that you give sixpence to your footman for I owe him for supper.'

'Nought! I shall pay you not a thing. That was not our arrangement and I have no intention of taking the last stair, *not* if you refuse to marry my niece!'

Jeremiah shakes his head, scowls at the Fish. 'Then my business here is finished.'

'Finished? What can he mean *finished*, Farley?'

The footman looks uneasily at Jeremiah. 'Sir,' he says, 'I believe it is the Cook you should be Curing.'

Jeremiah shakes his head. 'What has Mrs Soloman's cook got to do with any of this?' he asks.

'A great deal, I fear, sir.'

'What are you prattling about Farley?' asks Mrs Soloman.

The footman holds Jeremiah's eyes. 'Nothing of importance, your Ladyship.'

'Then cease distracting me so that Mr Goode can witness his success.'

But Jeremiah is already moving towards the door, feet echoing through the empty expanse of the house as he prays in silent bursts of pleading for the old woman to change her mind.

'What of my tonic? You cannot end your business now. *I shall be requiring more of that tonic! Much more…*'

Once outside the shrieking fades and Jeremiah walks east, towards London, towards a shop in need of a miracle, walking head cast down, battling through a winter that never seems to end.

I fear for your safety

Boswell tips out the contents of another gallipot into a hemp bag. 'St John's Wort, sir.'

'Named after John the Baptist and capable of relieving melancholy.' Jeremiah brings the bag to his nose. 'To determine whether damp has destroyed a herb's usefulness…' he inhales deeply. 'Use your nose. Some herbs became better with time whereas others rot too easily. The key is proper storage: porcelain containers with a lid that properly fits.' Jars purchased from a man called Bentley from Lancashire. They were not cheap, but for every four the fifth had been free. Ninety-five jars in total. Every one now belonging to Manners. He takes a deep inhalation of marshmallow leaf, still quite dry and potent. From certain decisions he reaps comfort.

Most gallipots, however, remain empty. Herbal suppliers call rarely these days. Word has got about. But in the absence of the travelling men with their cure-alls their blatant lies and occasional curses, there were of course small blessings to be found.

He tips the marshmallow into a bag. Stands and watches a mouse, perhaps a rat, scurry into the centre of the room, watches it collect something and scuttles back to its hole and for some reason he is left thinking of Miss Heart.

'It does not seem fitting that you—a gentleman—should go to gaol, sir. Is there nothing more that can be done? I remember all that you taught me but there is still much more for me to learn.'

'My luck has expired,' says Jeremiah taking his eye from the rat hole. Of course, he has relied too much on luck. Luck is a temperamental beast, whose claws rarely patter the cobbles of St Giles. As to his own luck, it has never previously concerned him, unless at the gaming tables. Preoccupation has lain instead with his patient's luck, or its lack. He had wanted to improve their lives, the wretchedness of it. But all he had ensured was his own portion of wretchedness. He had stood at the edge of a chasm trying to pull the parishioners out with a solitary rope and they had simply and effortlessly dragged him down into the abyss. And despite the parish giving him—*a supposed gentleman*—150 pounds, without Mrs Soloman's reward, without his compendium, there stood no obstacle between him and gaol.

'I still don't see how you lost your herbal, sir,' says Boswell. 'That might have saved you.'

'I told you I didn't lose it, someone stole it. Besides, I still have my notes.'

'But if you locked the compendium inside your case—'

'Boswell!' Jeremiah snaps, tracing the outline of the key in his waistcoat pocket with his finger. 'He stole the damned key.'

'You have the devil in your shadow, sir. You know my mother—'

'Another of your her enlightening quips?'

'No, sir.'

Boswell begins whistling. Jeremiah empties the remainder of cleavers—good for yellow jaundice—into a bag. A few more jars are sniffed and the herbs bagged.

'Do you remember the whore who wanted her child cut?' he says.

'I remember, sir.'

'Well, she kept the infant.'

'You must be relieved, sir?'

To have another bastard running around this already overcrowded city? 'I shall be happy when assured it is not left at my threshold. Keep your eyes wide.'

Boswell hands him a jar. 'That's the last one, sir.'

Jeremiah hands the remaining herbs to Boswell. 'Use all the bags. We have no more use for them. Any arsenic remaining we'll give to the rats.'

There was comfort in the repetitive motions of dispensing herbs into bags. He has not minded helping out in a task that would normally befall his apprentice. For a time he stops thinking that by the morrow he would be the owner of an apothecary shop less its contents. Further comfort is reaped knowing the contents of these pots will not end up in Manners' hands.

'Sir?'

'What is it, Boswell?'

'Last night I kept thinking about something Mrs Soloman's footman said to me.'

'Ignore the fellow's prattling. I told you, he is looking to benefit from the spinster's will.'

'Not him, but the cook, sir.'

'I beg your pardon?'

'Farley told me how the cook had been periodically slipping arsenic into Mrs Soloman's tea. Farley found in amusing that you could not comprehend her sickness.'

293

'And you didn't think to tell me this sooner!' says Jeremiah, veritably shaking.

'I did not know if it really occurred, since I had drank more than a bottle of Mrs Soloman's wine. But on the last visit I went down to speak with the cook and she did confess to me, sir, all drunk and weepy. She said, she had stopped positioning her mistress out of fear which was why Mrs Soloman had recovered enough to descend her staircase.'

Jeremiah does not know whether to feel relieved that he might still be in possession of an ability to heal (having it thoroughly eroded by Mrs Solomon) or whether he should wrestle the urchin to the floor.

'I did not want to tell you yesterday as you were very down at the mouth. But really you should feel glad, sir. For whatever you had done, the old hag would have remained sick.'

Jeremiah's anger spits and dies, acknowledges, 'Aside from Miss Heart, the house was full of liars. But then lies beget lies. I was not entirely honest with Mrs Soloman from the start, was I? Giving Miss Zeldin's tonic, claiming it as my own. A lesson has perhaps been served.' There is anyhow little time remaining to invest into each individual misery of his life.

'A lesson to stay clear of rich old spinsters, I should say, sir.'

'Something like that, Boswell.'

In his elaboratory he sits at his desk and takes out the accounts book. One new entry in a week: another bag of cleavers. Cleavers: a plant capable of choking to death any plant growing close to it. He had used it for many ailments. As with other plants, however, he had taken pains in distilling its plentiful uses on paper. Often people came to mind: Arnold Green who had drunk the juice and gained much needed weight, or the lamplighter who had been given cleavers and hog's grease for a swelling in his throat (doubtless caused by yelling Mary's name too loudly in the yard), but to translate these successes, based on little more than feeling into words, had proved harder than pushing a silk scarf through the eye of the needle. Too much breadth; too many individual differences. Drawing the minutiae of the plants was by far the easier task. Plants after all were less troublesome than people. He is glad the compendium is gone. Next time—if there is to be another opportunity—he shall refine his methodology; give himself over to the general.

He takes out a sheaf of paper but rather than begin again with Aconitum, he writes:

Dear Brigid,

He lets the pleasure of several possibilities flow through his thoughts.

I miss your skin, the scent of your hair, your body pressed against mine.

I wish to gather you in my arms, never let you go. Abide with me, Brigid. Abide with me.

He looks up. A magpie sits on the end of a shovel, wagging its tail.

I fear for your safety with the African. Set him free so that the villagers will cease leaving dead birds at your threshold.

He has not received a response from the first letter he has sent since returning from Dorset. This is the second of two written in the space of 2 days and not posted. He dips his quill, ink drops trail across the page, spreading like extensions to his thoughts. He takes another valuable sheaf of paper and begins a third attempt.

Dear Brigid,

London is greyer since my return. I failed my patient. Your tonic worked but I, alas, failed. I had, it would seem, been chosen for my weaknesses not my strengths. I intend to visit you before being taken to the bailiff's sponging house. I shall take the coach to Dorset. Wait for me.

I love you.

He looks up the magpie's iridescent feathers, crosses out this last part and writes,

My warmest affections,
Jeremiah.

A long absence from Society

Jeremiah walks to Grosvenor Square, despondent, defeated, the sole of his shoe flapping noisily. The sole, having been repaired earlier that day with a thin strip of leather, was held insufficiently in place by egg whites. The cobbler had been paid with a bag of lemon balm for persistent stomach pains. The egg whites had not been given time to harden (Jeremiah had worn the shoe home for his other pair remain in a farmhouse somewhere in Dorset), thus he walks with a continual flip-flap, flip-flap, as though his shoe had grown a tail, as though inner unravelling was beginning to show.

Wordsley's house, the largest in the square, burns brighter than daylight. Guests spill from the ballroom on the first floor onto the balcony, laughter rising and falling like crescendos of an unfamiliar ocean. Somehow, Jeremiah must climb out of his steep-sided abyss and imagine himself free from debt, from misery; the muddle of his existence exchanged for a night of trivia and charm, forgetting that at some point the rope tied about his middle will tug him back into the abyss again.

'Mr Goode?'

Jeremiah stands, in what he had presumed were the shadows, hands clasped behind his back, 'Miss Aldridge!' He clutches his misshapen hat, hoping it is too dark to see the holes in his periwig. Lucy is approaching, gaily laughing.

'We meet again! You are finally venturing out of your shop,' she smiles, coyly, yellow curls springing excitedly at the sides of her face. He takes her gloved hand, presents it with a kiss.

'I do venture out of my habitat from time to time,' he says, replacing his hat too quickly. 'Your mother she is well.'

'We have been through tiresome formalities, have we not?'

'Then might I say you appear in good health?' It is all he can presently manage.

'You are too kind, Mr Goode.' She links her arm in his, steering him through the carriages towards the bottom of Wordsley's steps. 'But should I not be ignoring you considering you blatantly turned me down?'

'I'm afraid—'

'You know exactly what I speak of.'

He sole flaps hard against the paving stone. He runs his tongue over his teeth. 'I thought it was you who turned me down.'

She taps his nose with his fan. 'Really? In which case we are even then!' She crosses the road. 'But I did not realise that you and Lord Wordsley were still friends.'

'If friendship constitutes going regularly to White's then indeed we are.'

'White's?' She smiles at a couple alighting from another carriage. 'Have you been going only to White's? How terribly dull.'

'You may remember my shop,' he says, then speaks about the long winter, about the difficulties for the poor in such climates, until he realises she is not listening, merely smiling at guests being deposited in ostentatious attire by their coaches and six.

'Peg Woffington! She played a male part in the Constant Coup at the Haymarket. Scandalous!' Lucy's hand is flung to her mouth as she glares towards the entrance. 'Do I see what I think I see?'

'Miss Aldridge?'

'Lord Wordsley employing Negroes!'

Jeremiah follows Lucy's gaze to the two white wigged men standing either side of the front door, poised like statues, faces inscrutable. 'I believe they prefer to be called Africans, Miss Aldridge.'

She taps his arm. 'Oh, you are so silly! But I am relieved to see that your absence from Society has not damaged your humour. By the bye, you heard my recent news, that I am now engaged?'

Confirmation of his sisters' chatter allows him to be pulled up the steps to meet the fiancé. 'Then I must congratulate you.' No pang of regret, or even envy follow only something akin to relief.

'My fiancé is Colonel Letchford-Briggs.' Lucy gestures to a tall man with a stiff moustache and small eyes lacking in any kindness. 'Have you two met?'

Jeremiah makes his greetings, relieved they have not.

'Your name,' says the Colonel, 'it's familiar.'

Lucy's grip tightens around Jeremiah's arm. He wishes for her to let go, *set him free for God's sake.*

'We are obstructing the entrance,' she says, pulling him inside, into the bright light and heavy din of people losing their reserve so that by dawn remaining respectability shall be waiting by the entrance to be collected like a neatly folded umbrella.

He keeps his face impassive. The colonel's pig-like eyes continue to bore.

'Goode,' the fellow says, tugging the ends of his moustache. 'I am thinking, for some reason, of the fool you were once engaged to, my dear. What was the fellow's name?'

Jeremiah meets the Colonel's eye, is forced to quickly look away again. All around guests are laughing, talking loudly, glaring with gemstones and heavily embroidered silks, faces whiter than if they had seen a ghost of their lost selves. For with or without masks, their characters are for the most part hidden. And Lucy, what does she want with him? Does the cat still need the mouse when it has found a new owner to tickle its ears? Or was it toying that counted and little more besides?

Lucy's fingers press into his arm. 'Refreshments?' she says, her voice scratching a path towards the salon. 'Let us go in search of some refreshments.'

The colonel's eyes continue to pierce. 'The man was a perfect fool. When I spoke of him to Lord Wordsley he described him as preferring plants over people.' Two identical circles of red appear on his cheeks, like cannon fire on a distant horizon. 'Lord Wordsley took him out every so often from pure pity. Knowing how he treated Lucy, I should say he deserves public disgrace!'

Indeed, one did not slip back into society for a night with the ease with which one pulls on a glove. He shall not remain anonymous for long. This is not White's where dice grip attention. This was the frivolous politesse of society. It had its demands, its expectations and it demanded, at the very least, one's soul.

'I shall join you in a moment,' he tells Lucy, prising his arm from her grip.

'I hope that's a promise,' she replies with a pout.

At the bottom of the mahogany staircase, he encounters Wordsley's wife, Agnes, not yet porting a mask, her timid eyes wide as if with dread.

'Once again people assemble to flaunt their wealth,' she tells him with a sigh.

He kisses her hand. 'Then I ought not to be here, Lady Wordsley.'

She smiles and he finds himself immeasurably grateful for what he takes to be the sincerity with which she tell him. 'Oh, one can be wealthy in so many other ways, Mr Goode.'

On the walk home Jeremiah attempts to weigh up the state of his existence. In one scale sits the heavy burden of debt, the loss of his compendium, Mrs Soloman's reward and, if a prig such as Letchford-Briggs was to believed, the most recent loss of his friend. In the other scale sits the image of Brigid.

Beautiful Brigid.

The loss of his father rests between the scales, tipping them between states of relief and grief. But one thing about a man in a state of desperation: he has not the slightest inclination towards self-pity. Self-pity is a form of indulgence and a man needs a sense of worth in order to indulge himself. Without self-worth Jeremiah is perhaps little more than the skeleton standing in the corner of his shop. Yet, stripped of everything, his profession, his pride and his ambitions, one thing remains, the one thing he formerly lacked and that is *love*. Jeremiah, it would appear, is deeply but truly in love—perhaps for the first time in his four and thirty years. And every paving post he kicks on the walk home from Grosvenor Square to St Giles is an attempt to quell the intensity of this feeling. One might say that love was serving as a timely distraction. On the other hand it might just hold the power to save him.

If such a living could be considered free

'Five guineas. That is all?'

'The most Mr Cummings pays for a pocket watch, sir.'

Jeremiah takes the money from Boswell then hands the waiting customer a bag of marigold petals. 'Tell your father a spoonful seeped in boiled water, thrice daily for a week,' he smiles at the boy, 'his ulcers shall be soon eased.'

The boy tosses a penny onto the counter—a penny he has been brandishing since entering the shop—and then runs outside and across the yard. Jeremiah envies him his ability to run, to escape. He recalls Boswell at a similar age, running into the shop in search of a cure for his grandfather's gout: a fast, thin sprat of a boy, halfway along the road to professional pickpocket. He had, at the time, reminded Jeremiah a little of Jasper whose mannerisms likewise remained as self-centred as a child's. Now looking at the boy, almost a man, it would appear seriousness emanated from him, and it seemed to be growing in proportion to the plumpness of Mary's belly.

'Five guineas,' says Jeremiah looking at the chain where his pocket watch had once hung; a watch with which Mr Cummings will make a grand profit. He removes the traces of dirt with spittle. 'I shall have to hide it from Manners,' he says, then muses, 'Perhaps I should also hide myself.'

'Where would you go, sir?'

He shrugs. 'The Rookery.' Though he thinks: Chideock, to a cottage, to the arms of his beloved.

'No room to be found at the Rookery, sir. Not much of anything to be found at the Rookery.'

Jeremiah looks to the coins on the counter, such objects he almost despises for all the misery they have brought. He picks them up and hands three guineas to Boswell.

'Soon there shall be nothing—' Hope halts him, unexpectedly tugging at his thoughts like a ragamuffin tugging at his coat tails. 'Tell Mary to prepare a good meal on my return.'

'Going abroad, sir?'

'Tell Mary to prepare a bedchamber too.'

'You are having a guest to stay?'

'If I had wanted someone to question my actions I would have employed one of my sisters as my apprentice.'

Boswell pulls a face of mock concern. 'But apothecary work is not for women, sir, you have often said so yourself.'

'And if nothing else I still possess the freedom to change my mind!'

Jeremiah glances up at the bleak December sky. He has finished administering the last of his herbs at the Rookery. After supper, he shall leave for Dorset by which time Manners will be too drunk to taunt or spy on him. With 5 days of freedom there is no time left to await Brigid's reply.

He crosses the road, heading back to Neal's Yard. A lady is crouched down to a crying child, her crimson dress spread over the ground like a leaking wound, out of place in a parish already bled of its colour.

'Miss Heart?' he says.

She stands, the child now regarding her with an ill-disguised look of admiration.

'He fell,' she says, rising from the ground, 'I was enquiring about his mother, or… his nurse maid but he appears, well, to have neither.'

'Here,' says Jeremiah, taking a ha'penny hidden at the bottom of his basket. 'Go back to your family.' The boy runs off, his knee miraculously healed, for there were other miracles money could accomplish in St Giles. 'Poverty makes them clever, Miss Heart.'

'I was trying to… well, to help him.'

'Spare yourself.'

She crosses a hand over her chest. 'I read, indeed… I read aloud from Deuteronomy 15:8 but he was wailing so loudly that he could not even hear me.'

'Save yourself the effort,' he repeats again; the Bible in these parts provided more frustration then help. 'You must not be fooled by their act.' He shifts the basket on his arm. 'And do not offer them a fathing unless you want to be robbed of your purse.'

'Thank you, Mr Goode. I shall remember your advice.'

She smiles generously, her eyes glassy with need. He can feel this need as a hollow space in his breast, not dissimilar to the space residing in her aunt's womb.

Then a boy cries, 'Black your shoes! Black your shoes!' and a barrow passes between them and something either finishes or begins—Jeremiah cannot discern which—but the world is let back in again as a cacophony of drabness and noise; light with plentiful shade.

'You realise what my answer will be,' he says as he gestures Miss Heart inside Neal's Yard, averting his eye from the emptiness of his shop's windows.

'Answer, Mr Goode?'

'If you ask me to attend your sick aunt.'

'Oh, I can easily imagine but my aunt's health is not my reason for calling.'

He gestures Miss Heart inside the shop. The bell trills and Boswell looks up from the counter, wide-eyed, mouth agape as if each time Miss Heart calls he is expecting another miracle.

'As you can see we are clearing out stock,' Jeremiah's tone is too cheery. Still, he wonders if she can see the mortar concealing the ever-growing cracks of his life. 'Out with the old and in with the new.'

Miss Heart's eye comes to rest on the alligator suspended above her head.

'Take him,' he says for want of anything better to say. 'We have no further use for the trifling tat of our trade.'

'Miss Heart has another big mouth to cope with at home,' says Boswell. They both turn to the boy, Jeremiah glaring with reproach.

'No, I have no use for an... erm... alligator, Mr Goode,' says Miss Heart. 'But it is nonetheless a kind offer.'

He smiles, though his offer hangs between them like a fine thread at which they must mutually stare before the inevitable snap.

'I have no use for the creature now,' he says. Neither can he stand here all day holding idle conversation; he has a shop to clear, final letters to write. 'So you have come to tell me that your aunt has had a change of mind about the reward?'

Another hue rises up from the frill of Miss Heart's collar and he thinks what great exercise for her veins all this blushing must be.

'Unfortunately,' she says, 'my aunt does not sway from her opinions so easily. She does, however, wish to dine downstairs in her dining room this Wednesday.'

To hide his surprise, Jeremiah wipes a finger along the old skeleton, Nicholas Culpeper. Out of all the useless objects in the room he shall miss this fellow the most. 'Then I wish your aunt well in her venture.'

'She wishes you to be there. Rather, my aunt wishes to invite you for dinner, Mr Goode.'

Next Wednesday was to be his last night of freedom, if such a living could be considered free. 'You must inform you aunt I am otherwise engaged.'

'In her usual manner she is quite insistent so if you would be able to respond in—'

'In writing, thus proving that your errand was carried out? Miss Heart, you must cease letting such a curmudgeonly woman govern your life.'

'I am happy to serve my aunt.' She fiddles with her bonnet. 'It is the least I can do.'

Until she marries you off. 'Miss Heart, I shall indeed come.'

Miss Heart tilts her head, regards him as if waiting for a 'but'. The thought of spending his last night unable to sleep, having consumed—if lucky—a stale piece of bread for supper, Mary and Boswell locked in embrace above his ceiling, however, requires no further explanation.

'I leave for Dorset today and shall return by next Tuesday,' he says.

'I shall tell my aunt to expect you, Mr Goode.'

He bows his head and opens the door.

'You do realise,' he says, running a hand through his loose hair, 'you do realise that the cook's intervention was beyond my control.'

'Of course, Mr Goode and I do believe the dinner may be my aunt's means of thanking you for brining cook's actions to her attention.'

'I see.' *Pity she will not thank him with money.*

'So we shall see you next week?'

'Indeed.' He bows low to Miss Heart acknowledging that it might be the last time he is expected anywhere.

His rational, empirical nature has all but left him

The stagecoach rocks but Jeremiah is far from sleep.

'I saw an angel,' says a boy with a pale, flat face sitting opposite.

'When?' asks the girl with ringlets.

'Just now.'

'Did not.'

'Did too!'

'He cannot help it, sir.' The girl hugs a basket of vegetables to her chest and rolls her eyes at her brother. 'He has spoken constantly of angels since learning to speak.'

If Jeremiah wanted proof angels did not exist he had only to look at this boy. A mongrel, he thinks. Either that or born possessed by the devil.

'*For he shall guide his Angels charge over thee.*' The boy points towards Jeremiah's arms, tightly folded against his chest, '*to keep thee in all thy ways.*'

The entire coach now stares. The lunatics: why did they always want to converse with him?

'We are going to visit my grandmother,' says the girl.

'And you!' The boy continues to point. '*Holy, holy, holy, the Lord Sabbath! The whole world is filled with His Glory!*'

The girl pulls in her lips. 'Sorry, sir.'

Jeremiah closes his eyes, the only protection afforded him. Even at these moments the image behind his closed lids is still there. Brigid's face: her full lips, her raven hair… Then her voice comes, as he sometimes does, as clear as the voice of his own thoughts: *I heal, it is what I do.*

Since when, he wonders, had every step turned into a pilgrimage towards this woman? Parts of his life had slipped away as easily as dried-up petals fall from a flower. What once had seemed so relevant, so essential to his existence—writing his compendium, gaming at White's, lying with Virtue—now seemed as relevant as those petals rotting in dirt. He had been alive to the magnificence of Nature not to that of living. Living required love. He could see that now. Looking back at his days, curing the parish, head bent over a compendium trying to make sense of his methods, he had been avoiding needing anything more. Even chiding Boswell was a way of declaring his lack of need for the boy. But he did *need* people. More specifically he *needed* Brigid, her love. Rather, he needed the freedom to love her and now this love had been turned inwards until it had become part of himself, until it had altered all that surrounded him.

Given his predicament, one might say his rational, empirical nature had all but left him.

'*I look to the sky, to the stars where a multitude of stars that did guide the shepherds…*'

The boy rants. Jeremiah drifts. At the next inn he is awoken by church bells and alights. He takes deep lungfuls of sea air, followed by a piss. The girl with the vegetables crosses the lane to say farewell, griping her brother's hand.

He has something to say to you,' she half-apologises.

'*Angels are but messengers from God*,' says the boy, narrow eyes almost closing, his flat face tightening into pain. '*Come to thee thy angels to offer up thy salvation.*'

Jeremiah sleeps, for how long he does not know. When he wakes again he is slumped against the coarse coat of a man. He apologises, and peers between the boards, rubbing his neck. It is raining. The horses' hooves are sucked from muddy potholes to the accompaniment of the driver's whip against water-slicked backs; a sound that breaks up the creak of the wooden shaft all too readily; a sound that enlivens his nerves.

'Where are we?' he asks with a yawn.

'Approaching Seatown,' says the man, who has served as his pillow.

'How far is it to Chideock?' If he were given a map he would not be able to point his location. For the first time in Jeremiah's life he feels set adrift: a ship without sails, rudder and barely any crew.

'About three mile. You have people here?' The man's inquisitiveness is like a blast from a stove and Jeremiah shifts his body to the side.

'No,' he tells him as another pothole rattles his ribs.

The man snorts. 'These roads too rough for London folk?'

'You are from around here?'

'I be from Charmouth.'

It may as well be Bengal for all Jeremiah knows of the place.

He takes his wig from his lap and puts it on and indulges the man's curiosity for his own sake. 'I am visiting a Miss Zeldin, from Chideock,' he says.

The man's laughter fills the coach with *hawfs* before he slumps back, resting his hands on the mound of his gut and laughter is replaced by bird song. Refusing to indulge him further, Jeremiah keeps his eyes to a slither of visible world between the boards.

At Seatown he alights. He knows he will have to inquire again about the whereabouts of Miss Zeldin's cottage but for now he walks inland, towards hills and dense forests, stretching his legs with such care it as though he must unwrap a body without spilling its contents. He breathes the sea-whisked air. He reminds himself of his passions, for plants, for healing, reminds himself there is not yet a place reserved for him in Bedlam. He keeps his eyes to the muddy track, placing one foot after another as he treks closer to his cure.

'They call her the Witch round these parts.'

His earlier travelling companion is there, walking briskly at his side, smirking.

Jeremiah asks, 'And where may I find her cottage?' Everything appears altered without snow.

'City folk, they do not object to a walk? My name is John Crocker but people call me Crock. I am a church warden at St Giles.' *St Giles, it would have to be.* 'My brother is from Chideock.'

Journeying with the man along a narrowing drover's way, Jeremiah listens to him talk of the eight martyrs of Chideock, put to death for their Catholic faith, about Lord Arundell who recently inherited Chideock from his Cornish cousins. He listens at length to the wrongdoings of the man's brother. But Jeremiah has no interest in this small-town talk and when there is a pause he says, 'Miss Zeldin in not a witch.'

'She gave the Cure once for my brother's daughter who was healed from close to death. My sister-in-law says the woman harbours something not right in her breast, says it is obvious from her complexion.'

'Her complexion?' asks Jeremiah, now disconnected from the rhythm of his own stride as much as from the opening and closing of his own mouth.

'Aye, as pale as moonlight, though she spends plenty time in her garden tending to her plants. The devil's skin some do say. People say too she has a dog for company.' The man pauses. 'A black dog. There is other filth I hear about but me, I do not live in the village. Anyhow, it does a man no good to speak of filth.' He points a finger. 'Ruins Lane where Chideock Castle and its moat can still be seen. My brother's house is made from them ruins.'

They continue up a small hill where from the top there is a view of the hamlet below. The man points to a cottage in a clearing where a brief break in the clouds reveals a rainbow floating above its roof.

'You'll find her there,' he says. 'And a pot of gold by the look of it!'

She harboured a slave

The cottage is a pretty place with creepers, it appears aloof, isolated. It is set back some distance from the road and its thatched roof conceals much of the façade.

He pauses, one hand on the garden gate. The man removes the piece of straw he has been chewing. 'There is no Mr Zeldin,' he says, with a wink. 'In case you were wondering and, nay, I do not think she is a witch in answer to your question.' The man shakes his head, tightening the string about his waist. 'A woman with a cold heart perhaps but not a witch. Still, that business is not for me.'

Jeremiah manages to thank the man. He continues up the road. 'But if we do not hear from you again,' he laughs, 'we shall think you are under her spell.'

Jeremiah stands for a moment outside the gate. It is not yet spring but there is a hint of its arrival in a wren's call and the determined shoots of snowdrops pressing up through the earth. Against this vast swath of nature he feels small, his hardships little more than a stitch in God's grand tapestry, a mere flick of the weaver's wrist. Yet he knows too that days with Brigid in them are the ones that remain filled with hope.

The gate opens and groans and swings shut behind. He slowly takes the narrow path to the door. Fleetingly, it crosses his mind that he might stay here. Hide here. Cease to exist here. Manners would in time forget about him. His apothecary shop would become something more useful to the parish: a boarding house curing the ills of man by the usual means: with drink and willing whores.

And he could spend the rest of his days in blissful contentment.

He notices a number of cracks in the cottage's walls. Tiredness washes over him as the path ebbs and swells beneath his feet. He knocks on the front door. A wood pigeon coos. His second knock is harder and wings flap in a nearby tree. His heart pounds and if he looked at his shirt he would see it waft to its rhythm.

Anticipation, however, is quickly replaced by foreboding. What if Brigid has a new lover? The *Praefacrus Horti*, Mr Rand? A fellow from the village, perhaps? God forbid, the African!

He raps on the front door in a manner now too loud for politeness. There is still no reply. He tries the latch. Locked. He sees a path winding around one side of the house. He follows it to the scullery, peers in through the window, sees that the purification and distilling apparatus gone. No pans. No bread upon the board. No Brigid, the door locked.

She is seeing a dying patient in the village. She is delivering a child. She is somewhere in this garden, tending to her herbs.

'*Brigid?*' He clears his throat, corrects himself. '*Miss Zeldin? It is I, Jeremiah.*'

The cuckoo calling from the woods begins to irritate him. Acid burns his stomach, travelling up his oesophagus, making him suddenly nauseous. He carries on past the muckheap to the barn, the low brick building where the African lived. He bangs on the entrance, the door shaking beneath his fist. He kicks it with his foot.

In the darkness his hand swipes at cobwebs. Pinpricks of light leak through gaps in the vaulted ceiling. He anticipates the African jumping out of the shadows and stands with his hands held out protectively before him, listening. Not a sound, not even those of Brigid's horse or goat can be heard, only the birds and that maddening cry of a displaced cuckoo.

Once his eyes adjust, however, he takes in the shrine: two yards across and three yards tall, comprising stripped animal bones, a sheep's skull at the pinnacle. On the wall: rudimentary pictures of the sun and moon and adjacent to this two interlocking circles, something he could recall drawing at school to demonstrate something, he forgets what. The Father, the Son and the Holy Spirit perhaps. Further along the same wall a low shelf where several sealed jars are arranged in height order, found on closer inspection to contain spiders, beetles, one solely given to a collection of dried ants.

Jeremiah lets out his breath.

He looks about at the bed on the floor and a table. He wanders across the straw-scattered floor and picks up the sheet of paper where *I am Tayo*, is written countless times in child-like script, the letters becoming increasingly smaller, sloping down one side of the page until at the very bottom they alter. His heart stumbles as he reads another name. The g curls snake-like towards the edge of the page. It could almost—

It is not possible!

It could almost pass for his script.

I am Indigo Goode, it reads. *I am Indigo Goode*.

He had not revealed his christened name, not to Brigid and certainly not to Tayo. He had been Jeremiah, Jeremiah since leaving home. Indigo was left alongside the memories he had neither inclination nor verve to burden himself with. People adjusted. These epithets society seemed to accept almost as readily as unfaithfulness.

Why then when examining the script closer does he feels caught out? Guilty. What other secrets lay in this barn buried amongst straw? Thoughts untether, circling above his head like the swift or the swallow too frightened to land. He thinks, *Who are you*?

He returns to the front of the cottage, peers into the parlour, stripped bare of its contents. Only the drug chest remains, its drawers heaped upon the flagstones. Brigid's carefully ordered herbs reduced to a few crumbs.

At the sound of footsteps he turns. A man, dressed in a sapphire blue coat carrying a musket, marches up the path; a man, it appears, unacquainted with fear. Both his cheeks are meshwork of broken veins, his brow deeply furrowed like a hound's.

'Who goes there?'

Jeremiah runs a hand over his face gazing meeting the fellow's *No popery* badge. 'I am looking for Brigid Zeldin. Miss Zeldin.'

'Looking for the witch are you? You won't find her here. Not anymore. Last seen in the stocks.' He gestures north. 'Up in the village. Word was she harboured a *blackie*. The village does not take kindly to such deceit.'

'Where do I find these stocks?'

'Stocks?' says the fellow examining the bore of his musket. 'She not be there now.' He continues to suck on a piece of straw. Jeremiah understands the urge to punch a person and would do so, if not for the musket.

'Where might I find her?'

'There was a frost. Many said she would not survive the night. Rumour was she was with child. The blackie, he escaped. Much injury did befall the woman. Cuts and bruises like sooty stains about her face from all the things thrown at her by villagers.' He shifts the musket onto his shoulder. 'Aye,' he says staring towards the facing fields. 'She harboured a blackie.'

'And after the frost?'

The man looks back at him, taking him in from his shoes to his periwig. 'After the sharp frost none thought she would survive. Most did not care whether she lived or died. They wanted to burn her as is appropriate for them that are called witches.'

'Where is she bur—' His voice cracks.

'Buried?' The man laughs. 'She not be buried. There was no body. Just empty stocks, locked when the squire discovered her gone at daybreak. He ordered Jack Johnson our smithy to repair them but they were ne'er a break in them. Found to be in perfect order. So what business do you have with the witch?'

'Business?'

She escaped.

'Are you sick?' The man laughs. 'Most need to be dying before trusting their lives to a witch.'

'I am Miss Zeldin's… friend.'

The fellow spits. 'Those that have the Devil in their shadow have no friends. Most are afraid of her and for good reason. There is no telling how many she cursed though some say the blackie did the curses. Myself, I believe they were of her own doing.'

A roe deer, pert white tail, walks out of the forest. Both men turn. The deer looks up, fear stilling its limbs, then it jumps, springing over the low stony wall and across the lane and over the fields.

Jeremiah clenches his fists. 'She healed your blessed village.'

The musket is raised. 'If she owes thee money, best speak to her brother. Her brother is dealing with her plate, her debts and the like.'

Jeremiah thumps the cottage wall. He storms out of the gate and uphill, heading towards the church tower, its square top just visible above the bare tree tops as the skies spills hesitant drops of rain.

'You are not the first,' the man calls after him. 'They were plenty others, men with hunger in their eyes just like thee!'

By the time he reaches the stocks—the usual means of publicly humiliating the villagers—anger flames into his throat and stings his eyes.

It is a sport to a fool to do mischief
to
Thine own wickedness shall correct thee

He recognises it as a conflation of Proverbs 10:23 and Jeremiah 2:10. He squats down to examine the locks. Two milkmaids pass by and seeing him on the ground, folded into the smallest space possible, they snigger. He examines his grazed and bloodied fist. *What did she endure?* He sits back on his heels, looks up to a clear oval shape in the overhead cloud and watches as it neatly closes up, obliterating the sun.

There is a man to see you about a book

When Jeremiah enters his shop three days later, thoughts still circle above his head so that his actions appear to belong to another: a person able to walk, pay greetings in the street, breathe. He opens the moneybox, peers inside and closes it again, having registered nothing of its contents. He opens the curtain to his elaboratory, removes his coat and hat, tosses them on the table then looks at the scene before him. It might well exist at the end of a long telescope: a mere blot on the horizon for all he can make of it.

Only after Boswell says, 'We did not know what to do with it, sir?' does he take in Boswell and Mary seated on stools before the fire with something on Mary's knee, a package of sorts.

'The baby, sir. We did not know what to do with the baby.'

The thoughts swirling above his head land with a thump. *Mary has given birth.* He, a man with no business, no prospects, shares a house with apprentice, maid and their baby!

'Does it cry?' he hears himself utter.

'Does it cry! Methinks we are in need of a board to strap it to. Pity we cannot strap something over its mouth.'

Jeremiah keeps moving through his elaboratory, up the narrow stairs, gait unsteady. In his bedchamber he lies on the bed, fully clothed, staring up at the canopy, waiting for the point when his mind will return to his body.

He remains here for the rest of the day in a state halfway between awareness and sleep. His dreams are of angels as black as ebony, wings as white as snowdrops. In his dreams Brigid visits his bedside. 'Hold no secrets,' she says, but reaching out to grasp her she has no more substance than mist.

After an unknown amount of time an insistent *rat-a-tat-tat* at his bedchamber door draws him fully awake. He opens his eyes and examines the crumpled linen in his palms.

'What is it?' he calls.

'There is a man to see you about a book, sir.'

'What book?'

'Your herbal I believe, sir.'

He gets out of bed wiping crusts of tears from both eyes. He opens the door, motions retarded as if moving through a thick, life-sucking syrup.

'Who is he?' he asks.

'An important-looking gentlemen with very fine whiskers,' says Boswell regarding him strangely. 'The gentleman says he wants to speak with you about your compendium.'

Jeremiah attempts to laugh. 'Did he find it strewn across London?'

'He wants to know if it is complete.'

'Complete? He would have more success getting thieves from the Welsh's Head to write out the Bible than wait for the completion of my compendium.'

Nevertheless, by the time he has taken his stairs the loss of Brigid stifles further disappointment. Too much effort is required in saying, 'How do you do?' to Mr Jacobs the bookseller who stands shifting his round form between one foot and the other like an exotic, badly drawn bird. With a brief grimace, Jeremiah slumps into his seat.

'Extraordinary number of wooden legs in this area,' the bookseller tells him, as he sits on a chair facing Jeremiah's. 'I am always surprised by areas of London I am unfamiliar with. Grub Street, for example, one would expect to be filled by writers. On the contrary, there are more ragged shoemakers there than any other profession. Now, of course, you must wonder why I am calling on you.'

Jeremiah picks up a shard of glass—all that remains of his brother's paperweight. He holds it up to the light to reveal dozens of tiny imperfections.

'Why?' he manages.

'Recently, on account of the cold,' says the bookseller, 'I have had more requests for herbals, or books concerning health, than ever before. I propose that if you complete yours to the best of your abilities before January is through, I am prepared to offer an advance for its copyright. In the future, naturally depending on the book's success, we may have to put the copyright up for auction at Stationer's Hall. I also belong to the Conger Club, a club comprising booksellers who collaborate to issue the more expensive works, you understand. But I am willing for now to pay between fifty and seventy five pounds depending on quality and length, considerably more than I usually offer authors publishing a work for the first time but, as I mentioned, demand for such a book appears absolutely assured. Now I propose we sell the herbal at a reasonable price and we shall print the price on the cover, to avoid it being sold for more. Alas, it does happen from time to time. Four pennies. The cost of a pound of sweet almonds. Affordable even to those inhabiting St Giles-in-the-Fields. Is it not?'

Jeremiah, immersed in the glass, does not notice the incongruity: that the parish can neither afford the luxury of almonds, nor do they read.

'As to the book's details—I am not a particularly pious man—but most would prefer that there is some allusion to God in the text. I advise you consider a biblical quote, perhaps on the first page. I have one here to hand.' He rummages through his case extracting a sheet of paper and clears his throat. '*He hath filled me with bitterness, he hath made me drunken with wormwood.* Lamentions. Something to that effect though perhaps something more cheerful or even a quote that bears personal relevance: *The message came to Jeremiah from the Lord... make a yoke and fasten it on your neck.* I shall leave the details to you. Bindings we can discuss on my next visit.'

Jeremiah runs a finger along the sharp edge of the glass. He mumbles, '*For the lips of an adulteress drip honey, and her mouth is smoother than oil / But her end is bitter as wormwood, sharp as a two-edged sword.*'

'That's the spirit! Anyhow I shall leave the details to you. So, I propose I return in two weeks to collect the manuscript. In the meantime I shall leave this bank note for thirty-five pounds. This is, you understand Mr Goode, exceptional for an unknown author and on account of the South Sea Bubble bursting, well, I am no longer given to advancing large copyrights but since you are blessed by good timing—great fortune bestowing you with a cold spell that has made London so terribly sick—I make an exception.' He stands, pauses, raising a finger to the ceiling. 'One more thing, the remaining sum I shall give to you upon receipt of the manuscript; the *full* manuscript.' He looks about. 'An interesting place you have here.'

Jeremiah places the shard of glass carefully next to his quill.

'Charming.' The bookseller squints at Jeremiah's bookshelves his nose still twitching. 'Quite charming!'

Following Mr Jacobs into his shop, Jeremiah senses his foot burning: a different sort of pain than that provided by frost: a gnawing, dull, heavy ache.

'You wish for a remedy for your gout?' he inquires.

The bookseller stops with an abruptness that causes Jeremiah to run into his back.

'Well I never!' he says.

'Horseradish root, parsley and wormwood.'

Jacobs scratches his whiskers. 'What a curious talent you have for Curing, Mr Goode. A curious talent indeed.'

'Some wormwood for the gentleman,' Jeremiah instructs Boswell. 'As for the other herbs,' he tells the bookseller, 'I am afraid we are sold out. Most of these jars surrounding us you'll find quite empty.'

'Herbs, that is what people need. Herbs and books! A busy winter it must have been for you,' says the bookseller. 'A busy winter indeed!'

Jeremiah stares back mutely, not knowing where he would begin on the subject of his winter.

'See you in two weeks then,' says the bookseller. 'And if my gout has by then been Cured I shall be selling your book myself!'

Reflected in your eyes

Jeremiah says goodbye, gripping the bank note with thirty-five added next to the pound sign along with the date and his name as if he had a claim upon it. Watching the round little man scurry through the Yard, he tells Boswell, 'Keep this safe until it needs to be returned to Mr Jacobs.' He hands him the note. 'And do not let Manners get his grubby paws on it.'

'The gentleman wishes to buy your compendium, sir?'

'There is no compendium, Boswell.'

'Sir.'

'I have nothing more to add.'

'If you do not mind me saying so, sir, you look like you've been dragged by a horse back from Dorset.'

There is an absurd desire to confide, to reveal something of his loss. Instead, he buttons his waistcoat and runs a hand over his stubble. 'It was a long journey,' he says, turning towards the vermillion curtain. 'Ask Mary to bring me some tea.'

'Mary is with the baby.'

He had forgotten about the baby. 'Mary's child cannot remain here Boswell.' *None of us can remain here.*

'It is not Mary's baby, sir. The astronomer says that the whore left it outside the shop. It spent all night in a drawer on the threshold until Mary found it at dawn. It is a miracle it survived.'

Jeremiah wipes a hand over his face. *Miracles, miracles, miracles.*

'What do you think we should do with it, sir?'

'For now, do whatever one is supposed to do with babies.'

Boswell sniffs. 'One more thing, sir.'

Looking at Boswell Jeremiah is reminded of the roe deer: a similar fear seems to reside in his body as if too might spring off into the distance at any moment's notice.

'I would have to be more of an imbecile than I am already not to realise Mary is with child, Boswell.'

Boswell straightens his back. 'Sir,' he says, eyes dropping to the floor. 'We…are looking for a position where we can live together as…as a family.'

The words seem rehearsed, yet Jeremiah senses his apprentices' determination. But confirmation he shall lose his apprentice is a great blow. Yet, sympathy is not something he is practised at. Action not sympathy had healed St Giles. Besides, Boswell is almost a man. He will learn that hope matters more than sympathy, certainly much more than regret. For hope alone keeps a man marching forward into these unyielding battles.

'Naturally you cannot be bound to me if I am no longer here,' he says. 'And living as a family is perhaps too much to ask from an employer in London. But I shall write to my old employer Mr James. He knows every apothecary in London. It shall perhaps be easier having a more predictable apothecary to guide you in your studies.'

'But I have learnt much from your methods, sir. And Mary? Apprentices, you say yourself, are forbidden to marry.'

Jeremiah watches the post boy cross the yard, open the shop door and toss a letter to the floor.

'Mary cannot accompany you,' Jeremiah says, retrieving the letter.

'But she is with child, sir.'

'Her child must go to one of the new foundling hospitals. Mary must look for employment elsewhere.'

'There is no employer that wants a mute and deaf maid.'

'She is no longer deaf.'

'But she is mute.'

'And plenty of unmarried gentlemen want a maid as handsome as Mary.' Perhaps it is not to late to enact a cure for her silence.

Boswell bangs the counter with his fist. 'Gentlemen, they will want their way with her. I cannot let that happen to Mary. Do you not know what it is to love a woman?'

Neither speaks but there continues a silence, a terrible empty silence.

Jeremiah clears his throat. 'You should…' He clears his throat again, 'you should do well to remember that this counter is not yours, nor mine

315

for that matter. Now tell Mary to fetch me some tea. I have much to arrange before Manners next calls.'

He returns to his desk and stares up at the desolate winter sky.

Of course he must now write the letter he does not wish to write, that his father had doubtless anticipated him writing.

Dear Mother,

If I do not have one hundred pounds by Thursday I am to give up my existence to a debt collector at whose house I will remain until the court have settled the terms of my prison sentence. I ask that you lend me this sum with the assurance it shall be repaid as soon as I am able. With proper advertising of marvellous Cure-alls I feel sure I shall have a profitable business before the year is through. In addition, a bookseller wishes to publish my herbal, that is, once it has been written.

He pauses, wondering whether he ought to be more specific: emphasise he does not intend relinquishing freedom to reign over the prattle of his sisters, amid the tittle-tattle of Dulwich society. He intends to remain here in St Giles where he has, strange though it may sound, found a sense of belonging.

The letter he ends with Brigid's words.

My purpose in this life, Mama, is to heal. Whether it is a fate ordained by God I cannot be certain. I only know that it is a fate to which I have grown somewhat proficient.

Yours affectionately,

Indigo.

'Go to St Giles and disappear,' his father had told him after he had given up physic for the profession of apothecary, after he had delayed marriage to Lucy, and so far as most of society was concerned he *had* disappeared. Now, with his father dead, what did he have left to prove? He cared not a jot if anybody thought him dead. Yet, the desire to cure this parish could not be so easily surrendered and in that regard he had more in common with his father than mere feet. Yet, his means and methods remained his own, methods soon to be abandoned at the threshold of Manners' sponging house.

He sits back in his seat. A school lesson comes to mind, how he had learnt that the power of gravitation acts proportionally to the quantity of matter in bodies, a truth which Sir Isaac had demonstrated by experiment. The sun at the centre of the planetary system attracts bodies in a direct ratio of their quantity of matter combined with their nearness. Sir Isaac was bold enough to compute the quantity of matter contained in the sun and in every planet; and in this manner showed, from the simple laws of mechanics, that every celestial globe ought by necessity to be where it is placed. With or without his father he is here in St Giles. Even with the luxury of choice he would remain thus. As to who shall act as his sun, well, it is not a problem that he need consider for long. Immediately, he takes his quill and begins writing another letter, one he shall never post.

Dearest Brigid,

I am not in the habit of writing letters to a woman, or for anybody for that matter (though the debt collector has recently heard from me more than most), but it seems I have no choice but to write to you for I miss you, Brigid. I have Cured many but in all this time I have been ignorant of my own sickness: I was deeply deprived of love. But now I have seen myself reflected in your eyes and, a blessed miracle has occurred! I no longer feel abhorred by what I see—for you, Brigid, have made me a better man. When I am with you ...

He dips the quill, determined.

'... *my soul is more than content. It is rendered* ...'

He forces the nib forwards.

'... *in a state of miraculous Completion.*'

He wipes the loss from his eyes and opens the letter recently delivered by the post boy, eye falling immediately to the signature at the bottom. He then re-reads the letter several times amid the wild clattering of his heart.

Perhaps you have some knowledge of witches

Jeremiah has come to see life as a serious of motions he must enact towards its conclusion. He is not unlucky or blessed, neither wise nor dumb. He merely resides on Earth in a state of incompleteness, the sweet taste of love on his tongue, not yet displaced by the bitterness of its loss. Thus, as he walks towards the city, the numbness now familiar, it is as if—like this great sleeping city—he must wait for the thaw. Yet whether even the warmth of spring will melt the blessed icicle piercing his heart he cannot say, nor think of.

He enters the low door of *Lloyd's Coffee House*, in Lombard Street, in the shadow of Exchange Square. He stumbles over a stair, pays his penny charge and takes a few steps up to a larger, brighter lit room swirling with tobacco smoke. Through the haze he makes out customers sitting, writing, reading the shop's newspapers, some bidding with raised voices, nearly all smoking Cutty pipes as they sip their coffee from generous sized dishes. On a table beside the fire (not that a fire is necessary with the room giving off steam) earthenware pitchers are laid out beside unclaimed pipes. A large Bible remains unopened. Above the fire hangs a coffee pot, bubbling with Turkish coffee, and to the right further shelves of dishes. Beneath is placed a Parliamentary ordinance prohibiting drinking and the use of bad language: a rudimentary rule and one rarely reinforced.

Having chosen an empty corner of a table, Jeremiah sits down, already sickened by the smoke and the heady stench of stewed coffee. He looks about at the customers. In St Giles he has grown used to men unburdened by periwigs. These men in their lavish wigs and embroidered waistcoats brag loudly, appearing indistinguishable one from the other. They are, he supposes, proper men whose skirmishes with the world are marked by successes. Most boasted how coffee improved virility but the women, on the whole, feared its effects. Aside from the Turkish woman straddling the shop's emblem, women are absent from these establishments. They believed coffee heathenish. Culpepper had written in his herbal of coffee's usefulness for purging and on this point Jeremiah agreed. Back in his elaboratory, with himself as his subject, he had freely tested the stuff and in large amounts found no better use for it than cleansing but it likewise increased his anxiousness and so or this reason, he remains on the side of the women.

As with Jonathan's—one of the many coffee houses his father had taken him to as a boy—Lloyd's is a place where rich merchants gather on benches and Windsor chairs to broker their stock and converse on shipping news as if the tides themselves were under their govern. He remembers sitting in awe as bags of snuff, or elephant's feet captured and brought back from Africa and the Orient, were sold to the highest bidder as the candle burnt out. He remembers the servant on the pulpit reading the paper for the company's amusement. He remembers watching his father's face as a fishmonger sat cheek by jowl, talking politics, degrees of distance taken up again once outside the shop. He had read the Lloyd's List to keep him from boredom, glimpsed pamphlets such as *The Doctrines of Chance* and one in particular he remembers claimed passions instilled by Nature rendered the mind incapable of entertaining anything aside from its own astonishment, before his father had whipped it from his hand.

He now takes out the letter, examining for the 100th time the signature of the man who has summoned him here. After a time a voice inquires, 'Mr Goode?' He looks up to see a man wearing the white hat ribbons of Jacobite sympathies. Jeremiah immediately recognises the dark eyes, thickly lashed, and a mouth wearing the same half-smile.

'I am Conrad Zeldin. How do you do? Let me fetch you some coffee. You shall have a dish?'

Jeremiah shakes his head.

'It quickens the heart and lifts the spirit, Mr Goode.'

'I do not doubt,' says Jeremiah, knowing his spirit was beyond such remedy.

Conrad Zeldin smiles. 'I am glad, though surprised, that you came.' He places a package on the floor and removes an olive green coat, which he hangs across the back of a chair.

Jeremiah shrugs his mouth. 'You said that it was urgent.'

'Urgent was in fact my sister's word. But why did you not respond to my letter?'

He could ill afford the penny post. 'I have been busy.'

'Busy is the usual state of existence for a gentleman in this City, is it not? Are you certain you will not take a coffee? It is truly very good. The pot renewed every hour, or so we are told.'

Wishing not to prolong his reason for being summoned, Jeremiah agrees to a dish. The brother is tall and slim, and has a way of standing chin tipped heaven-bound like his sister. He fetches the drinks, returning with two green dishes, one of which he places on the table in before Jeremiah. Seated opposite, he takes out a pipe.

'She wrote to me,' he says, tapping used-up tobacco onto the tabletop, 'before they came for her. She knew they would come, eventually. That is the trouble with life, is it not Mr Goode, that most things are eventual. We tell ourselves otherwise, of course. We fool ourselves that death is under our dominion not God's, but eventuality is the curse of this life.' He holds Jeremiah's eye then unexpectedly laughs.

'There is no need for your concern, Mr Goode. I am not aware of Brigid being dead.'

Jeremiah breathes again, takes a sip of his coffee: a bitter, almost unpalatable liquid. 'Then do you know where she resides?' Unwittingly, he pictures Brigid publicly humiliated, an image that has frequently haunted him these past few days and absurdly long nights.

Conrad Zeldin continues filling his pipe with tobacco. 'No, I do not.' The sentence displaces further words from Jeremiah's thoughts. He watches the brother put away his silver box of tobacco. 'She mentioned you though, in a previous letter though. Goode, the apothecary. That is you, is it not?'

He nods.

'But not a physician?'

He has no wish to hold polite conversation with this fellow. 'I had and still have a preference for plants over people.' He cradles the dish in his palm. 'How does she fare?' Though he means to say: are you certain she is *alive*?

'The letter I received was sent before she was sent to the village stocks. Please excuse me a moment.' Conrad Zeldin crosses to the fire where he lights a spill that he uses to light his pipe. Another man, in a viridian coloured coat, with chocolate stains about his mouth, pats his back and they converse at length.

Jeremiah sips his coffee, picks up a pamphlet and sets it down again. He recalls another coffee shop he had visited with his father as a boy: Batson's: a coffee house for physicians where beneath mahogany shelves of hair tonics, snuff, caramels and toothpowder made from dried up coffee-grounds—as well as other useless stuff he now knows an apothecary must sell if he wished to keep his business profitable—he had watched physicians hover over patients like crows over carcasses. Graduates came to Batson's to learn from the more experienced who in turn learned from other physicians on such subjects as the *infallible* methods of preventing the spread of plague from

320

France to England. His father, wearing his red coat and short sword—the garb of the physicians—enjoying the coffee drank at his patients' expense, ensuring his meetings with patients ended in costly surgery and all the while Jeremiah had sat beside him feeling some pain or other, from one particular body or other, not knowing quite what to do with it.

He twists his bowl in the palm of his hand, his heart beginning to beat faster. A thought occurs, at once frantic yet obvious: *she might be dead.*

When Conrad Zeldin returns, he is smiling, eagerly puffing at his pipe.

'My apologies. A friend wanted to speak about the Prussian invasion of Silesia. He has relatives in Austria. War it would seem is imminent.' He settles on his seat. 'Tell me, Mr Goode, did my sister speak of our family?'

He could mention how Brigid had spoken of a drowned younger brother, her father's cotton mill, an older brother whose wife liked to frequent shops, but says instead, 'We had other things to speak about,' in a tone to imply whatever passed had been a private matter.

Conrad Zeldin inhales deeply on his pipe. 'Well, you shall hear the truth from my lips. My father came over to England from France in 1700. He struggled to learn English but worked hard and was favoured by the owner of the mill where he found steady employment. In time, he was offered a share of it. He met my mother at this mill. She was maid to the former mill owner. She was from Ireland, Mr Goode, and I suspect she shared with my father a sense of being the outsider. It is a feeling, I have come to learn, that can penetrate many a generation.' He pauses to sip his coffee. 'When Brigid and I were young our mother fell sick. Bedridden for many years. It was, I suspect, how Brigid developed her interest in healing. She travelled to and fro from Ireland in search of Cures from our maternal grandmother. Despite her efforts, my mother died. Brigid suffered. She felt herself somehow to blame as women are wont to do. Not long afterwards my father—not being a man to take care of himself, or indeed children—married again. This time a woman from the village, much younger than my mother. From her, I believe, my father finally attained a sense of belonging. They had one son: Henry. Brigid or I were much older than Henry and had very little to do with him, until one day Brigid took Henry for a walk. Millworkers saw them set off along the riverbank of the river that fed the mill. Some time later she returned, but alone. Henry was found by the workers early evening. He was a healthy, able young boy yet he was found face down in the water. Brigid gave her inadequate excuse but never spoke further on the subject. My father, devastated, sent her away to a nunnery in County Cork where she lived for many years until, that is, we learnt of her escape.' A distant look crosses Conrad Zeldin's face as he stares into the flames. 'I was living in London by the time I received news of her in Chideock, a village not far from my father's mill. I am not certain how she managed to afford the rent with no income of her own, but my suspicion is that she is kept by a gentleman in London.' He looks back at Jeremiah, his black eyes having lost their previous gleam. 'A gentleman from the Physics Garden in the village of Chelsea. You know of such a place?'

Jeremiah struggles with a nod.

'I went there, conversed with this Mr Rand myself. It was clear he had visited Chideock. He informed me that my sister was writing a herbal and that he would do all he could to help her publish it. It was not my place to tell him that my sister had never cared for what was expected of her or that she cared nothing for the opinion of others. However, Mr Rand, I suspect, had little knowledge of my sister or indeed what the village thought of her. But,'—he puffs several times on his pipe—'apparently, every place harbours its witch. I have no fond feelings for my sister, Mr Goode, as you have perhaps gathered.' He takes a longer puff on his pipe and straightens his frown with a question. 'Pray, are you from London?'

Doubtless he wonders if Jeremiah is another of his sister's keepers. Jeremiah does not respond.

'If not, then perhaps you have some knowledge of witches. To my mind they are women who on account of experiencing a sensation in their body, or thinking a particular thought, believe it to be true. My sister was such a person, Mr Goode.'

Jeremiah, face impassive, kicks the sawdust at his feet.

'Have you served an apprenticeship in your profession, Mr Goode?'

He blinks; he cannot manage more.

'Then you will understand the importance of an education. Brigid, alas, believed she could educate herself. She made plentiful mistakes, Mr Goode. A child almost died on her having administered a herb too strong for its body. She was lucky. But there is a limit to a person's luck. It is not a thing to be relied upon.'

There is a long pause. Conrad Zeldin gets up again and crosses to the fire to relight his pipe. Jeremiah stares ahead, eyes no longer absorbing his surroundings, they have turned inwards towards pain. He is barely aware that Conrad Zeldin has joined him until he slides a paper-wrapped object across the table.

'This, you might say, is a record of her so called *healings*.' He pushes the package closer to Jeremiah's elbows. 'Most of the herbs she tested on herself. No person could doubt my sister's tendency toward martyrdom and I fear whatever experimentation involved in producing such a work is credited to this. What surprises me is the quality of the drawings. From what I understand, Mr Rand assisted Brigid when it came to acquiring specimens but these drawings were done by her hand alone. The quality of the workmanship is impressive and I am not generally given to such appreciation, least of all where it concerns my sister. As to whether the herbs effectiveness,' he laughs, loudly, briefly, 'well, I shall not be putting them to any test. I place my hands in the educated physician, Mr Goode. Not in the hands of a witch. That said, I have counted almost a thousand specimens. It must'—he pats the book— 'be of great interest to a man such as yourself.'

Martyr, symmetry and peace

Jeremiah places a hand over the brown paper and it is like touching a body whose heart has ceased beating.

'You may open it if you like. I had it bound. One must make concessions when death is a possibility.'

Jeremiah takes out the herbal bound in brown leather, gold lettering. Reads, *A complete Herbal containing five hundred plants taken from life and used in the practice of the physick* as though it were a poem.

'I have spoken again to Mr Rand since Brigid's disappearance.'

Jeremiah's eyes narrow. Had the *Praefacrus Horti* heard from Brigid? On three occasions Jeremiah has visited the Physic Gardens, waiting until it was dark, until he was asked to leave but whilst there he had spoken to no one.

'Alas, neither he nor Dr Faversham, another gentleman she seemed to be...' He pauses, inhales deeply, '... in close association with has heard news from Brigid. But I do not think her dead. Brigid is a survivor. However, Mr Rand affirms that, even in her absence, the herbal must find a bookseller to publish it. He professes to never having seen a book of its kind so complete. He seems to think it shall make a great profit. But that is not why I am here. I am here, you understand, on account of Brigid requesting it to be placed in your hands in her... shall we say... absence. My sister trusted very few, Mr Goode. Perhaps she saw some kind of symmetry between your two lives: you both share ...' He takes a deep puff, holding Jeremiah's eye, '... a love of plants do you not?'

Jeremiah pulls the book closer, turning over the first page but is not met by Archangel but by Afterbirth. Brigid's compendium was in order of diseases! A most clever though now obvious way to order a herbal. Why had he never considered it? The agonising over methodology might have been avoided if he had given each disease several choices of herbs with which to cure it!

'You will find a letter at the back addressed to you.' Mr Zeldin pushes back his chair. 'It is a pity for Brigid she does not try to make contact. She has come into some money from an uncle who had favoured her as a child. Perhaps you will pass this message on if you meet. Now forgive me. I must be at Jonathan's Coffee House in Exchange Alley, and then I am back at Lloyd's again, for we meet here in the afternoons. The coffee, you do agree, is very good?'

Once alone Jeremiah takes out the letter from the back cover, instinctively bringing it to his nose though it smells only of leather and ink, nothing of Brigid. He unfolds it and reads slowly.

My dear Jeremiah,

Do you remember how you spoke of my herbal and I said that it would most likely be read if a man wrote it? Well I now place it in your hands so that may be so. Only Mr Rand knows of its existence and it shall be your word against his. I doubt that he shall notice it is mine anyhow. He was too preoccupied with telling me how I should be conducting my life than to pay much attention to what I produced with it. Women do not sit astride horses, Miss Zeldin, he would tell me too often. Thus, it shall be a herbal written by Jeremiah I. S. Goode, which seems fitting for such a work. I do not consider it a great accomplishment, however, not when other women are able to produce such things as children but I do hope that in your hands, and the hands of those that read it, it shall be put to use to accomplish many healings. For I know, as I know that my own name is Brigid, named after the goddess of the same name you might remember, that there is more to healing than purging and bleeding and that for every sickness there exists a corresponding plant in Nature capable of Curing it. I know too that good health is what God intended for us all and for such a purpose He thus provided Nature as our humble, obedient servant. Knowing in my heart that you shall enact my request I breathe freely in these final hours of misery.

Although my last days in Chideock were spent with a broken heart, I hold tight to the hope that it shall eventually mend and that you too, Mr Goode, shall find everlasting peace within your soul.

Go freely,
Brigid.

Once the bitterness subsides, Jeremiah finds the coffee has profound effects on his thoughts. Loose words rattle against the edges of his mind: *martyr, symmetry, peace …* words looping into other words, forming equally uncomfortable associations. His head swells, ripening with thoughts that press against his skull. He places the package under his arm and hurries out of the coffee shop.

Jeremiah catches up with Conrad Zeldin at the General Post Office. He has stopped to buy a Holloway cheesecake.

'I wish to say more,' Jeremiah tells him, catching his breath.

Conrad Zeldin swallows, wipes his mouth with a kerchief. 'Go on.'

'I knew Brigid but for a short time,' he says, competing with the volume of the moneylenders' cries.

'Short is often sweet.'

Jeremiah secures a footing on what he knows he must say. 'I know Brigid—'

'Coffee,' says Conrad Zeldin, purchasing another cheesecake, 'makes me hungry. Let's walk.'

325

They walk beyond the Bank of England where nine streets converge, weaving in and out of the moneylenders—men who toy with money as other men toy with dice—and Jeremiah walks beside Conrad Zeldin holding Brigid's herbal to his chest like a shield. 'I know Brigid was put on this earth to Cure and, like me, would never intentionally harm another. It is not... '

'I must say, Mr Goode,' interrupts Conrad Zeldin through a mouthful of cheesecake, 'you seem to know very little of my sister. People may change but their past cannot be altered. Oh, my sister did Cure. Indeed she did, Mr Goode, but only to make amends with God. You know, I assume, about the Negro?'

Jeremiah falls silent, distracted with straightening the peak of his hat.

'Do I interpret your silence as no?'

Jeremiah clears his throat 'he had rescued a man after a shipwreck. He tended to her garden as payment.'

'Is that what she told you?' Another burst of brief laughter. 'Oh, there was no such rescue, Mr Goode.' Conrad Zeldin's expression is now heavy with scorn. 'The Negro was former footman to a certain Captain Archer. He became Brigid's lover as he had once been the lover of Captain Archer's wife. As you can imagine, no man in all Dorset wanted a wife that had murdered her half-brother. But Brigid made do with what arrived on her threshold: make do with the hungry or the cold.' He narrows his eyes. 'Or those that, for whatever reason, needed the arms of a compassionate witch.'

He stares for an uncomfortable amount of time. In the light of day Jeremiah sees they are not as dark as Brigid's but show the same depthless, detached grey he had briefly observed in her outside her barn on the day he had almost discovered Tayo.

'Then, of course, she found you, Mr Goode.' Conrad Zeldin wipes crumbs from his mouth, laughing again his unexpected laugh. 'But I would not give another consideration to my sister. She is not deserving of the attention.' He lifts his hat. 'She was not the goddess she believed herself to be—she was, however, the Devil's imp. But look! You got a book out of it! Even the Devil does good work from time to time. Good day to you, Mr Goode.'

Ample candlelight

February 1st, St Brigid's Day—the patron of babies and printing presses and poets. A day to mark the beginning of the Celtic spring. With the days lengthening a little, the lamplighter, sits on a rung, waiting for dusk to descend, a sense of urgency all but gone from his body. He eats an apple, his ladder leant against the apothecary's shop. Jeremiah salutes to him as he crosses the Yard wearing his shiny new riding boots.

'A proper gentleman now!' the boy cries.

'What do you want?' asks Jeremiah, with a smile. 'Still overcome with passions for my maid?'

'Nay,' replies the lamplighter, wiping his face and smearing it with soot, 'I did listen to your words.'

'My words?'

'That you spoke about love not existing when a man was properly grown.'

Jeremiah scrapes the muck from his boots. 'I have been known to be wrong.'

'I got a dog.'

'And this is satisfactory replacement?'

'Aye.'

Jeremiah laughs. 'I shall have to remember that. Or perhaps I shall offer you further advice.'

The young man shrugs. 'I can see she's with child, sir, and that too… well, it persuaded me to get a dog.'

'I do not want to give advice about Mary, there are many more Marys.' Jeremiah rests his arm across the boy's shoulders. He has been drinking, but not at White's, not with Wordsley and though not exactly drunk he feels intoxicated with life's possibilities. 'I offer you advice about love.' The boy's nose wrinkles at this. 'There comes a point—as a man—that love takes hold of you,' he says, swaying with sentimentality, 'and when it does you must pursue it, with all your heart pursue it. Disappointment may follow, yet it matters not. What matters is that you have experienced something heaven sent, a force, and your soul has reached beyond its earth-bound limits. For a time it shall restore your faith in life and in God, for this love—' He pats the boy's back—'builds hope and only with hope do we understand grace.'

'It's a bulldog, sir. It's won more money than I've been paid in two years.'

Jeremiah overpays the boy then lets himself into his shop. Still feeling generous, he turns back. 'A message?'

'Tell her… tell her she can come to watch my dog fight. When he wins I will buy her a silver pin and one for the baby.'

Jeremiah smiles. The boy is perhaps learning about love after all.

He enters his shop and inside his elaboratory, awash with ample candlelight, he pauses to admire his new drug chest comprising thirty-two drawers, each brimming with fresh herbs. The herbs are stored alphabetically. Such order produces comfort. He steps over the stacks of new books, all bound in amber-coloured leather with gold lettering on the spine. He settles at his desk. Outside, in the yard, the light dims, but the yellow heads of the daffodils do not immediately fade. Jeremiah links his hands behind his head, staring out of the window, feeling as he has done of late that this is his home, that the profession of apothecary is his fate. It does not bring the bliss of contentment discovered in Chideock, for such a feeling is now lost to him, but peace touches his core and for now simple peace shall suffice. He knows too that as contentment begins to unfold he shall discover Brigid, self-sufficient and fearless, at its centre. Each new day unfurls his love a little more. It is not a dead love but a growing love. At times, he imagines an angel had visited him; one who had given him the task of comprehending God's grace.

On his finger his grandfather's diamond ring—redeemed from the pawnbroker—catches the candlelight. One day it shall perhaps adorn the finger of his wife but such propositions lie in the future. For now he is happy to settle his debts and remain a free man. He has returned the pair of boots to Dorset, boots that allowed him to journey to Chideock to arms that encircled him with hope, with forgiveness and he dispatched two gallipots to the farmer's wife as promised. If nothing else the man affirmed to him that even his own death he could battle against. There is much to be grateful for.

Time and again he returns to the Catholic church of St Anselm and St Caecilia where he offers up prayers, subdued by the perverse attachment to old customs, the solemnity of its Latin mass. Whilst there he meditates on God's mercy, God's grace, two things he now holds in high regard. Then, at fortunate times, he senses her presence beside him, a gently kind loving force so palpable it seems to contain life and with it comes comfort. He imagines her smiling at him, as though what had happened—his salvation at the eleventh hour—is but an anecdote he shall one day comprehend. But for now he feels blissful in her presence particularly at night when together they swim within the warm womb of his dreams, naked and entirely cleansed.

He opens a letter from his mother and reads it in part.

Dearest Indigo,

I hope this finds you well. We are exhausted after a long day spent at the wedding of Lucy Aldridge. Lucy was a charming bride. She wore her grandmother's wedding dress with a Spanish lace veil…

He jumps forward a paragraph.

The father of her new husband, Colonel Letchford-Briggs, apparently owns much of Yorkshire and does seem a most suitable match for Lucy. I wish them…

… It was both a surprise and a pleasure to see Lord Wordsley after so long. He talked with liveliness about the prospect of your opening a second apothecary shop in Fleet Street with his aid. His wife seemed very comely and none of the things I have heard or indeed imagined about her.

… I apologise once again for the circumstances that render me by the Law not to loan you money. However, I am much relieved that your herbal was completed in good time and that you did not suffer greatly. I am sure the stay at the debt collector's house is something you shall soon put behind you. With God's strength and plentiful prayer most things can be accomplished, dearest Indigo. You are attending…

… Jasper is thrilled about the prospect of a visit. He has been packing paper and ink most of the morning. I hope that he shall not be much trouble. His absence will allow me to give some consideration to the girls' futures, for since your father passed away he is not keen on spending time in his room alone but prefers us to accompany him to places that he wishes to draw. Incidentally, Reverend Alcock, it seems, has taken a keen interest in your sister Rose. Violet seems to think their piety is well matched. For the short term, I shall not wish for your work to be disturbed by your brother. Thus, if he…

The shop bell rings. Jeremiah looks up from the part read letter. The silhouette of a sparrow hawk passes before a full moon. He closes the amber-coloured book open on the desk to its dedication, *To Brigid, the Goddess of Healing,* and crosses the elaboratory, through the boxes of herbs he has yet to unpack, and shifts tiredness aside to make way for whatever complaint has found its way over his threshold.

As for us, we have intruded long enough on one man's struggle in a city brimming with such tales. It is the nature of this beast to lure a man in before spitting him like gristle, only to grant him a place at the head of the table with a plate of delicacies the very next week. But one person's journey towards joy is another's misery. There was to be no last supper with Mrs Soloman. With the agony of Brigid's disappearance to absorb Jeremiah, the evening had been quite forgotten. Thus, as his feet take tentative steps amongst London's streets like an angel unused to the solidity of the earth, seeking new methods, new herbs—not giving in to the persistent travelling salesmen and their Cure-alls—yet providing the parish with much needed cures (more often for free), far away, in the village of Chelsea, a lady sobs, chastising herself for thinking she was capable of wooing such a gentleman. For after Cook had ceased poisoning her aunt with arsenic and pig's fat, her aunt had returned to health with renewed bitterness. Miss Heart now suffers her failings, brandished at the end of her aunt's accusatory finger. But over in Covent Garden, a young prostitute is happy to see her old customer again for with or without the brilliant on his finger Jeremiah remains a gentleman, one with pretty blue eyes, not as sad as they once were.

But wait! Perhaps, we depart too soon. That tinkle above the door seems more insistent than usual. Let us follow Jeremiah, cursing his apprentice, as he sweeps through his curtain.

'Boswell!' he calls out uselessly into the distant wail of babies and the unending clatter in the scullery. They are preparing to move: to a friend of Wordsley's who requires a gardener and a milkmaid. It transpired there was worse a man might do than confront a friend—a rake in the process of transformation—about the extent of his pity.

In the shop a cloaked figure stands before the open door. The wind blows through, scattering papers on the counter as the bell continues to trill.

'Please,' says Jeremiah closing the door, 'Come inside.'

He glances across the yard, to a man—black as ebony, African—who waits before the alchemist shop, tapping a foot against the wall, head tipped to the Heavens. The hooded figure steps inside the shop clasping at the edges of its cape, Jeremiah collects the loose pages from the floor, the skeleton of Nicholas Culpepper regarding him curiously.

'How may I help…?' he says, hesitating, for he cannot yet discern the sex of this customer.

'I have come about the position,' the woman says, barely above a whisper.

'As you can see …' *What can she see with her head bent low and the cloak all but covering her face?* '… this is an apothecary shop, madam. Doubtless he should point her in the direction of Mrs Marizio's boarding house, newly opened after the death of the astronomer who had, as predicted, a month later followed his pigeon to heaven. 'Young ladies frequently find work in this establishment,' he says, 'paid well for their efforts, from my understanding.' Rather, the boarding house had restored Neal's Yard with renewed life, plentiful Covent Garden 'gout', not to mention plenty of custom as the bagnio's apothecary.

She tells him, still whispering, 'No, you misunderstand me. I would like to apprentice here.'

He clears his throat and replies gently, 'I am an apothecary, madam. That is not work for women, not in London.' But for some reason he is thinking of the trajectory of winged creatures, of interludes of happiness: a little flight, a little wading through mud.

The cloaked figure throws back her hood, lifting her face towards his, its radiance quite overwhelming.

'I heal,' she says, ''tis what I do.'